SELZNICK'S GIRL FRIDAY

A NOVEL OF 1939 HOLLYWOOD

MARTIN TURNBULL

This book is dedicated to

COLE HORSFALL

because everything is a cue for a show tune.

DISCLAIMER

1

Santa Catalina Island
California
August 1938

As Polly Maddox stood at Catalina's highest overlook, she discovered the blistering August heat had rendered the telegram in her hand a damp relic.

Oh dear.

Thankfully, it wasn't meant for the mayor of Avalon or the town's police sergeant, or even Mr. Wrigley, scion of the chewing-gum dynasty who owned almost the entire island. Papa wouldn't relish the sight of his soggy dispatch, but a heartfelt "Sorry!" and a quick kiss on the cheek would fix that.

Polly laid the telegram out on her flattened hand. Perhaps in the ten minutes she had before setting out on the trail back into town, the sun might bake it dry. The ink had bled into the paper, blurring the words, but they were still legible.

TO: ELROY MADDOX
FROM: JUDD HARTLEY
AMELIA ARRIVES ON SS AVALON AUGUST TEN STOP
THANK YOU FOR TAKING HER IN STOP
LOIS AND I APPRECIATE YOUR HELP STOP

In the two years Polly had been working for Pacific Wireless as one of Catalina's telegraph operators, she had developed an ability to read between the lines.

If Judd and Lois Hartley were such good friends of Papa's, how come he had never mentioned their names in the sixteen years he and Polly had lived on the island? Polly supposed Amelia was their daughter, but if the girl needed to be sent away, was she in trouble?

The telegram wasn't drying fast enough. Polly grasped the top corners carefully between her thumbs and forefingers and waved it in the warm breeze. The telegram was none of her beeswax, of course, but if she didn't work in the telegraph office, how would she have known what was going on under her own nose?

What if she hadn't been the operator on duty? When might her father have told her about this newcomer? When the girl was standing in their kitchen, clutching her battered cardboard suitcase?

Papa was as jovial as a puppy and candid as an open book; it wasn't like him to be so secretive.

She gingerly slipped the telegram into her pocket. It was time she delivered it to him.

* * *

Polly and her father, Elroy, lived in a bungalow down the tranquil end of Sumner Avenue, but his office was on Metropole, smack-dab in the heart of Avalon. He was the accountant for the Santa Catalina Island Company, through which Wrigley administrated all public works, private ventures, and philanthropies he and his wife oversaw.

Elroy beamed when he spotted his daughter. "Doodlebug!" He detected the telegram sandwiched between her fingers. "Why, Miss Maddox. A personally delivered telegram?" He made a show of patting his pockets for a nickel tip.

Before she reached his orderly desk, she smelled the rich, rosy aroma of his Carnaval de Venise cologne steeping the air. She slid the almost-dry telegram toward him. "I have questions."

He picked it up. "Dropped this in Avalon Bay, did we?"

"I hiked up to Three Palms, but hadn't counted on getting so sweaty." She studied her father's face as he read the message, but saw nary a twitch to interpret. "Who's Amelia?"

"Judd and Lois's daughter."

She flopped into his guest chair and slung a leg over the armrest to feign nonchalance. The chances were good Polly would have been the one to take down the message anyway, so why was Papa being uncommonly tight-lipped? Some sort of monkey business was going on here. "And they are . . .?"

He dropped the telegram onto his blotter. "You were only five when your mother died and we moved here. Before that, I used to work for—"

"City of Angels Distillery."

Okay, now he's chewing his lower lip, which means he's trying to buy himself some time. If I sit here long enough, silent as a gravestone, he'll come clean.

It didn't take long.

"City of Angels is owned by Judd Hartley."

"He was your boss?"

"Yes."

"You've never mentioned him. What gives, Papa? Did you leave on bad terms?"

"No, no, nothing like that. You see, Doodlebug, I was heartbroken over your mother's passing and needed a fresh start. The Hartleys were part of what I wanted to leave behind. That's all. And would you at least try to sit like a lady?"

Polly slid her leg off the armrest and demurely crossed her legs at the ankles, although she wasn't sure why she needed to act all prim and proper. Catalina Island's eligible bachelors certainly weren't lining up outside. Still and all, Hartley's telegram gave her the heebie-jeebies. "After sixteen years, they contact you out of the blue?"

"I couldn't have been more surprised myself."

"And they're sending this Amelia to Catalina—why?"

"The girl's gotten herself into a pickle. It's easy to fall prey over there on the mainland. You know what I've always told you."

"Bad Los Angeles. Dangerous Los Angeles. Treacherous Los Angeles."

"I don't recall describing it as treacherous."

"I was extrapolating."

A quiet smile surfaced. "You and your vocabulary. All those books you read."

What else was she supposed to do with her time? Nobody had offered her even so much as a token of friendship. Not at high school. Not during the pottery classes at Catalina Clay. Not in typing school.

The Avalon townsfolk hadn't been outright rude to her. Polite nods and the occasional bland "Good morning" here and there were as far as it went. She used to wonder if it was because she was the only freckled-faced, pale-skinned redhead on Catalina. But she had long since given up trying to figure out how to make them see she was an amicable, affable, agreeable girl who didn't deserve their cold shoulders. Meanwhile, she had evenings to fill.

"This pickle Amelia's gotten herself into—" she began, but her father cut her off.

"Day after tomorrow, I'd like you to meet her at the pier and take her to the Hotel St. Catherine, where she'll be working as a housekeeper. Listen to me, Doodlebug. Be friendly and welcoming, but not *too* friendly and welcoming."

In other words, Polly wanted to say, treat this girl the way people have treated me for as long as I can remember. Nobody deserved *that*, but she trusted her father enough to accept that he had a good reason for sidestepping every question she'd asked him.

"Can do," she said, rising from the chair. "I thought I might see *Marie Antoinette* at the Casino Theatre tonight. They say Norma Shearer is quite marvelous. Care to join me?"

"I wish I could." He laid a hand on the half-dozen ledgers stacked to his right. "But this'll be a late one for me."

* * *

Stepping onto Metropole Avenue, she felt a slight cooling of the air as the sun burned an orange hole into the late afternoon sky.

The girl has gotten herself into a pickle.

As everyone past the age of puberty knew, this was a euphemism for a girl prematurely finding herself in the family way. Polly had only heard about such girls or read about them in books. She'd never encountered one in person.

How scandalous! Her heart beat a little faster at the thought of encountering a—a—what would they call someone like Amelia Hartley in the movies? Polly stretched a hand across her mouth.

You're about to meet a fallen woman.

2

Polly's shift at Pacific Wireless started at seven a.m. In a town only eight blocks by three, her morning walk took her just fifteen minutes. Before the heat of summer sent the tourists scurrying to the beach, Polly enjoyed her stroll along the freshly hosed sidewalks, watching the shopkeepers prepare for another day of hawking snow cones and renting pushbikes to sunburned vacationers.

Miss Trent from Rozika's Beauty Shop possessed a shining head of platinum-white hair and always smiled the same perfunctory smile. No teeth. No warmth.

Turning up Sumner Avenue, Polly passed balding, pear-shaped Arthur, who ran Abernathy's Radio Sales and Repair. His good-morning smile held a little more warmth than Miss Trent's, but hardly enough to melt candle wax.

On Beacon Street, she encountered Karina from The Kit and Kaboodle. Her sign alluded to hidden gems for adventurous treasure hunters. In truth, it was a load of junk that Avalon's townsfolk no longer wanted or day-trippers had left behind in their rush to make the last steamship home.

And finally, a trek up Northwest Hill to the telegraph office.

Pacific Wireless's overnight operator was already tugging on his hat. With his unkempt beard and wrinkled shirts, Polly suspected Winslow was an insomniac who slept all day to avoid people, and, like her father, had relocated to Catalina to leave an old life behind.

Polly was only five when her mother had died of a burst appendix. All she had of Mama was a slightly fuzzy honeymoon snapshot—Flora had moved her arm as the shutter had snapped. The black-and-white photo with its shades of gray revealed nothing, so Polly had had to take Papa's word for it when he assured her that she had inherited her mother's freckles and cinnamon-red hair.

"Good morning!" Polly waited for Winslow's usual grunt that passed for conversation. She hung her straw sun hat on the peg that her coworker's newsboy had vacated. "Anything I should know—"

Winslow had already left.

A tinge of warmth in the wind drifted through the open doorway. Catalina was in for another scorcher. Thank goodness she spent her days perched on a hill that caught every breeze blowing across the ocean.

The first hour brought no distractions, so her thoughts drifted to the mysterious Amelia. What was with all of that vague business about Polly not to be too welcoming? And how was she supposed to pick out one girl from among the thousand passengers the *Avalon* deposited on Steamer Terminal pier?

What did fallen women look like? In the movies, she'd be one of those blowsy dames with her cleavage on display and reeking of drugstore perfume. That type sauntered off the pier, accompanied by men a dozen years older, displaying diamond tiepins that glinted in the sun and sporting trimmed mustaches to convince themselves they resembled William Powell. Polly called them "weekend getaways." Get away from wives. Get away from husbands. Get away from hotel detectives.

"Not too busy, I hope?"

The voice belonged to one of the few people on Catalina who deigned to talk to Polly.

Zane Grey was famous for his tales of the Wild West, cowboys and horses, cactuses and tumbleweeds. An enthusiastic fisherman, he'd first visited Catalina on his honeymoon and loved it so much that he'd built a vacation home, dubbed The Pueblo, a stone's throw from the telegraph office.

He thumped an inch-thick stack of pages onto the wooden counter.

"This one took longer than usual, didn't it?" she asked.

He contorted his lips into a jagged line. "Some of them gush out of my fingertips like holy water on a Sunday morning. But others are more like the Virginia Woolf quote about writing a novel, how it 'involves an agony of spirit not easily borne.' Let's just say I'm glad it's finished."

After Polly had given up on the dream of befriending someone in her pottery class at Catalina Clay, she had taken up the piano. A previously unsuspected hidden talent had emerged under the tutelage of the island's music teacher, whose praise had encouraged Polly's hopes of being invited to parties where she could accompany singalongs. But not even the local amateur dramatic and musical society had asked her to play for them.

However, one unsuspected benefit had emerged.

"You're skilled with your hands; you should take up typing," her teacher had commented. "There's always a call for that."

So off she traipsed for private lessons with Catalina High's typewriting teacher and in short order, she had become the fastest, most accurate typist on the island. Yet again, she had hoped people would come to her with their typing needs. Yet again, disappointment.

With one surprising exception.

Not long after she had started work at Pacific Wireless, Zane Grey had appeared at the office saying he'd been told she could type eighty-five words a minute and would she be interested in earning some money on the side?

Polly read the title of Grey's newest tome out loud. "*Raiders of Spanish Peaks*. Where are the Spanish Peaks?"

"West of my right ear and east of my left." He smiled at his little joke. "I'll warn you now: Lots of revisions, corrections and I-changed-my-mind-put-it-back-the-way-it-wases."

Polly threw her hands up in mock horror. "Not the dreaded back-the-way-it-wases."

He ran his fingers through his thick, unruly hair, which was parted down the middle. "Which is why I brought this." From inside his jacket, he produced a gift wrapped in baby-pink paper. "One part bribe, one part thank-you, one part advance apology."

She tore at the paper until it revealed a bottle of perfume topped with an etched glass pyramid. "L'Heure Bleue Eau de Toilette by Guerlain. Oh! Mr. Grey!"

"According to the Bullock's Wilshire salesclerk, the top notes are anise, bergamot, and lemon. Base notes include vanilla and sandalwood. Whatever that means."

She flipped the pyramid and breathed in its heady fragrance. "It means that you have divine taste in scents."

"Promise me you'll wear it often and not save it for special occasions."

What special occasions? I've never even been on a date. "Of course I shall, but you needn't have."

"You haven't seen the manuscript yet."

"I rather enjoy a challenge."

"No rush." He rapped his knuckles on the counter, once, twice, thrice. "I saw you yesterday when I was bringing my boat in. You go up to Three Palms a lot, don't you?"

Polly was used to being ignored, so his comment startled her. "It's a lovely lookout."

"Toward Los Angeles."

"Yes, that's right."

"But you don't go there. Why's that?"

"Papa insists there's nothing for me."

"For starters, there are bottles of Guerlain." He stared at her, his thick eyebrows knitted together. She could tell what he was thinking: *Everyone shuns you. What's keeping you here?*

"My father was in Long Beach the day of the horrible quake in 'thirty-three. He was getting a shave when bricks came tumbling down like the walls of Jericho. Said he'd never been so scared in all his life and rushed back to Catalina first chance he got."

"And yet he goes to the mainland every couple of months."

"Yes, but—"

"Doesn't he offer to take you?"

"I've never asked him to."

"Aren't you the least bit curious?"

"I've seen all I need to see in movies and newspapers." As soon as the words left her lips, she winced inwardly, wishing she hadn't sounded like a gosh-darned drip. *Of course* LA wasn't how it appeared in movies. Maybe it was better, but it was probably worse. That's what Papa had assured her. "And anyway, I wouldn't think of leaving my father alone. Who would fix his fish chowder the way he likes it?"

Her attempt at a goofy joke crash-landed on the counter between them. His gift was thoughtful, but this line of questioning made her uncomfortable.

"Okay," he said, "but promise me one thing."

"I will be wearing L'Heure Bleue the next time you come in here."

"That would be nice, yes, but I want you to think about this: Nobody is an island."

3

Three shrill blasts from the SS *Avalon* were the signal for two dozen teenagers to start rowing their dinghies toward the steamship where they'd jump into the ocean, whooping and hollering at the passengers, who, in turn, tossed coins for the energetic kids to dive for.

Polly watched them foam the water in a frenzy of grabbing hands and kicking feet. Years ago, before the typing lessons, piano lessons, and pottery lessons, she had tried to convince Papa to let her join the tradition. But no amount of sweet-talking, pouting, begging, or even the silent treatment had changed Elroy's steadfast "Absolutely not!"

A Mexican band serenaded the passengers as they filed down the gangway—gloved women in wide-brimmed straw hats, men in Panamas and espadrilles, all with the usual suitcases, parasols, and picnic baskets. Without a photo or description of the mysterious Amelia, Polly wasn't sure what she was looking for. All she had to go on was her father's laissez-faire "You'll know her when you see her." Why? Polly had wanted to ask. Because she'll be the only pregnant woman?

A few maybes passed her by, but none of them was traveling

alone, nor seeking Polly, nor appeared to be expecting. But then she spotted the girl that made her realize Papa had known what he was talking about.

If a baby were tucked inside that white, snug middy blouse, it certainly wouldn't be showing any time soon. Her sky-blue poplin skirt flared around her shins as she strode toward Polly with the confidence of an Olympian sprinter.

"Dear ol' Dad told me Elroy Maddox's daughter would meet me at the dock, but he might have mentioned"—she waved her hand in a wide circle around Polly's face—"this."

The bold copper-red hair cascading from beneath Amelia's hat was more striking than Polly's softer cinnamon, but it fell to her shoulders in curls and waves the same way Polly's did. Their faces also narrowed to a sharp chin, which Polly disliked on herself, but it suited this girl.

"Are you as shocked as I am?" Amelia asked.

"Why, yes."

"How old are you?"

"Twenty-one," Polly replied.

"I'm twenty."

"So we're not twins separated at birth."

"But we could be sisters, don't you think?"

As tourists and getaways jostled past them on the sidewalk, the young women stared at each other. They were the same height, but Amelia's blue eyes contrasted with Polly's hazel ones. And she lacked Polly's freckles. Lucky so-and-so. Papa had always insisted they gave a person character, but Polly hated them.

"Cousins, at least," Polly said, still looking Amelia up and down. We're not related, are we? she thought. We couldn't be actual cousins—could we? "If this was a screwball comedy starring Carole Lombard and Myrna Loy," she said, "we'd find out in some far-fetched, wacky way that we were related, and hilarity would ensue!" She nudged the suitcase with her knee. "I'm to walk you to the St. Catherine."

They skirted the last of the stragglers and headed along the street that paralleled Avalon Bay.

"Has your dad ever mentioned mine?" Amelia asked.

"Never."

"I had to crowbar the facts out of Pop. He told me how your dad worked for City of Angels until you guys moved here. My mom told me about your mom. Tough break, kiddo."

Aside from the odd passing reference, Papa rarely mentioned Mama. Even when Polly had asked direct questions. What was her favorite food? Did she like to play tennis? Good at embroidery? Could she sing? Papa's answers had always been so evasive that Polly had long given up asking. But this Amelia, with an appealing rasp in her voice and her go-get-'em fiery red hair, already felt like family.

"My mom's a redhead," Amelia continued. "Like rust in the sun. And she's glorious proud of it." Amelia let out a giggle. "My dad and yours went for redheads, so here we are!" She threw one arm into the air. "On Catalina where the seagulls are hungry, the sun shines all year round, and reckless gambling types can hook into a high-stakes poker game anytime they want." She put her arm down again and looked at Polly. "But that's nothing new to you, being Elroy Maddox's daughter and all."

Papa's job as the accountant for the Santa Catalina Island Company kept him at his desk for long hours. Polly wanted to probe Amelia further about her "high-stakes poker game" comment, but Papa had been clear: Don't get too friendly.

They had reached the hotel, where the manager was standing on the front porch. "Mr. Pembroke," Polly said, mounting the steps to the veranda, "this is Amelia Hartley."

"Thank you, Polly," Pembroke replied. "We're awfully glad to have you on board, Miss Hartley."

"Thank you. I'm glad to—"

"We're fully booked all week, so there's no time for dilly-dallying."

Polly knew an exit line when she heard one. She wished Amelia good luck and trotted back down the steps. As she blended in with the sightseers and fun-seekers, she slowed her pace to a languid stroll.

Hooking into a poker game is nothing new to Elroy Maddox's daughter.

What had Mr. Hartley told Amelia?

More to the point: What had Papa not told *her*?

4

The next day, a picture postcard arrived. The last time Polly had heard from Clark Gable had been in the early spring when he'd written to say he was about to start *Too Hot to Handle* with Myrna Loy and how he wished Margaret Mitchell had never written *Gone with the Wind*.

Three years had passed since those glorious summer weeks he'd lived on the island filming *Mutiny on the Bounty*. His memories of that gawky kid who'd helped him pass notes to Joan Crawford or deliver bottles of Mad Ox bourbon were bound to fade like photographs left in the sun, so it was no surprise that his postcards —each one featuring a different view of Los Angeles—arrived less frequently now.

This new one featured the Culver Hotel, a six-story building of red brick with a gigantic neon sign on the roof.

Dear Polly, it read in Gable's neat handwriting, *I got around to seeing* The Adventures of Robin Hood. *What a crackerjack picture! But you won't catch me wearing tights, so let Errol Flynn have the glory. Ha! Right now, Carole is making French toast, but from all the swearing, I assume it's her first time. If I die of poisoning, tell the cops! Your friend, Clark.*

It was coming up to ten o'clock. She didn't need to report for work until noon, so maybe Amelia would appreciate a familiar face, if only for a minute. Or five. Or however long it took to ask her what poker games had to do with being Elroy's daughter. Papa had worked late the previous night and hadn't arrived home by the time Polly had headed to bed, and he'd already left the house by the time she'd rolled out of bed this morning.

The St. Catherine's front desk clerk told Polly she'd find Amelia round the back, which meant they'd put Amelia on the most tedious of all hotel tasks.

Polly found her leaning against the laundry wall, a cigarette pinched between her lips as the metallic drums of the three huge Speed Queen washing machines rumbled like stampeding bison. She looked up from the magazine in her hands. "Hiya, cuz."

The way she said 'cuz.' A small knot clotted at the base of Polly's throat. "I had some free time, so I thought I'd stop by."

"That's mighty decent of you."

Polly waved a hand at the laundry shed. "Got you doing the donkey work?"

"I don't mind. This arrangement isn't forever."

"You must be glad to be out of Los Angeles. I hear it's awful."

A flare of confusion crossed Amelia's face as she held up her magazine. The front cover of *Modern Screen* featured an illustration of Bette Davis in a red halter-neck bathing suit. Along the bottom ran a banner: *SCHWAB'S—PHARMACY TO THE STARS.* "Ever heard of it?"

"Even us yokels out here in the middle of the ocean know about Schwab's." Polly hadn't a clue what the place was.

Amelia flicked through pages until she arrived at a four-page spread. The headline read, "This Sunset Blvd. Drug Store Is Hollywood's Favorite Hangout!"

"I'll be part of that crowd one day." Amelia tapped a sub-headline and read out loud. "'Why Schwab's Pharmacy Is Where Actors, Actresses, Screenwriters, and Columnists Get Acquainted, Get Friendly, and Get Discovered.'"

It all made sense now. Amelia wanted to be an actress. Of course she did. Look at her. We might share a passing resemblance, but she possesses the extra glow that cameras eat up with a spoon.

Amelia handed the magazine to Polly. The article's photographs showed a packed drugstore. Customers filled every stool of the long lunch counter that ran along its right-hand wall. Behind them, a human bulwark pressed in close.

"Won't it be hard for talent scouts to pick you out of the crowd?" Polly asked.

"Pick me? No! I won't be there for *that*."

"Don't all pretty girls in Hollywood want to be movie stars?"

Amelia retrieved the magazine. "You won't catch me slouched over a chocolate malted, hoping some casting-couch creep notices me. No sirree, missy. I want to *work* there." The girl was someone with a plan to get what she wanted and the gumption to go after it. Her inadvertent baby must have gummed up the works. "The absolute last thing I want is a pleasant life."

Polly blinked slowly. "You don't?"

"I want a *fascinating* one." Amelia took a final drag of her cigarette and ground the stub into the cracked asphalt. "Schwab's is Hollywood's unofficial meeting place, right? All sorts of interesting people flock there: actors, writers, cameramen, scenery designers, makeup artists. My husband will be game to hike the Rockies. Maybe he collects shrunken pygmy heads or speaks nine languages. Willing to try Japanese food, fly a plane to the Argentine, or paddle a canoe around French Polynesia."

Polly had never met anyone who talked like this. "You'll meet someone like that at Schwab's?"

Amelia tossed her *Modern Screen* onto the back porch. "Those Speed Queens are done with their racket. I need to go hang sheets in the drying room."

"How about I give you a hand?"

Amelia gave a start, her eyes widening. "You're volunteering?"

"I know how heavy those wet sheets are. I worked here almost every day a few summers ago when MGM filmed *Mutiny on the Bounty*."

"Sounds like slave labor."

"It wasn't all bad. I met *this* guy." Leaving Amelia to read Gable's postcard, she walked into the laundry. How could she have forgotten that comingling smell of linen, lye, and ammonia?

Amelia appeared in the open doorway. "This friend of yours, he isn't Clark Gable, is he?"

"He is."

"Gable? Is your *friend*?"

"I have friends." Well, one. Sort of. She hadn't gone out for hot fudge sundaes or to a movie with Zane Grey because it would be improper to be seen around town with a married man forty-five years her senior. Why add to the townsfolk's disdain? She opened the first washer and hauled out the damp sheets. "Clark happens to be famous, is all."

Amelia tackled the second Speed Queen, piling more sheets into the huge hamper. "If they don't cast him in *Gone with the Wind*, there'll be rioting in the streets."

"Well, then"—Polly waved a hand in front of her nose; Amelia had used too much ammonia—"you should stock up on pitchforks and flaming torches."

"He doesn't want the role?"

"No. And he'll fight like the devil against getting cast."

"Do Louella and Hedda know this?"

"*I* certainly haven't told them."

"Oh! You're funny!" She lumped the last few sheets into the hamper and grabbed its handles. "You being pen pals with Clark Gable gives me palpitations. Tell me everything and leave out no details."

When Polly had first spotted this girl down at the pier, she'd doubted she had anything in her arsenal that would impress. *Thank you, Clark!* She hoisted a leaden hamper and led Amelia into the drying room. "MGM filming here was a terrifically big deal. They even built a replica of the *Bounty*. Along with Clark, Franchot Tone, and Charles Laughton, we had a whole pack of actors and extras and crew. Plus hangers-on and visitors, one of which was Joan Crawford."

"She and Clark—"

"That's right. But she was also making goo-goo eyes at Franchot. So, when Joan showed up with Marion Davies—"

"All hell broke loose?"

"It put a wrinkle in Clark's plans, which meant I spent that summer running all over, passing notes back and forth between Clark and Joan and Franchot and Marion."

"You were living in a French farce!"

"Until Clark and Franchot found they had more in common than they suspected."

"Like what?"

"Womanizing and drinking, which is where my father's bourbon comes in."

"Mad Ox, right?"

Polly swiped her hand across the sweat seeping from her forehead. She'd forgotten how hot the drying room could get. Her father only sold his brand of bourbon on Catalina, but she'd forgotten how the outside world knew about his side business, too.

"The *Mutiny* crew nearly drank us dry. Between delivering love notes and Mad Ox to dressing rooms and hotel rooms, I was pretty busy, and Clark was grateful for my help."

"You must be tops with him if he's still writing to you three years later."

What a halcyon time it had been to be the girl who'd made Clark, Joan, Franchot, and Marion smile every time they opened their hotel room doors. How many times had she wished that summer could have gone on forever?

They began slinging sheets over the lines, pulling them flat.

"Speaking of my father," Polly said, "what did you mean when you implied he's connected with gambling?"

Amelia's face was blank as an empty dinner plate. "What do you mean what did I mean?"

"That remark about high-stakes poker being nothing new to Elroy Maddox's daughter. I think I'd know if my own father ran a . . ." Polly's voice petered out when she caught the slack-jawed astonishment filling Amelia's face. The look disappeared as quickly as it had come.

"Don't listen to me." Amelia turned to the next sheet. "I'll keep my trap nailed shut tighter than a clamshell with lockjaw."

Despite the stifling, humid air, a cold sweat broke across Polly's face. "Please tell me what my father's up to."

"I overheard my folks talking, is all."

"About what?"

Amelia bit down onto her lower lip. "A place called Ningpo—but I may have heard it wrong."

"The *Ning Po* is an old Chinese pirate ship moored in Cat Harbor over at the Isthmus"—Polly swung a hand northward—"thataway."

"It's on a pirate ship?"

"What is?"

"The gambling joint your father runs. Roulette, blackjack, and California's longest-running craps game. That's what Pop said."

Polly slung another sheet over the next stretch of rope and ducked behind it. She needed a moment to digest how oblivious she'd been all this time. Did everyone on Catalina know about Papa's gambling den? Those getaway girls and their diamond-studded boyfriends definitely would. She felt like one of those mushrooms that grows in the dark and someone had just switched on a light bulb. "How long's he been doing this?"

"How long has he been selling Mad Ox?"

"He started two years after Prohibition began."

"You knew he was a bootlegger, right?"

Polly had been about twelve when she'd put two and two together: Prohibition had applied to islands like Catalina as well as the mainland, which meant Papa's bourbon hadn't been strictly legal. But it was found everywhere in Avalon. Nobody cared. Not even Sergeant Blackburn, who more or less singlehandedly ran the four-man police department. And now Polly knew why. Compared to running California's longest craps game, Elroy Maddox's low-key bourbon operation was a big fat nothing.

Amelia frowned. "Haven't you been to this Isthmus place?"

Polly had vague memories of going there with Papa not long after they had resettled on Catalina, but not since then. She worked six, sometimes seven days a week—the local telegraph had to have someone on duty.

Polly shook her head.

"I only know all this because I eavesdropped on my parents," Amelia said. "How about we mosey over there and check it out for ourselves?"

"You'd do that with me?"

"I don't have a day off until next Wednesday." Amelia lifted another sheet from the basket. "Can you wait until then?"

Could she wait nearly a week? Polly wanted to sprint to her father's office and confront him on the spot. Though she was burning with curiosity to hear his reasons for keeping all this from her, Amelia's suggestion felt like a more levelheaded approach.

"Sure."

After all, you're nothing if not levelheaded.

But maybe that was part of the problem.

5

The road across the island was the old winding, unpaved stagecoach route. Amelia reached forward to pat the neck of Ol' Jim, the most serene of all the horses available for rent at Hansen's up the canyon by the bird park. "Have you really never been to this place?"

Polly gently tightened her legs against her horse's flanks. "I wouldn't blame you for thinking, 'How can someone who lives on an island the size of a postage stamp not have visited a spot that's so close?'"

Several times, Polly had come close to confronting her father over this gambling business, but each time she'd held herself in check. All she had to go on was an eavesdropped conversation from someone she'd only just met. If she was going to fling implausible accusations around like confetti, the least Papa deserved was a well-thought-out case. "I feel like a foolish little bumpkin who's never stopped to wonder what sits outside her cardboard box."

"To be fair," Amelia said, "Avalon is a pretty agreeable box. Off the top of this straw sunhat you've lent me, I could name twenty LA neighborhoods a heck of a lot worse than this place. Especially during the worst of the Depression." She sucked in a lungful of warm sea air and let it out slowly. "Oof! Those Hoovervilles."

Polly tightened Heidi's reins to give Ol' Jim a chance to catch up. "Hoovervilles?"

"You don't see them around much anymore now that conditions are improving. But back in the day, they were these shantytowns that sprang up. People got so desperate they'd cobble together shacks and lean-tos out of scrounged-up shipping crates, planks of wood, discarded furniture. They'd plug holes with trash, and line the walls with newspaper and homemade glue. No heat. No running water."

Los Angeles is no place you want to visit, Papa had told Polly, always with the solemnity of a funeral director. You're much better off on Catalina.

Amelia continued, "My mom was always telling me: 'You best be thankful, young girl, that your father could make legally licensed products like sacramental wine, near-beer, malt syrup, and wine bricks.' I must have heard *that* speech a thousand times."

As they continued along the summit of Middle Ranch Road, they could see the mainland. They'd soon be heading downhill toward the Isthmus. Polly's grip on the reins tightened with every clop of Heidi's hooves on the gravel path.

"*Was* all that stuff legal?" Polly asked.

"Prohibition was such a farce. But surely you saw that, even all the way out here. Especially with your dad's famous Mad Ox bourbon."

Polly gave a tight shrug. "Mad Ox is famous? For what?"

"Being available only on Catalina. Your pop's a genius at marketing. People get excited when they see it on the mainland. 'Oooh! You've got Mad Ox? Can I have a shot? I've never tried it.'" She snapped her fingers, causing Ol' Jim's ears to twitch. "Your last name is Maddox, and your dad makes Mad Ox. What a dummy I am for not seeing that sooner."

No worse a dummy than I am, Polly thought.

As the ground beneath them sloped down, a fetid whiff of seaweed blew past. They were nearing their destination now. But was she ready for whatever lay in wait down there? No. But wasn't it time she found out?

* * *

The trail brought them to the flatland of the Isthmus itself. To the leeward was Banning Harbor, but their destination—Catalina Harbor, known to the locals as simply Cat Harbor—lay across a half-mile stretch of dirt, the end of which would present them with a view out to Ballast Point, where the *Ning Po* sat, moored in the still water.

A hundred and forty feet long, weather-beaten, and gouged with dents and chips, the Chinese pole-junk didn't look as though it could withstand many more winter storms. Other than that, it looked pretty much the way it did in the old photo that hung in the foyer of the St. Catherine. But as Heidi and Ol' Jim ambled down the last stretch of gravel, a sinking feeling in Polly's stomach twisted into a nauseous knot as she counted the tables. Twelve in total. Arranged dockside in three rows of four.

Roulette.

Blackjack.

Craps.

And a few she didn't even recognize.

A broad, rectangular expanse of concrete shone in the sun; it was inlaid with three-inch-square Catalina Clay tiles—pink roses against a pale-yellow background. Ketchup-red umbrellas stood at the ends of each table. A bar decorated with bamboo poles was set back from the water. Behind it stood a large cabin with a corrugated-iron roof. Decorative torches, like the ones angry villagers used in monster movies, dotted the landscape. They were extinguished right now, but their flickering light would add an exotic mood come nightfall.

It wasn't hard to picture well-heeled weekenders crowded around each table, betting outrageous sums, not caring if they lost because, damn the Depression and forget the Hoovervilles, *they* could afford to have some fun.

Polly and Amelia slid from their saddles and tied Ol' Jim and Heidi to a driftwood railing.

It was all true. Amelia hadn't misheard. Papa ran an illegal gambling outfit. Tucked away from prying eyes where the local police could turn a convenient blind eye.

Polly felt Amelia's hand press lightly on her left shoulder. "Hoping for an empty beach?"

A slow-burning fury seared Polly's chest. "I bet all those townsfolk laugh at me behind my back. 'How does Polly the moron think her father paid for all her pottery lessons and piano lessons and typing lessons?'" She slapped her hands to her cheeks. "Oh my God! I'm the village idiot!" Polly eyed the large cabin behind the bar. "What do you think's in there? I'm so mad I want to bust it open with my bare hands."

"In that case." Amelia hooked her by the elbow and marched her across the sand.

Polly's curiosity, already at boiling point with her frustration over Papa's deception, fueled every stride until they arrived at the cabin door. Polly gave the handle a vicious yank and found it padlocked. The lock was pockmarked with dings and dents of rust. Polly looked around. A rock the size of a small cannonball caught her eye. Three vigorous clobbers later, and they were inside.

An odd tang hung in the air. Astringent like vinegar, but heavier, denser. Smoky, too—cigars, not cigarettes. And a hint of something musky, but pleasantly so, like opening an old book and breathing in paper and printer's ink.

Polly felt to one side of the door and flipped a light switch. Metal shelving ran along the right-hand wall. Bottles of Mad Ox bourbon filled most of it, but there were other brands, too—Old Hickory, Glenmore, Four Roses, Early Times—as well as every other type of liquor. Gin, vodka, vermouth, rum, brandy, and tequila stood shoulder to shoulder the entire length of the shelf.

"Nothing from City of Angels, I see." Amelia plucked down a bottle of Mad Ox bourbon and ran a finger over the image of the ox that was Papa's trademark. "Where does your dad make this stuff?"

"The still is a little way out of town, near the cemetery. As I'm sure you know, it's a stinky process, which is why it's out yonder."

"He's an accountant, isn't he?"

A bookshelf made of wood polished to a high sheen stood in the far corner. "For Mr. Wrigley's company."

"Does that mean you get all the Juicy Fruit you want?"

"I prefer Beech-nut gum, but that's an admission no local makes out loud."

"Wrigley is king around here?"

"In a benevolent-despot sort of way." Polly headed for the bookshelf, making her way past tables jammed with jars full of arbitrary oddments: ink, sugar, glue, thumb tacks, pens, a magnifying glass, clothes pegs, several rolls of ribbons. "I haven't met him, but Papa says he's decent to work for. He trusts my dad enough to let him do his job without much interference."

Polly inspected the neatly stacked contents. Mostly accountancy ledgers and old books with cracked spines about how to distill whiskey, bourbon, and scotch. Below them was a shallow tray filled with maps of Catalina, the Channel Islands, and the California coastline.

Amelia opened a wooden box that held black roulette chips. "I don't see any devious skulduggery going on here."

"My father told me about none of this," Polly snapped, "so it *all* counts as skulduggery, if you ask me."

Amelia threw up her hands like a shield. "It's him you should be asking."

She wanted to think that Papa had an excellent reason for keeping all this from her, but what if his reason was unsavory or even repugnant?

"They even show movies way out here?" Amelia pointed to a pair of film cans on the bottom shelf, then bent and picked up the topmost one. The lid was a little rusted and the frayed label too worn to make out anything other than odd letters. "There's a C and maybe an A that might also be an H—or an M?" She ran a finger along the bottom edge. "Is this a date?"

Polly squinted at the can, but the numbers had badly faded. "Nineteen eleven? Fourteen? Seventeen?"

"Sweet Jesus!" Amelia let out a shrill giggle. "What if it's a stag film?"

Polly had no idea what stag films were, but from her new pal's scandalized tone, she suspected they weren't nature documentaries. She replaced the film can on the bottom shelf and wandered back to the rows of liquor. "I've always seen my father as a pillar-of-the-community type. Donates to all the charity drives, attends public ceremonies. And now I find out he runs"—she swept a hand in a wide arc—"this."

"It can be pretty disheartening when your parents disillusion you."

Was Amelia talking about getting packed off to an isolated island when her parents learned she was in the family way? Polly didn't look forward to the conversation she'd have to have with Papa, but it paled compared to the one this girl must have had with her parents.

Amelia popped the cork stopper of a half-empty bottle of Benedictine brandy and inhaled its aroma. "Is there someone you can ask about all this? Other than your father, I mean."

Polly looked at the floor. Amelia was the first friend she'd ever made, but admitting that felt like a sure-fire way of bringing it to an unceremonious halt. If only she had one person she could turn to.

Oh.

Wait.

Of course.

6

The peak of the day's summer heat had abated by the time Polly arrived at the steep staircase leading to Zane Grey's hilltop pueblo.

Might he resent the interruption? What if he were in the middle of a thorny story whose words had only begun to trickle? Maybe she should call first. But risk one of the island's telephone operators listening in? No thanks. A note? Yes, that would probably be better. Ask him when he'd have some time to chat.

But would she get any sleep tonight knowing that the answers to all her questions lay in the bedroom down the hall, and that she hadn't challenged Papa as soon as he had walked in the door?

Her visit to Cat Harbor had flipped her upside down, teetering her from fear to trepidation to shock to disappointment. Riding an emotional seesaw was exhausting. She should've swiped one of those Mad Ox bottles.

"Coming or going?" The familiar voice boomed down the canyon. Mr. Grey stood with his right hip leaning against the wrought-iron railing. "Not even your speedy little fingers could've finished *Spanish Peaks* already." He waited until she had reached the upper landing. "You look like you might benefit from some of my wife's lemonade."

He told her to take a seat in the living room as he fetched a couple of glasses from the kitchen.

Grey had modeled his sprawling home in the style of the Hopi Indian adobes. Thick walls and high ceilings ensured the rooms stayed cool even after a long August day, which was a blessed relief for Polly, who longed to unlace her riding boots to relieve her hot feet.

Grey joined her on the sofa, which was upholstered in a dark-green-light-green geometric pattern. He set the tray with glasses and a plate of molasses cookies on the coffee table. "Take a good, long swig before you tell me what in tarnation has got you all riled up."

Mrs. Grey's lemonade was a refreshing balance of sour and sweet. Two sips and Polly already felt better.

"I saw something today that's thrown me for a loop."

"The two-headed shark Cap'n Reggie swears he sees at least once a summer?"

Reginald Hawthorne was Catalina's most skilled deep-sea fisherman. From May through October, he skippered mainland fat cats on his *Queen of the Seas* for a day of wide-open ocean, high-priced fishing poles, and the tallest tales those spoon-fed moneybags had heard all year.

"I was over at the Isthmus. I've never been out there before."

"You don't say?" The squint in Grey's eyes betrayed his surprise.

She deposited her glass on a cowhide coaster. "I've come here because I need the truth."

Grey hung his head as though to say, *And now that task falls to me.* He sighed, somewhat theatrically. "Several people have suggested to me, over the years, that you had no idea of Elroy's activities. To which I replied that you were one of the smartest girls I know and I doubted you were in the dark."

"So imagine how big a fool I felt when I got to Cat Harbor and I saw for myself."

"I'm sorry you had to experience that."

"Is *everyone* aware of what my father is running over there?"

Grey's nod was reluctant. "Uh-huh."

"How long has it been going on?"

"He started bootlegging a year after the two of you moved here. It was Prohibition, so folks turned a blind eye because it meant they could enjoy decent bourbon. I don't think it surprised anybody when he got busy at the *Ning Po*."

"When was that?"

"Coupla years later, I reckon. So, 'twenty-six, maybe?"

Polly would have been around ten, graduating from picture books, playing with dolls, giving imaginary tea parties, and wondering why none of her schoolmates invited her over to play. Had she found the answer to why she'd been a pariah all this time?

"Did people approve of the gambling?" she asked.

"Prohibition was a law nobody agreed with, so cooking up moon was one thing. Gambling, well now, that's something else again. Some folks disapproved, but it soon drew free-spending vacationers. Hotels benefited. So did the cafés, the stores, people like Cap'n Reggie, and Rozika's. After Prohibition ended and Elroy went legit with Mad Ox, most of us thought that'd kill the tourist trade, but the opposite happened. Legal hooch combined with the *Ning Po* drew even more crowds."

Nobody would have expected ten-year-old Polly to catch on, but when Prohibition was repealed, she was sixteen. What excuse did she have? Utter nincompoopery was a flimsy defense.

"Is this why everyone ignores me?"

Grey ducked his head. "You're the fallout of everybody turning a collective blind eye. Individually, most people are against gambling. But as a community that benefits from it, they're willing to look the other way. You're a reminder of their hypocrisy, which they swallowed by telling themselves that you were happy to benefit from all the proceeds flowing into the Maddox family coffers."

"What proceeds? That private yacht I keep moored off Casino Point?" She fought against the surge of resentment building inside her. All those solo school lunches. All those evenings listening to

The Jack Benny Show by herself. "This stinks worse than last Friday's mackerel."

"I get it, lassie. I do. Maybe they wouldn't treat you quite so poorly if they knew what your father did on the QT."

Even further off the record than running a gambling outfit? A generous splash of Mad Ox wouldn't have been the worst thing Mr. Grey could have snuck into Polly's lemonade glass. "What else has he been up to?"

"You know the fire that ripped through Avalon in 'fifteen?"

Polly and Elroy had moved to Avalon seven years after the terrible fire that razed six of Avalon's best hotels, along with the Pilgrim Club, the Tuna Club, and the Bath House, as well as virtually every home between Hill Street and Whittley Avenue. Polly still remembered the blackened telephone poles, the charred remains sitting in abandoned lots, and scorched walls dotting the town like rotting teeth.

"What about it?"

"That inferno scarred the town so deeply that even now, many old-timers still don't like to discuss it. Elroy knew it, so he paid for the last of the remaining ruins to be carted away and the area re-landscaped."

Polly felt light-headed. Papa had done that? She'd need every second of her forty-minute walk home to regain her equilibrium. "Nobody knows this?"

"Nope."

"How come you do?"

Grey grinned slyly. "That's what happens when you have Philip and Helen Wrigley over for cocktails and you inadvertently serve too much Mad Ox. I'm only telling you now so that you don't condemn your father for operating outside the law."

"What I resent is that he never trusted me enough to tell me any of it."

"He spread the word that what he was doing out at Cat Harbor was hush-hush-nod-nod-wink-wink."

"But why?"

"To protect you."

"From what?"

Grey paused. "Life's ugliness, I suppose. You were only five when you landed here. You'd lost your mother. You were like a little doll that needed protection and coddling."

"I'm twenty-one now. How much coddling do I need?"

"Elroy will always think of you as his little girl. So when you run home and condemn him for it—and I can see by your ruddy glow that you're about to do exactly that—I suggest you don't rush to hang, draw, and quarter him."

Polly looked down at her empty glass. "I'll try."

"I'm not letting you out of here until you promise me you'll give him a fair trial."

It took some effort to meet him in the eye. "Fine."

"Let me hear the p word."

"I promise."

He winked at her. "Now, go home and have it out with him. Then get to work on *Spanish Peaks*. My publisher is real strict with deadlines."

Polly rose from the sofa and thanked him for his honesty. Mr. Grey's revelations had left her feeling flattened under an avalanche she hadn't seen coming. Maybe she'd take the long way home and stretch out those forty minutes.

The sun was inching down over the mountains when she stepped out onto the front patio. It was nearly seven o'clock. Papa rarely made it home before eight on Mondays, so that gave her an hour to prepare for whatever lay ahead.

7

The crack of splintering wood woke Polly from a restless sleep.

Another followed, louder than the first.

Where was it coming from? The back of the house? The front? Surely not Mr. Anderson from next door? North of eighty with a catastrophic wound from the Great War running down his arm, he was incapable of wielding an ax if his life depend—

CRACK! More splintering wood followed by a loud BANG!

Were they under attack? From whom? The Japanese were thousands of miles away.

Polly scooped up the robe she had slung across the end of her bed after she'd waited up for her father to arrive home. She'd been able to keep her eyes open until midnight, but he hadn't showed. Slipping on her robe, she grabbed her hardbound copy of *Gone with the Wind*. Not exactly a baseball bat, but the brick of a book had heft.

She called down the hallway. "WHO'S THERE?"

"Sergeant Blackburn."

Polly tightened her grip. "What's going on?"

"Please join me in the foyer."

A briny breeze blew past Polly. "Did you break down my door?"

"I'll politely ask you one more time. Join me in the foyer."

Polly dropped the book and tightened the sash around her waist. Blackburn, a six-foot-two brick wall of a man, stood in the middle of the vestibule, the fractured remnants of the front door crackling under his boots. The three men behind him were not the remainder of the Avalon police department.

"You could've knocked like a normal person," she told him.

"Sorry, Miss Maddox. Not today."

This 'Miss Maddox' business sounded menacingly formal. "Why are you all here at—" She glanced at the grandfather clock in the parlor. "It's not even six."

The man behind Blackburn stepped into view. He was shorter by five or six inches, but emitted a call-the-shots aura. "My name is Whitaker. I'm with the vice squad, and—"

"From the mainland?"

"Yes, miss. I'm the deputy in charge of this raid, and—"

"We're being raided by the LA Sheriff's office?"

"Polly." Blackburn held up his hand. "This'll go a lot easier if you let Captain Whitaker do his job."

Polly cupped her hands to her mouth. "FATHER! YOU'D BETTER COME HERE. NOW!"

There was only silence.

"Miss Maddox," Whitaker said, "it's obvious that your father isn't home."

The morning winds gusting through the open doorway cooled the cold sweat breaking across Polly's skin. "Why are you here?"

Whitaker produced a sheet of folded paper from inside his jacket. "I have an arrest warrant for Elroy Maddox, and a search warrant to seize all papers and physical evidence connected to his running an illegal gambling establishment on the *Ning Po*."

Polly snatched the orders from him. "If you think I'm his accomplice, the joke's on you. I only found out about what's been going on over there yesterday. That's right. *Yes-ter-day*." She spat the syllables at the unvarnished skepticism stretching across Whitaker's face. "I'm acutely aware of how implausible this must sound, but it's the truth, so it'll have to do."

"Polly," Blackburn had tempered his voice, "you appear nowhere in those orders. Captain Whitaker and his team are after your father, and only him."

"But Sarge, you don't—he can't—"

What could she say, though? Papa was guilty of running an illegal gambling operation out of the *Ning Po—Oh my God, Papa's on the lam!* Polly felt like a sea turtle whose shell had been ripped away by a belligerent tiger shark.

She stepped aside. "Go ahead with whatever you're here to do."

* * *

No longer able to listen to the vice squad ransacking her father's office, Polly stepped onto the porch where she sat in one of the rocking chairs she and her father would sit on occasional summer evenings and polish off vanilla-raspberry swirl ice cream from Beaumont's. She should be enjoying the cool morning air, but instead she had to sit here and recover from a sock in the jaw like she was Joe Louis.

She ran her eyes down the first part of the list of the nineteen charges that Captain Whatever-his-name-was had handed her:

- Ownership of gambling equipment
- Operation of an illegal gambling establishment
- Profiting from illegal games of chance
- Contravention of the Volstead Act
- Manufacture of intoxicating liquors
- Transportation of intoxicating liquors
- Sale of intoxicating liquors

Good lord. Some of these charges dated back to Prohibition. Sure, Papa had been breaking the law, but Prohibition got shown the door five years ago. What was the point of all this?

She turned to the twinkling waters of Avalon Bay.

The Casino.

Steamer terminal pier.

Pleasure pier.

Visitor information booth.

Children's playground.

Wait a cotton-picking minute.

Polly had gazed out over this vista for fifteen years; she knew when something was missing.

She slipped off the chair and stood at the edge of the porch.

Captain Reggie enjoyed his post-fishing rum punch too much to roll out of bed in the pre-dawn hours like some of his *Queen of the Seas* customers would have liked. All the locals knew he broke his seven-a.m. rule for no one, no how.

And yet today it wasn't bobbing in its usual berth on Pleasure Pier.

Behind her, Blackburn cleared his throat. "Not too much longer."

Polly kept her gaze on the *Queen*'s empty mooring. "When can I expect the vice squad to replace our door?" *Listen to yourself, Doodlebug,* she could hear Papa say. *Sassing the police sergeant like he's the town bum.*

Was the sergeant worried about his job? For years now, he'd turned a convenient blind eye to Papa's bootlegging and beachside gambling. But now they were on his doorstep. "Manufacture, transportation, and sale of intoxicating liquors." She rattled the paper at him. "What do they think this is? Nineteen twenty-seven?"

Blackburn leaned against the porch balustrade. "That was my first question. Why charge Elroy now?"

"What'd he say?"

"He buttoned his lip, but good."

"What's your gut feeling?"

"That someone might have it in for your father."

How could anyone hold a grudge against Elroy Maddox? *Or maybe Papa wasn't so mild-mannered, after all.* "What am I supposed to do now?"

"Let the river of justice run its course."

Whitaker appeared in the doorway. "We're done." He stepped to one side as his squad marched single file out of the house, each man carrying five boxes apiece.

"Gadzooks!" Polly exclaimed. "Is there anything left?"

"We only confiscated what we've deemed necessary and will return it to you in due course, unless it's crucial evidence in a criminal case."

The word—criminal—was a bucket of cold water drenching Polly's outrage.

He closed his spiral notebook with a well-practiced flick of the wrist. "One last question, Miss Maddox." Inquisitive neighbors were emerging from their houses, content to stand and gawk from the safety of their front yards. "It would be in your best interest, and your father's, if you told me where he is."

Polly raised her eyebrows in her best Stanwyck impression. "You think *I* know?"

"Affirmative." Whitaker played the steely silence game, hoping she'd succumb.

She thought again of *Queen of the Seas'* vacant berth at the pier. "I honestly haven't the slightest clue."

The best he could manage was a brusque nod, then he jutted his chin toward the police car parked out front. "Whenever you're ready, Sergeant."

Polly waited until Whitaker was out of earshot. "You believe me, don't you, Sarge?"

"If you learn of your father's whereabouts, tell me. I don't want to arrest you for being an accessory after the fact."

The accumulating neighbors reminded her that she was now smack-dab in the middle of the most gossip-worthy news to happen on Catalina Island since the fire that had burned down half the town. She watched him follow the gravel path to the waiting squad car.

Accessory after the fact.

Well now, isn't that peachy.

8

The two girls sat on weather-battered seats in the abandoned amphitheater overlooking Avalon Bay that had once hosted summer concerts crowded with locals and tourists. Polly took a generous swig from a bottle of Mad Ox bourbon to sandpaper the rough edges off her ghastly day. "For medicinal purposes, you understand." She handed it to Amelia, who followed suit.

"After the day you've had?" The sunset had turned Amelia's copper-red hair silver, as though she were an entrant in a Jean Harlow lookalike contest. "The more medicine, the better."

This lightheadedness that Papa's bourbon caused was quite pleasant. Little bit floaty. Little bit giddy. No wonder people traveled from the mainland for it. "I appreciate this more than I can tell you."

"I'm glad you called. Besides, that's what pals are for, right?"

Polly splayed her arms along the back of the bench seating behind them. "What am I going to do?"

Amelia tilted her chin toward the setting sun. It shone down on her face like a spotlight. "How many boxes did they haul out?"

"Fifteen? Twenty? Nine hundred and sixty-three?" Already the details were blurring like a watercolor painting left in the rain. "I'm surprised they didn't take Papa's typewriter ribbons."

"I hate to say it, Polly Wolly Doodle, but that flatfoot might be right about someone holding a grudge against your pop."

Papa's bourbon was loosening the stays of her inhibitions in a rather delicious way. "He didn't even leave a note. A clue. A scrap of paper. Telephone number. Nothing!" Polly's throat dried up. She took another shot of Mad Ox. "And now I have to walk into McNally's Hardware and order a new door with customers whispering behind their hands. You don't know what it's like to be from a place where everybody knows everybody's business."

Amelia let out a derisive snort. "It doesn't matter if you live in a three-donkey burg two hundred miles north of Billings, Montana, or on Fifth Avenue at Thirty-ninth. There's no escaping the grapevine."

Living in Los Angeles wasn't much different from living on Catalina? Polly looked up at the dusk sky. Could Papa, wherever he was, see the same tapestry of emerging specks?

"However," Amelia added, "you can escape this place."

Even in the face of what had happened, panic at the prospect of leaving the only home she'd ever known seized her. "Leave Catalina?"

"Go to the mainland. With me. Tomorrow."

"But what about the baby?" Polly winced. She should have waited for Amelia to bring it up first. Gosh, Papa's hooch sure knew how to loosen a girl's tongue.

"Baby?" Amelia stared at her, puzzled, and then realization dawned. She cradled her hands to her stomach. "You think I'm knocked up?"

Polly felt her face flush. "Papa said you'd gotten yourself into a pickle, which is the same as saying you'd gotten yourself into trouble. And we all know what that means."

"No, no, no!" She set the bottle down between them and flattened her palms onto her thighs. "Remember how I talked about wanting an interesting life? Well, there was this fella. Quite the rake. Fancy clothes. Fast cars. You get the picture."

Polly nodded, although she didn't get the picture at all. What did she know, socked away on Catalina Island where the worst crime the local boys could commit was to filch a stray baseball one of the Chicago Cubs had lobbed during winter training.

"I swallowed all his guff about where he got his money. A little stock market, a little investing, a little inheritance. I can't believe I was so pea-brained that it never dawned on me he was a racketeer."

"You were dating a gangster?" Honestly, Polly scolded herself, could you sound any more like Rebecca of Sunnybrook Farm?

"Not big-time or anything. But in the neighborhood." Amelia blew a raspberry. "I suspect part of me liked to think I was in some ripped-from-the-headlines Warner Brothers picture. My upbringing was so everyday, run-of-the-mill that this diversion was kinda thrilling—until the night I wised up. Ever heard of the La Brea Club?"

Polly shook her head.

"It's a classy joint at La Brea and Third. One night Jimmy says to me, 'I've gotta go meet my boss.' I didn't know his boss from a hole in the wall, but I tagged along. Jimmy walks into the club like he's been there a thousand times. We go straight through to the back and it's a gambling den. Furs, diamonds, tuxedos, money flying everywhere. Jimmy points to his boss and says they have some business to do, so meanwhile go get some cigarettes. Now, I might be naïve, but I'm no halfwit. His boss was Longie Zwillman. Ever heard of him?"

"I don't think so."

"Good. Keep it that way. Mobster. Big-time. Bad news. Real bad. So now I'm thinking, 'Uh-oh! I'm out of my depth.' But before I can plan my escape route, the goddamn vice squad shows up."

"What happened?"

"Everyone's scattering like cockroaches, but some of the goons started shooting. Naturally, vice doesn't take that lying down, so now bullets and bodies are flying all over."

Polly stared at her, speechless. "Did Jimmy get hit?"

"Right in the chest. Didn't kill him, but one of the bullets got his lung. The raid made all the papers. Aggie Underwood had a field day." Aggie Underwood was a *Herald-Express* crime reporter, known for her fearless coverage of the gruesome, the grisly, and the ghastly, which meant, from time to time, she bumped fenders with the mob. "She said the cops were seeking the redhead in the sea-foam-dress." Amelia directed both thumbs at herself.

"What did they want with you?"

"They thought I had information that might disappear if Jimmy died."

"About what?"

"A huge stash of tommy guns."

"Where?"

"Jimmy didn't share his comings and goings with me, but try telling the cops that."

"And did you?"

"Heck, no! But I told my parents. It was Mom who suggested I go hide out at Catalina until the heat was off."

"But you said that I should come to LA with you tomorrow."

Amelia rocked her head from one side to the other. "While you were getting your door busted in, I was reading Aggie's report about how a La Brea Club raid gangster died of his wounds. The dumb bastard got pneumonia. Must've sneezed that bullet into his lungs. The end. But not before he gave the cops what they wanted."

"They found the stash?"

"Oooh, yeah. Last year, CBS opened their new radio studios on Sunset, right near Columbia Studios. Out back of it, they built a couple of utility sheds. One of them was filled with spare parts for microphones and whatnot. But the other? Jackpot! Aggie's been having a grand time."

Polly was trying her best to keep up with this rapid-fire turn of events. Was life in Los Angeles always like this?

"So now," Amelia continued, "I'm free to go home. The only question that remains is: You coming with me?"

A chilled ocean breeze shot down the amphitheater's hillside. Polly jumped to her feet. "It's time we got back to town."

They got to their feet; Polly picked up the nearly empty Mad Ox bottle and they set off down the road. Mt. Ada threw the path ahead into dark shadows.

"It's a big change, I know," Amelia said as they walked. "Little Catalina to the big smoke. But with your pop gone, what's keeping you here?"

But my whole life, Papa's told me LA is bad. LA is trouble. LA is dangerous. And now I'm supposed to leap in like some daredevil movie stuntman? "First Papa disappears, then I do. Won't that look suspicious?"

"In the first place, you're not facing charges. And in the second place, you're not disappearing. You're heading over to the mainland for a change of scenery."

"What would I do when I got there?"

Amelia barked out a laugh. "The head housekeeper at St. Catherine told me you're the world's fastest typist, so I'm sure Western Union would snap you up." She picked up a pebble and catapulted it to the patch of dirt where the old bandstand used to be. "When does the *Avalon* leave for LA in the morning?"

"Eleven."

"And now Miss Maddox has a deadline."

* * *

It was well after ten p.m. when they parted company. Jack's Steak House was still open, but otherwise the town was deserted—thankfully. Polly didn't possess the energy to pretend to ignore anyone's judgment.

Could she pack a bag and wave goodbye to her old life from the deck of the *Avalon*? Catalina hadn't exactly welcomed her into its warm embrace, but it was all she had ever known. Did she *want* to do it? No. What she *wanted* was for Papa to come back to the island and face the music.

She rounded the corner onto her street, so lost in thought that she didn't notice the figure standing on her porch until she had stepped onto the gravel path. Zane Grey rapped his knuckles against some planks of wood leaning against the front wall of the house. "I brought these over as a makeshift door until you can get a new one from McNally's."

Another reason she couldn't up and leave. Even though hardly anybody bothered to lock their doors on Catalina, she couldn't very well leave the house open to the world, could she?

"Aren't you thoughtful?" She reached around the door jamb and flicked on the light. "Coming in?"

"I'd better."

Polly didn't like his grim tone, and waited until they had settled on the sofa before she asked him what was on his mind.

"Weeks ago, the Wrigleys invited the missus and me over for dinner."

Philip Wrigley had only ever nodded at his accountant's daughter. There had been no need for him and Polly to have a conversation. "I imagine dinner at the Wrigley ranch is quite the swell affair."

"He showed me the full rundown of charges."

"He already had them *last week*?"

"Officially, they were listed as preliminary charges."

"All nineteen? I'm still getting my mind around them."

"I'm sorry to have to tell you this, Polly, but there are now twenty-seven. These additional charges are"—he hesitated for an uncomfortable moment—"more serious."

Leaping lizards. "Such as?"

"New allegations have since come to light." Flippancy dripped from every syllable.

The memory of those deputies carrying out twenty evidence boxes played in Polly's mind. "Allegations of what?"

Grey took a deep breath. "Embezzlement."

Polly shot forward onto the edge of the sofa. "From who?"

"The Santa Catalina Island Company."

"My father has always said that Mr. Wrigley is the perfect steward of this island. What reason could Papa possibly have to steal from him?"

Grey shook his head.

"How much is he supposed to have made off with?"

"Thirty-five thousand dollars."

Polly gasped. "Papa's no embezzler!" Even saying those words out loud felt ridiculous. The drama of the day's events had taken its toll. She could feel the last remaining bead of energy seep from her as she thudded back into the sofa. The tom-tom of an approaching headache throbbed at the base of her skull. "I don't know what to say."

"Time for some good news," Grey said. "Mr. Wrigley agrees."

Finally, a semblance of sanity. "With what?"

"With you—that your father is no embezzler. In the sixteen years Elroy has worked for the Company, he's not given the Wrigleys any cause to worry."

"He must've known about bootlegging Mad Ox and the *Ning Po.*"

"Not too thrilled about it, naturally, but it brought people to the island. However, embezzlement—"

"—can't be ignored."

"Indeed. He produced one of those broad accounting ledgers and showed me where three pages were missing, and . . ."

Oh, cripes. "And?"

"And listed on pages before the missing ones were payments to Myer-Harris Haberdashery."

"Has anyone called them?"

"Evidently, there's no such business registered with the city."

Oh Papa. Why didn't you stick around? "Doesn't look good, does it?"

"There is, however, someone called Meyer Harris Cohen. That's Meyer with two e's, whereas Myer-Harris has just the one. Meyer Harris Cohen is more widely known as Mickey Cohen."

The name meant nothing to Polly, but the wild-eyed look on Grey's face told her that it meant something to *him.*

"Mickey Cohen is a Chicago mobster. Rumors are rife that Cohen is about to arrive in LA to work for Bugsy Siegel."

A startled "OH!" flew out of Polly. "Oh. No. Not Papa, no."

"Probably to set up race wires. So, if Elroy has embezzled

thirty-five grand to give to Mickey Cohen and, by extension, to Bugsy Siegel, then he's in deep because Siegel is allied with Jack Dragna."

"Do I even want to know who that is?"

"He's the mafia kingpin in Los Angeles. He's the one who runs those gambling ships off Santa Monica."

Hot tears prickled the backs of Polly's eyes; her breath came in short, harsh wheezes. "All of this is circumstantial."

"Which is why Mr. Wrigley prefers to believe in Elroy's innocence."

I can breathe again! "He's on our side?"

Grey was quiet for a moment. "The evidence is stacked against your father, Polly. If he's guilty, Mr. Wrigley will not hesitate to cooperate fully with the investigation, which I think is fair enough. But then I asked him if he had any connections inside the DA's office."

Polly's emotional seesaw had stretched into a roller coaster. "Please tell me he does."

"He's Mr. Wrigley. Of course he does. He plans to call in a favor and get a delay in the charges being officially filed. He felt pretty sure that he could get a three-month grace period."

A three-month grace period was three months longer than Polly thought she had to try and fix whatever she could. If she could. "I'll take it."

"Meanwhile, however, all of Elroy's effects are frozen—real estate and personal, which means you'll no longer have access to anything in this home or at his office. Both will be off limits, and any attempt to breach the perimeter will constitute breaking the law. I've spoken to Sergeant Blackburn and asked him to give you until midnight to get some things together."

"What happens then?"

"He will be returning to cordon off the house."

His words felt like a punch in the solar plexus. "I'll be locked out of my home?" The grandfather clock showed she had less than ninety minutes to pack. And go where? The answer shone like a neon sign: To LA with Amelia and find her father. Assuming he was in the city. Which he probably wasn't.

It was a big town, however, with tons of places to hide. Whether he had moved there or moved on, she needed to see if she could find him and help clear his name before it was too late. She had a sinking feeling that it would prove to be a colossal waste of time, but she wouldn't forgive herself if she didn't at least try.

9

Polly peered at the tower clad in pale turquoise tiles through the back window of the taxi she and Amelia had taken from Long Beach. "Was that the Wiltern Theatre?"

"I thought you'd never been to LA."

"I haven't."

"And yet you know the Wiltern?"

"It was on one of the picture postcards Clark sent me."

For the past hour, Los Angeles had unfolded like a perpetual diorama of palm trees and neon signs. Well-dressed pedestrians walked their dogs past elegant homes with manicured lawns. Open-air convertibles shone in the sun, gliding past with a sense of purpose that she couldn't help but envy. With its bright red streetcars, girls on bicycles in floppy sun hats, and ornate churches whose spires reached into cloudless skies—this was big, bad LA? Where were the rundown tenements and ramshackle boarding houses? This city was hardly the forbidding den of iniquity Papa had always cautioned her against.

I could have been coming over here all this time.

Amelia retrieved a compact from her purse and checked her lipstick. "It still slays me that Clark Gable is your pen pal."

They passed a barn-sized building on the left with half a dozen arched windows, its name painted in three-foot letters: FOX STUDIOS.

Polly pressed a gloved finger to the glass. "Is that a movie studio?"

"Yep." Amelia dropped the compact back into her purse. "It's Twentieth Century-Fox now after William Fox went belly up during the Depression."

"Was it terrible back then?"

"Sometimes, yeah. Lines for soup kitchens, people on every corner selling apples or oranges for a penny." Amelia tapped their driver on the shoulder—"Take a left on Beverly Boulevard and a right on Bronson"—then returned to Polly. "Used to be Okies all over the place, living in their jalopies held together with spit and string. It's not so bad anymore. Now, listen: we need to talk about my folks."

"Do they know you're coming home?"

"I sent them a telegram first thing this morning."

"Did you tell him I was coming too?"

"Yep. And I bet they're dying to see what you look like."

Polly found it faintly unsettling to not be seated at her Pacific Wireless desk—but not so unsettling she wouldn't have swapped this taxi ride for all the powder puffs at Max Factor. "I bet they're relieved it's all over."

Amelia stared out the window as the taxi turned left onto a major thoroughfare with two lanes in each direction, making it three lanes wider than almost every road on Catalina. "We'll stay there an hour. Two hours tops. Then we exit stage right."

Mild panic tightened Polly's throat. Were they homeless?

"I've made the break," Amelia said. "I'm not going back there again. Not to live, anyway. Look, they're perfectly nice. Honest, they are. But they want me to have a regular life. Marriage. Kids. Thanksgiving dinners. The usual ball of wax."

"And you don't?"

Amelia's eyes crinkled at the edges. "When I was twelve, I went through a poetry phase. There was this one poem that socked me right between the eyes. Get a load of the final verse." She sat up straight and cleared her throat. "'Not for me will the hours pass, dulled with the pallid hues of muted pastels. Make my sole rotation on life's carousel radiant with primary colors.'" She let a whole city block roll by before she spoke again. "There's a little fellow they've been trying to pair me off with since the day I got my first monthly visitor."

"A little on the dull side?" Polly asked.

"I'd rather read the Congressional Record of eighteen twenty-five. Twice. In Latin. Standing on my head."

"Hence the Schwab's plan?"

Amelia elbowed Polly. "You get it, don't you? Nobody else seems to."

Growing up in a house with two parents, siblings, and probably a hamster or two didn't sound to Polly like the worst way to pass a childhood. But Los Angeles was unfolding around her like a rainbow-colored picnic blanket, whose every corner whispered a promise of unforeseeable adventure. "I get it."

After telling the driver to take a left on Maplewood, Amelia said, "I have a pal. He's got a house on the end of Hollywood Boulevard, which wanders up into the Hollywood Hills. His dad had tuberculosis, so they converted their side porch into an open-air cure. We can stay as long as we want. It'll be cool at night, but that's what blankets are for. Meanwhile, we'll get jobs and can look for a place."

Maple trees thick with leaves, swept driveways, and well-maintained homes lined Maplewood Avenue. Amelia directed them to the third house from the corner. Freshly painted pale green with white trim, it looked to Polly the sort of place she'd be inclined to run toward, not from.

The clang of the front gate set off a cacophony of barking from inside the house. "That's Jewel and Cookie," Amelia said. "Or as I call them, Death and Destruction."

"They sound awfully glad you're home."

"They'll only jump on you like you're their personal bale of hay for the first forty minutes."

The front door swung open, unleashing an Irish setter and a

golden retriever, both of them pressed their paws against Polly's chest, their meaty breath filling the air.

Amelia hauled them off her. "Down, you crazy hounds of the Baskervilles. Down!"

Jewel and Cookie ignored her until a louder, sterner voice called out from tiled patio, "HEEL!"

A clean-shaven man in a striped shirt with an Arrow collar and light brown suspenders snapped his fingers twice. The dogs dropped onto all fours.

"That's about as civil as they get, I'm afraid." A woman in her early forties appeared next to him.

Amelia stayed rooted to her patch of gravel. "Hiya, Pop. Hiya, Mom. I'm back."

Mr. Hartley stayed where he was, but Amelia's mom stepped off the porch. The sun glinted in her bright red hair, the exact shade of her daughter's. Her amiable smile dropped away suddenly. "POLLY!" Amelia's mother drew her into a hug. "You've fairly taken my breath away," she exclaimed over Jewel and Cookie's rambunctious barking and Amelia's ineffectual orders to quit making such a racket.

"Hello, Mrs. Hartley," Polly said.

"Please, call me Lois," the woman said, releasing Polly to arms' length and turning her from side to side, giving her a thorough once-over. "Pardon my stupefaction, but the last time I saw you, goodness, you were such a little bitty cherub. No more than five years old. And look at you now." She twisted around to address her husband. "Isn't she the spitting image of Flora?"

Polly couldn't remember the last time Papa had even said her mother's name out loud. Hearing it now made her inhale sharply.

Judd Hartley shook her hand warmly, if perhaps a little stiffly, as his austere face melted a little at the edges. "Lois put on a pot of coffee when we saw the taxi pull up."

They led her and Amelia into a living room strewn with newspapers, clothes, and toys, where a woman was bent over a hotel-sized laundry basket. Shorter than Amelia, and with dead-straight brown hair that hung past her shoulders, she bore the harried look of a woman who couldn't remember the last time she'd slept through the night. Lois introduced her as Amelia's older sister, Faith, who waved a hand toward a sleeping baby nestled into the end of the sofa.

"And this is my darling little Chester," said Faith, as she scooped up a mountain of clothes off the dining table. "Sorry. Today is laundry day."

The window at the rear of the house opened onto a backyard with four mature lemon trees that filled the room with a sweetly bitter smell. Under the trees, an identical pair of prepubescent boys were running around on the lawn, screaming as loudly as their lungs would permit. Using baseball bats as horses, they were playing cowboys and Indians, but with those nests of strawberry blonde hair, it wasn't clear who was the Indian and who was the cowboy.

"And those mouthy heathens are my brothers, Samuel and Sebastian," Amelia said. "Swear to God, those two generate more energy than the Boulder Dam."

This tumultuous house, with its unruly dogs baying at an imaginary moon, rowdy boys caught up in the Battle of the Little Bighorn, scattered toys, and whopping piles of laundry, couldn't have been more different from the quiet, orderly Maddox household. A few days ago, the thought of living in a house like this might have overwhelmed Polly. But now that she was here, surrounded by Amelia's boisterous family and smack-dab in the middle of a city swarming with a million people, she felt invigorated and exhilarated over the possible paths her life might now take—even though wading through those million people to find Papa felt like a task of Biblical proportions.

As Lois set the table with sugar and creamer, and a platter of plum tarts from the icebox, Judd said, "So, tell me, how's your father? Well, I hope?"

Polly and Amelia exchanged wary glances. There was no easy or quick way to tell him what had happened over the last twenty-four hours.

"Papa worked for you at, what's it called? City of Angels Distillery?" Polly began.

Judd nodded sternly, as though it pained him to dredge up the past. "He started with us a year or two before the Great War. Right away, he proved to be our best salesman. He had that knack with people, you know?" Polly nodded. Yes, she knew.

"We were sad to see him go," Lois said, "but after your darling mother died of a burst appendix, your father announced he wanted a fresh start and was moving the two of you to Catalina. To us, it sounded like a fine idea."

It occurred to Polly that she'd never asked her father why he had decided on Catalina. The island was all she'd ever known, so why question it? "Do you know why he moved us there?"

"I expect it's because we all spent a memorable summer out there together, living in those semi-permanent tents. They were part wood, part canvas. Is Tent City still there?"

Polly nodded.

She paused, lost in memories it seemed to Polly. "We didn't hear from him much, which was understandable. Fresh start, and all that."

"A while later," Judd continued, "we began hearing fuzzy rumors about how a still had started up on Catalina, known as Mad Ox."

"We thought, 'Must be Elroy!'"

"And then we heard he'd taken on a silent partner and they were in it fifty-fifty."

"A partner?" This was news. Papa had never mentioned a partner. "Who?"

Lois shrugged. "I don't know. But he was obviously doing well for himself. We were at a party once. An industry bash thrown by a big muckety-muck from Columbia. Or was it RKO? At any rate, deep into the night I snuck out the back for a breath of fresh air. There were at least a dozen bottles of Mad Ox lined up along the fence, and I thought, 'Elroy must be making scads of money.'"

"I can see why he continued to make it after Prohibition came to an end," Judd added. "He was smart to manufacture exclusively on Catalina. Your dad always knew how to sell booze, I'll give him that. But tell us. How is the ol' so-and-so doing?"

The news of Papa's embezzlement would have whipped around the island by now, and would likely reach the mainland before long. There was no point holding back from these folks. Polly was still positive he was innocent. There *had* to be a perfectly reasonable explanation. But three years of sending and receiving carefully worded telegrams had taught her plenty about human nature. Everyone at home had already assumed the worst about him.

Laying out the events of the past few days was an arduous slog that felt like she was describing someone else's life, but Polly felt lighter somehow, unburdened, when she arrived at, "And that's what brings us to your doorstep."

"I can see how tempting it must have been to set up a gambling joint far from prying eyes of the police. But—" Lois shook her head slowly— "embezzlement? It's been quite some time since we've seen your father, but that doesn't sound like his style at all."

Polly breathed a quiet sigh of relief. At least she wasn't the only one who refused to condemn Papa. "He left the island without telling me."

"You mean he—" Lois put a hand to her throat. "He's on the run?"

The tremulous hesitation in Lois's voice made Polly question whether the woman was telling her everything she knew. It was a lot to assume, but if an opportunity presented itself to get Lois alone, Polly would take it. But that might be hard in this three-ring circus of a household.

"You know," Judd said, rubbing the line of his distinct jaw, "if you've come over here to try and track down your father, you might ask George Stevens. He's currently directing *Gunga Din*."

Polly doubted she could walk up to a movie studio and talk her way onto the set of a high-profile movie. Then again, an hour ago she'd had no idea how to track down her father, but now she had a lead. "Why him?"

"Because Elroy and George were palling around back when

Stevens was a gag writer on the Laurel and Hardy shorts for Hal Roach."

"Oh, Judd, that was twenty years ago," Lois said.

"If you have any other suggestions—"

"I was reading in *The Hollywood Reporter* that Edmund Goulding is at Warner Bros. preparing an Errol Flynn picture, and after that, *Dark Victory*, with Bette Davis. He's absolutely one of the most well-connected men in—"

"ABSOLUTELY NOT!" Judd thumped the table; several plum tarts bounced off the platter. Even the twins outside ceased hostilities long enough to peer through the window. He fixed Polly and Amelia with a flinty glare. "I categorically forbid you girls having anything to do with that man."

Until this moment, Amelia's father had matched his daughter's perfectly-nice-perfectly-conventional description, so this outburst caught Polly unprepared.

Amelia said, "If you want to lay down the law, you should at least present a robust case."

Judd restored the tarts to their plate. "Several years ago, Goulding was embroiled in a scandal in which it became known that he possessed a penchant for voyeurism and for bacchanals involving both sexes—"

"Orgies?" Amelia cut in, too gleefully for her father's liking.

"He got himself exiled to Europe," Judd said, pointedly ignoring her. "After a period of time, he returned, unrepentant, to MGM, where he insisted they honor their contract. So L.B. Mayer assigned him to two minor pictures before casting him adrift. The man is bad news, and you, my dear daughter, have already flirted with danger, and look where it got you. I cannot forbid Polly from doing anything, but if you're smart, you'll heed my advice." He turned his attention back to Polly. "While it's admirable that you've come looking for your father, I strongly recommend you find another way."

The dining room fell into what Polly assumed was a rare silence until Lois stood abruptly. "There are no sheets on your bed, Amelia, but in the linen closet—"

"We're not staying, Mom."

"You're what?"

Polly's heart sank; she wanted to take Amelia aside and beg her to change her mind. This household was unruly and chaotic and the opposite of what she was used to, but wouldn't it be better than a closed-in TB-cure porch? Amelia, however, was already on her feet.

"We've got digs all organized, haven't we, Pol?" She flared her eyes at Polly. *This is our cue to amscray.*

Polly reluctantly got to her feet. "It's been lovely meeting you. Hopefully I'll see—"

Amelia prodded her toward the front door where they had deposited their suitcases.

"But Amelia, darling . . ." Lois had to shout over the racket Cookie and Jewel were making; the dogs had commenced howling over the movement of humans towards the front door. "What's the address? Is there a telephone? How can we contact you?"

"We haven't even talked about the close call with that—fellow," Judd added, raising his voice over the din.

"I don't have the telephone number memorized yet, but I'll call you with it. Promise. And Dad, the less we say about 'that fellow,' the better, okay?"

"How do you plan on paying for these lodgings?"

"I'm getting a job at Schwab's, and Polly's a virtuoso at the typewriter, so it'll take her all of six minutes to get a job."

After a flurry of goodbyes and assurances that they'd be in touch, Polly soon found herself standing on the sidewalk, a suitcase in one hand and a dozen questions bouncing around her skull.

"This way." Amelia took off west along Maplewood.

Polly hurried to catch up. "I know your parents' place is—"

"—an uproar morning, noon, and night."

"But they mean well, don't you think?"

"In their way."

"I'll admit that your dad's a little on the stern side—"

"It ain't that." Amelia kept her focus on the sidewalk. "I've lived my whole life in Faith's shadow. Little Miss Perfect with the Straight A's. Little Miss Art History Degree from Wellesley. Little Miss Married Her High School Sweetheart. I'm the also-ran daughter."

"I'm sure your parents don't look at you as—"

"And then the twins came along. God, what a nightmare handful they've been from the start. They suck up all the air in the room, leaving nothing much for me. I KNOW!" She threw up a hand to stop any interjection. "I sound like a whiny little brat. Nobody listens to me. Boo-hoo for Amelia. I'll get over it, I promise. But for now, that's how I feel. I need to strike out on my own. Make *my* way in the world. And I'd have thought you of all people would know how that feels."

Before today, Polly wouldn't have described herself quite like that. But now that she was off the island, miles and miles away from everything and everyone she knew, she had caught a glimpse of how she appeared to other people. "You're right."

Amelia stopped abruptly and dropped her suitcase on the sidewalk. "I am?"

Polly nodded. "We're both starved for attention."

Amelia stared, hard, her mouth slightly agape. It was almost as though the girl were a mirror, reflecting back at her a whole new Polly Maddox.

"This place up on Hollywood Boulevard," Polly said. "Is it far?"

"Highland is a few blocks ahead. We'll flag a taxi there easy enough."

Polly picked up Amelia's case and handed it to her, then grabbed up her own. "Let's get going."

10

The sign—*SCHWAB'S PHARMACY*—stretched the width of the drugstore's front windows. Amelia patted down hair that didn't need fixing and tugged at the Peter Pan collar of her emerald-green blouse. "I haven't gotten any schmutz on it, have I?"

"That depends on what schmutz is," Polly replied.

"I'm guessing there aren't many Jewish yentas where you're from."

"Santa Catalina Island isn't exactly the Lower East Side."

"It means little stain or smudge."

"In that case, you're schmutz-free."

"Now that you've joined the real world, you might want to learn a bunch of Yiddish. From what I've heard, Jews are streaming out of Europe to escape those Nazis. If they can write or act or play a musical instrument, Hollywood's their best chance at a job." Amelia turned back to her reflection. Above her, the words *BREAKFAST, LUNCHEON,* and *DINNER* in cursive neon tinted her hair a bright tomato-red.

Though the two girls looked similar, Amelia possessed a sparkle that twinkled like a halo and followed her like a spotlight. Her eyes danced with the glee of whatever excitement might lie beyond the next corner, and her smile, filled with white, milk-fed teeth, was always on the verge of parting wide to unleash a contagious cackle.

Imagine breezing through life like that, Polly mused. Nothing to lose. Everything to gain. I could stand to learn a thing or two from this go-getter.

"Why are you gawking at me?"

Amelia's question plucked Polly from her swirl of ponderings. "Because it's past nine-thirty and I haven't eaten anything since your mother's plum tarts yesterday. Can we go in? I'm famished."

* * *

Even the Crescent Beach Bar and Grill on its rowdiest Saturday night would have trouble competing with the verve and exuberance of this place. Glass shelving filled the eastern side of the retail area. Tubs of Woodbury's Facial Cream stood alongside artfully arranged Vitalis hair tonic, Barbasol, Bavarian chocolate bars, and —yes, of course, there it was—Wrigley's spearmint chewing gum.

Amelia elbowed Polly. "Empties at the far end!"

As Amelia led her toward a pair of unoccupied seats, she caught snippets of conversation.

"Have you seen Norma Shearer in *Marie Antoinette* yet? Irving'd be proud."

"When Chamberlain meets with Hitler in Munich, what's the bet he gives that crazy thug the Sudetenland like it's a chunk of the Paramount backlot."

"I can't believe Hughes cut Lindbergh's time to Paris in half."

Polly and Amelia slid on to the vacant seats next to two guys in houndstooth sports jackets with open-necked shirts and country-club tennis tans.

Polly canted her head toward them. "Are they the interesting men with interesting lives you had in mind?" she said, sotto voce.

Amelia stole a furtive glance. "Could be. Don't bother with the menu, though. I've already decided what we're having."

"Shall I guess, or is this a surprise party?"

An approving smile. "You can snap off a quippy comeback when you want to."

Polly gave her a rueful smile in return. If anybody in Avalon had taken the time to engage her in conversation, they might have given her more than a bare-minimum good-morning nod. "Would I be right in thinking quippy comebacks are a handy skill in these here parts?"

"Yes indeedy." Amelia ran a fingernail down her menu. "I can't stand drippy-droopy, wishy-washy, namby-pambies with Jell-O backbones, can you?"

A waitress with Clara Bow curls and Jean Harlow eyebrows approached them, a stubby pencil poised over her pad in anticipation. Amelia rattled off their order: number two club sandwich, number five club sandwich, whole avocado on the side, and two coffees—unless Polly preferred Postum instead? No, Polly did not.

Amelia surveyed their fellow diners, and then drew Polly's attention to a mismatched couple walking through the front door. "See what I mean? Interesting people!" A handsome young man in his mid-twenties and a mid-fifties woman seated themselves further down the counter. "What's their story, I wonder."

With Lois's tarts a distant memory, the bewitching smells of burgers, fries, and grilled ham made Polly hollow with hunger, so she was glad for the distraction until their breakfast arrived. "Mother and son?"

The woman had marcelled her hair into a coif that even the matrons of Catalina Island would have deemed old-fashioned. She hadn't gone gray yet, but from the wattle of skin sagging beneath her chin, Polly guessed it wouldn't be long now. She wore expensive clothes, but none of those beiges and browns flattered her. Nor did the cut of her two-piece suit. It may have done ten years ago, when that style had been popular in the late-flapper era, but now it just made her look like someone's maiden aunt. It wasn't as though Mother couldn't afford to update her wardrobe, Polly thought acidly, if that diamond ring on her finger was a reliable indication.

Her companion excused himself and crossed over to the retail side of the store.

"Look at the way he moves," Amelia whispered. "I bet he does a mean rumba."

He had his back to them now. Keeping his spine straight as a conductor's baton, he ran a fingertip along a shelf of cosmetics. "Maybe," Polly said, "he's one of those guys who dances behind Judy Garland and Alice Faye?"

They didn't get a clear glimpse of him until he'd selected a jar of Evening in Paris face powder. He possessed a full head of thick hair, black as pitch, shiny as licorice. His eyes, sapphire blue, sparked with mischievous charm as he rejoined his companion and placed the powder in front of her. She unleashed a piercing yip. Just when Polly thought he couldn't get any more handsome, dimples dented each cheek as an amiable, almost conspiratorial smile emerged.

"I've changed my mind," Polly said. "Rich aunt with favorite nephew."

"See how that jacket sits squarely on his shoulders, and drapes down his torso in easy folds?" Amelia observed as he took his seat. "I'll bet you ten bucks it's bespoke vicuna."

Polly wasn't entirely sure what vicuna was, but it sounded expensive. "He's got style to match his looks."

"Oodles. But she's not his doting aunt. They don't resemble each other. Not around the eyes. Not around the nose."

The handsome young man waved his teaspoon in a circle like it was a magic wand and snuck a droll comment out of the corner of his mouth. The woman feigned outrage and slapped him across his shoulder.

Amelia clutched Polly's forearm. "He's her *gigolo*!"

"No!"

"Good-looking. Well-dressed. Charming. Amusing. Moves like a dancer. And you know what they say about guys with rumba hips."

An actual gigolo? Out in the wild? In bespoke vicuna—whatever that was. *Honest to God, Papa, when I track you down, I'm going to scold you so hard for keeping all this from me.*

As she continued to watch the strange pair, an odd sensation enveloped her body. Almost like an eggshell—stiff, but brittle. She could almost feel it cracking as she shifted in her seat. Not a shell, she decided, but a crust. *And that cracking sound is you chipping away at the crust you didn't realize you had cocooned yourself into.* Polly took a deep breath, perhaps a deeper one than she'd ever been able to take before.

"Who gets the five and who gets the two?"

The question came not from their waitress but a man in shirt-sleeves and an apron with the Schwab's logo across his chest. Amelia directed him to place the chicken sandwich in front of Polly and took the corned beef for herself. "I told your waitress to take a break because I wanted to introduce myself. My name is Leon Schwab."

Amelia's fork slid from between her fingers and clattered against her plate. "One of *the* Schwab brothers?"

"The one that runs this place, anyway."

"Mr. Schwab!" She sat up straight and pushed out her chin. "This is your lucky day!"

Schwab rested a hip against his side of the counter and crossed his arms. He took his time giving Amelia the once-over, though there was nothing lascivious about his wandering eyes. "Lucky, huh?"

"You don't know it yet, but"—Amelia leaned forward to redirect his attention—"I'm your new favorite waitress. I've had tons of experience dealing with slow eaters, messy feeders, reluctant payers, and wisenheimers of all stripes who assume it's okay to sass waitresses and assume they won't get as good as they give. I can think fast, talk fast, move fast. I can add up a check quicker than you can say 'boiled ham on rye,' and I have more stamina than Seabiscuit."

Amelia had delivered her word-perfect pitch with the right emphasis on all the crucial words, but Schwab merely gazed at her, glassy-eyed. "Sure, kid." He tilted his head toward a woman near the kitchen hatch who had made the most of her generous cleavage and peroxide rinse. "Give your details to Ida."

"Thank you, Mr. Schwab! I appreciate—"

"I'm probably way off the mark here, but I must ask," he said, turning to Polly. "You're not Flora Maddox's daughter, are you?"

A muffled cry lodged itself in Polly's throat. "How could . . ." The shock of Schwab's observation had robbed Polly of her voice.

"A boy never forgets his first crush; you're her spitting image."

Polly shifted her wide-eyed stare to Amelia. *Start talking. I can't speak right now.*

"What an amazing coincidence," Amelia said, her tone suddenly suspicious. Not that Polly blamed her. They had come in here with the express purpose of getting her a job, and now Polly had hijacked the spotlight. Was Mr. Schwab feeding her a pickup line?

"Not so coincidental as you might expect," he replied. "Back when I was a kid, LA wasn't so big as it is now. The movies hadn't even come to town yet. Everybody's folks belonged to one club or another: Rotary, Knights of Columbus, Odd Fellows. My grandparents and yours belonged to the Moose Lodge, and so my mom and yours became quite pally."

"When you were still a kid?"

He rewarded her joke with a lopsided grin. "I was eleven when I first met your mom. I thought she was crackerjack. Always over at our house, she was, lending my folks a helping hand in our huge garden. Gosh, they were always out there planting, weeding, watering." His eyebrows clenched together. "You must be the same age now that she was back then. Gosh, but you're the spitting image. You must get that a lot, though, huh?"

Polly shook her head.

"But you must have family snapshots," Amelia's voice was back to normal now.

"Only one. Mama's in the background, so she's a bit blurry." That single photo was the sum repository of all Polly's memories of her mom: blurry and in the background.

A warm tide washed over Polly. Papa had tacitly deemed his

life before Catalina off limits, so she had never brought it up. Never asked about her mother. Never gone looking for photos stashed in their backyard storage shed. And yet on her first day off the island, here she was in the middle of a crowded, rowdy jamboree, and her first conversation was with someone who had nothing but loving memories of Flora Maddox. What a magical place this Los Angeles was.

"Did you ever meet my father?"

"Oh, sure. He got many of us through the Dark Ages. That's what we called Prohibition on account of we didn't know where our next drink was coming from." Schwab jacked a finger into the air. "But we could always count on plenty of Mad Ox bourbon at one of Cohn's parties."

"He's talking about Harry Cohn," Amelia said, "the head of Columbia. *Real* powerful."

If Cohn was always so well-stocked with Mad Ox bourbon, maybe he might know where Papa was. "Are my father and this guy good friends?"

"No idea," Schwab said. "But Mad Ox has always flowed wild and free at his parties."

"I'm trying to track down my father."

"He's gone missing?"

Polly leveraged the elation in hearing her mother's name into her brightest smile. "Nothing so Dashiell Hammett as all that. But if this Harry Cohn knows my father—"

"You'll be lucky to get near him." Schwab punched each word with the rancor of a losing prizefighter. "And *un*lucky if you do."

Polly couldn't imagine her amiable father being chummy with a guy like that. "What's wrong with him?"

Schwab and Amelia exchanged a look too brief for Polly to grasp.

"Ruthless," Amelia said. "Devours girls like us for breakfast and spits our bones out before lunch."

Leon tilted his head down the length of the counter. "I'd better throw myself back into the fray."

"Thank you for introducing yourself, Mr. Schwab."

"Call me Leon. In my book, Flora's daughter is family."

"I can't tell you how much I appreciate it."

"One question before you go," Amelia said. "Who's the Beau Brummel with the duchess?"

Leon's smile stopped short of a smirk. "Ludlow Sinclair."

"A made-up name like that? He's got to be an actor."

"You'd think so, but no. He often comes in here, mostly after dinner hours. Always in the company of an older, respectable woman."

"Gigolo?" Amelia asked.

Schwab shrugged. Ida called out his name, so he took off down the lunch counter.

"See?" Amelia picked up the closest half of her corned beef sandwich and watched Ludlow Sinclair light the tip of a long, thin cigarillo his companion was holding out for him. "What did I tell you?"

11

A week later, Polly and Amelia walked along the Hollywood Boulevard sidewalk at a window-shopper's stroll. The crowds were thinning now that the lunchtime rush was over.

"If you want a job at Schwab's," Polly said, "shouldn't we be there as often as possible?"

"Coffee and donuts are cheaper at Newberry's five-and-dime." She tapped the *L.A. Times* tucked under her arm. "Two donuts will buy us more time to read the want ads. And besides, Leon Schwab is a sharp character. It's not good to come across too needy."

"We're sleeping in a TB porch in October. We *are* needy."

"Pah! And besides, the Santa Anas will start blowing soon."

"The what?" Polly asked.

"The Santa Anas. You know, the devil winds."

"They sound fun."

"They blow in from the hot desert this time of year. They'll warm us up, but can be sudden and blustery, so you gotta watch 'em." Amelia nudged Polly and pointed up at a Western Union sign farther along the boulevard. "All you need to do is tell them you type ninety words a minute and you'll have a job quicker than you can say 'Zing went the strings of my heart.'"

Now that circumstances had liberated Polly from a cage whose bars she had never truly noticed, why would she work for another telegraph company? If she was going to spend her days taking and transmitting telegrams, she might as well catch the *Avalon*'s afternoon run back to Catalina.

As a duo of nannies steered identical baby buggies around them, Polly's thoughts returned to that line of poetry Amelia had quoted.

Make my sole rotation on life's carousel radiant with primary colors.

The friendship she had yearned for her whole life had fallen into her lap like an unexpected Christmas present, and she had no intention of letting it slip away.

But it was those primary colors that had already cemented Polly to the mainland. The sunflower-yellow of the taxicabs. The conch-shell-pink of the Beverly Hills Hotel. The blood-red booths at the Gotham Delicatessen. Catalina had its fair share of hues, of course. The wildflowers in spring. The Casino's ocean-inspired friezes. The tiles on the roof of the Hermosa Hotel, which were so intensely red they almost looked permanently aflame. Life in Avalon was hardly a sepia-toned Pickford movie, but it was nothing like the Technicolored cyclorama now surrounding Polly.

"I'm keeping Western Union up my sleeve in case we get down to our last two bits."

"Fair call. Meanwhile"—Amelia unfurled her newspaper—"did you read what Hedda Hopper has to say about Errol Flynn being cast as Rhett? *Robin Hood* is cleaning up at the box office, which means he might—"

"As Rhett Butler? I can't see it."

"Nobody can, but if Gable puts his foot down, Selznick'll have to look elsewhere."

Like every other American old enough to read *Gone with the Wind*, Polly had been following the saga-without-end that casting the leads had become. She was glad David Selznick hadn't settled on any of the early contenders. Would Tallulah Bankhead, Joan Bennett, or Katharine Hepburn be able to make Scarlett jump off the screen in the same way she jumped off the page? Polly didn't think so.

But contemplating anyone else for Rhett Butler was a fool's errand.

The two girls were now in front of Belle Apparel Millinery, which offered an array of hats in every material, style, and color. The cheapest Polly saw was $11.95, which put it, and every other hat, far beyond the reach of a pair of girls headed for a five-and-dime to save on coffee.

"Say!" Amelia leaned a shoulder against the glass. "You've got Clark's address. Why don't you write to him? Maybe he can wrangle you a job at MGM. Wouldn't that be swell?"

"It would," Polly admitted, "but he's talked a lot about how people always want a piece of him. A favor for this, a favor for that. I suspect he's still writing to me because I've never asked anything from him."

Amelia's face fell into a frown. "You're right. You don't want to be some awful bottom-feeding bloodsuck—" She grabbed Polly's arm. "Ohmygod! Look!" She craned her neck around an incoming trio of sailors in crisp uniforms, white caps jauntily perched at the backs of their heads. "The guy at Schwab's. Mister Vicuna."

"What about him?"

"He walked into Kress's. Come on." Amelia rushed her down the sidewalk, past a music store and a yarn shop until they reached a window display featuring cardboard cutouts of witches, ghosts, and jack-o'-lanterns.

They put their cupped hands to the glass and peered in. The natty young man with the finishing-school charm and movie-star name stood out among the pencil sharpeners and lunch boxes, packets of hairpins and bags of marbles. He had stopped at a display of tin wind-up toys to inspect a Bakelite figurine of Felix the Cat.

"I'm surprised a guy like that would shop in a store like this." Amelia opened the door and ushered Polly in. "I had him pegged as the Bullock's kind." She pretended to inspect a packet of sewing notions wrapped in yellow cellophane. "This makes him far more interesting."

Polly had seen advertisements for Bullock's department store in the occasional Los Angeles newspaper that had strayed into the Maddox household. The womenswear was always so sleek and modish. The next time they went window shopping, she thought wistfully, couldn't they do it there?

Amelia ditched the notions back onto the counter. "We've been caught."

Polly executed a slow one-eighty rotation. Close up, the sapphire of his eyes was even deeper, the cut of his jawline sharper, his smile more beguiling than before.

"Well," he said, "if it isn't the Cherry Sisters from Schwab's."

Coming from almost any other man, a line like that would have sounded like well-rehearsed smarm designed to soft-soap girls into giving up their telephone number—or worse. But he had a boy-next-door charm with take-me-or-leave-me appeal that Polly hadn't counted on.

"On account of your red hair," he said, filling in the silence. "You stood out like a pair of Roman candles."

"How flattering of you to notice." Polly had meant her rejoinder to sound like the sort of witty repartee Ginger Rogers might have exchanged with Fred Astaire when they met for the first time. But were they flirting? Was this a flirting situation? Polly had zero experience with the opposite sex, so what the heck did she know?

"I hope your companion wasn't jealous," Amelia trilled.

Yes, Polly decided, we're definitely flirting. And with a gigolo, no less.

He let off a genial laugh. "She can be, but not with me. Ria and I don't have that sort of . . . bond."

That word, "bond," struck Polly as an odd choice. Especially since he'd paused to choose it. "What sort *do* you have?"

His eyes narrowed as he shifted his weight from one foot to the other. "Professional."

A young mother juggling a squirmy toddler and an infant squeezed past them. They left in their wake the stink of baby vomit and day-old diapers, instantly dissipating the cheeky, playful air.

"I admired the jacket you were wearing at Schwab's," Polly said, changing the subject.

"Thank you."

"Custom-made, was it?"

"Sunset House."

"The one owned by the *Hollywood Reporter* guy?" Amelia asked.

"You know your men's haberdashers."

"About a year ago, my father got his hair cut at the barbershop down the back. He commented on how expensive the clothes were. 'High-quality merchandise at high-quality prices,' were his exact words. Did Ria pay for yours?"

Polly was sure Amelia had tried to be cutesy, but her wisecrack slapped the affability from his face. His eyes took on a steely irritation and dropped to the newspaper tucked under Amelia's arm. The top half of Gable's face peeked out from under her sleeve. "Ria's last name is Langham."

The name meant nothing to Polly, but Amelia yipped. "Otherwise known as Mrs. Clark Gable," she told Polly.

The flintiness in Sinclair's eyes was already thawing. "Not for long."

"Carole Lombard, huh?" Amelia nodded knowingly. "Ria's refusing to let him go?"

"But David Selznick can't cast him as Rhett if he's carrying on an open affair with"—Polly lowered her voice to a whisper—"his mistress!"

"Correct. But Clark's unaware that Selznick and Mayer—" He broke off. "I've already said too much."

"Then let me say it for you," Polly said. "Selznick and Mayer are in cahoots because Selznick wants him for Rhett, but that can't happen while he's married to Ria but carrying on with Carole."

Sinclair slow-blinked. "You're not just a pretty face."

Polly felt a blush slink onto her cheeks. "I assume this is where you come in?"

"Ria knew her days were numbered the moment Carole sidled into view, so Mayer pays me to make her feel wanted and included. Trouble is, she's dead set against divorce."

"I take it that it's your job to smooth the path to the negotiating table?"

"More like 'convince her to accept the inevitable.'"

Quite the diplomat, aren't you? Polly thought. I bet Ria loves spending time with you. All the right honeyed words, with enough sincerity to make them stick. I bet you take the time to point out how much you like her brooch or perfume, or how flattering you think her new hairdo is.

"And if you do your job properly," Amelia said, "everybody gets what they want."

"She'll score a generous settlement. I'm there to entertain and escort. It pays well, so if I turn it down, some other escort will say yes."

Polly and Amelia gaped at each other. *So he's an escort, not a gigolo? Is there a difference?*

"Is there much competition for a job like that?" Polly asked.

"Enough. Most men over the age of forty don't like to dance or go to the opera or the symphony. All they want is to sit in a corner with their cronies, smoke their Partagas Cubans, drink their Courvoisier, and swap insider trading tips. Meanwhile, their bored wives languish at home with their needlepoint, wishing they were at the Biltmore Bowl dancing to Paul Whiteman and his orchestra. That's where we come in." He flashed that smile again, wide as the Pacific, bright as the California sun, and designed to impress those lonesome wives.

But why would someone like this talk to a couple of nobodies like us? God knows I'm a babe in the woods when it comes to making whoopee, but after he takes them dancing, does he really take them to bed? Polly sensed no lechery or lewdness radiating from this guy, though. No hint of a lady-killer. Maybe he already had a sweetheart. Maybe he didn't go for redheads.

"So," Amelia piped up, "you got a name?" Of course, they already knew his name, but protocol was protocol.

"Ludlow Sinclair. And you?"

After Amelia had introduced them, she elbowed Polly. "Tell him about your Clark Gable connection."

"Oh, yeah?" he said warily.

His flattened tone told Polly that she really shouldn't.

"Polly here, she's from Catalina," Amelia went on, oblivious to their discomfort. "She was there when MGM went on location to shoot *Mutiny on the Bounty*."

"Oh, yeah?" That tone hadn't gone away.

"And they became pals. Such pals, in fact, that he's still sending her picture postcards. And now that she's living here, she's hoping to connect with him again."

"You want me to ask Ria to ask Clark for a favor?" His tone was downright cold now.

"I wouldn't call it a favor, exactly," Polly said.

"Gable doesn't want to know anything about me. Mayer's paying me to keep Ria happy, and that's as far as it goes. However, speaking of movies"—he faced Amelia more squarely now, his tone warming again—"have you thought about auditioning for the *Pretty Pennies* remake?"

Amelia stared at him blankly.

"Next year will be the fiftieth anniversary of the first projection of moving pictures, as well as twenty-five years since DeMille came to Hollywood to film *The Squaw Man*. His picture gets all the attention; however, *Pretty Pennies* was also made in 1914, *and* it was made entirely by women—director, scenarist, camera operator, lead actress. Caused an absolute sensation wherever it played. Along with *Squaw Man*, it proved that nickelodeon customers will sit through longer films. There are no copies left, just a few publicity stills, so David Selznick wants to remake it and has announced he's holding auditions. He plans to cast an unknown, and in his character description, he describes—well, *you*."

Amelia's lips had turned down at the edges. "Flattering as that is, Mr. Sinclair, I have no desire to become an actress. Go outside and swing a tomcat by the tail. You're bound to hit half a dozen aspiring actresses. It's a job at Schwab's I'm after."

"You should have asked Leon Schwab for one."

"I did, but he gave me his standard answer."

He handed her a knowing wink. "I throw him a lot of business in the way of prescriptions. My lady clients love their Benzedrines to get out of bed in the mornings, and their Seconals to help them fall asleep. If I have a quiet word to Leon, maybe we can move you up Ida's pile."

According to Papa, all Hollywood people were solely preoccupied with scrambling to the top of the dog-eat-dog heap. Or was that another notion he'd gotten wrong?

"You'd do that for me?" Amelia asked.

"Absolutely! But I've read the character rundown. It truly does read like it's describing you."

Had the guy not been standing in front of them, Polly would have asked Amelia, What's the big deal? He might get you the job you want, so one little audition seems a small price to pay.

She did wonder, though, why this well-dressed Samaritan was so willing to go out of his way for a total stranger. "Not to be too mercenary about it," she said, "but what do you care if some girl you hardly know gets cast in a Selznick picture?"

He threw up his hands as though he were in a stickup. "You got me. I confess."

That was more like it. Maybe Papa was right about Hollywood people; he'd told her, more than once or twice, "Everybody over there has an agenda."

Sinclair peered down the aisle toward the lunch counter, where three uniformed nurses were slipping off their stools. "How about I buy you two a cup of coffee?"

Amelia was already marching toward the rear of the store. "And donuts."

Once they were settled, Sinclair placed his hands on the table in front of him and interlocked his fingers. They were long and tapered, and perfect for playing the piano. Besides cutting a smooth rug, Polly was willing to bet he played decent ragtime.

"One of my other regulars is Marjorie Selznick, who is married to David's brother, Myron."

"The talent agent?" Amelia nudged Polly. "Very successful."

"And a terrible lush," Sinclair continued. "But at least he doesn't overwhelm his secretary with memos like his brother does. Between *Gone with the Wind*, the *Pretty Pennies* remake, and this new project David's considering, called *Rebecca*, Marjorie tells me his secretary, Marcella, is drowning. She's a fast typist—sixty-five words a minute—but it's not fast enough. At any rate, Marjorie's awfully unhappy and would love to be more involved in her husband's business." Their coffees had landed in the middle of his speech. He raised his cup and blew on it. "I was thinking that if she could be the one who finds the unknown lead in *Pretty Pennies*, it might help patch things up between them."

"Ah!" Amelia said. "So that's your hidden agenda for spilling beans you ought not be spilling to complete strangers."

"Oh, I don't know," Polly told her. "As far as agendas go, it doesn't seem so atrocious."

"You'll show up for an audition?" he asked.

"You'll have a word with Mr. Schwab?"

"First chance I get."

"When will that be, exactly, Mr. Sinclair?"

He bit into his donut. "First of all, none of this 'Mr. Sinclair' jazz. It's Ludlow, okay? Second of all, I have a day job, so it'll be one evening this week. Promise."

"I've often wondered what escorts do by daylight." Ten minutes ago, Amelia had never met one, and now she was making out like she hired one several times a week.

"I work at NBC Red, where I do sound effects on *Dick Tracy*."

"I'm impressed." Amelia clinked her coffee cup to his. "Are you the one who makes horsey clippety-clop sounds and police sirens?"

As she and Ludlow talked about the pressure of performing a nationally popular radio show live to air, Polly's mind strayed to David Selznick's harried secretary. Sixty-five words a minute didn't sound so fast to Polly. She typed seventy-five if she put her mind to it. Eighty-five if she concentrated. Her typing-class record was ninety-one.

If Ludlow wasn't already doing Amelia a favor, Polly might have asked him for an introduction, but she didn't want to push her luck. But landing a job like that was worth taking a shot because it sure beat the heck out of working for Western Union.

12

David Selznick's office was housed in a small wing of a long, wide building with eight two-story columns spaced across the front. The reception office's window looked out over the manicured lawn and knee-high hedge that lent Selznick International Pictures some breathing space from the unrelenting traffic along Washington Boulevard.

To Polly's amazement, the telegram she had sent to Selznick's secretary had resulted in orders for her to present herself at ten the following morning. And so now here she sat in a borrowed suit, borrowed blouse, and a new hat from the bargain basement of a department store at Hollywood and Vine.

A maelstrom of activity eddied around her. The continuous racket of competing typewriters battled with the chatter of a teletype machine. A stream of people flowed in and out, holding script pages, photographs, and sketches of elaborate dresses pinned with swatches of material. Too busy, too preoccupied, too distracted, none of them gave Polly a second glance.

She smoothed the hem of Amelia's skirt over her knee. What a difference from the quiet, predictable life she had led on Catalina, where each day, each season, each year melted into the next.

"You must be Miss Maddox."

The woman was standing in front of Polly was dressed in a suit of pale pink with a full skirt and an unadorned blouse.

Polly swung to her feet. "Yes, ma'am."

"I'm Mrs. Rabwin. Follow me."

She was already seated at her desk by the time Polly stepped into her office. "Ninety words a minute? Is that accurate?"

"If I put my mind to it, yes, ma'am. *Ninety*." Polly leaned as heavily on the number as Rabwin had.

The desk telephone jangled. Mrs. Rabwin picked it up and barked out a series of orders stern enough to impress a drill sergeant. Dropping it back into its cradle, she said, "Teletype machine?"

Polly lowered herself onto the chair. "We had little call for it at Pacific Wireless, but I'm sure I can figure it—"

"Suppose I gave you this." She held up a page filled with handwritten notes and a name—Kay Brown—scrawled across the top. "Could you type it up before eleven a.m.?"

Polly checked her watch. It was twenty of. "Assuming those hieroglyphics are legible, yes, I believe so."

"You're confident," Rabwin noted. "I like that."

I have nothing to lose, Polly thought. At the very least, I can eat dinner tonight, warmed by the knowledge that I've spent an hour in the place that shall soon be filming *Gone with the Wind*. "You don't get far in this town without confidence."

That made the woman smile. Another phone call. Another set of barked orders. "How did you come to hear how desperately I need the fastest typist in the West?" The woman stared. Not blinking. Not moving. Almost challenging.

Should Polly tell her that she knew the fellow her boss's sister-in-law paid to take her dancing? Was it common knowledge that Marjorie Selznick employed an escort? Was it socially acceptable for the wife of Hollywood's most powerful talent agent to admit she uses the services of a man like Ludlow?

Marcella Rabwin, Polly decided, was a no-nonsense woman with neither the time nor inclination for playing games.

"Ludlow Sinclair told me."

Rabwin blinked the blink of someone caught off guard. "You know Ludlow?"

"We got chatting at"—Kress's five-and-dime sounded a bit tacky, so Polly revamped the truth—"Schwab's. He was there with Ria Langham, and Marjorie's name came up. She's the one who told him you're swamped with enough work to sink the *Lusitania* all over again."

For the first time, Mrs. Rabwin's smile held some warmth to it. "Isn't he a marvel? And a godsend for women like Marj. And poor Ria, too. Imagine being stuck at home while your husband is heralded as the King of Hollywood."

"Do you think she knows Mr. Mayer is paying Ludlow to squire her around town to butter her up over the divorce?"

Mrs. Rabwin fanned herself with Polly's telegram. *I see,* her face appeared to say. *You* are *in the loop, aren't you?* The telephone rang again. She yelled for someone to pick it up, then faced Polly once more. "I'd like to hire you."

"Wonderful!"

"Providing."

"Yes?"

"You can start immediately."

"Certainly."

"By which I mean right this very second."

"You haven't even seen me type yet."

"Let's consider this afternoon your typing test."

Polly's new boss led her back into the outer office where another typist sat—a rather harried-looking woman named Hazel. Next to her stood an empty desk with a covered typewriter. Mrs. Rabwin transferred a stack of handwritten notes from Hazel's in-tray to Polly's. "All these need to be typed up before you leave tonight."

An entire afternoon to type up a bunch of notes didn't sound so hard.

Dropping her pocketbook into the bottom drawer, she slipped the cover off her typewriter, and picked up the first sheet.

Draft #14—re: Negotiations with MGM to acquire GONE WITH THE WIND in the event Selznick International Pictures runs out of funding.

Goodness gracious! I've had been here fifteen minutes and I've already seen confidential information Louella Parsons and Hedda Hopper would stab their mothers for. My, oh my. I'm going to enjoy working here. Very, very much.

* * *

Polly rotated her wrists to ease the ache, something she'd never suffered during her three years at Pacific Wireless. She might have finished by six o'clock, but Marcella kept adding more and more memos. How did this Mr. Selznick get any work done if he sat at his desk all day dictating?

Still, they made for interesting reading: orders to track down a Swedish movie called *Intermezzo*, suggestions for Scarlett O'Hara's dress in *Wind*'s opening scene, a list of potential sets to be used for the burning of Atlanta, and a recap of the current status of the screenplay, which was nowhere near finished.

But now it was almost eight o'clock. She was mid-yawn when Marcella strode into the room. "How about we call a truce on the paperwork for today?"

Polly nodded. "How often do the streetcars run this time of night?"

Marcella fixed her with an approving once-over. "I threw you in at the deep end and you didn't even wince."

"Not that I let you see, anyway."

"If you can't swim in the deep end, you have no business being here."

"I'm from Catalina. We're all splendid swimmers."

"I need girls with stamina." Marcella's eyes flickered to Hazel's empty desk. "Your colleague might not have what it takes, but I suspect you do."

Polly lifted her chin in the hope it made her look strong and willing, even though her fingers felt like they were about to snap off. "You can count on me."

Marcella rattled the sheet in her hand. "I have to teletype Kay, our East Coast story editor. She's waiting to hear from me."

"Isn't it eleven o'clock in New York?"

"Remember what I said about stamina?"

Good Lord in heaven. These movie people worked harder than Polly had ever imagined.

"Kay's the one who hounded David until he bought *Wind*. Let me get this off to her and I'll walk you out." Marcella disappeared into the teletype room. "And don't worry about the streetcar. I'm putting you into a taxi."

Polly retrieved her hat and purse, and wandered into the corridor. Framed movie posters lined the walls: *Manhattan Melodrama, David Copperfield, A Star is Born, Nothing Sacred*—all of them featuring the credit *Produced by David O. Selznick.*

She came to the one Ludlow had mentioned.

The poster for *Pretty Pennies* featured a redhead with her back to the audience. She wore a plum-colored bathing suit. With no sleeves and curved audaciously low, revealing several inches of bare flesh below the neck, it must have been daring for 1914. Bright copper coins filled the girl's left hand.

They made Polly think of the kids who greeted the SS *Avalon* and encouraged passengers to throw coins into the ocean. How desperately she'd wanted to be one of them. Oh, Papa, would it have been so terrible?

"Are you lost?"

A rather large, ungainly man stood behind her.

"No." She crushed her purse to her stomach as though it were a shield. "I'm waiting for Marcella. She had an urgent teletype for Kay Brown."

He pushed a pair of gold-wire-framed glasses up his nose. "I sometimes suspect our Miss Brown never sleeps." He rolled onto the balls of his feet and rocked back as he fidgeted with loose change in his pocket. "Has Marcella hired extra help? I told her she can do anything she likes as long as she doesn't bother me about it."

"Oh!" Polly exclaimed. "You're Mr. Selznick?"

A gentle smile playing on his lips indicated it had been a while since he had encountered someone who had no idea who he was. "And you are . . .?"

"Polly Maddox."

He looked her over. "How long have you been working here?"

"Nine hours."

His roar of a laugh was hardly in proportion with her reply. He jerked the hem of his tweed waistcoat and narrowed the space between them until he drew close enough for Polly to see her reflection in his glasses.

What was he doing?

She felt the heat of his hand slide onto her behind.

That's happening? Right now? What should I do? If I pretend like nothing's going on, won't it encourage him?

Not that she knew what came next. But whatever he was doing, he shouldn't be doing it.

She took a step to the left. "And on my first day, too!" She tried leavening her rebuke with a bubbly giggle. "At least give me enough time to find the commissary."

He sucked on his lower lip as he jerked his hand away and returned it to its pocket.

Is he about to cry? How fragile can this man's ego be? "Mr. Selznick, while I'm flattered—"

"Do you still have that olive-green gown? The one with the ruffled sleeves."

Polly tried to hide her look of bafflement. He had just described the outfit she'd had made for her high school senior prom. Papa had even permitted her to wear lipstick and mascara. She had walked to the prom, sure that one boy, some boy, *any* boy, would ask her to dance. But nobody did. Unable and unwilling to become a dreaded wallflower, she had left early, hung the dress in her closet, and had never worn it again.

"How do you know about that?"

"Your father carried around a photo of you wearing it. He'd show it to anyone who stood there long enough, describing its color, and how beautifully it suited you."

Polly retained only a dim memory of posing for that photograph. "You knew my father?"

"Most bootleggers were skunks out to chisel buyers with substandard product. But Elroy's bourbon was always dependable. I haven't seen him lately. How's he doing?"

Why am I only now learning that Papa carried around that photo, and learning it from someone who was a complete stranger until he laid a desperate hand on my rear end? "He's fine." Until she located Papa, bland responses to that question would have to suffice.

"Listen," he lowered his voice even though not a soul was around, "let's pretend that clumsy pass of mine never happened. I wasn't even serious."

A heck of a ploy if he didn't mean it. Were all men like this?

Selznick jangled his loose change again. "I suffer from a compunction to make a pass at every girl in the office and am always horrified when they say yes because I love my wife."

"Why do it, then?"

He shrugged. "It's expected of me?"

"How many women take you up on it?"

His shoulders dropped as he stopped monkeying with the coins. "Not many. But some. Then I have to go through with it. And after that, I have to deal with the horrible guilt over cheating on Irene, who is a saint. Life can get so complicated, can't it?"

Polly peered down the corridor. How long did it take to send a teletype? She turned to the *Pretty Pennies* poster. "I hear you plan to remake this."

"It's the picture that got my father into the business way back when. Alas, I have a clearer memory about the dinner afterwards than the movie itself. I wish he'd thought to retain a print." Selznick sighed. "But dear ol' Dad was never mindful of the future."

"He didn't keep a copy of his very first movie?"

Another sigh. Less sincere, more resentful. "My father was far more concerned with enjoying the profits of his labors."

Ludlow was right; the redhead in the poster looked like Amelia. But could he get her an audition? Did it matter now that Selznick himself was standing next to her?

"I will say this about him, though," he said. "He didn't care a whit that *Pretty Pennies* was made by women. It was his path into the movies. He would have gone on to greater success, but the men running the film business conspired to kick him out on his tuchus. So me and my brother are making it our mission to restore the Selznick name."

Who'd have thought that she and David Selznick would share the mutual urge to restore their fathers' reputations?

"Speaking of fathers," Selznick said, his voice wistful now, "if I had a buck for every time Elroy bailed me out of holes I'd gambled myself into . . ."

Wait. What? If Papa had enough money to bail out David Selznick, why would he need to embezzle from Mr. Wrigley?

"Bit of a gambler?" she asked lightly.

"When I've convinced myself I'm on a winner's streak, there's no dissuading me. But your dad, he's a fine, upstanding fellow. I can't tell you how tickled I am that fate has sent his daughter to work for me."

Even though Papa had never brought up Selznick in conversation, they had clearly enjoyed a trusting friendship, so maybe Polly could trust him too? "I wish it were under more pleasant circumstances," she ventured.

"How so?"

Polly outlined the events leading up to Elroy's disappearance and how she was over here trying to find him. "But he's the needle and Los Angeles is the haystack."

"I'm sorry to hear this. I've been so preoccupied with *Wind* that I hadn't heard of Elroy's troubles. I tell you what. This weekend Irene and I are throwing my brother a fortieth birthday party. I expect a lot of people there will know your father. Maybe one of them can help you pick up on his trail."

"Thank you," Polly said. "That would be wonderful."

"Do you have someone to escort you?"

"Yes. I can ask my friend Ludlow."

Selznick cocked his head to one side. "Sinclair?"

Was there nobody Ludlow hadn't met? "Is that okay?"

"He'll know half the people there. Including my sister-in-law, Marjorie." He clapped his hands together. "And speaking of wives, I ought to get home to mine before she stops talking to me altogether. Good evening, Miss Maddox."

Polly bade him farewell and then returned to gazing at the *Pretty Pennies* poster and wondering about how to go about asking Ludlow for this favor. Would he expect her to pay him? If he did, how much did he charge? Even if his fee depleted her savings, might he be worth the investment? If even one of the guests knew where Papa might be, Polly had little doubt Ludlow could extract that information.

Speaking of money, it dawned on Polly now that Marcella hadn't mentioned her salary. What did typists make over here? And if they expected her to work until nine in the evening or until her fingers fell off, whichever came first, shouldn't she be earning more than what Pacific Wireless had paid her? She heard heels on the hallway floor and turned to see Marcella approaching.

"Sorry that took so long," Marcella said, fixing her hat in place. "I should've anticipated Kay would have questions."

She peered at Mr. Selznick's office. "I heard you and the boss talking. How'd that go?"

"He was very nice."

Marcella raised a skeptical eyebrow. "Did he make a pass?"

The world's most awkward one. "Not that I noticed."

"Glad to hear it," Marcella said as she guided Polly toward the exit. "If he ever does, come straight to me and I'll fix his little red wagon."

Polly gripped her purse extra tight. "We didn't get around to talking salary."

"With so much going on, we didn't. And that's my fault." They stepped outside to a cloudless night blazing with stars. An ocean breeze whipped past their faces. After being cooped up in that office, Polly was grateful for the October nip tingling her skin.

"How does thirty sound?" Marcella said.

"A week?"

"I can't go over forty."

Compared to the seventeen fifty a week she'd been making at Pacific Wireless, thirty sounded like a king's ransom. Forty was more than enough for her and Amelia to start looking for a place of their own.

"Forty'll be fine," Polly said. "Oh, and by the way, Mr. Selznick invited me to his brother's birthday party this weekend."

"That means he likes you." Marcella stopped to slip on her gloves. "Irene Selznick knows how to throw a swell affair, so you'll have a marvelous time. But don't gape at the famous faces."

A frisson of excitement spiraled around Polly's chest. "I'll try my best."

"I tried my best, too—and failed miserably. Come on, the taxi stand is this way." They headed toward Washington Boulevard. "And when you get home, head straight to bed. If you thought today's workload was unusual, you'll be in for a shock."

Polly didn't care. She had an exciting job, a decent salary, and a boss who took no guff from anyone. Not even from David O. Selznick—or his little red wagon.

13

Amelia drew a circle with her fingernail against the glass counter of Sunset House Haberdashery. "Are you sure it's okay to bring an extra guest to this shindig? You've only been working at Selznick a week."

"Nobody'll stop us at the gate when they see we're with—" Polly wiggled her fingers in Ludlow's direction.

With the methodical precision of a diamond cutter, he was now eliminating unacceptable candidates among the twelve neckties the salesman had laid out.

"I don't care how we get in," Amelia said. "This'll be my first big Hollywood party."

"Mine, too."

"I'm super excited."

"Me, too," Polly said, although it wasn't outside the realm of possibility that she was only on the guest list because he was so embarrassed over his lumbering attempt at a pass.

The salesman, a cultured gent sporting a paisley silk pocket square and leaving a trail of Vitalis hair tonic in his wake, approached them. "He's narrowed it down to three possibilities."

"Are all guys this fussy?" Amelia asked.

"Most of my customers have more money than taste. They

come in here, point to the first suit they see, and tell me, 'That'll do.' Unfortunately for them, they didn't have an Uncle Fedor like Mr. Sinclair does."

Polly looked askance at Amelia. *There's an Uncle Fedor?* "Fedor is on his—father's side?"

"Yes, the vaudevillians."

Ludlow's family was in vaudeville? "Did you ever see Fedor do his act?"

"Sadly, no. Song-and-dance man. High class. Top hat, tails, patent leather shoes, walking cane."

"I bet he had a willing pupil in Ludlow," Amelia said.

"You'd win that bet. Fedor taught him how to dress, speak, walk, dance. All the social niceties. And a good thing, too, after what happened to the circus during the Depression."

Vaudeville and the circus?

"What do you think?"

Ludlow had chosen a claret-colored tie with a subtle pattern of tiny gray anchors arranged in a diamond formation to go with his new suit.

Polly ran a finger down his lapel. It was smoother than moon-kissed jazz. "What is this made of?"

"Gabardine," the salesman replied. "Italian. Milan, to be specific."

"Thanks, Norman," Ludlow said. "I need some time to walk around in it."

Amelia waited until the salesman had withdrawn. "Sounds expensive."

"The most expensive suit they have in stock."

"Bit of an overkill for a garden party, isn't it?"

"This is an investment. Norman told me that ever since Mussolini took power, the output from the Italian factories—cars, wine, suits—has all gone downhill. And if war breaks out in Europe, there'll be no more for the foreseeable future."

"How much is it?"

"Seventy-nine ninety-five."

"That's a fortune!" Polly blurted out.

"I took Ria to the Cocoanut Grove last night. She'd heard from her lawyer that Clark's about to make a tremendous divorce offer, so she was in the gayest mood. And when she's like that, she's ridiculously generous. Tipped me an extra twenty."

Amelia pulled a deadpan expression Buster Keaton would have envied. "We're in the wrong business."

"She was especially titillated last night because Bugsy Siegel stopped by our table to compliment her emerald brooch. Suddenly she was a twittering schoolgirl."

"The gangster? Was at your table?"

"He gets his hair cut here." Ludlow pointed out the barbershop at the rear of the store. "The main barber is a fellow called Harry Drucker. He knows everybody who's anybody, and he told me Siegel is real particular. Shave, facial, haircut, and manicure. The works."

"Otherwise"—Amelia drew a thumbnail across her throat "—it's cement shoes for you."

Mention of Bugsy Siegel threw Polly back to that awkward conversation she'd had with Zane Grey about Papa's payments to a Myer-Harris Haberdashery. She made her way into the barbershop, where she encountered a portly chap in a white smock reading *Variety*. "Mr. Drucker?"

"If you're looking for a beauty parlor, there's one—"

"I was wondering if you've heard of a haberdasher called Myer-Harris."

Drucker shot her a wary side-eye. "Where'd you hear that name?"

"From my father, Elroy Maddox."

Drucker folded his *Variety* and gestured to the vacant chair next to him. "I was sorry to hear about the trouble Elroy's gotten himself into. Embezzlement!" He sucked air between his cigar-yellowed teeth. "That's a curly one."

Polly's heart filled with lead. Those charges were already public? "He didn't do it."

"Your dad's a swell guy. Anybody'll tell you that."

"I'm desperate to find him, but this is such a big city."

"He's around here some place," Drucker said. "I had someone in here last week who saw him."

The haystack got smaller. Polly slid forward until she was on the verge of spilling out of her chair. "Were they sure?"

"Him or someone who looked like him."

"Oh." The haystack swelled again.

"You're here with Ludlow, aren't you?"

"I am."

"The big Selznick party?"

"Yes. The person who saw my father, will he be there? Who was it? Can you give a name?"

"I get a dozen or more customers in my chair every day, so it's hard to keep track. But it was an A-list type—or runs with that crowd, at least. I'd bet my best pair of clippers one of them will know your father."

"Myer-Harris sounds like a gambling front, or code-name, or password, don't you think?"

Drucker didn't answer straightaway. Was he sizing her up? She had read somewhere that men treated their barbers as trusted father confessors, so she kept quiet, willing herself to not blink.

"Myron's brother, David," Drucker said at last, "he's a high-roller. Bets bigger than he can afford. The crowd he hangs with is the same way. Be discreet and casual when you bring up your father in conversation. Like you don't care one way or the other. Gambling debts are a funny thing. Selznick, Mayer, Schenck, Zanuck, Wilkerson—they're always borrowing and owing and repaying outrageous sums to each other, but rarely talk about it."

"So I should ask around," Polly said, "but don't mention the subject that nobody talks about?"

Drucker cracked his first smile. "If you come up empty-handed, try Dave's wife. She's one of the sharpest, most straight-talking people in Hollywood."

"So, this Myer-Harris so-called haberdasher—"

"Take my advice, young lady. Steer clear of anything connected to Myer-Harris."

"But my father—"

"Go to Selznick's party. Lay your girlish charms on thick. See who spills what and take notes." Drucker consulted the clock above the pair of mirrors. "You'll have to excuse me. I've got Mr. Wilkerson coming in any minute, and nobody keeps the landlord waiting."

* * *

Mr. Selznick's house sat on a U-curve in the folds of Beverly Hills. A gravel driveway led to a white two-story Georgian home with few embellishments other than a fanciful portico of wrought iron surrounding the front door. Music from a string quartet floated through the air. Polly, Amelia, and Ludlow stood at the foot of a curving staircase, its mahogany banister so freshly polished it reeked of beeswax.

To their left, the foyer opened into a vast living room decorated in creams and rose-quartz pink. Past a pair of French doors at the far end, Polly could make out knots of people scattered across a lush green lawn, engaged in lively chatter. The first person she glimpsed looked like Fay Wray; she was dressed in a lingonberry silk outfit and talking to Lionel Barrymore.

Polly looked down at her dress. Or rather, Amelia's. The beige chiffon had passed muster in the dim light of the TB-cure porch, but compared to Fay Wray, she now felt dowdy and old-fashioned. "I feel like the poor country cousin."

"Hardly," Ludlow scolded. "You look lovely."

"Says Mister Seventy-Nine Ninety-Five," Amelia lobbed back. "I'm with Pol." She plucked at the skirt of a poplin sun dress, off-white with a haphazard pattern of muted cherries. She had tried to jazz it up with a sky-blue scarf, but hadn't achieved the casually whimsical effect she'd been hoping for. "We come across like scullery maids who have raided some dusty trunk in the attic."

"Where are my two spunky girls from Schwab's?" Ludlow landed his hands on his hips, creating loops with his arms. "'Tis time we sally forth."

. . .

The trio hadn't taken ten steps into the backyard before Una O'Connor and Elsa Lanchester proffered warm, if somewhat baffled, good-afternoon smiles before sailing past. A passing waiter stopped to offer them champagne coupes of Dutch courage. White patio furniture filled a large square porch where people dressed in fashionable pastels convened in clusters of threes and fours. One of them appeared to be Ronald Colman, radiating relaxed confidence.

"These people think of themselves as phonies?" Polly murmured into her coupe. "They look quite comfortable living a life of success and luxury."

"Don't forget," Ludlow replied, "most of these people are actors whose job it is to convince you otherwise."

Polly clinked her glass against his; the chime was deep and resonant. "Why are you so kind to us?"

Ludlow redirected his gaze from Myrna Loy back to Polly. "What a confounding question."

"Is it?" The tiny bubbles glided over Polly's tongue, so sweet and refreshing that they made her wonder if she'd ever tasted real champagne. "We were a couple of strangers at a lunch counter."

"My clients are much older, much richer, much more *everything*," Ludlow said, his voice deeper now. "But they need my services. It's a transaction. You and Amelia don't, so the pressure's off."

"What pressure?" Amelia asked.

"It's nice to be nice for no reason other than I genuinely like you."

Polly stared at Ludlow. *Really?*

He stared back. *Yes, really.*

"Don't look now," Amelia said, "but Katharine Hepburn is close enough to toss a cucumber sandwich to us. But who's that with her?"

Hepburn was the only woman in slacks. Dark brown and baggy, they looked comfortable. She was deep in conversation with two women. One of them wore a sun dress of hip-hugging cream cotton, and possessed sharp, intelligent eyes that flitted around the crowd. The other had a long face and lightly marcelled hair.

"Edna May Oliver," Polly said.

"No, the other one."

"Your hostess, Irene Selznick," Ludlow said. "Later on, we'll make a point of thanking her for her hospitality. But for now, let's mingle."

Following his lead, Polly strolled across the plush lawn, nodding to various people, some of whom she recognized. ZaSu Pitts had catapulted herself into a spirited discussion with someone Polly didn't recognize about how the Independent Theater Owners of America had taken out print ads condemning a myriad of stars as "box office poison." Even though three of the stars listed—Hepburn, Dietrich, and Astaire—were within earshot, ZaSu and her friend weren't taking the trouble to lower their voices.

Ludlow, naturally, proved himself an expert at working the crowd. He dragged Polly and Amelia from one conversation to another, complimenting women on their outfits—"Correct me if I'm wrong, but you bought that at I. Magnin, didn't you?"—or their perfume—"The citrus-floral combination in the new Elizabeth Arden was *made* for you!" The men received warm congratulations on recent professional successes they'd had—"Casting Fred MacMurray opposite Ray Milland was genius!" or "You were sublime in *Nothing Sacred*, Mr. March." If no other obvious topics presented themselves, he professed his love for Selznick's champagne and praised the delectable potato puffball appetizers.

Polly admired his skillful ability to join conversations at the opportune moment, rarely interrupting, always waiting for lulls in chit-chat. She observed his smooth transitions between different groups, armed each time with fresh opinions and probing questions. He looked so thoroughly at home among these Hollywood elites that every last one of them would've assumed he'd been attending chic fêtes like this his whole life.

Predictably, most of the chatter was about *Gone with the Wind,* specifically over casting Paulette Goddard as Scarlett O'Hara.

"Polly here can shed light on that," Ludlow announced to a quartet of older women who had married well, if the quality of their manicures was a reliable guide.

The brunette bent forward toward Polly with a conspiratorial look on her face. "Friends with Paulette Goddard and Charlie Chaplin, are you?"

The idea that she could be chums with Chaplin made Polly giggle. The fine French champagne she'd been downing as though it were soda pop had probably helped. "I work for Mr. Selznick."

"Which one?" the platinum blonde asked. "The ruthless agent, or the twerp who thinks he can wrestle a brick like *Gone with the Wind* onto the screen?"

"The twerp," Polly quipped back, and then bit her lip, appalled at her unthinking disloyalty to the man who had shown her nothing but kindness—outside of his clumsy pass, which she hoped he'd forgotten as quickly as she had forgiven. "He's very sweet, though."

"Is the script not even finished yet?"

Around Mr. Selznick's office, strict confidentiality governed supreme, no matter how heated the argument nor how insignificant the detail. But Polly had never been encircled by people, eyes bulging with eager expectation in the hope of a succulent tidbit they could rush home and tell their friends.

"I spent all day yesterday typing up the latest draft."

"So it *is* finished!"

"Depends on what you mean by 'finished.' When Marcella saw the page total, she said, 'If they film that, it'll be a six-hour movie.'"

"Nobody's bladder is *that* cavernous." Ludlow's riposte sent the four women in a fit of hooch-fueled giggles. "We haven't wished Myron happy birthday, so if you'll excuse us?" He guided Polly and Amelia through the crowd and then raised his hand to attract Myron Selznick's eye.

Shorter and rounder than his younger brother, the central

player in this fancy garden party was, oddly, standing by himself. "Mr. Sinclair." He slowly shook Ludlow's hand. "A delight," he said, but with a faintly perplexed tone, presumably about how his wife's paid escort had wrangled his way past the gate.

"I'd like to present Polly Maddox."

"My brother mentioned that Elroy's daughter now works for him."

Polly shook his hand, searching his face for signs that her boss had also told his brother about the embezzlement charges, but she saw only mild amusement.

"And this," Ludlow continued, "is Amelia Hartley, whom I firmly believe you should take on as a client."

She forced back a gasp. "You do?"

"Amelia would be perfect for the *Pretty Pennies* remake." Ludlow turned to her with a smirk. *I told you I'd get you an audition.* "She looks like the original lead."

As Ludlow continued to pitch Amelia, Polly noticed Irene Selznick excuse herself and her husband from their huddle with Hepburn and Oliver. Stopping at the French doors, Mrs. Selznick poked him in the chest. His only response was to shrug until she marched into the house, leaving her husband no choice but to follow in her wake.

Although clearly not in the sunniest of moods, Mrs. Selznick had shaken herself free from her guests, so perhaps this was Polly's best chance.

She excused herself from the group and headed across the lawn to the house, but hadn't made it halfway there when a dark-haired man in wire-rimmed glasses blocked her path. "You're Polly Maddox, aren't you?"

The man ordained to direct *Gone with the Wind* had been a frequent visitor to Mr. Selznick's office, but he'd always spoken with Marcella, and ignored Polly and Hazel. But that was nothing to hold against the fellow, who was, after all, juggling so many flaming clubs.

"Mr. Cukor!"

His was the soft hand of someone who hadn't done a lick of

manual labor. "Most secretaries in David's office barely last a week, but it appears you're made of sterner stuff, so I offer my condolences."

Polly assumed he was referring to Papa until she caught the mischief glinting in his eyes. "How kind of you."

"David's work ethic is like a tumultuous roller coaster with no brakes. How onerous it must be to toil in his office, banging out those endless memos."

From his clipped, educated speaking voice, Polly figured he would appreciate a dash of French. "Strictly entre nous, it *is* a lot." She saw his mouth twitch, just slightly, in appreciation. "But nothing I can't handle."

"Let's chat again in three months, when I shall ask if you still feel that way."

"I love my job, Mr. Cukor."

"Tell me, Miss Maddox, is it true David recently screened *A Yank at Oxford*?"

"Twice. I got called in for the second screening to take notes."

It would have been Marcella's role, but she had been too busy putting out fires over the Box Office Poison fracas, so she had pressed Polly into service. It was the first time the two of them had been alone since his bungled pass, so she had been more than a little apprehensive. She needn't have worried, though. As soon as the MGM movie had started, he thought of nothing else.

"Notes on casting, I assume?" Cukor ran a thumbnail across his teeth. "Please tell me he's not considering Robert Taylor as Rhett?"

"Casting, yes, but not Robert Taylor."

"Maureen O'Sullivan?"

"The other actress. Vivien Leigh."

"For *Rebecca*?"

"For Scarlett."

"WHAT?!" Several nearby heads turned. Cukor waved back affably. "That girl is as British as tea and crumpets," he said through a taut smile. "Go on."

Aw, jeez. Have I gone and blabbed the one secret I should've kept mum about? But he's the director!

Cukor slapped the side of his leg in frustration. "Two whole years I've been leading the search for Scarlett. And yet I hear about this from the new kid on the block. No offense," he added curtly. "Keep going."

If Mr. Selznick hadn't yet shared his thoughts about Miss Leigh with this gentleman, it wasn't Polly's place to speak for him. "You need to take it up with the boss."

"God almighty, girl, you took the notes. Don't stop now."

"But—"

"I'm begging you."

Desperation mixed with annoyance strained the features of Cukor's face. How was she supposed to ignore it? "She's a genteel English rose, but if you turn the sound down, she's how I pictured Scarlett O'Hara. But that's the trouble with Scarlett: everyone seems to have a different picture of her."

"Does David agree?"

"When the screening room lights came up, he said, 'Give her a month with an accent coach and she could nail the part.'"

"I can't tell you how grateful I am for this news."

"You didn't hear it from me."

"I would've heard about this eventually; you happened to be the first. However . . ." He charmed her with a conspiratorial wink. *Why does everybody in this town have a 'however' tucked up their sleeve?* "I'm hoping you'll be my eyes and ears in David's office." Her reluctance must have shown on her face. "Nothing unethical, naturally. He rushes headlong in all directions, so he might forget. *Wind* is a monstrous project sprouting a million tentacles, and as the director, I'd be unspeakably grateful."

You don't have to agree to anything, Polly reminded herself. Mr. Selznick is your boss, and he deserves your loyalty. You've said too much. If he'd wanted Mr. Cukor to know about that Vivien Leigh girl, he would have already told him.

With his marmalade-colored ascot tied with stylish precision, his jacket tailored to flatter his chunky frame, and his brown suede wingtips teamed with begonia-red knitted socks, the man oozed worldly sophistication to a degree Polly hadn't ever encountered, not even in Papa, and for that reason alone she liked him.

But to be his office spy? Wasn't that asking too much?

"I can't make you any promises."

"Consider it merely a request. By the way, are you any relation to Elroy, of Mad Ox bourbon and *Ning Po* fame?"

"I'm his daughter. You know him?"

"Of course—even though I resist frittering my money away when the house always wins. Gambling is more David's thing."

"I'm trying to track down my father."

"You've lost him?"

"Long story."

Cukor hummed quietly to himself. "Aren't they all?"

"Someone advised me that if anyone might know his whereabouts, it'd be Mr. Selznick's wife."

"Nothing escapes that woman. David is lucky to have her. I've heard your father has gotten him out of more than one financial scrape."

"I've been told that gambling debts are *the* unspeakable character flaw."

"Indeed they are, which is why you're smart to tackle his wife instead. Hollywood husbands rarely give their wives credit. Best of luck, my dear."

She thanked Cukor and slipped into the house before anybody else could ambush her. It wasn't ideal to approach a woman while she was playing hostess to a hundred people, but Polly knew she might not get another chance.

A woman's voice, strident and insistent, hurtled through an open door down a short corridor to the left. As Polly approached, she heard a man's voice, too. She tiptoed closer.

"It's bad enough that you gamble such vast sums. The least you can do is come clean to me when you lose."

"We are in the middle of a party," David countered. "This is neither the time nor the place to thrash out—"

"There is *never* a right time!" Mrs. Selznick's voice climbed half an octave. "*Gone with the Wind* alone is a lot to grapple with, but now you're adding *Rebecca* and *Pretty Pennies*."

"I can't wait until I've finished *Wind* before I start the next project."

"You're always doing a million different things for a million different people, with no time or energy left for your wife or your family. A family who, might I remind you, can't afford for you to be throwing money away like it's tissue paper. Especially now that the mob is involved."

Polly took a step backward. Eavesdropping wasn't good manners. Even if it was accidental. But now that Mrs. Selznick had brought the mob into the conversation, Polly found it impossible to sneak away.

"Stop listening to gossip," Mr. Selznick snapped.

"You think it's a coincidence that Billy Wilkerson sold the Trocadero to the mob?"

"It's only a rumor that Hahn guy is mob-connected."

"Open your eyes, David. He's a front for Bugsy Siegel and Mickey Cohen, and everybody knows it. And what about that hustler from Catalina Island?"

Polly clamped her hands over her mouth.

"He's no hustler," Mr. Selznick retorted. "He bailed me out more than once, as you well know."

"I also know he's with the mob somehow."

"No, you don't. Not for sure."

"People don't go on the lam on a whim. And now I learn his daughter is working in your office. I suppose that's merely a coincidence?"

"Yes, it *is*," he insisted. "I was floored when I figured out who she was. I hope you at least believe that."

An alarmingly lengthy pause followed. Had one of them left the room via a different door?

"Are you hoping this girl can lead you to him?" Mrs. Selznick asked.

"The thought has crossed my mind, yes."

"And if she can't? Is she out of a job?"

Polly felt as though she had pushed her luck as far as she could. For now, it was enough to know that Mrs. Selznick believed her husband wasn't aware who Polly was when Marcella had hired her.

It was time to beat a silent retreat.

Outside, she scanned the crowds until she located Amelia sitting alone on the patio, sipping champagne at the edge of a wicker chair. She plunked herself down and snatched the coupe from Amelia's hand. "Where's Ludlow? I have jaw-dropping news."

"It'll be a minute before we're likely to clap our peepers on Mister Popular again."

"Why?" This French champagne really was top-notch. Polly emptied the glass. "What's he done?"

"It's not so much *what*"—Amelia tittered like a naughty schoolgirl—"but *who.*"

14

Marcella flopped onto her chair like an overworked rag doll. "He's done it!"

Polly looked up from Mr. Selznick's memo about a British director named Hitchcock. "Who's done what?"

"Our lord and master has set a date for the burning of Atlanta."

"At last!" Polly noted the skeptical lines etched around Marcella's eyes. "When is it?"

"December tenth."

"Two months, huh?"

"He's buying himself time. God only knows when principal photography will begin, but burning Atlanta to the ground will generate a blaze of publicity that should keep all the Louellas and the Heddas and the Sheilahs and the Kathryns busy."

"And buy *us* time to retype a dozen more drafts of the script." Polly's fingers ached at the thought of tackling that monster again.

"Oh, Miss Maddox," Marcella said, reaching for her jangling phone, "we'll be lucky if we have to type out only another twelve versions. Do they sell typewriter ribbons by the ton?"

Polly returned to the memo in which Mr. Selznick needed three pages to say, "I might hire Alfred Hitchcock for *Rebecca*." After two weeks in this job, she was starting to suspect that these copious memos were his system of working through the ideas that constantly cascaded through his mind.

After finishing the *Rebecca* memo, she moved on to one about a Swedish actress Selznick wanted to star in his English-language *Intermezzo.* Much of the memo was about how much Mr. Selznick hated the girl's name.

As she sandwiched a sheet of carbon between two Selznick International letterheads, her mind wandered to yesterday's birthday party. Irene Selznick's words—"that hustler from Catalina"—still stung. He might be a lot of things, she told herself as her fingers flew across the keys—*Her name is too German, especially with what's going on in Europe at the hands of Hitler and his Nazi bullies*—but my father is no hustler.

While they had waited for Ludlow to reappear, Polly and Amelia had mingled with actors and actresses, screenwriters, costumers, and producers, along with people who didn't appear to have any job at all. But the one opinion they all shared was that David Selznick had gotten lucky when Louis B. Mayer's daughter agreed to marry him.

"He's like an octopus with arms flung out in all directions," an older woman with a shock of purple hair had proclaimed, "but I hear his doctor has prescribed Benzedrine. I'll bet my favorite hat it makes him seem like he's got *sixteen* arms." Polly didn't know what Benzedrine was, but surely his personal physician wouldn't prescribe anything dangerous? "Irene, however, is a sensible counterbalance," Mrs. Purple Hair had continued, "but who knows if she'll last the distance? I mean, filming on *Gone with the Wind* hasn't even started yet."

If Irene Selznick thought Elroy was a shabby little street hustler, should Polly even bother approaching her? Mr. Selznick had defended Elroy, so she had his sympathy. But Mrs. Selznick would give her the straight dope. Marjorie and Ludlow were well acquainted, and she was married to Myron and was sister-in-law to David, so wouldn't he have a more nuanced insight into that family?

Regarding Miss Bergman's command of the English language, it's been my experience that many Scandinavians speak passable-to-good English, but in case Miss Bergman is not one of them, we might need to find her a language coach.

Polly's mind drifted back to the party. What a revelation it had been to watch Ludlow flit from W.C. Fields to Billie Hartley to Jimmy Durante as though he'd known them his entire life. But his actions had shocked Polly—and puzzled her, too.

According to Amelia, he had circled a certain stylish gent in his late forties like a lion on the Serengeti, approaching his quarry, radiating charm and then leading him to a quiet nook. "I may not be the most worldly woman in Christendom, but I know a seduction when I see one," Amelia had said. "And I know what a flirtation looks like—*and* what an exchange of calling cards between two attractive Dapper Dans means."

"Ludlow is . . . queer?" Polly had asked her. "He escorts women around town but goes home with men?" Amelia's response—"I guess"—had been strangely comforting to Polly. At least she wasn't the only Naïve Nancy here. "So he doesn't sleep with his clients? Makes sense, I guess. The husbands needn't fear their wives' escorts will seduce them."

As the string quartet had floated a dreamy version of "It Don't Mean a Thing if It Ain't Got That Swing" over the crowd, Polly and Amelia had stared at each other, wrestling with the idea that their witty, sophisticated, fashion-plate friend bedded men.

Our natural inclination might be to plaster Miss Bergman with makeup and restyle her hair as we force her to endure the usual Hollywood glamour treatment. However, I suspect hers will prove to be a natural beauty, so please show restraint when filming her screen test.

When Ludlow had at last reappeared, his necktie had been askew and his hair rumpled. "You won't believe who I've met," he had murmured. "Edmund Goulding!"

"The guy my father forbade us from approaching?" Amelia had asked.

"The one who'd been banished to Europe because of his"—Polly had whispered like a melodrama villain—"orgies!"

"Yep. The two of us have been crossing paths recently. It wasn't until today that I figured out who he is. By that time, it had become clear he was lusting after me."

"You returned the affection?" Amelia had asked.

"I like charismatic people, and that guy oozes with it. Plus, with all his shady social connections, I figured if anyone might know of Elroy's whereabouts, it'd be him."

"LUDLOW!" Polly had slapped her hands to her cheeks. "Tell me you didn't proposition Edmund Goulding on *my* account?"

She hadn't been prepared for his lighthearted chuckle. "I never do anything I don't want to do. If I can enjoy a fun encounter with someone I find attractive and at the same time acquire useful information, I call that a productive use of my time."

"And?" Polly asked.

"Your father came to Edmund for help."

Polly's heart thudded against her ribs. "When?"

"About a month ago. He told Edmund he was hiding from the authorities and asked if Edmund would take him in."

"Did he?"

"Yes, but only for a few weeks. And then the vice squad started snooping around, so he had to give Elroy the bum's rush. And get this: Edmund asked your boss if he had any suggestions about where Elroy could hide. Selznick told Goulding to get Elroy to call him, but by the time he got home from work, Elroy was gone."

Papa had been so close and yet so far. Frustration had threatened to overwhelm her, and she wanted to escape this party she'd looked forward to all week.

It wasn't until later that she grasped how Goulding's story hadn't lined up with what she had overheard. If Mr. Selznick had found a place for Elroy to hide, why would Irene bring up Selznick's motives for hiring Polly "to see if she can lead you to him"? She would never get the answer to that question until she confronted Selznick, but if the conversation didn't go well, might it put her out of a job she was growing to love?

I feel that Ingrid Bergman is a rare actress, so we must proceed with discernment. After Intermezzo, *please be on the lookout for roles that suit her unique appeal. She can light up the screen better than most current actresses.*

Polly unthreaded the finished memo from her typewriter. Marcella cupped her hand over the telephone receiver glued to her ear. "I'm on hold with the Culver City Fire Department. He wants the Bergman memo on his desk, pronto."

Polly walked into his office to find Mr. Selznick staring at four large tablets sitting on the palm of his left hand. At his elbow stood a large glass bottle labeled *Benzedrine*. "I shouldn't take so many at a time, but it's the only way I can get through the days."

She wasn't sure why he felt the need to justify his decisions, but when she spotted the two cigarettes burning simultaneously in his overflowing ashtray, she didn't bother to censor her words. "You ought to pace yourself."

He gawked at her.

Had she overstepped her boundaries?

He returned two of the tablets to the bottle. "My wife says the same thing."

Any lingering tendrils of indecision evaporated. If Polly was going to approach a Selznick for help, she would get further with Irene. But Irene Selznick was sharp and direct and suffered no fools. Polly would have to approach her boss's wife in the right way—even though she hadn't the slightest idea what the right way might be.

15

Ludlow was saving a seat for Polly at the lunch counter, but it was Amelia's powder-blue uniform with the Schwab's logo stitched onto the white collar that was hard to miss.

"When I left for work this morning," Polly said, sliding onto the stool, "you didn't have a job. What happened?"

Amelia made a grand display of laying a menu in front of her. "Mr. Schwab called at eleven to say 'Can you be here by twelve?' I'm replacing a waitress who had to leave town at the last minute to—*ahem*—'care for an ailing spinster aunt.'"

"Does this mean that when the girl comes back in"—Polly held up nine fingers—"you'll be out of a job?"

"That's more than enough time for me to show the boss that I'm utterly indispensable." She picked up her order pad. "But for now, please excuse me. I have customers!" She bounced down the counter to greet a couple of Navy officers.

"She'll be smiling for weeks," Ludlow said.

Polly nodded. "And now that she's got money coming in, we can afford to get a place together. Last night, I saw an ad for an apartment near Robertson and Pico."

"Not too far from the studio. It'll be handy when you have to stay late, which, I'm gathering, is quite often."

"I don't mind. The work is stimulating and Marcella calls for a taxi home if it gets too late."

"Robertson and Pico, huh?" Ludlow appeared to be lost in thought.

"Is it near you? Wouldn't it be great if we lived close by?"

It had occurred to Polly and Amelia that Ludlow was secretive about where he lived. For someone so charming and gregarious, it was an odd quirk.

"I'm not sure, but Beverly Hills might extend as far south as Pico. If it does, that'll put you inside Beverly Hills, in which case you're required to act unspeakably ritzy." His skillful deflection told Polly that the subject of his home situation was a walled-off no-man's-land.

"My goodness, that sounds fancy." From Catalina Island to Beverly Hills in—had it only been six weeks? All these changes left her breathless. It was almost as though she were the stand-in for someone else and any minute now, the marquee star of this movie would be tapping her on the shoulder and saying, *I'll take it from here*. "You'll have to start watching your manners around us."

They laughed at the absurdity of her warning the most well-mannered young man in Hollywood to watch his p's and q's.

"Did you get caught up in last night's radio drama?" he asked.

"I only heard a bit of it," Polly said. Marcella had never called her into work on a Sunday, but Mr. Selznick had decided his protracted analysis of the four actresses still left in the running—Paulette Goddard, Doris Jordan, Joan Bennett, and Katharine Hepburn—couldn't wait until Monday. When Polly had realized he'd excluded that British actress, she keenly regretted mentioning her to Mr. Cukor.

"I got called into work in the middle of the afternoon," Polly went on. "Marcella and I didn't finish till well after nine, so I missed all the hysteria. Did people truly believe Martians were invading us?"

"By the thousands."

"But why would they choose New Jersey? That would have been my first tip-off right there."

"I must say, Orson Welles put on a hell of a show. And besides, Grover's Mill is near Princeton. Maybe they planned to kidnap Einstein and pick his brains over his theory of relativity."

The first Polly had heard about the national uproar was when a studio runner had charged headlong into the office, breathlessly insisting they turn on the radio to hear a breaking bulletin on a New York radio station. "If Martians had figured out how to fly a spaceship all the way to New Jersey, I doubt they'd need to pick Albert Einstein's brains for anything." She closed her menu. "Seeing as how you're here, there's something I'd like to ask you."

Ludlow turned in his seat to face her more squarely. "I'm listening."

Polly splayed her hands flat onto the counter. "Marjorie Selznick is a client of yours."

"That's right."

"Is Irene?"

"David's wife? Nah. She already has a regular. With your boss so preoccupied with his work, she's been keeping Tom busy. Why are you asking?"

"I suspect she might be able to help me to track my father down. But I don't want my personal problems to spill over into my work life."

"Smart move."

"So, I was thinking maybe"—she started tearing the corners off her paper napkin to keep her fingers occupied—"oh, who knows what I was thinking. Forget I asked."

"Would it help to know Irene and Tom have a standing date?"

"Where? When?"

"First Monday of the month, he takes her to Culver City where they enjoy a set-menu chicken dinner at King's Tropical Inn. It's inexpensive and unpretentious, which means they can relax. If you don't want to take the chance your boss will overhear, King's is your best bet."

Polly scooped up the paper shreds and dropped them into a glass ashtray. "What are you doing next Monday?"

"Why, Miss Maddox!" A sly smile glided onto his handsome face. "I thought you'd never ask."

* * *

When Ludlow had said "King's Tropical Inn," Polly had imagined a quaint, pocket-sized tavern tucked away in a side street, perhaps a little rundown, but in a fun, slumming-it sort of way. So Polly wasn't the least bit prepared as Ludlow pulled up outside a huge building, covered in white tiles and crowned by a dome that itself was capped by a seven-foot cupola.

A faintly Polynesian tune greeted Polly and Ludlow as they stepped into the foyer. He asked for a table near the dance floor, and they were soon following the maître d' deeper inside the cavernous place. The ceiling was a deep purple, as though the last vestiges of the setting sun had departed for the night, leaving a summery night sky.

"Are these stars and clouds moving?"

"Welcome to King's, where you come for the fried chicken but stay for the stars."

Their bamboo table was nestled between papier-mâché palm trees whose fronds formed a canopy. Ludlow hugged the drinks menu to his chest. "I assume you're a bourbon girl?"

"Because I'm Elroy Maddox's daughter?"

"And that's the last time I'll assume anything about you."

"I've spent my whole life cooped up on the same tiny island. Why bother leaving if I'm doomed to repeat the same old routine?"

"I'm impressed," Ludlow said as their waitress approached. He ordered a couple of sloe gin fizzes.

"Does that mean we'll get drunk slowly?"

"It ain't that kind of slow, honey." He cast a quick look around the tables circling the dance floor. "I don't see Tom or Irene yet."

He checked his watch. "It's nearly eight. They should be here by now."

"We're not in any rush, are we?"

He returned his attention to her. "What shall we talk about?"

"How did you get your *Dick Tracy* job?" Talking about work was a roundabout way to get where she wanted to go.

"Ah!" An impish spark flittered in his eyes. "My first client was a rather nervy, high-strung woman named Fanny, whose husband runs NBC Red. She was a handful, and he was looking for someone to show her a good time."

"And give him some peace and quiet?"

"You get the picture. We had an enjoyable evening at Chasen's."

"She wasn't so bad, then?"

"Not after a couple of Brandy Alexanders. All she wanted was to vent about her frustrations over her husband's long hours."

"Sounds like Irene Selznick."

"As well as every client I've ever taken out for a night on the town. These men . . ." His eyes drifted away for a moment. "They get so wrapped up in their careers and successes, their power and influence and, of course, money. They lose sight of the wives who love them and the children who need them, so you have to wonder what it's all for."

Is he talking about his own father? "So it was Fanny who found you a job on one of her husband's shows?"

"Not quite. Fanny raved to her neighbor, whose sister is Helen Lewis, who plays Tess Trueheart. She's best friends with the secretary to the head of advertising for Tootsie Rolls, which is *Dick Tracy*'s sponsor. He was the one who called the producer and asked if he had a job opening for what Fanny had described as a 'bright young man bursting with potential.'"

"And who was the bright young man?" Polly deadpanned.

Ludlow threw a matchbook at her; she caught it in her left hand.

"Your family must have been happy for you to get a job on such a popular show," she said.

His smile faltered. His "Yes, they were" was less than convincing.

"Are they in showbiz, too?"

He mounted one of his professional smiles as the waitress approached with their drinks. He told her they weren't ready to order dinner yet, and when she'd departed, he raised his glass to Polly. "Here's to fleeing Catalina."

"It's not a prison." Or at least it hadn't felt like one. But now that Polly had escaped its gravitational pull, she could see Ludlow had a valid point. Still, she'd feel disloyal to her entire childhood if she didn't defend it. "It's a most agreeable place. Lots of space, hiking, sailing, horseback riding, clean air, and fresh fish."

"So I hear."

"You've never been?"

"Gosh, no. Too rich for my blood."

"It doesn't have to be." Sharpened with lemon juice, Polly's sloe gin fizz had a pleasant, tingling bite to it. She took another sip. "There are these tents with wooden floors. Very comfortable. They go for eight dollars a week. Shared with three other people, that's only a couple of bucks."

She expected him to wryly ask, "Do I look like I'd enjoy camping?" but instead, he hovered over his drink as though to shield his thoughts from the carved tiki god perched on a shelf next to them. "I've had my fill of living the rough life."

The tone he'd switched to was the polar opposite of his usual sparkling, uplifting banter, leaving Polly to wish she hadn't poked the bear of Ludlow's past.

"And then along came Uncle Fedor!"

Her course correction did the trick. "You know about him?"

"He came up when I was chatting with Norman at Sunset House. Taught you all the social graces, I hear."

"And thank God he did, too. I don't know where I'd be without his tutoring."

"Neither do half the neglected wives of Hollywood." Relief filtered through her when she saw Ludlow's easygoing smile return. "Ditto their boring husbands, who I imagine sit around private clubs goosing pretty waitresses—or worse."

"Put it this way: wives make for more congenial company."

"But at the end of the night, you'd rather go home with men?"

Ludlow's cocktail froze midway to his lips. "Is Miss Santa Catalina Island shocked?"

Polly waved her glass around in what she hoped was a blithely sophisticated manner. "A little. At first."

"But then?"

She had no idea what sloe gin was, but she was fairly sure her tastebuds would soon be demanding another round. "I assume your clients' husbands feel secure knowing that you're not in danger of seducing their wives."

"Oh, but I do seduce them."

Polly gulped down the rest of her gin to disguise her shock. So much for blithe sophistication. "You do?"

"I can tell when the woman is open to shelling out for extra services."

"How?"

"You'd have to be dumber than a barrel of mud to not see the signs." He ran a fingernail along the bamboo pole lining the edge of their table. "These women are so starved for physical affection that they're willing to do anything to get it. *And* pay any price," he added with a wink. "So I charge them. A lot."

Polly stared at him, trying not to let her jaw hang open. Whatever had happened to Ludlow's family during the Depression, it couldn't have been a heartwarming story worthy of a Lubitsch comedy. But if Ludlow had been his family's main breadwinner, in whatever inventive ways he could conjure, well, then, she admired him all the more. Especially after what he'd revealed when he had joined them on the patio at the Selznicks' party that evening after rendezvousing with Edmund Goulding.

"Somebody's got to pay for all your gorgeous clothes!"

She meant to sound playful and a little facetious, but her snappy comeback only provoked a return to the dark cloud Polly had glimpsed earlier.

"I'm squirreling away as much of it as I can."

"For your family?"

She caught the split-second flare of surprise in his eyes before he smothered it with charisma. "Families—can't live with them, can't live without them, right?"

Before she had a chance to respond, the house band of six brightly costumed musicians started playing a Dorothy Lamour tune, "The Moon of Manakoora." Sweeping gracefully to his feet, he gave a half-bow and urged her to stand. Squiring her onto the dance floor, he swept her into a half-turn before sliding one arm around her waist and raising her right hand into place. She felt the heat of his torso along her body. Was this normal? Was this how it was to rhumba with a man? He shifted his arm to adjust their trajectory around a slow-moving couple. A nudge of the hip and a squeeze of the hand, and they moved as one. A whole conversation passing without a word.

Now I get it, she wanted to yell to the stars meandering across the ceiling. Now I see why women pay to be chaperoned around town. If I were married to a man who worked seventy-hour weeks, I'd pay anything!

"Irene and Tom have been seated," he whispered into her ear, momentarily breaking the spell. "Follow my lead."

He piloted her toward Irene's table. Tom was a handsome Gary Cooper type with wavy blonde hair too wiry to be tamed by hair pomade. Its curls bobbed as he leapt to his feet and greeted Ludlow with a heartfelt handshake and a slap on the back.

Next to him, dressed in an unadorned gown of black crêpe de chine, was Mrs. Selznick, who remained seated as Ludlow introduced Polly to her. "Good evening, Polly," she said, then turned her attention once more to Ludlow. "Mr. Sinclair, I was hoping we might get acquainted at Myron's birthday party, but there were so many people."

"As the hostess, I'd imagine it would have been hard to say hello to everyone."

"A skilled hostess can surprise her guests."

Polly wasn't sure what to make of Mrs. Selznick's cryptic

rejoinder, but she couldn't shrug off the inkling that her boss's wife rarely missed a trick.

"Please excuse Tom and me for just a moment," Ludlow announced. "I've just spotted someone I'd like him to meet."

The two men melted into the crowd before either Polly or Mrs. Selznick could respond. Polly took Tom's vacated seat. She didn't have long with this woman, but now she wasn't sure where to start.

"How are you settling in at work?"

"Fine, fine," Polly replied over the band's version of a Gene Autry number, "Song of the Islands." "Thanks to Marcella."

Mrs. Selznick nodded. "That woman is a marvel who should be canonized at the first opportunity. She speaks highly of you, by the way. Evidently, you're the fastest typist north of the equator, which is what Mr. King of the Memos needs. Ghastly, isn't it, the sheer volume of them?"

"I have a theory," Polly began, then wished she hadn't. She was sure the woman wouldn't hesitate to put Polly in her place if she talked out of school.

But Irene Selznick's eyes gleamed with intrigue. "I do so love a good theory."

Polly rested her elbows on the table and leaned forward. "I suspect those memos aren't so much about disseminating information as they are about your husband formulating his thoughts about the millions of details and decisions he needs to make every day."

"Jumping June bugs!" Mrs. Selznick clapped her hands together. "You *are* whip-smart, aren't you?"

"Honestly, Mrs. Selznick, I was worried that I might come across as too know-it-all."

"My husband has enough yes men. What he needs are smart people who aren't afraid to say, 'That's a dumb idea.' Or if he's mid-rant, perhaps a tactful 'I suggest you think about that some more.' Can you do that for me?"

"I'll try."

"And"—she ducked her head, sending a lock of her dark

brown hair spilling onto her forehead—"has he made a pass at you yet?"

My goodness, Polly thought. The daughter of Louis B. Mayer, the most powerful man in Hollywood, was no different to every other wife who frets about her husband straying outside the marriage. "No need to worry on that score," Polly equivocated.

"It's no secret that David's a profligate gambler. He gets that from his father. Myron, too. They're incorrigible, the pair of them. Which'd be fine if they had wealth like DeMille or were loaded like Pickford. If only they didn't gamble it away every time they find themselves within a five-mile radius of a deck of cards. But what do they care? They're not the ones lumbered with running an expensive household with two growing children on an unpredictable budget."

At the party, this woman had radiated an intimidating aura of chic majesty paired with candid pragmatism. But Polly now found herself reassessing her impression. Irene Selznick was unflappably sophisticated in all the ways Polly aspired to be. Even more surprising, she felt she could be honest with the woman who considered Papa to be a hustler.

"I do hope you'll forgive me," Polly said, "because I assure you it wasn't intentional, but I overheard the argument you had with Mr. Selznick during the party."

"And what you don't realize is that when someone stands in the hallway outside our library, the fireplace mirror catches their reflection."

The volume of the chatter in this place felt like it ratcheted up a notch. "You saw me?"

"Knowing I had an audience egged me on. At the time, I wasn't aware who you were, but goodness!" She released a surprisingly girlish laugh. "I let him have it, didn't I? Right between the eyeballs. Well, good. I'm glad. He had it coming. I have no regrets."

"And does your husband hope I can lead him to my father?"

"Oh, that." Irene swiped the smoky air. "A wild accusation flung in a heated moment. I could tell he was being honest when he said that it surprised him to learn the new girl in his office was Elroy Maddox's daughter."

"As surprised as I was to hear you call my father a hustler with connections to the mob."

"Are you telling me he isn't?"

"Not as far as I'm aware."

"We don't know everything about our parents. Nor should we." Her steady gaze lost its focus. Was she thinking about how her own father hadn't risen to the head of MGM by playing Mr. Nice Guy? Her rumination was short-lived. "If it makes you feel any better, I suspect David doesn't *need* to find Elroy, but *wants* to."

"For what purpose?"

"Loyalty or some such thing. Your father carried my husband's substantial gambling debt more than once and thus saved our familial bacon. And I'm not saying that I'm ungrateful for that. Quite the opposite, in fact. But that was before these rumors started surfacing around town."

"About Papa?"

Mrs. Selznick regarded her somberly for a moment. "Tell me, Polly, is it true the authorities are preparing to charge Elroy with embezzling thirty-five grand from the Santa Catalina Island Company?"

Polly stared into her lap. *There's that number again. Will it always feel like a slap in the face?* "Last I heard, they were merely accusations."

"They're probably waiting to catch him. It'll have more impact in the papers."

"That's why I want to get to Papa first. I didn't know about gambling on the *Ning Po*—"

"You didn't?"

Skepticism dented Irene's brow—not that Polly blamed her. She, herself, was still trying to comprehend how she'd missed every sign all those years.

"I can see why the authorities are suspicious. But embezzlement doesn't fit Papa's personality."

"You're his daughter, so naturally you want to think the best of him." Irene's face softened as her cynicism receded. "If your gut tells you embezzlement doesn't seem right, go with that."

"Do you have any suggestions about where I might look for him?"

The dance floor cleared out a little as the band shifted to a slow "Give Me Liberty or Give Me Love." As couples wended their way around the dance floor, Irene mulled over Polly's question. She sat up straighter when an idea took hold. "What about his sister?"

"Whose sister?"

"Elroy's."

Polly struggled to conjure up details of Papa's mystery sibling who had gone into show business against the direct wishes of their strictly religious parents. Polly couldn't recollect which arm of showbiz, though. Opera, musicals, vaudeville, burlesque—it had all been shameful devil's work to Grandpa and Grandma Maddox. "I wouldn't have the first clue how to go about finding her."

"Couldn't be simpler." Irene dismissed her objection with a brusque shoulder raise. "Go to MGM."

"WHAT?" Several heads turned to see who'd erupted louder than the band. "My aunt works down the street?"

"When Yip Harburg and Roscoe Arlen were writing songs for *The Wizard of Oz*, they needed a vocalist to help them with phrasing and arrangements. Cora is one of their favorite vocalists because—"

"Cora! Yes, that's her name!"

"She has a five-octave range. Can sing anything, in any key, by sight, with no rehearsal." Irene lowered her voice when she saw Ludlow and Tom approaching their table. "And don't worry about getting onto the lot." Irene winked at her. "Sometimes it pays to have a movie mogul for a father."

16

MGM was only a mile from Selznick International, but for a girl whose in-tray filled up faster than she could empty it, the studio might as well have been a hundred miles away. Even if Polly had the time to take a lunch hour, how could she possibly get over there, hunt down her aunt, and get back to her desk in time? And now that Mr. Selznick had announced a date to film the burning of Atlanta, memos, lists, and press releases were landing on Polly's desk at an accelerated pace. "We need to hang on for dear life until we've incinerated Atlanta," Marcella had told her. "Then things will subside from insane to merely maddening."

As desperate as Polly was to get onto the MGM lot, several weeks whirled by without her finding an opportunity to absent herself. She was starting to despair when Marcella dropped her telephone receiver into its cradle and turned down the radio. It had been playing all morning, broadcasting reports of Nazi atrocities taking place across Germany, an explosion of violence and destruction that the newscasters were calling *Kristallnacht.*

"You have been summoned!"

Polly skimmed the memo in which Selznick had detailed a list of combustible sets: *The Last of the Mohicans, King Kong, The Garden of Allah,* and *Little Lord Fauntleroy*. "This one'll be at least four pages. Mr. Selznick can't think I've already finished—"

"Not him. The missus. You're needed at MGM."

Polly lifted her fingers from the typewriter keys. "What for?"

"That Prohibition picture they're filming. Two screenwriters came to blows over the logistics of rumrunning to and from the Channel Islands. Fisticuffs and everything. When word reached Mrs. Selznick, she reminded Jim Taggart, who heads up the writing department, that you're from Catalina and that your father is Elroy Maddox."

Were these alleged fisticuffs a story Irene had ginned up?

"It's half past eleven. Why don't you head down there now? We'll call it a two-hour lunch break. Lord knows you've earned it."

"But what about this memo?"

"Leave it in the typewriter. I'll finish it first chance I get. And if his lordship doth protest, I'll tell him to take it up with her ladyship."

* * *

With Polly and Amelia now earning steady paychecks, they'd gone halves on a second-hand Chevrolet coupe, a little on the bumpy side with a chorus of rattles and clanks, but it got them where they needed to go, each of them driving it on alternate days. Polly braked at MGM's main gate and gave her name to the guard. He produced a small square envelope of velvety smooth paper with a handwritten note inside.

Ignore the bunk I invented about the writers' fight. You should find your Aunt Cora in the music department.

Good luck!

I.S.

Venturing into the MGM lot felt like the first day at Selznick—but much bigger and ten times busier. An aura of mystique overlaid the workaday scene of a wardrobe assistant carrying a tower of top hats and an animal trainer leading a train of three camels toward the backlot.

Polly found the music department easily enough. A pair of men in shirtsleeves sat in a square lobby with mismatching sofas and armchairs lining the walls.

"Nothing against Thorpe," one said to the other. "He was doing a better job than Taurog would have done." He noticed Polly approach. "You lost, honey?"

"I'm looking for Cora Maddox."

"She's assisting Gale Sondergaard for her Wicked Witch screen test. Rehearsal room two."

The door had a square window made of extra-thick soundproofing glass. Polly watched Aunt Cora take Sondergaard through a series of threatening witchy poses—arched fingers and hunched shoulders. Slender, with a high forehead and unlined face, the actress looked more like Disney's evil queen in *Snow White*. She'd have to endure hours of torturous makeup to turn her into a menacing hag.

Aunt Cora stood in front of her pupil, arms crossed and lips pinched into a thin line. She gave another instruction. Sondergaard adopted a new pose, sticking out her limbs at awkward angles, like the branches of a gnarled tree, and threw back her head to laugh.

By contrast, Aunt Cora held herself with the resolute bearing of a prima ballerina. Tall and thin, with hair dyed jet black, she bore no resemblance to Papa. Polly had pictured the Maddox family's bad apple as looking like she'd been dragged through life's mud and come up ready to punch the nearest bystander. But this woman, with her dramatic eye makeup and fingernails lacquered in deep carmine, projected the aura of someone who took no guff. Polly cracked open the door.

"It's time you got yourself to your screen test on Stage Twenty-Seven," Aunt Cora was telling Sondergaard. "They're building the

Munchkin Village, so good luck ignoring all that hammering." She waited until Gale had murmured her thanks and left the room.

"Hello." Polly waited for signs of recognition, but when they failed to appear, she added, "I'm Elroy's daughter."

Cora barely moved, not even to blink. "From what I recall of your mother, you look just like her."

This exotic creature with her gray-blue eyes remained glued to her spot on the floor, forcing Polly to close the space between them. "And that makes you my Aunt Cora."

Any hope of a joyful family reunion dissolved when Cora Maddox stiffened like a telephone pole. Irene's inspired suggestion had ended up a mortifying fool's errand. Polly could only stare, still as a pond and mute as the moon.

"I'm sorry." Cora's apology sounded strained but gracious. "It's just that you took me by surprise."

"Imagine *my* surprise when Irene Selznick told me I'd find my aunt here." A cruel accusation to level at someone who was trying their best to make amends, but not inaccurate.

"You live here now?" Cora asked.

"I work for David Selznick."

"Oh!" She pressed her palms to her temples. "I'm such a skunk!"

"How long have you been living in LA?"

"Almost three years."

"And you didn't contact Papa?"

Cora stared at Polly, her face a battleground of surprise and remorse. "Did your father not tell you I'm the scandalous *bête noire* to be avoided at all costs?"

"Papa didn't talk about you much."

"Amounts to much the same thing, doesn't it?"

"Not to me. As far as I'm concerned, you're a blank slate."

Cora drew back, her lips parting as she absorbed Polly's words. "Did Elroy send you? Are you his ice-breaking emissary?"

Now that Polly had met this sylph-like vision, sleek as a swan with the aloof air of a sphinx, she had more questions than she had arrived with. "I don't have a lot of time, but perhaps we could visit a few minutes?"

Cora's response was a mute nod. When they'd settled onto a pair of stiff-backed wooden chairs in the corner, she asked, "Where should we start?"

"How come you're living in LA again?" Polly asked.

"Well, you see, when vaudeville died—"

"I thought you were an opera singer."

"Shows how far I've fallen." Cora made an apathetic swishing motion with her hands. "A tale of woe for another time. When my staunch pal, Roger Edens, tracked me down and offered me a job, I said yes. I'd have been an imbecile to turn down a chance to work at the richest studio in Hollywood when we were all still mired in the Depression."

"And you're no imbecile."

Cora's rigid body thawed a little. "My job is invigorating and productive, but it's not full time, so I take in singing students. At first, I was positively gangrenous with shame."

"What's so degrading about teaching?"

"Dear heart, when you were once the prima donna of the New York Opera, teaching other people to sing betokens the end of your performing career." She gave a resigned shrug. "It was that or—God help me—burlesque. Turns out, I rather enjoy teaching. Between it and this studio work, I make a decent living." Her face fell into a solemn pout. "But it never occurred to me your father would want to hear from me."

"Why not?"

"Because our dogmatic, God-fearing parents turned him against me. All they ever told him was 'Cora is bad. Cora is corrupt. Cora must be avoided.' Why would he question it?"

She sounded like Papa's warnings: "Los Angeles is bad. Los Angeles is corrupt. Los Angeles must be avoided." But, Polly knew now, he was flat-out wrong. "Maybe you should have let *him* make that decision."

Cora pretended to inspect her immaculate nails. "You're right. I should have. But"—she looked up again—"let's rectify that. Is he still on Catalina? I could go visit him—why, whatever's the matter?"

Polly took her through the past couple of months and how she had sought Cora out, hoping she might know where Papa might be.

"I suppose I should read the papers more. But embezzlement? I cannot fathom my baby brother sinking so low. Do you have anything to go on?"

"Just one thing, but it's slim pickings." Polly told her about the entry in the Island Company's books for Myer-Harris Haberdashery, but how no businesses were registered with the city by that name, and that Meyer-with-an-e Harris Cohen was more widely known as Mickey Cohen.

Cora's eyes, already made large with thick eyeliner, widened with surprise. "The mob?"

"I refuse to believe Papa would willingly get involved with them."

"If they want to move in on your operations, you're not offered a choice." Cora tapped her chin for a few moments. "What was that haberdashery called?"

"Myer-Harris."

"I'm sure I've encountered it before."

"It's a fake name on a ledger to hide a thirty-five-thousand-dollar embezzlement, so I can't imagine how—"

"From Gable."

"Clark?"

"He's working on *Idiot's Delight*. They've got him performing 'Puttin' on the Ritz.'"

"I bet he's mortified at having to perform a song!"

"Talk about my most reluctant pupil. But I got him there." She tapped her chin some more. "Yes, yes. I'm sure Myer-Harris came from him." She rose to her feet and beckoned to Polly. "We're off to Stage Twelve."

Polly checked the clock above the rehearsal piano. She'd

already been gone an hour and a half, and she still had to drive back up Washington Boulevard, where work was bound to be piling up higher than the *King Kong* sets Mr. Selznick was planning to torch. But, a little voice whispered in her ear, how many times will you be in the same room as Clark Gable?

* * *

Cora led Polly onto a nightclub set cluttered with small round tables and matching chairs with semi-circular backs.

Clark stood off to one side, dressed in a dark double-breasted suit with wide lapels and even wider shoulder pads. Teamed with a black shirt and white tie, the outfit made him look like Hollywood's version of a gangster. Deep in conversation with a man in a red sweater, he didn't catch sight of Cora until they were twenty feet away.

"Well, if it isn't my savior!" He immediately abandoned his discussion. "Don't tell me they want another production number."

"Relax," Cora reassured him. "I've come in search of information that only you can provide."

Polly stepped forward, awkward as the schoolgirl she'd been that summer four years ago. "Remember me?"

"POLLY!" He scooped her up into a hug. "My favorite pen pal!"

She breathed in the licorice scent of his Sen-Sen breath freshener. "I wasn't sure if you'd recognize me."

His response was to hug her even harder. "Haven't I been sending you postcards regular as the Super Chief?"

That thick black hair, that square jaw, that slightly skewed smile. She'd almost forgotten how much more captivating he was in person.

"I see you survived Carole's French toast."

His "HA!" turned the heads of several stagehands preparing for the next shot. "You know what? It wasn't half bad. Tell me, though, what're you doing here?"

As Polly brought him up to speed, activity around them intensified. Aware she couldn't hold him captive too long, she skipped over a few details. "And so, I'm left with one single, solitary clue."

"Clark," Cora said, "do you remember the day I was teaching you how to hold your cane during 'Puttin' on the Ritz' and you mentioned Myer-Harris?"

A sudden look of wariness came into his eyes. "Uh-huh."

"To what did it refer?"

Wordlessly, Clark led them to a secluded nook behind the set where the lights scarcely reached. "It's a password to a gambling joint originally launched down back of Mattson's of Hollywood."

"The menswear store in Wilcox?" Cora asked.

He nodded. "But it's always on the move to avoid the vice squad."

"Where's it now?"

Clark shrugged.

Another dead end. The time was closing in on one-thirty. Poor Marcella must have been tearing her hair out. "I'll keep asking around," Polly told him.

"Got yourself a job?"

"At Selznick International."

Clark let loose a hoarse laugh. "If that don't beat all. You know who's most likely to know where that roving casino is?"

It took Polly an anxious heartbeat or two before the answer slapped her across the face. "Are you serious?"

"The most reckless gambler in town. How about this: If he knows the location, then the three of us—you, me, and David—"

"Mind if I tag along?" Cora cut in.

"Correction—the *four* of us will see what we can unearth."

"You'd hobnob with the man who's heckled you, harassed you, and hounded you into taking a role you were dead set against playing?"

"Carole said to me, 'You may as well resign yourself to the inevitable.' She's been suggesting I make time to see David outside of work to improve our relationship while we're filming *Gone with the Goddamned Wind*."

"She's right, you know," Cora said.

"Carole usually is. So, do we have a date?"

"We do," Polly replied. "But I must get back to my typewriter."

"The memos?"

"Oh, Mr. Gable." She planted a grateful kiss on his famous cheek. "You have no idea."

17

"Oh, boy!" Mr. Selznick half-climbed, half-stumbled into the back of Cora's road-weary Packard. "I'm in trouble with the lady of the house!"

"What is it this time?" Clark asked. "The gambling?"

Cora pulled away from the curb of his Beverly Hills mansion. "Or because the husband is leaving the neglected wife at home for a night on the town?"

"The latter," Selznick replied, "made worse by the former."

"You could've asked her to join us."

"Jeffrey and Daniel are still too young to be without their mother."

"Did you ask *her* about that?"

Polly snuck a side-peep at her gutsy aunt. Not everybody had the audacity to sass the son-in-law of the man who signed her paychecks. Selznick's response—the squeaky giggle of a naughty adolescent—told Polly all she needed to know. Like Clark Gable, who had confessed to a couple of whiskey-and-sodas, the producer of *Gone with the Wind* was already half-sauced.

"I have good news," Clark announced. "Ria has accepted my settlement. All three hundred grand of it."

Polly and Cora swapped dumbstruck goggle-eyes. *How much did he say?*

"Twice divorced." He had turned morose. "No wonder the public thinks movie stars are fickle jerks who can't stay married more than two minutes."

"But now you are free to tie the knot with Carole," Polly told him, "whom everybody adores."

Selznick let out an exasperated snort. "Yes, but how can I cast Clark Gable and Paulette Goddard when they're both shacked up with people they're not married to?"

Cora braked at the lights out front of the Beverly Hills Hotel. "What about that British girl I hear rumors of?"

"Don't make me laugh," Clark scoffed. "There'll be rioting in the streets."

"At least she's married."

"Yes, but not to the chap she's humping," Selznick said. "He's about to start filming *Wuthering Heights* for Goldwyn."

While Polly agreed that casting a Brit as the ultimate Southern belle was madness, she could only picture that actress she had admired so much in *A Yank at Oxford*. "Will she be coming with him to LA?"

"As soon as her ship arrives in New York, she'll catch a flight to the coast. Myron is driving Larry to Clover Field for the big reunion." Selznick let out another schoolgirl giggle. "Cukor warned Myron that Larry and this Vivien girl might be schtupping in the back seat of his brand-new Lincoln convertible en route to the hotel."

"Hell's bells!" Clark thundered. "I'm playing second fiddle to a British Scarlett with a director who's gonna turn it into a goddamn women's picture."

Selznick, Cora, and Polly burst out laughing. "*Wind* isn't just a goddamn women's picture," Selznick said. "It'll be the supreme goddamn women's picture of all time. Listen, I know you hated being in period costume—"

"You saw *Parnell*, right?"

"Enough shoptalk!" Cora turned off Hollywood Boulevard and

onto a side street, where she braked outside a nondescript building. "We're here."

Clark peered into the murky nighttime shadows. "Didn't this used to be Club New Yorker?"

The four of them gathered into a half circle around a plain door framed with small black-and-white tiles. Selznick knocked and waited for it to crack open wide enough to reveal half a face. The eyeball took in Selznick and Gable. "Sorry, fellas, but I still need the password."

"Myer-Harris."

When the door swung open, lively chatter, a trumpet solo, and a billowing cloud of cigarette smoke rushed to greet them.

"Now remember," Gable said to Polly, his voice low and brotherly, "you can encounter all types in a saloon like this. If any lowlife gives you trouble and I'm not within hooking distance, knee 'em in the groin. Don't warn 'em. Don't hesitate. Don't hold back. Got it?"

Polly hoped defensive maneuvers wouldn't be necessary. But if they were, would she have the wherewithal to follow his advice? She doubted it, but nodded anyway.

Teeming with gamblers, the room stretched to a velvet-draped back wall. Polly assumed the manicured ferns and potted miniature palm trees filling the corners were there to distract the crowd from the obvious fact that someone had gussied up this room as cheaply as possible in case it became necessary to vacate in a hurry.

The foursome picked their way through a maze of tables hosting poker, blackjack, craps, roulette, and a horse-race betting board off to one side. The mood in the room shifted as people noticed Clark Gable and David Selznick walking among them. Nobody fawned or gaped at them like regular folks, however. This spiffy crowd liked to give off a detached nothing-impresses-me air, but even Polly's unseasoned eyes registered that they couldn't divert their gazes.

"Big surprise. It's the unholy trinity." Selznick contemplated three men standing next to a large potted fern near the roulette tables. "Wilkerson, Cohn, and Balaban."

Polly whispered into Cora's ear, "Who are they?"

"The tall chap with the clipped mustache is Billy Wilkerson. He owns *The Hollywood Reporter*. The short guy who looks like he ought to be a carnival freak-show barker—that's Harry Cohn, who runs Columbia. And with them is Barney Balaban, head of Paramount. I teach his son piano. The kid's only nine and is already showing remarkable musical abilities."

Striding past them was someone Polly wouldn't have guessed she'd encounter in a high-stakes place like this. She excused herself and caught up with him. "Remember me?"

"Polly!" Leon Schwab fussed with the cuffs of his off-the-rack jacket, probably the only one of its type among this ritzy flock of peacocks. "I'm surprised to see you here."

"I wanted to thank you for giving Amelia a job."

"She's lucky the girl she replaced had been so . . ." The man flushed.

"Careless?" Polly suggested.

"Indeed. But Amelia has proved to be an excellent employee. My customers love her."

"I must confess," she said over the rattle of a craps table behind them, "I wouldn't have figured you for the gambling type."

"Compared to these cardsharps, I'm strictly amateur hour. I enjoy the occasional flutter, but I'll bet you a sawbuck I'm the lowest spender here. I never gamble more than I can afford and always pay my debts."

"Now that I have your ear, I want to say how touched I was that I made you think of my mother. She died when I was so young that I have no memory of her."

"Flora was a living doll." A wistfulness filled his eyes as the high rollers around them plunked down more for a hand of poker than Polly earned in a year. "I can still hear her laugh. Gosh, oh my . . . Nobody laughed quite like her."

Polly wanted to kiss him on the cheek, but it felt somewhat inappropriate. "I'd love it if you'd share a memory of her."

Schwab didn't hesitate. "Your parents' wedding."

"Somewhere out in the countryside, wasn't it?"

"At the Mount Lowe Tavern, north of Pasadena. Such a lovely ceremony. Outdoors, in the alpine setting of the San Gabriel Mountains. And your mother!" Schwab broke into a dreamy smile. "So lovely. You could have been her stand-in."

Is that why Papa never talks about Mama? Do I remind him too much of her? "Tell me more."

"Your father marched up to me later, well in his cups by then. Started on about the setting, and how glorious it was, filled with such breathtaking natural beauty. And it was, to be sure, but I'm a city guy. I like sidewalks and honking horns and hot chocolate fudge sundaes. What did I care about hiking trails? So I nodded and listened as he talked about how if he wasn't doing so well at the City of Angels Distillery, he'd find a job as a park ranger or run a place like the Mount Lowe Tavern. Anything that would let him live in nature."

All this was news to Polly, but it explained the attraction of living on Catalina Island, where unspoiled nature unfurled in all directions.

"I suppose," Schwab said, "you're here tonight because you heard about the fight he was in. You're a week too late, I'm afraid."

"He was *here*?" Polly gripped her pocketbook extra hard. "In a fight?"

"One of the croupiers told me your father got into a terrible dust-up with Harry Cohn."

Polly swiveled to where Cohn had been talking to the head of Paramount and the *Hollywood Reporter* guy, but they were no longer there.

"Punching, slugging, headlocks," Schwab continued. "Got so bad it spilled out into the parking lot."

Polly couldn't picture Papa slugging it out with anybody. "Who won?"

"Cohn is a streetwise son-of-a-gun who knows what to do with his fists. Never take on that bully unless you're sure you can win."

"And Papa? What happened to him?"

"Apparently your dad didn't so much walk away as stagger."

"Poor Papa!" She caught sight of Cohn's white-gray hair at a blackjack table. "I need to ask him what happened."

Schwab restrained her. "He's been losing all night, so he's in a foul mood—even more than usual. Tell him you're Elroy Maddox's daughter and I'd fear for your safety."

"What's he going to do? Take a whack at me in public?"

"Harry Cohn is not above hitting a woman. Promise me you'll steer clear of him."

. "Fine." She could see Cora scanning the crowd now; Polly told Schwab that she needed to go.

"Take care of yourself, young lady," he said as she headed off.

"There you are!" Cora said as she approached. "I lost you in the shuffle."

"I ran across Leon Schwab."

"As in 'Pharmacy'?"

"He told me my father was here last week and got into a fight with Harry Cohn."

Cora winced. "That can't have ended well, but it proves he's still in LA."

A thought struck Polly that made her feel as though she had taken a step closer, and yet at the same time, a step farther away. She looked around for Schwab, but couldn't see him amid the milling crowds. "The day I first met him, he brought up Harry Cohn's name."

"In what context?"

"He mentioned how Cohn always had Mad Ox at his parties."

"Perhaps it's his favorite brand?"

"He made it sound as though it was the *only* brand."

"Polly, darling, you've got a funny look on your face. What's circling your noodle?"

"My roommate's mother told me that back during Prohibition, Papa had a silent partner."

"Cohn?"

"That's what I'm thinking." Now that she had articulated her theory out loud, it sounded on the far side of far-fetched. "I missed Papa by a week, so I'm probably clutching at straws."

But Cora was looking thoughtful now. "Just now I got talking to a gal I know from MGM. She works on hairpieces and false eyelashes, and she asked me who the redhead was that I walked in with. When I told her you're my niece, she said, 'Elroy Maddox's daughter? That's a funny coincidence because Elroy was here last week.' She mentioned nothing about a fight, but did say he arrived with a companion. When I asked her what the woman looked like, she pointed to you and said, 'That girl could be her daughter.'"

What kind of fugitive from the law brings someone to a public place where he's likely to be recognized? The desperate kind, Polly decided.

"I don't suppose you have a twin I don't know about?" Cora said.

"No, but my roommate and I resemble each other."

"How closely?"

"Enough to be cousins."

"Does Amelia resemble her mother?"

"Oh yes. She inherited her mother's red hair and—oh golly."

"Golly?" Cora clutched Polly's arm. "What golly?"

"Amelia's mother, Lois, is married to Judd, who Papa used to work for before we moved to Catalina."

"So Elroy and Lois have a history."

Polly nodded. But what was Lois doing with Papa? And if she knew of Papa's whereabouts, why hadn't she told Polly?

18

As Polly and Amelia walked up the Hartleys' garden path, Cookie and Jewel barked loud enough to rouse a coma patient.

"Nervous?" Amelia asked.

"Nah," Polly lied.

The day before, the girls had moved their sparse belongings into the apartment Polly had found at Robertson and Pico. It was a little cramped for two people, but sunny, conveniently located, and affordable. On the drive over, they had batted around possible explanations of why Lois had been with Elroy that night. None of their theories had been the least bit plausible.

"She's an FBI agent and he's a stool pigeon!"

Or worse: "He's a mobster kingpin who's unaware that she's an undercover ace reporter using him to get a scoop!"

Lois held the two eager dogs by their collars as she opened the screen door with a dexterous kick to the handle. "You'd think these two would've calmed down in their old age." She waited until Amelia had closed the door behind her before liberating them. "How did the move go?"

"Fine, fine." Amelia handed her a card with their new address.

She waved the card like a miniature fan. "I'm always happy to see you, of course, but you could have mailed this to us."

"We had another reason to drop by." The girls sat at the dining table and waited for Lois to follow suit.

"I wanted to ask you," Polly said, "when was the last time you saw my father?"

Lois's "My goodness!" sounded a little too forced. "When did your mother pass away?"

"Nineteen twenty-two."

"There's your answer, then."

"Are you *positive*, Mother?" Amelia urged. "It wasn't more recent than that? Like, for instance, at a secret casino off Hollywood Boulevard?"

Lois molded her lips into a wide "O" from which she prepared to launch her denial, until she took in the unblinking faces of the two young women in front of her. "Obviously you know I was there."

"Why did we have to hear about it from Polly's aunt?"

Lois's eyes bulged in genuine surprise. "Cora?" she asked Polly.

"We met the other day at MGM."

Amelia slapped the table. "Don't change the subject."

"Okay. Fine. I guess you deserve to know."

"You *guess*?"

Polly laid a hand on her friend's wrist. "How about we just listen?"

Lois bit down on her lower lip for a moment, the way people do when they've got a complex story to tell but don't know where to start. "First of all, I swear it was the first time I'd seen Elroy in a very long time. From out of the bluest blue, he sent me a telegram asking me to meet him at the bar of the Altadena Town and Country Club. Considering what's been going on, I was shocked that he'd pick such a public place. But he asked to meet at four p.m., when hardly anybody is there. And I have to admit that I was curious."

"How'd he look?" Polly asked.

"A little disheveled, but not too bad, considering. He explained that to clear his name he had to get to Harry Cohn—but not at the studio. Somehow, he knew that Cohn goes to that illegal backroom casino on the first Saturday of every month. He didn't want to take a taxi in case the authorities tracked him down."

"So he asked you to do it?" Polly ached to run to him and tell him they'd fix everything together.

"The more I tried to talk him out of it, the more insistent he grew. In the end, I caved. I suppose you know about the fight, too? I could do nothing to stop it. I could only pick up the pieces and drive him back."

"Could he walk? Was he bleeding?" Polly said, trying to keep the anguish from her voice.

"No blood, no broken bones. Nothing that a week's rest in bed wouldn't fix.

"But Papa could have asked one of any number of people."

Lois half-turned away from the girls. Her fingers found the edge of the checked gingham tablecloth and fidgeted with the corner.

"Outside of that telegram you sent about me, you and Pop hadn't seen him in years," Amelia said. "What're you not telling us, Mom?"

As though sensing the room thicken with tension, Cookie and Jewel sat themselves at Lois's feet and looked up at her expectantly.

Lois dropped the tablecloth corner and forced herself to look at Polly. "Your father was quite the dashing young man in the distillery's early days."

Polly knew so little about Papa's life before Catalina. Finally, she had a chance to fill in some blanks. "A real go-getter, huh?"

"To say the least. Blessed with all the pep and zip to go out and take on the world. It was why the business did so well."

"I smell a 'however' coming on," Amelia said.

"Yes, well, after a while, it became obvious that Elroy was love-struck." Two rosettes of color bloomed in Lois's cheeks.

"With *you*?"

"Is that so hard imagine? I was a lovely young chickadee too, once upon a time."

Amelia raised her hands in surrender. "Just seeking clarification."

"But Judd and I were already courting, with plans to marry. I was flattered but firmly rebuffed his overtures.'

"What did Pop say?"

"Your father was clueless to all the signs—until that awful night when Elroy made his big romantic declaration of love."

"What did he do?" Polly asked.

"The LA Aqueduct had been built to deliver water from up north. The day they opened the spigot, a huge crowd gathered to watch. Judd couldn't go for some reason, so Elroy took me. As the first wave of water cascaded down the channel, Elroy produced flowers and chocolates and a bracelet and declared his undying love for me. Right there in front of everyone as the water splashed and gushed past us."

"Sounds like a scene from a movie." Polly couldn't picture Papa being so wildly romantic. Maybe because she'd never seen him acting mushy over anyone.

"I let him down as gently as I could. Naturally, he'd been invited to our engagement party. I didn't think he'd come, but he did. And that's where he met your mother, Polly."

"She came with Papa?"

"No. Flora was there on the arm of one of the other salesmen. As soon as she walked in the door, everybody was saying 'Ooo, is that your sister? Is that your cousin?' The fact is, we did look uncommonly similar. And I liked Flora. Everybody did. A couple of months later Elroy and Flora were courting. I was relieved—"

"Even though his new girlfriend resembled you?" Amelia asked.

"I tried not to think about that. And besides, they seemed happy. The next thing I knew, Judd told me Elroy and Flora were getting married."

"It happened that fast?" Polly said.

Lois shifted in her chair, no longer looking at Polly or Amelia. Instead, she bent down to pet the dogs.

Amelia cocked her head to one side and eyeballed Polly. *Do you get what my mother means?*

Reality slapped Polly in the face like a cold apple pie. "Shotgun-wedding fast?"

"Yes, dear, I'm afraid it was."

"I was conceived out of wedlock." Polly needed to hear the words out loud from someone in the know. Yet another skeleton in the closet to add to Papa's list. "I hear the wedding took place up in the mountains above Pasadena."

"After the scene at the Aqueduct, Elroy had distanced himself from Judd and me, so we barely knew anyone there. But yes, it was a charming wedding. Elroy continued to work for Judd, but they kept their distance, which I thought was a shame, because around the time Flora gave birth to you, I fell pregnant with Amelia. I rather hoped you girls would become playmates. But it wasn't to be. We suspected Elroy might strike out on his own, but after Flora died, Elroy announced that he had to get out of LA and away from all the memories. He'd secured a new job working for Mr. Wrigley and was moving to Catalina with you."

"Pol looks like she could do with a drink," Amelia announced. "And frankly, so could I."

"I'm fine," Polly insisted. "And besides, it's ten-thirty in the morning." But even as she tried to shift the focus, she could feel the color ebb from her face.

"Amelia, the cooking sherry's in the end kitchen cabinet," Lois said. As Amelia fetched fortification, Lois continued. "About a year or so later, we heard stories of a bootleg bourbon called Mad Ox, and so we figured Elroy had found Catalina perfect for making bootleg. Then we heard about a casino on the *Ning Po*. I figured all-night poker games with vacationers who don't have to work in the morning and a moonshine outfit out of reach of the long arm of the law—what a perfect place for Elroy to set up shop."

Amelia set a filled glass in front of Polly, who reached for it with a shaky hand. She wasn't a great fan of sherry—cooking sherry even less so—but she felt trampled by all this news. She took a sip —at least it was dry sherry. "Do you know where my father is?"

"If I did, I'd take you there right now."

"When did you last see him?"

"The night he tangled with Harry Cohn. He refused to go to a hospital, so I took him back to the country club."

"It must have gotten late by then."

"At least two a.m. He said that he was staying nearby, but he left it at that. He didn't want me to be in a position to rat him out."

"So you left him there?" Amelia said. "All banged up like that?"

"It's what I led him to believe." The smallest of smiles creased Lois's lips.

"You *followed* him? Mom! How very Sam Spade of you."

Lois flinched. "I'm afraid I didn't make a good Sam Spade. I followed him a few blocks north of the club to where the hiking trails head up into the mountains. It was quite dark and there's more than one trail, so I didn't get far. Sorry, Polly, but I lost him almost immediately."

A doleful silence settled over the table until Polly recalled Leon Schwab telling her about her parents' wedding.

"Is the Altadena Town and Country Club far from the Mount Lowe Tavern?"

"Where your parents got married?" Lois asked. "Yes. Those hiking trails I mentioned—the main one leads up to the tavern. Or at least used to. The place closed down a few years ago after the terrible fire."

"You think maybe your pop's living there?" Amelia asked.

"I can't imagine it's the least bit habitable these days," Lois countered.

"So the police aren't likely to think of it."

"You're not going up there, are you?"

"I won't sleep until I've at least taken a look around."

"Those trails in the Angeles Forest, they're no walk in the park," Lois warned.

"I've never hiked a step in my life," Amelia burst out, "but I can't let you go up there alone."

What a relief. Polly wasn't looking forward to tackling unfamiliar hiking trails by herself.

Lois said nothing as she pinched her lips together and ran a fingertip around the edge of her glass. When she faced the girls again, an air of resigned surrender had settled over her. "In that case, you both'll need sturdier shoes."

* * *

Amelia's labored breaths rang out from several paces behind Polly. "I didn't figure you for the outdoorsy mountain goat type."

"I'm from Catalina Island. It's all outdoors."

Amelia huffed and puffed some more. "You're sure we're following the right trail? Because this is kinda steep, and rocky, and—and—I want to be sure we're not making all this effort only to find these ruins are three canyons over."

"Your mom told us to take the Rubio Canyon trailhead. As long as we see a sign for the Rubio Pavilion, we're on the right track."

"And did we?"

"We saw an old, weathered sign with two words on it. First word ended with an 'o,' and the second one started with what looked like a 'p.'"

Amelia grunted. "Close enough."

The mid-afternoon sun seeped through the thick overhang of the tall trees bordering the rough trail. Though it was early December, the weather was unusually mild. In fact, if it got any warmer, Polly would have to shed the woolen sweater Lois had insisted she take.

Polly wasn't a big believer in women's intuition, but what if her hunch was right? What if Papa was hiding out in one of the cabins, cozy as a puppy and thrilled to see her? What would she do? What would she say?

First, I'll hug him. Then I'll check he's okay. And when he reassures me that he is, I'll hug him again, hard as I can for as long as I can, until he begs me to let him breathe.

And if her hunch was wrong? That was, after all, the most likely outcome. The farther she and Amelia trudged up the rough track, the more outlandishly romantic the idea sounded. Elroy Maddox takes sanctuary in the place where he got married and takes shelter in a fire-ravaged cottage under a caved-in roof held up by cracked walls and desperation, but he doesn't care because deep down he always wanted to be a park ranger.

"I wish Ludlow was with us," Polly said.

"I dunno, Pol. He comes across as strictly cocktails-in-the-back-of-the-Duesenberg. Top hats at Silverwoods, neckties at Oviatt's, shoes at Bullock's. Meanwhile, you and me are clambering up hillsides like we're Swiss mountaineers."

The trail curved into a hairpin hook turn before growing even steeper. "Yes, but he always seems to know the right thing to say at exactly the right time."

"He's got the gift of the gab, that's for sure. And he's found a way to make it pay. More power to him, I say. But boy howdy, don't ask him about his past. He closes up like a clam at low tide."

Polly turned around. "You've noticed that too, huh?"

Amelia flopped against a dead oak tree. "One time, we got to talking about schools. I told him all my stories: my crush on the geography teacher; Dwight, the schoolyard bully with the buck teeth, Wednesday afternoon detention."

"Did he return the favor?"

"In theory. But, gosh, I dunno. His stories were all so"—she seesawed her hand—"so ordinary, so everyday. No particulars, no quirky details, nothing specific."

"Like a well-rehearsed story?"

"Uh-huh. Eventually, I thought, 'Oh, I get it. The past is Taboo Territory. No visitors allowed.'"

Fifty feet from where they stood, the trail bent slightly to the left, then opened out into a huge clearing. A stone wall rising four feet ran along its western edge—the fossilized remains of what had once been a building larger that some of the bigger homes Polly had seen in Beverly Hills. But the fire Lois had spoken of had reduced the rest of it to a tumbled-down mess of charred planks and broken glass glinting in the sun.

The girls crept closer, twigs and branches cracking beneath their shoes. "Your mom was right." Polly ran a hand over the brick wall. "This place is uninhabitable."

Past the tangle of scorched rubble and encroaching tentacles of Mother Nature, a line of half a dozen cabins stretched into the distance. The first couple had been as fatally incinerated as the main building, but the two behind them still had most of their walls and passably intact roofs. And the two behind them looked virtually untouched. It was the final one that had caught Polly's notice. Inside the open window stood a yellow candle, its flame dancing in the late afternoon breeze.

Polly broke into a run.

Please let it be him. Please let it be him.

Twenty feet from the cabin she could hear a voice singing.

Fifteen feet from the cabin she could tell it was a man's voice.

Ten feet from the cabin she could tell it was her father's voice.

Five feet from the cabin she could see the cabin door was ajar.

She jumped onto the porch and peeked through the gap.

As a bedside radio played a languid version of "I Get a Kick Out of You," Elroy was taking a dark blue box to a square dining table where a small electric generator sat. The rusty hinges chirped as she pushed the door wider. When he looked up and saw Polly, a mix of horror and delight, surprise and relief flashed across his face.

"Doodlebug?"

He needed a shave and a haircut, fresh bandages around his right hand, and the services of a Chinese laundry. But other than that, he was "PAPA!" She threw herself into his arms. His shirt smelled of carbolic soap, cheap cigarettes, and something metallic. Was it blood?

"What're you doing here?" His voice trembled from the weight of his dismay.

"I've been looking for you," she replied. "For weeks. The

charges. Embezzlement." Words were tumbling from her now. Each one cracking as it slipped out.

"But how did you find me?"

"It hasn't been easy." Amelia stepped forward.

Polly drew her into their huddle. "Papa, this is Amelia."

"Judd and Lois's girl," Papa said.

She grabbed Polly's hand. "You've got a hell of a daughter, lemme tell you."

Pride battled confusion in his eyes. "I sure do. But how—"

"Everyone helped me. Not only Judd and Lois, but Leon Schwab and David Selznick. Cora too. She—"

"My sister?"

"She lives in LA." Papa's grip around Polly's shoulder slackened as he absorbed the shock of missed opportunities. "Works at MGM, but I can tell you about that later. For now, I want to know about these charges. Are they true?"

Papa offered up a watery smile. "I tried to shield you from all of it—"

"The embezzlement, Papa. Thirty-five thousand. Tell me you didn't do it."

"I suppose everyone assumes I'm guilty."

"No, sir," Amelia cut in. "You'll be pleased to know that everybody's reaction is the same. 'That doesn't sound like his style at all.'"

Elroy looked to his daughter for corroboration. Polly nodded, tears now stinging her eyes.

"Misplaced, I'm afraid."

Papa's admission jerked through Polly like an electric shock. "What are you saying?"

The courage to look her in the eye deserted him. "It's true."

"What?" He can't know what he's saying. These past weeks have been too much for him.

He sucked air in through gritted teeth and braced himself with tightened fists. "Thanks to Longie Zwillman."

Polly turned to Amelia. "Isn't that the guy from the La Brea Club you were telling me about?"

"The original Mister Bad News."

Back to Papa. "What's he got to do with this?"

"When I moved us to Catalina, I found myself living in the perfect place to bootleg what I knew best: bourbon. But I didn't have the capital. At City of Angels, we'd been doing business with Harry Cohn and the two of us got talking one day. I floated my idea, not expecting him to do anything, but he offered to front me the money and said we'd go fifty-fifty on the profits."

"Let me guess," Amelia said. "He reneged on the agreement?"

"On the contrary, he was a thorough professional all the way through Prohibition. Why wouldn't he be? We were making good money, and he had a dependable supply of decent liquor for all his parties at the studio."

"What about the gambling den on the *Ning Po*?" Polly asked. "Was he fifty-fifty on that, too?"

"Nope." Papa dismissed this idea with an unequivocal shake of his head. "All he said was, 'I admire a guy who gets off his rump 'cause it's tough to get ahead in this cockeyed world.'"

All this information felt like quicksilver seeping through Polly's fingers before she could grapple with what had been going on around her while she had been sleepwalking through her own life. Polly wanted to sit down, but the only chair was the one next to the rumpled bed, and it looked as though it might come to grief in the next windstorm. "But what about after Prohibition ended?"

"Business as usual."

"Was embezzlement business as usual, too?" Polly hadn't meant to snap at her father like that, not after how hard it had been to find him, but it was better than slapping him across the face, which is what she wanted to do.

"Of course not. That came later, when Longie Zwillman put the screws to me."

"But why? And why you?"

"He wouldn't tell me, but I put two and two together when I learned that years before Harry had borrowed money from the mob to buy out his partner at Columbia, and that Zwillman was his go-between. And now suddenly, fifteen years later, there he was, putting the squeeze on me to the tune of thirty-five grand. Meanwhile—surprise, surprise—Harry wouldn't return my calls."

"Are you saying that the mob forced you to embezzle from the Company? Or that Harry Cohn did?"

"Yes? No? Both? Neither?" Papa rolled his eyes. "Not that the authorities care. My fingerprints are all over the Company's ledgers. So, I made a run for it so that I could—"

"ELROY MADDOX!" A deep voice amplified by a bullhorn pierced the room. "THIS IS THE LOS ANGELES SHERIFF'S DEPARTMENT." Sheriff

"Papa!" The cops had been following her? She had led them to him! Not once had she looked behind to make sure they'd been alone.

"WE ARE GIVING YOU TEN SECONDS TO COME OUT WITH YOUR HANDS OVER YOUR HEAD."

"There's a window in the bathroom." Papa pointed to a closed door in the rear of the cabin.

"MADDOX! THIS WILL ALL GO MUCH EASIER IF YOU DO IT VOLUNTARILY."

"All I need is ten, fifteen seconds to make a break for it." His eyes darted around the room, wild with panic, as he backed away from Polly.

"No, Papa, NO!" Polly stepped toward him, but he raised his flattened palms to halt her progress.

"I don't want you caught up in all this. I never thought you'd track me down." He attempted a smile, but it was a feeble effort. "But you're my clever little Doodlebug, aren't you?"

"Papa, please don't leave. I'm begging you. Come clean with them, tell them the whole story. I'll stand by you, no matter what. I promise, Papa. I won't—"

"All you have to do is go out there. Distract them." He was halfway across the room now. Almost at the bed. "By the time they realize you're not who they're looking for, I'll be through the windows, in the woods, and out of sight." He spun around and brushed away the pillow, revealing a dark gray handgun.

"Papa! What are you thinking?"

"Don't worry, Doodlebug. It's not loaded." He waved the gun like it was a flag on the fourth of July. "Just for show!" He jerked a thumb toward the bathroom door in the corner. "Stall 'em and I'll—"

The cabin's door disintegrated into a thousand shards as a burly cop in a green uniform invaded the room, his service revolver already cocked and raised. "GUN!" Then he spotted Polly and Amelia off to the right and hesitated for a split second.

Polly glimpsed Amelia flying toward her. They tumbled to the floor in a painful muddle of elbows and knees. In the chaos, Polly tried to meet her father's gaze, but Amelia kept her head pressed down as a deafening hail of bullets erupted around them.

19

Hazel stopped typing when Polly walked into the office. "You're back," she said, but it was more of a question.

Polly placed her handbag in the bottom drawer of her desk. She had expected this conversation all morning, practicing what she would say. Not until she had stepped through the studio gates had she decided simplicity was best. "And ready to work."

"So soon?"

That word—*soon*—sucker-punched Polly in the chest. It felt like a month had crawled by since that awful day up in the mountains.

She could still hear the bullets hit Papa with a sickening thud.

She could still feel Amelia's arms crush her as momentum thrust them downward.

She could still sense the floorboards shudder as Papa's inert body collapsed to the floor.

"There are only so many days a girl can stare at the walls."

"You sure?" Hazel asked. "Because if—"

Polly shut her down with a single glare. *I'm begging you. Please let's not talk about it.*

For a week she had felt like that fragile eggshell that had been cracked open, spilling her guts out in a clotted, ropy tangle. Days had blended into nights only to become daytime again without her noticing. Everything had felt so utterly pointless she hadn't found the strength to leave her bed.

Two days ago, she'd made it as far as the kitchen to burn herself some toast.

It wasn't until yesterday she had noticed how badly she reeked.

This morning, she had pulled herself together, showered and dressed, and had ridden the streetcar without rupturing at the seams. And she wasn't about to let that happen now that she had made it all the way to her desk.

Polly slid the cover off her typewriter as she had done every morning. Consistency and routine. That's what she craved.

She was folding the cover into a neat pile as Marcella trooped into the office like a general. "Yesterday's efforts have been for naught—OH!"

"You said to take as much time as I needed, which I appreciated—"

Marcella was suddenly by her side. "You haven't been eating. Skin and bones, isn't she, Hazel?"

Polly had only stood in front of the bathroom mirror long enough to brush her hair, and not a second more. "My roommate has been making me chicken soup," Polly told them. Her voice sounded like it was coming from another room. "The same recipe Mayer's mother uses in the MGM commissary."

"It was all you could stomach, I should imagine," Marcella said, her voice soft and maternal. "Can't say as I blame you after everything that's happened."

How much did Marcella and Hazel know? Amelia had refused to show her any of the papers, insisting, "They're full of guff and fibs."

Polly would be eternally grateful for Amelia tackling her to the floor and holding her down. Once the shooting had stopped, brave, daring Amelia had hauled her to her feet and hustled her out of the cabin. She had tried to look back, but Amelia had kept her facing forward. "No, Pol, it's awful." The early evening air had prickled her skin and stolen her breath, but it also cleared her mind enough to answer questions from some faceless, nameless police detective. And when Amelia had decided enough was enough, she had tossed their address to the nearest uniform and had held Polly's hand as they tackled the downhill path that had now seemed twice as treacherous.

"Did you get the flowers?" Hazel asked. "We requested white lilies with carnations and the pale pink roses."

"I did, thank you. It was very thoughtful."

"Did you add vinegar to the water?" Marcella asked. "It makes them last longer."

The sweet fragrance of their bouquet still filled the apartment. "I did, and it does."

Two days after the shootout, the city morgue had called to say she was free to collect the body. And put it where? she'd wanted to ask.

Good ol' Ludlow to the rescue. He had swooped in and made arrangements with a crematorium. The brushed pewter urn he chose now sat on the bookshelf in the living room. That night, Judd and Lois had arrived with food, and Cora had shown up with three bottles of Chablis. Polly had picked at her supper, grateful for the company, but longed for everybody to leave.

Marcella patted Polly's shoulder. "I won't lie. It's a relief to see you. However, we have lots of work to do, so I need you to keep up your strength. I'm talking corned beef sandwiches, brisket, or that smoked tongue salad they now have in the commissary. Comes with Monterey Jack cheese, pickles and cole slaw. Just the thing to build you up again."

"I'd prefer the salmon, if it's all the same to you."

"Anything you want. Now, before you high-dive back into the fray, are you *sure* you're ready?"

Polly had spent the week alternating between staring into space and crying. Amelia had done her best with that chicken soup and occasional Chapman's Fancy ice cream. But then Polly had remembered how the night was coming up when old sets were to be incinerated to recreate the burning of Atlanta. How could she leave all that work to Marcella and Hazel while she was sprawled out on the sofa like a listless sloth?

"Ready, willing, and able, ma'am."

Marcella tipped her head toward the boss's office. "It's quite possible the schedule of final screen tests I've been juggling is about to be thrown out the window. Would you believe—"

"MARCELLA!" Selznick roared. "GET IN HERE!"

She rolled her eyes. "Like I've got nothing better to do than play referee." She hurried into Selznick's office.

Hazel crushed a *shhh!* finger to her lips. She tiptoed to the doorway, pulling Polly behind her until they were hugging the wall.

Myron told his brother, "You're being pigheaded. As always. You haven't started filming yet, and until you do, you have plenty of time to make a final decision."

"Burning down Atlanta tomorrow night is our signal to Hollywood that we've started," Selznick snapped, "so don't lecture me on—"

"Unless you plan on throwing Scarlett into the blaze, tomorrow's bonfire is irrelevant. Meanwhile, you haven't even clapped eyes on the girl yet."

"Stop pushing Vivien Leigh on me."

"Okay, but here's what you want if—"

"Don't tell me what I want. Jesus, Myron, I can see why Zanuck banned you from the Fox lot over Loretta's contract. You don't know when to quit, do you?"

"A strong contender for Scarlett has been in LA for ten days and you haven't even made the time."

"You've signed her as a client along with Olivier, so you're hardly impartial as to what constitutes a strong contender. We haven't heard from Ray or Eric or Howard yet. What do you guys think?"

Ray Klune, the production manager, Eric Stacey, the assistant director, and Howard Greene, the cinematographer, had been filing in and out of Mr. Selznick's office for weeks. None of them were wallflowers when it came to venting their opinions, but casting was outside their purview.

"I'm telling you, Dave," Myron almost sounded like he was about to punch his brother, "the girl has a special magnetism. You absolutely must see her before you decide."

"Oh, sure!" Selznick slapped his desk. "I'll make time. Let's say anywhere between two-thirty in the morning and two-forty-five."

"Go screw yourself, you sarcastic ass."

Myron stormed out before Polly and Hazel could scamper back to their desks. Ray, Eric, and Howard followed close behind. Polly was at her typewriter by the time Marcella emerged. "Those Selznicks," she muttered. "They're like a couple of rams locking horns."

"May I make a suggestion?" Polly asked her. "Why doesn't Myron take Miss Leigh to watch the filming? From what I understand, there'll be a lot of waiting around, so Mr. Selznick will have an opportunity to engage with her. It strikes me that—"

Selznick, hearing her voice, poked his head through the doorway. "My sincere condolences."

"Thank you, sir."

"I overheard what you said."

Polly felt a slight blush coming on. "I was only thinking out loud."

"Please go on."

Polly stared at him, momentarily at a loss for words. She felt unsteady, like she was still groping her way out of a darkened room, and wished she'd stayed in bed with the covers over her head. Who was she to tell David O. Selznick what to do? But then she thought, *Screw it. I've survived a police shootout that killed my father. Nothing's impossible anymore.*

She cleared her throat. "Think of it: Selznick meets his Scarlett O'Hara by the flames of Atlanta. You'll have press there. Imagine the coverage."

Selznick sought out his trusted lieutenant with an inquiring look. "What do you think?"

Marcella didn't hesitate. "You'd be a fool not to."

Another idea hit Polly. "She'll be extremely nervous to finally meet you, so don't make a big deal about it."

"And how should we do that?"

"Your brother should take her and Mr. Olivier out for dinner, and then over dessert he should drop into the conversation, all casual like, 'Hey, it's only nine o'clock. Wanna see a fire?'"

A smile slowly surfaced on Selznick's face. "Miss Maddox, it's marvelous to have you back."

* * *

Polly mounted the steps of the makeshift viewing platform the studio carpenters had built especially for tonight. She tightened her inadequate coat. "It's colder than I expected."

"Don't worry." Marcella ran a finger down her checklist. "There'll soon be a great big fire to warm our rumps."

Ahead of them, the towering *King Kong* gates were catching the wind like pirate sails, rocking from side to side, threatening to topple over. The foreman called for reinforcements. Polly counted fourteen men lined up along the base, inching each gate into place.

"Do me a favor," Marcella said. "Look around. Keep it nonchalant. Tell me if George is here."

"Cukor?"

Marcella nodded. "He and Mr. Selznick had a knock-down, drag-out shouting match this morning. I want *nothing* to upset the boss tonight."

Toward the rear of the wooden platform, Cukor was talking to a woman with lively, intelligent eyes who reminded Polly of Irene Selznick. "He's over there"—she inclined her head toward the pair—"speaking with a dark-haired woman. I don't recognize her, but she looks smart as a sleuth."

Marcella discreetly followed her gaze. "Kathryn Massey. *Life* magazine. Though why she left *The Hollywood Reporter* is beyond me."

"Is it good that they're talking?"

"As long as she's not bothering Mr. Selznick." Marcella pulled her knitted hat down over her ears. "And remember, you've got a job to do."

Earlier that day, Selznick had asked Polly to come to the filming so that she could "keep a close eye out for Myron, Vivien, and Larry." He had so much on his mind, he explained: the seven Technicolor cameras he'd borrowed, the enormous conflagration he was about to initiate, the Culver City police and fire departments, the press, and the safety of the Scarlett and Rhett stunt doubles. Overshadowing tonight's events was Mr. Selznick's declaration to the world that production was underway.

"Civil War pictures don't make money," the naysayers had warned.

"*Gone with the Wind* is unfilmable," they'd scoffed.

"A better title for this white elephant is *Selznick's Folly*," they'd jeered.

He was out to prove them all wrong. Every doubter, critic, and detractor. But Polly sensed the agony that kept her boss up at night. What if all the effort leading to this evening failed to ignite interest in the film? Selznick had no more discarded sets. There could be no second takes, no try-agains.

Polly threaded her way through the growing crowd as Ray Klune shouted instructions to clear the area. "We are ready for fire number one. Cameras are rolling." She reached the rear steps as he yelled, "And . . . ACTION!"

Firemen swarmed around the six engines parked to the left, readying their equipment. Stagehands lined up across the field waved in succession. As the last man raised his hand, Klune called, "GAS!"

Polly gripped the rough wooden railing. *Please don't turn into a limp misfire.*

A low rumble throbbed the ground, and Polly felt the air vibrate. And suddenly a series of four explosions rent the night air. Polly held her hands in front of her face as the heat reached her. She turned around to see two men and a woman emerge from a midnight-blue Lincoln and head for the steps. Polly waited until they were halfway up before she greeted them with an energetic "WELCOME!"

"Polly, isn't it?" Myron said. "I fear we're too late for the fireworks."

"That was the first go-around," Polly said. "Two more—"

An almighty crack cut her off. One end of the blazing set buckled as a brave stuntman shepherded a reluctant horse and buggy along the entire length.

"Good heavens!" said the woman. "They can't be but twenty feet from it all!"

Vivien Leigh wore a dark velvet Tyrolean hat that dipped close to her right eye. As stray embers floated around her, the glow from the flames lit her delicate face, stunning Polly into silence.

She's mesmerizing. She's flawless. She's Scarlett.

"They need to get forty minutes on film."

Olivier adjusted a white cashmere scarf around his neck. "That's a lot." He stared at the spectacle, unruffled and unimpressed—and, Polly guessed, uninterested.

She looked over her shoulder in time to see Selznick run a finger along the arm of his glasses. It was their secret sign. "Mr. Selznick is dying to meet you." She led the three of them through the thicket of crew, press, staff, and hangers-on who wanted to say "I was there when" until she drew close to Selznick.

"Hey, genius," Myron said to him. "I want you to meet your Scarlett O'Hara. This is Miss Vivien Leigh."

Polly withdrew and inadvertently backed into George Cukor.

"That's her, isn't it?" he asked in a voice scarcely above a whisper. "The limey."

Polly nodded, unable to turn away from the woman.

"I'm already picturing her Scarlett to Clark's Rhett." George rubbed his hands together in eagerness. "That scene in the library where Scarlett and Rhett meet for the first time!"

Polly looked askance at him, then turned back to the sight of the renegade movie producer meeting the woman who Polly felt should be his leading lady.

"Come with me." Cukor led her to a vacant pocket of the platform and faced her more squarely. "What did that look mean?

Please don't play games. You recall our conversation at Myron's birthday party?"

"I remember saying I couldn't make you any promises."

He acknowledged her with a terse nod. "I don't want you to break any confidences you've shared with David or Clark or whoever."

"Okay, but"—she drew closer to him—"you didn't hear it from me."

"Scout's honor."

"Are you aware that Gable is far from thrilled with the prospect of you as director?"

George frowned. "I directed him on *Manhattan Melodrama.* We got on perfectly well."

"Making a crime picture. Gamblers, guns, and all things manly."

Realization dawned on his face. "But *Wind* is a woman's weepie."

"Which you'll throw to—" Polly wiggled a finger in Miss Leigh's direction.

He watched her and Selznick chat and joke and flirt and charm as they swayed back and forth through their wary Will-He-Can-She mating dance. After a time, his expression turned into an indignant scowl. "In all the endless meetings I've had with Selznick and Gable and Kay in New York, not to mention everybody else, this is the first time anybody has addressed the issue head-on."

"I'm sure you know how to handle him."

"He's not that hard to figure out. But this is *Gone with the Wind*. The stakes are higher." George hadn't taken his eyes off Vivien Leigh. The woman glowed as brightly as the wall of flames behind her. "She's ideal, isn't she?" Suddenly he started as though someone had trod on his foot. "Oh! Polly!" He turned away from the performance unfolding at the other end of the platform. "I was so distracted that I neglected to offer my condolences over your father's passing."

Just when I'd managed not *to think of Papa for twenty consecutive seconds. Maybe next time I can shoot for thirty.* "Thank you. It's been . . ." But the words to describe the past week deserted her.

"And you were right there. I can't imagine."

"I had some time with him before—" Her voice cracked. She pointed a gloved finger toward Selznick. "I wouldn't have been able to track Papa down had it not been for him."

"I see," Cukor replied.

But it was his scornful, almost mocking tone that pulled Polly up short. "What does that mean?"

He flapped his hand nonchalantly. "Oh, nothing."

The scores of crewmembers scurried around the field to prepare for the next firestorm. The cameramen surrounding the enormous Technicolor cameras threw themselves into action.

Cukor watched the frenzy for an uncomfortably long moment. "David might have his own agenda with finding your father."

Jamming an unlit cigar in his mouth, Mr. Selznick had abandoned his Scarlett to concentrate on the next shot.

"Agenda for what?"

"Take what I'm about to say with a grain of salt, but have you heard of a movie called *Pretty Pennies*?"

"The one he wants to remake? Sure, I have."

"Do you know the story?"

"It's about a girl who dives for pennies thrown by steamship passengers."

"Where are these ships?"

"Avalon."

"And who's from Santa Catalina Island?"

The way Cukor had taken the time to call Polly's home by its full name hinted that he was making a point. But what point? "*Pretty Pennies* came out in nineteen-fourteen, years before we moved there."

"There's a rumor that only one copy of *Pretty Pennies* exists, and that Elroy had it."

"He what?"

"Just a rumor, mind you, but mighty persistent."

"I doubt that. I mean, I certainly never saw it." Someone with a bullhorn barked out an order to evacuate the field. "And anyway, my father was on good terms with him. Why wouldn't he have handed it over?"

Cukor shrugged. "All I know is that deep in the bellies of David and Myron burns the desire to restore the family name. It drives everything they do. And if they can do it by remaking the picture that kicked off their father's career, all the better."

As crewmembers rocketed in all directions, the assistant director commenced counting down from thirty. Everyone turned their attention to the second phase as Atlanta fell victim to Sherman's march to the sea. Everyone but the redhead from Santa Catalina Island.

20

When Polly walked into Kreiss's Coffee Shop in the Beverly Wilshire Hotel, she thought only of the hot chocolate fudge double banana split sundae with whipped cream and peanuts that Amelia had promised would cure whatever ills she might be suffering from her twelve-hour day.

In the week since Polly had returned to work, Marcella had kept her promise to fill Polly with brisket and smoked tongue. It had done the trick. The gradual return of Polly's appetite had helped her ramp back up to speed.

All decked out in black and gold, Kreiss's high ceilings and mirrored walls reminded her of Carver's Ice Creams back home in Avalon, on Crescent Avenue near the Green Pier. Mr. Carver claimed he knew his way around an ice cream churn better than anyone else on the island. It wasn't an empty boast, but the ice-creamy aroma in Kreiss's smelled that teensy bit richer than the bouquet in Carver's eight-table nook.

Amelia had thrown her new winter coat over her Schwab's uniform. She hollered "YOOHOO!" across the restaurant as Polly strolled in. "Your banana split is on its way." She beckoned Polly over to the table where she sat with Ludlow.

"What a delightful surprise." Polly slid onto a cherry-red chair and turned to Ludlow. "Shouldn't you be out with some deep-pocketed lady friend?"

"I was," Ludlow said. "Constance DeMille and I were at Paris Inn. Cecil's filming *Union Pacific* in Utah, so she was at a loose end."

Polly eyed the unfinished waffles on his plate. She hadn't eaten a bite since noon. "What happened?"

"We were having a marvelously convivial time until she started talking about her husband's film of *Cleopatra*."

"The one from a few years ago?" Gosh, those waffles looked good. Would he mind if she helped herself? "That seems out of the blue."

"Not after a head-turner sauntered into the place like she was the second coming of Gloria Swanson."

"Anyone you knew?"

"No, but Constance did. Miss Ingenue was someone ol' Cecil had a fling with during production, so Constance came down with a headache."

"That's a shame."

"Not especially." Amelia giggled. "Right, Luddie-pie?"

He blithely blew Amelia a kiss. "I'm Luddie-pie now," he dead-panned to Polly. "Call me Luddie for short. At any rate, Constance paid me a full evening's fee for one hour's work."

Amelia stirred her pink milkshake with a straw. "I pity women like her. Sure, she gets to swan around town as Mrs. DeMille, with all the privileges that entails, but—gosh, I dunno. Seems like a high price to pay."

Polly grabbed an unused fork. "May I?" She stabbed at Luddie's waffle and tore off a chunk. "I feel like I haven't eaten since Labor Day."

He pushed his plate toward her. "They must be working you extra hard after you burned Atlanta to the ground and discovered Scarlett O'Hara all on the same night."

These two didn't know the half of it. When word spread that a British outsider had thrown her velvet Tyrolean hat into the ring, the telephones hadn't stopped shrieking.

"Marcella has hired two new girls," she told Amelia and Luddie. "They face each other close enough to bump heads if they lean too far forward over their typewriters." She turned and stared longingly toward the kitchen. Where was her sundae? These left-over waffles wouldn't keep her ravenous hunger at bay for long. "Meanwhile, did you see the *Examiner*?"

Working in Hollywood's busiest office gave her little opportunity or energy to brood over anything that didn't involve *Gone with the Wind*. But she couldn't avoid the *Examiner*'s stinging headline.

GAMBLING KINGPIN AND BOOTLEGGER CHARGED WITH EMBEZZLEMENT

"The guy who runs those floating casinos off Santa Monica might be called a 'kingpin,'" Luddie scoffed, "but what your father was doing on the *Ning Po* hardly qualifies."

Polly pushed the waffles away as the soda jerk arrived with her banana-split dinner. It needed an extra-large ceramic bowl to fit the mountainous dessert. She shoveled a pile of scrumptiousness into her mouth. "You'll get no argument out of me."

"And besides," he added, "how can they charge someone with embezzlement when he's no longer with us?"

"Someone somewhere has figured out an angle. And I must too if I'm to clear Papa's name."

"Any ideas?"

"Oh, sure." Polly waved her spoon around like it was Lady Macbeth's dagger. "All I need to do is place a person-to-person call to this Zwillman character and order Harry Cohn to get back to me. I haven't had a full night's sleep since the Mount Lowe Tavern . . ."

But Luddie wasn't listening anymore. Neither was Amelia. They were facing off with a pair of young men seated at the neighboring table.

"Would you like us to speak louder?" Luddie asked. "Or would it be easier if you joined us?"

Polly couldn't tell if they missed the sarcasm in Luddie's question or ignored it in their haste to squeeze in around a table built for two.

"I'm Benji," the sandy-haired one said, "and this here's Gil."

"Pleased to meet you." Gil sported a head of dark curls, the type that would have resisted Brilliantine's power to slick down and flatten. But oh my, wouldn't it be heaven to run one's fingers through them?

Luddie introduced the three of them and asked Gil what he did for a living. "We're at Paramount. Benji is an art director."

"Working on *Beau Geste*," Benji added.

"And you?" Polly asked Gil.

His teeth looked like a slightly ramshackle picket fence, but his smile was warm and friendly. "Most recently, *Union Pacific* for Mr. DeMille. Before that, I built the stagecoach in *Stagecoach* for United Artists, and next I'll be at MGM to work on *The Wizard of Oz*."

"You get around."

Benji laughed. "You're speaking to Hollywood's foremost maker and restorer of horse-drawn carriages and coaches."

Hollywood people, Polly had noticed, defined themselves by what movie they were working on, as though it were a declaration of value.

"Our ears popped up when we heard you're with Selznick," Gil said. "I don't suppose you were there when they set fire to those sets?"

Polly looked down at her food. It was already half gone. How did that happen? Also, would it be so gauche if she ordered a second? "Why, yes, I was."

"So, this British actress—does she stand a chance?"

The last task Polly had worked on that evening was the script for Jean Arthur's final screen test, which Mr. Selznick had wanted to rewrite, although Polly wasn't sure why he was bothering. She had seen a draft of Vivien Leigh's contract with Myron. Every sentence had been meticulously crafted as though her casting were inevitable.

But she couldn't share such classified information with Amelia and Luddie, let alone complete strangers. Even if they were cute. Especially that curly-haired carriage builder. But all four of them were looking at her, their faces filled with such intense expectation that she felt obligated to feed them a scrap.

"Well." She paused for dramatic effect. *Look at me! I'm a Hollywood insider now!* "From where I was standing, Mr. Selznick looked captivated."

"Enough to give her a screen test?"

"The telling sign is"—she put on a show of looking around to see if anyone could hear them—"if Mr. Selznick or Mr. Cukor orders a Technicolor test. Only serious contenders get those."

"Your secret's safe with us!" Gil had an appealingly wide-open face. His ears stuck out a bit too far, rather like Gable's, and suited him in the same way.

Benji rose to his feet and pushed his chair back into position. "I have an early call tomorrow."

Gil followed suit. "If you're going anywhere near the Pan-Pacific, I'd love a lift."

Benji picked up their fedoras. "It's been a pleasure." He tossed the dark gray one to Gil, who hesitated a moment, then turned to Polly. "There's bound to be a great number of horse-drawn carriages needed for *Gone with the Wind*. Maybe put in a good word for me with Mr. Menzies?"

Polly wasn't sure William Menzies had the authority to hire and fire. "I can't imagine he'd listen to me. Especially seeing as how I barely know you."

"Easily fixed." He produced a pencil from inside his jacket and wrote his name and number on a paper napkin.

Polly stuffed the paper into her pocket as Gil and Benji exited through the tall glass doors and disappeared into the hotel foyer. "This talk of DeMille gives me an idea," she said to Luddie. "Do the Hollywood wives all know each other?"

"They know what philanderers their husbands are," he replied. "Looking the other way is an occupational hazard."

"But do they turn to each other for support?"

"Only their fellow Mrs. Moguls know what they go through."

"How would you feel about asking Mrs. DeMille if she knows Mrs. Cohn?"

"Does this have anything to do with your hunch about Harry Cohn?" Amelia asked.

Polly scooped up the last of her banana split. Her stomach had finally caught up with her spoon, and she realized it had been more filling than she'd expected. What a relief that she wouldn't need to embarrass herself by ordering a second. "He's powerful and ruthless and scary, so I can't take him on directly. Not that I have a bona fide plan. All I know is that sitting around doing nothing is no option."

"No, it isn't." Quiet admiration filled Luddie's face. "Your idea of getting to Mrs. Cohn through Mrs. DeMille—it's such a Hollywood chess move."

"So you'll call her, Mister Luddie-pie?"

"Leave it to me, Miss Polly-Pol."

21

The piebald gelding swung around to scrutinize Polly as he chewed the bit threaded across his mouth.

"What's his name?" she asked the stable attendant.

"Rumormonger, but we call him Mongo." He ran a firm hand down Mongo's muzzle. The horse shook his head, raising it high enough in the air to pull himself out of reach. "Mrs. DeMille left instructions to saddle him up especially for you."

"Why him?"

"You must be Polly." The statement came from a stiff-backed woman, her white hair knotted into a tight bun and an austere expression engraved on her face. She sat astride a thick-bodied pinto with a gentle light in his eyes that Mongo lacked. "I'm Mrs. DeMille."

"Thanks for agreeing to meet with me—"

"Ludlow assured me you were an experienced horsewoman."

Experienced, yes, but only with weary nags like Ol' Jim and Heidi. "I grew up on Catalina. We ride horses all over." She inserted a foot into a stirrup and hoisted herself up. The horse stamped his hoof, raising a puff of dust. "There, there, Mongo," she cooed. "We'll be good pals, you and me."

"Let's shove off before Griffith Park is overrun with picnickers who wander wherever their carefree minds take them." Pulling on her left rein, Mrs. DeMille led her horse toward a trail next to a copse of eucalyptus trees.

Polly repeated under her breath Luddie's warning from the previous night. "Constance is a forthright, commanding woman with full knowledge that she is Mrs. Cecil B. DeMille. You'll find her thoughtful and generous once she lets her guard down."

The trail ambled around manzanita bushes and jacaranda trees before rising up a moderate incline. Farther along the path, the slope steepened to a more challenging angle.

"Ludlow indicated you'd like to speak with Rose Cohn."

"Yes, that's right. I'd be so grateful if—"

"For what purpose?"

"I believe her husband may have been in business with my father. However, I need more substantial proof than a hunch."

"Elroy Maddox, may he rest in peace."

It was neither a question nor a request for more information. Did she expect a response? Mongo was falling behind. Polly gently squeezed his ribs to encourage him to giddyup. He ignored her. "My father ran a bootleg operation during Prohibition."

"Mad Ox was one of the better moonshines, as I recall."

"I've recently learned my father needed a silent partner."

"And you think Harry might be able to identify this partner?"

"I believe Harry Cohn *is* the silent partner."

Mrs. DeMille pulled on her reins and waited for Polly and Mongo to catch up with her. "Has Ludlow explained the connection between Mrs. Cohn and me?"

Polly shook her head.

"My husband was at MGM, where he made three unsuccessful films, including his remake of *The Squaw Man*. It was a horrible time; desperate men do desperate things. He sought comfort in the arms of a little strumpet who he'd cast in all three movies. He was also under the spell of high-stakes gambling and was at an all-night poker game that Harry Cohn also attended. My husband is a skilled player, but on this particular occasion he had a run of bad luck. His debt ran higher and higher, so he decided Cohn was cheating. His suspicions grew and grew until his temper overheated and he started throwing accusations across the table. It became disgracefully ugly and ended with Cecil signing an IOU to Cohn for thirty-five thousand dollars."

Polly gasped. "In one poker game?"

Mrs. DeMille nodded grimly. "Not long after, he moved to Paramount and released *The Sign of the Cross*, which was a tremendous success, and he was back on the upswing. Then I heard the strumpet had started working at Columbia, so I went to Rose Cohn and cautioned her. Rose confronted the girl, warning her to stay away."

"And did she?"

"Quite the opposite. The little tramp went out of her way to seduce Harry. On the bright side, though, she gave him crabs. Rose and I bonded over that. We feel most protective of each other, which is why I insisted you and I meet first." The initial frostiness in Mrs. DeMille's voice had melted. Not a lot, but enough to signal that Polly was making headway.

The pinto took off up the hillside, leaving Polly to follow. "Come on, Mongo, ol' pal. Don't fail me now." The piebald neighed softly and fell in behind.

"How are you acquainted with Ludlow?" Mrs. DeMille asked.

"My roommate and I were at Schwab's when he came in with Ria Langham."

Polly wasn't sure if it was seemly to drop names like that. But weren't they in Hollywood, where careers were made on the ability to drop them into a conversation?

The woman broke into her first smile. It wasn't a dazzling movie-star beam, but it was not without warm sincerity. Polly wondered if Mrs. DeMille would smile the same way if she learned Luddie had swapped calling cards with a libertine like Edmund Goulding.

"How very like Ludlow to take Ria to a place like Schwab's. All us married ladies wish our men knew how to behave like him. He knows how to make a woman feel special."

Polly couldn't help but wonder: Had he slept with Ria? And

what about Rose Cohn? From what she could make out, their husbands appeared to be quite free from conscience when it came to straying outside their marriages. No wonder Luddie and his fellow escorts were so busy.

When the bridle trail widened into a level opening, Mongo trotted a little faster until he'd caught up with the pinto. "So, what do you think?"

Mrs. DeMille snapped out of her reverie. "About what?"

"Introducing me to Mrs. Cohn?"

"Rose said that if you had won Ludlow's recommendation, that was enough for her. However, I wanted to be sure, so I volunteered to be the scouting party. We're to meet her in about an hour and a half."

"We *are*?"

A pair of pigeons cannonballed out of a huge azalea bush, bright with crimson petals.

"I assume David doesn't have you working Sundays, too?"

"Not as a rule. I'll need to run home and change into a more appropriate outfit."

Polly and Amelia had spent more than an hour piecing together an ensemble of pants, sweater, and jacket in more or less matching shades of green, all sufficiently thick to keep the chill of the early December morning at bay. But she doubted it was fancy enough for someone who spent more in a single shopping expedition at Bullock's Wilshire than Polly and Amelia did on a month's worth of groceries.

Mrs. DeMille passed a cursory eye over Polly's ensemble. "It's fine for a casual afternoon tea at the Ambassador."

"I do so appreciate this huge favor," Polly said. "Thank you, Mrs. DeMille."

"We ought to get a move on before your horse snacks on that crepe myrtle over yonder."

"What'll happen to him if he does?"

"It'll take two Wallace Beerys to pull him away. Oh, and one more thing."

"Yes?"

"You may call me Constance."

* * *

Rose Cohn had already taken a seat at a corner table of the Lido Room off the main lobby. Polly assumed the lacy concoction she wore was expensive, but it was the color of boiled potatoes and looked a little on the dowdy side, which meant she was a prime candidate for Luddie's brand of companionship.

Constance ordered a large pot of tea and a "generous plate of those delicious petit fours—and be sure there are a couple of the coconut ones. Last time I didn't get any, and I was terribly disappointed."

As their waitress hurried away, a string quartet embarked on a Strauss waltz. "I understand you work for David Selznick." Mrs. Cohn said. "I'd imagine Myron is in and out of that office all day. What are they like to deal with?"

Not yet five minutes in and already this conversation had veered off into a direction Polly hadn't foreseen. Was this a trap? A test? Did this woman revere or loathe the Selznick brothers? Polly felt loyal to David. Myron, however, she could take or leave, but it had become clear that although they often butted heads, the brothers viewed Hollywood through an us-against-them lens.

"Well, Mrs. Cohn," she said, choosing her words carefully, "I must admit they're a bit of a handful—but in a good way. They're filled with fierce ambition and determination, which I find admirable. It certainly makes for a lively place to work."

"I can only imagine." A hint of tart amity twinkled in her eyes. "I'm asking because of *Pretty Pennies*."

"You know about that?"

"My interest is purely mercenary. My husband is currently grooming a starlet. Her name was Margarita Cansino, but Harry's changed it to Rita Hayworth and dyed her hair red. Not subtle like yours, but a bright, flaming red." She tsked loudly, though what she disapproved of, Polly wasn't sure. "He's put her in *Only Angels Have Wings*, a Cary Grant and Jean Arthur picture they're about to start shooting. He's hoping David will cast her in *Pretty Pennies* because he's got nothing else for her."

Constance harrumphed. "God forbid those sons of bitches have a contract performer sitting around inactive for more than seven and a half minutes."

"But now I understand that Myron's lining up his own redhead for the role," Mrs. Cohn continued.

Polly kept her hands folded on the table. Was she referring to Amelia? But Amelia had only said yes to humor Luddie. "I hadn't heard that."

"It's like this British actress we keep hearing about for Scarlett. She's Myron's client, too. So, if he's got someone on the inside track for *Pretty Pennies*, I'd say Harry's got little chance of putting Rita over. And I can assure you, my husband hates to lose."

Constance landed a light hand on Polly's wrist. "Tell Rose what you told me about your father."

"Poor Elroy!" Rose exclaimed after Polly had caught her up. "I was positively aghast when I read what happened to him. But embezzlement? How shocking."

Polly pushed aside that final image of Papa before the cop opened fire. "You knew my father?"

"He supplied the best bourbon in town, so he was often at the big parties."

The waitress materialized at their table, laden with trays of food. Polly said nothing until after she had set out their tea and tiny cakes and departed as discreetly as she had arrived. "My father hinted to me that his troubles all hearkened back to your husband."

Rose sighed as she filled their cups. "What's he done now?"

"Has he ever mentioned the sum of thirty-five thousand dollars?"

"My husband rarely talks to me about business or finances."

"This would have been more along the lines of a gambling debt."

Rose narrowed her eyes and tapped her wedding ring against the side of her bone china teacup. "Harry and Elroy maintained an amicable and beneficial arrangement. But then their partnership soured."

"Recently?"

"No. A couple of years ago. We were celebrating the success of *Theodora Goes Wild* at Lou and Frank Capra's New Year's Eve party, so it must have been nineteen thirty-seven."

"Soured, how?"

"Well, you see, that year was shaping up to be an important one. Harry had Frank's *Lost Horizon* and Leo McCarey's *The Awful Truth* coming up. He'd sunk a ton of money into them—especially *Horizon*, with that mammoth monastery set. He needed huge successes, so he was even more combative than usual. Naturally, he dealt with it by getting disgracefully drunk."

"How disgraceful?"

The question came from Constance, but the disquiet in her voice made Polly put down her cup. It rattled the matching saucer.

"He grew belligerent," Rose declared, "which is even worse than his sober belligerence. He ended up in a dreadful altercation."

"With my father?"

"No, someone I'd never seen before. My husband is a child of the New York streets; he knows his way around a fistfight. But not that night. *He* was the one left sprawled out on the gravel driveway, bleeding like a pig, so this confrontation ate at him. After that, he conducted a lot of closed-door telephone conversations."

"You didn't tell me this!" Constance said. "Conversations with whom?"

"Johnny Roselli, Bugsy Siegel, Mickey Cohen."

Constance fell back in her chair. "No wonder you clammed up."

"I was so horrified I stopped listening on the kitchen extension."

Polly hadn't heard of Johnny Roselli, but there were those other two names again. The deeper she dug, the more she felt like she was excavating a grave.

"Did your father ever mention those three?" Constance asked Polly.

"No, but I've been learning so much about him I was blissfully unaware of."

Constance tut-tutted. "Men are so skilled at keeping secrets."

Rose fixed Polly with an unflinching stare. She looked like someone who was connecting dots that, until this moment, had been merely a mass of unrelated spots. "Elroy might have been a bootlegger and run the *Ning Po*, but those crooks make your skin crawl—like my husband, who thinks nothing of screwing people over. I'm surprised nobody's run over him. Especially at the moment. He's got this movie coming up, *Mr. Smith Goes to Washington*, and he's been shoveling sackfuls of dough into it."

Polly bit into one of the petit fours. The thick layer of dense coconut sandwiched between thin slices of sponge cake and dipped in chocolate was delicious, but Polly was too worked up to enjoy it. "You said this souring between your husband and my father started at that party. Why do you think that?"

"He'd always been a member of Harry's wider social circle. But after that night, I never saw Elroy again." Rose set down her teacup. "Tell me, Polly, what is it you really want?"

Finally, a question she could answer. "To clear my father's name. He told me he was close to getting the evidence he needed to resolve this embezzlement charge, but then the raid happened. I'm not even sure how they can charge someone who's no longer alive—"

"Who is he supposed to have embezzled from?" Constance asked.

"The Santa Catalina Island Company."

"So Philip Wrigley is looking to recover the money from Elroy's estate. And that means until he lifts any charges, the authorities will have seized your father's assets."

"What about his bank accounts? The distillery had several with—"

"Down to and including his piggy bank."

"If I returned to Catalina—"

"I imagine you'll be barred from retrieving a damned thing."

Polly had no plans to return home, but the idea that she might never step inside their house again sank her into a gloomy hole.

"Have you found anything at the tavern?" Rose asked.

"I couldn't go back there! Not after what happened."

"Perfectly understandable," Constance said. "I'd imagine that the police would have confiscated every last shred of evidence."

Rose strummed her fingertips against her cheek. "Not unless he hid it well. You know him better than anyone else, so I'd imagine you'd know where he was likely to conceal any evidence he'd uncovered."

But did she know Papa better than anyone? Some days, it felt as though she didn't know him at all. And should she revisit the site where—Polly couldn't say the words. Not even to herself. The prospect of poking through whatever the cops had rejected as worthless trash was more than she could grapple with.

But at least she wouldn't have to do it by herself. She wasn't friendless Polly Pitiful anymore, was she?

"Look, Rose," Constance trilled. "You've given Miss Maddox food for thought. I think our work here is done."

Polly picked up what was left of her tiny cake. "You're right about these coconut ones. Do you think we could get some more?"

22

A stiff wind blew through the leaves of the towering oak trees looming over the hiking trail. Polly turned up the collar of her new overcoat. "This'd be more fun in July."

At Polly's request, Amelia had taken the lead. "I feel like I'm on a thrilling adventure."

"Let's not count our chickens."

"I think you're brave for coming back," Luddie said, from directly behind her. "Regardless of what we do or don't find."

Polly looked over her shoulder. *Thank you for saying that.*

"I'm surprised David Selznick gave you time off," Benji said.

"Yeah!" Gil added from the rear. "I hear he works his staff harder than General Pershing."

It was Luddie's suggestion that Polly invite Benji and Gil along. "Combing through trash and debris avoids all that gauche first-date awkwardness."

She hadn't even mentioned how she'd been trying to think of an excuse to call Gil so that he could take the hint and ask her out. But somehow Luddie knew. Luddie always seemed to know. "Most Saturday afternoons I'm hammering away at my typewriter, but Mr. Selznick has stopped work on everything else because the *Wind* script isn't finished yet."

"You set a match to all those sets, and the script isn't even done?" Benji asked.

"Hasn't he had three hundred and forty writers on it?" Gil asked.

"Stop reading Louella Parsons," Polly told him. "It's only been three hundred and four."

"Including Scott Fitzgerald."

"Yes, but—" Polly caught herself. Out here in the wilderness among friends, it was too easy to blab confidential details surrounding the movie. Especially when the number of people dismissing the project as a misguided money pit grew with every passing day. "My boss prefers to be involved in all aspects of production, including the script."

"You sound like one of those memos you're always typing," Amelia called out.

"You're jealous because you can't type at all." Benji was trailing her. Very closely, Polly noted.

"Oh, please!" Amelia took a playful swipe at him. "Nobody can compete with Miss Lightning Fingers."

Benji didn't have a standard handsome face, but it was not without its charm. He looked like he might take a cross-country trip, hike the Swiss Alps, or recite Shakespeare: the type Amelia had avowed she was looking for. Gil, on the other hand . . . Now *there* was someone Polly could go for. Good-looking, but not movie-star charming. Friendly without being fawning. Chatty but never sought to dominate the conversation.

"Miss Lightning Fingers can't cook a pot roast anywhere near as delicious as Miss Schwab's," Polly said, "so I'd say we're even."

"For the record," Gil said, "I make a darned decent tuna noodle casserole. I took my mom's recipe and perfected it."

"What did you add?" Amelia asked.

"How about I have you girls over and we'll see if you can guess."

Gil winked at Polly. A slow, deliberate wink. The man was flirting—wasn't he? Nobody had flirted with her before. She looked at Luddie for corroboration. He was staring, his lips curled into a knowing smile.

Luddie. Always. Knows.

"We're here!" Amelia announced.

Wait. What? Already? Polly hadn't given herself time to gather her courage. The thrill of her first flirtation drained away as the dilapidated Mount Lowe Tavern emerged out of the underbrush.

Luddie wrapped a tender hand around her elbow. "Slow and steady does it."

The cops had thumbtacked a sheet of sheriff's stationery to the front door of Elroy's hideaway.

CRIME SCENE
DO NOT ENTER

The rest of the proclamation told members of the public that the cabin was the scene of a felony and that "all persons not employed by the Los Angeles Sheriff's Office" were forbidden to enter.

"To hell with that." Polly pushed open the door.

Elroy's hideaway was the chaotic shambles Polly was anticipating, but the police hadn't picked it as clean as she had expected.

"What are we looking for?" Gil asked.

A fair question. "Anything that looks like it doesn't belong here. Especially if you find it stuck up the chimney or behind that mounted moose head."

Polly made it halfway into the room before her breath stuck in her throat. She stared at the blood-stained spot where Papa had fallen, already dead when he hit the ground. She went to turn her back on it, but Luddie urged her forward. "Don't look away."

Everyday odds and ends were scattered across the cabin: a couple of hats, copies of *Drums Along the Mohawk* and *Anthony*

Adverse, a Carpenter's Drive-In matchbook, a shoehorn. How very like Papa to go on the lam with a shoehorn like he was taking a transatlantic cruise.

Most of the remaining detritus the cops had left behind consisted of papers and documents. None of them mentioned Mad Ox, Cohn, Siegel, Zwillman, or the *Ning Po*.

Turning over a cushion on the sofa, she unearthed the necktie she had given him for Christmas the year MGM had come to Catalina to film *Mutiny on the Bounty*. She had made piles of money in tips that summer, so her gift had been the nicest tie for sale on the island. A deep steely blue with fine diagonal silver stripes, it suited him and he'd frequently worn it. It warmed Polly's heart to know that in his dash to escape, he'd grabbed this particular one.

"I've found this." Benji held up a photograph. "It's not evidence, but it's interesting."

It was the high school prom photo Mr. Selznick had told her about. Polly stared at it, lost in the memory of her excitement that night. How grown-up she'd felt. How much she had looked forward to being asked to dance. She still felt the steel blade of disappointment pressing against her throat after she had left early and walked home alone, berating herself for being so foolish as to believe any of those pimple-faced juveniles would give her the time of day.

"I don't believe it!" Amelia stood at a chipped, rickety bureau where Papa's briefcase lay open. She held another photo in her hands. "This you gotta see."

It was a creased, sepia-tinged image of two girls, their hair in long Mary Pickford ringlets, wearing wide straw sun hats and muslin summer dresses dotted with buttons and bows. On the back an inscription in meticulous copperplate read, "Lulu and Bernice during filming of 'Pretty Pennies,' 1914." Amelia tapped the girl on the left. "My mother's high school nickname was Lulu."

Thanks to a swarm of press releases Mr. Selznick had dictated over the past few weeks, *Pretty Pennies* was now often mentioned in the newspaper columns, making much of how 1939 would mark the twenty-fifth anniversary of the first film his father had produced.

"Who's Bernice?" Gil asked.

"That'll be the first question out of my mouth the next time I see my mom," Amelia said.

Intriguing though this photo was, it didn't help clear Elroy's name, so they kept looking.

And looking.

And looking.

In every drawer, under every chair, behind every bookshelf and cupboard. Even up the moose's nose. But they unearthed a big hatful of nothing. As the fading light outside lengthened the shadows, Polly reminded everyone how the trail back to the parking lot was arduous enough, let alone in the dark. She placed the tie, the shoehorn, and a few other items into Papa's briefcase, snapped it shut, and led them outside, clutching the briefcase to her chest.

As soon as they had left the clearing behind them, Gil made his move. "Sorry it was such a bust."

Polly needed to inject some levity into what had been a futile exercise. "If you had been William Powell, and I had been Myrna Loy, we might have come away with a burned match or typewriter ribbon that turns the case on its head."

"Nothing ventured, nothing gained, huh?"

"People usually say that when they've gained something better than a necktie and a shoehorn."

"Listen, could I take you out some time?"

Polly tightened her grip on Papa's briefcase. It had happened! At long last, someone had asked her out! "I would like that." She let him have his moment of joy before she socked him with the reality of asking out a Selznick girl. "The trouble is, I might be forced to cancel seventeen times before I get off work early enough to have dinner."

His smile didn't dim. "I'll take my chances, which will improve when I start on *Wizard of Oz*. We'll almost be neighbors."

She shifted the briefcase to her left hand so that it no longer formed a barrier between them. "What sort of horse carriage do they need?"

"At some point somebody rides through the Emerald City behind the Horse of a Different Color. They've got one, but it's ancient."

"Just a patch-up job?"

"Not just any patch-up job. This particular carriage was originally presented to Lincoln during the Civil War."

"What?" The guy had dropped this detail into the conversation as though it were as commonplace as the pebbles sliding under their feet. "*President* Lincoln?"

"Uh-huh."

Now that she'd had a chance to study him up close, she saw a rather earnest fellow underneath that cornucopia of silky curls. As if that wasn't appealing enough, he also possessed initiative and enterprise, but without the smug hubris of the boastful maestros that filled Mr. Selznick's waiting room.

And the cherry on the sundae of his appeal was his occupation. 'Carriage maker' sounded old-timey, but in a good-old-days way.

Since moving to Los Angeles, Polly had seen the bachelor wolves on the make in drugstores, theaters, office buildings, nightclubs. Loaded with charm and confidence, they rarely wasted an opportunity to use it on any female between eighteen and sixty. Never on Polly, though, and she was fine with that. But this guy who built wagons and restored carriages was a throwback in all the best possible ways.

He must have taken her smile as an encouraging sign. "If you ever need a bookshelf or a coffee table, I can knock one together in an afternoon. Although, if you want a secret compartment, that'll take all day, plus dinner afterwards."

"Secret compartment? In a bookcase?"

"You'd be surprised how many people ask for that."

After another couple of turns in the shadowy path, she got to thinking. If Elroy had been running an illegal gambling operation, might he have had one somewhere? Maybe even in his briefcase?

Was it too outlandish? Too cloak-and-dagger-spy-movie, a ruse dreamed up by a fanciful screenwriter? But if people asked for one in their bookcase . . .

"Did anyone think to bring a flashlight with them?"

"You mean like this?" Benji handed her a weighty one.

She rested the briefcase on a fallen tree trunk and popped it open. As she shone the light around its interior and ran her fingers around the edges, she pitched her idea to the group and asked if it was too far-fetched. Yes, they agreed, it was, but they encouraged her to keep looking anyway.

For what, though? A hook? Tab? Button? Lever? Spring?

But it revealed nothing.

"Nope," she announced. "Let's keep going."

She closed the case and handed the flashlight back to Benji, and they set out along the trail again, falling into a hush. But as they did, though, an image came to Polly.

When she had first encountered Elroy in the cabin, he'd been holding a box. She couldn't quite picture it now, but she had a powerful impression that it was like a miniature traveling trunk.

"Does anyone remember seeing a small trunk? Tiny, about the size of a bread box."

"It was under the coffee table," Luddie said.

"Did you look inside?"

"I . . . did . . . not."

It wasn't like Luddie to be so tentative. "What are you not telling me?"

"It was . . . splashed with blood."

Oh, God. Anything but that.

No, she told herself. This was no time to be squeamish. "We have to go back."

"Pol!" Amelia protested. "We're losing the light. Isn't this trail perilous enough?"

"I'll meet you all at the car. Mind if I take this?" Not waiting for an answer, she took Benji's flashlight from him and headed up the hillside, thankful to hear the others fall in behind.

Back inside Papa's cabin, she charged to the coffee table. There it was. A miniature chest, dark stains showing in the shaft of light. Its brass hinges squeaked quietly as she opened the lid.

"Anything there?" Amelia asked behind her.

Polly handed over two fountain pens and continued to feel around the sides, the top, and the bottom. Wait! Did her prodding fingers sense it give way? A tiny bit? She pressed harder until she felt it pop. The bottom of the box swung down like a second lid.

"Holy moly!"

She spied a folder of papers in the box's fake bottom.

"What are they?" Luddie asked.

"No idea," Polly slid them into the briefcase, "but it's almost nighttime and we've only got one flashlight."

"And," Benji added, "I can't remember the last time I changed the batteries."

* * *

Amelia flung open the Hartleys' front door. "MOM!"

Lois appeared from the kitchen, a striped apron tied around her waist. "What hellfire crisis—" Her scolding withered when she saw the photograph Amelia held aloft. Outside in the backyard, Cookie and Jewel were working themselves up into a conniption fit. "Where did you get that?"

"Among my father's possessions," Polly said, "up at the Mount Lowe Tavern."

"And on the back," Amelia flipped the photo, "it says, 'Lulu and Bernice during filming of *Pretty Pennies*, nineteen-fourteen.'"

"My goodness gracious me. Has it been that long?"

"Who's Bernice?"

The shrill screech of a kettle erupted in the kitchen. "You're welcome to have tea, but will one of you fetch those baying hounds of the Baskervilles before Old Man Vincent complains to the police again?" She hurried away to shut off the stove.

By the time Amelia had corralled Cookie and Jewel into the house and settled them down with a fresh pair of bones, Lois was pouring tea into matching cups and had set out a plate of oatmeal cookies. Her smile took on a nostalgic tinge as she scrutinized the photograph. "Those awful sausage curls. Who'd have guessed flappers were coming?"

"Who's the other girl?" Polly asked.

"The star of *Pretty Pennies*. We were on the set that day. Gosh, what a lark that was. Your father took this."

"Pop was there too?" said Amelia.

"Yes, but I meant Elroy."

"Can we back up to the beginning?" Polly asked.

Lois laid the photograph flat on the kitchen table, pinning its four corners with her fingertips. "Bernice was my best friend. We'd graduated from Hollywood High. Back then, Hollywood was a hick town, so we assumed we'd marry farmers, but then DeMille arrived to film *The Squaw Man*. We got curious about what it was like to shoot a motion-picture show, so we started hanging around the set—which was a barn over on Selma."

"You watched them shoot *The Squaw Man*?" Polly said, awestruck.

"Nobody knew what they were doing. The flickers had barely been invented. Anyway, Bernice caught the eye of Sibyl Langley. She'd been the stage manager during *The Squaw Man*'s Broadway run. When Jesse Lasky announced they were going west to film it, she jumped at the chance. But she questioned every decision Cecil made."

"I bet ol' Cecil didn't like that," Amelia said.

"He was still a nobody, but even back then he resented people questioning his authority. Their little spats led to bigger and bigger ones until she quit. Somehow, she ended up on Catalina, which is where she conceived *Pretty Pennies*. After she returned to the mainland, she contacted everyone in the directory to fund her picture and finally approached the one who said yes: Lewis Selznick."

The joke around the office where Polly worked was "All roads lead to Selznick." Evidently, there was more truth to it than she had ever guessed. "If this was nineteen-fourteen, my father had already joined City of Angels."

"That was the summer when everything changed."

Lois was choosing her words more deliberately now. What was she not saying? "Papa was around when Sibyl cast Bernice?" Polly asked.

"Most definitely. Once she'd found her lead actress, the movie went into production. Putting films together back then was so much simpler. By the time Flora arrived on the scene, life had become somewhat complicated . . ." Lois flicked the edge of the photo with a fingernail as her comment trailed off.

"Complicated, how? Because Elroy carried a bit of a torch for you?"

"Well, yes. Not only that, but what Elroy didn't realize was that Bernice had fallen for him."

Polly said, "Let me get this straight: Bernice loved Elroy. Elroy loved you. You loved Judd. You were caught in a love triangle!"

"Love *quad*rangle," Amelia corrected her.

"Yes, yes, it was all rather messy," Lois said, "but we avoided talking about it. We were Victorians. None of this blab-everything flapper attitude for us. *The Squaw Man* became a colossal hit, and you couldn't live in LA and be oblivious to D.W. Griffith shooting *Birth of a Nation* all over town. The flickers were so fresh and exciting. And now my best friend was going to star in one. It was all such a jolly lark!"

Joyful nostalgia had animated Lois's face as she had recounted that long-gone, thrilling summer. That is, until Polly watched it ebb away.

"And so *Pretty Pennies* went into production," Lois continued. "First on the mainland and then over to Catalina for the location shots. I had nothing better to do, so I tagged along. The cast, the crew, the hangers-on, we all rented a bunch of those semi-permanent tents with wooden floors in the camping ground. Tourist season was over and we had the run of Tent City. It was quite wonderful. And then one day, Judd and Elroy showed up unannounced. 'On a whim,' they said. I was thrilled because Judd was with me. Bernice was thrilled because Elroy had appeared."

"That must have been awkward," Amelia said. "All things considered."

"We were a silly band of misfits, but it was all such fun, we carried on regardless." Lois's face softened as she gazed wistfully at the photo. "Elroy took this in front of the Pilgrim Club. Very exotic, it was. Turkish rugs, green leather club chairs, paintings of all kinds. They had a chandelier in the main room that was rumored to have cost three hundred thousand."

"I remember hearing about this," Polly said. "Gambling house, wasn't it?"

"The owners loved to boast they were operating a miniature Monte Carlo. The Pilgrim Club is why Elroy set up operations on the *Ning Po*. The island had nothing that came close after—" Lois's face hardened. "I suppose it's time you knew."

"Oh, God, Pol!" Amelia slapped her hands to her cheeks. "This doesn't sound good."

Polly was suddenly filled with a desperate yearning for an easier, simpler time. Back on Catalina, all she had to worry about was sending and receiving telegrams, returning library books on time, and choosing Papa's birthday gift. No surprises. No secret gambling dens. No puzzling photographs. No vice squad raids. And no police shootouts. Maybe the quiet life had its advantages, after all.

Almost immediately, a reprimanding voice sounding like Aunt Cora launched in her head. "Quiet life—ha! It didn't have burgers at Schwab's, elegant Hollywood garden parties, or horseback rides with Mrs. DeMille, not to mention flirting with carriage builders whose curly hair you're dying to run your fingers through."

"Do you have any more of that sherry?" she asked.

Amelia sprang up from her chair as though her rear end had caught fire. "Don't stop now, Mom."

Halfway through a sigh, Lois turned it into a groan. "After filming on *Pretty Pennies* finished, Sibyl threw an end-of-production party. Elroy brought along his Kodak Brownie. They were still quite novel then, and he took photos every chance he got." She tapped the photo. "Including this one. The night started out gay and lively, but as everyone got a bit drunker, things took a vicious turn. And all the secrets came tumbling out. Bernice loved Elroy. Elroy loved me and hated how I loved Judd instead. Judd resented Elroy's feelings for me and became paranoid that I was stuck on Elroy. It took a lot of effort to convince him I wasn't, but of course Elroy didn't want to listen."

"How did he react?"

"He got so angry, so belligerent. But that's how he became when he drank. Some men are like that. Some turn into teddy bears; others turn into Atilla the Hun."

"Not true!" Polly slammed down her glass. Some of her sherry splashed onto the polished wood. She'd wipe it up later, but Lois's accusation had sparked a fierce need to defend Papa's reputation. "He was no Atilla the Hun."

"I'm sure you—"

"I was around him every day. I never, *ever* saw him drunk."

Lois fixed a hard eye on Polly. "That's because after that night he never drank again."

"But he ran—"

"A bootleg distillery? Ironic, huh?"

But—but—but—

Polly stared back at her, slack-jawed.

"Polly dear, your father became an expert on how to fake it because he could barely live with himself after what happened that night."

"Jesus, Mom," Amelia groaned, "what the hell went on between you people?"

"Judd and Elroy started out ribbing each other, but the teasing became squabbling, which became fighting. And then the fighting escalated into brawling so bad we got thrown out. We headed for the Metropole because their bar stayed open late. But without street lighting, it was dark. The woman who operated the camera —Zara, her name was—she produced some candles that she still had on her for lighting the last scene. She lit them and handed them around, and off we went. We had only gotten as far as the Rose Hotel and were ducking behind it for a shortcut when Judd and Elroy started up again. Whatever Judd said to him, it made

Elroy worse, and he started taking swings. Wilder and wilder they got. Everyone cursing like sailors."

Polly dropped her head into her hands. Papa had always had a kind word for her about a new dress or a recipe for chicken and dumplings she'd tried for the first time. Rarely gossiped. Rarely complained. Always well-groomed.

But *this* Papa? Drunk? Throwing punches? Cursing?

"Elroy worked himself up into a lather. He got so mad that he knocked the candle out of Judd's hand. It sailed through the dark and landed on the grass. I can still see it. Then Elroy threw his candle at Judd. Neither candle went out, though, so then Elroy picked them both up and menaced us with them."

"What did you all do, Mom?"

"We'd had enough by then, so we headed home to Tent City. I assumed Elroy would follow us, but he didn't. When I looked back, he was standing there, wavering in the winds blowing off the beach. Like a rag doll, he was. I said to Judd, 'We're not leaving him there, are we?' But Judd had steam shooting out of his ears and said, 'He can go to hell.' It was past two a.m. by the time we got back to camp and dropped into our cots. Next thing I know, all this screaming and shouting and panic woke us up. Bernice and I scrambled out of our tent and found the whole town was on fire. The Pilgrim Club, the Metropole, Tuna Club, Bath House, all up in flames."

Polly pushed her chair away from the table, its feet scraping the linoleum like nails on a chalkboard.

Papa a jealous brawling drunkard was bad enough, but this was too much.

By the time she and Papa had moved to Catalina, seven or eight years had passed since the notorious fire that had destroyed half of Avalon. She could remember seeing the charred remains of buildings left standing where they'd burned. What happened there? she'd asked Papa. Oh, he'd replied after an uncomfortable pause, a terrible fire.

She fell against the kitchen sink, fighting back tears. "I can't believe he went back."

"Irresistible urge to return to the scene of the crime?" Amelia suggested.

"I'd like to think he wanted to make amends," Lois said. "Is it true he became a pillar of the community?"

Polly nodded. "He sponsored all sorts of things. Baseball little leagues. The Miss Avalon beauty contest."

"You'll be pleased to hear he also redeemed himself by rescuing all the *Pretty Pennies* footage. Including the climax. If he hadn't, there'd have been no picture. By the end of filming, Sibyl had run out of money. She couldn't afford to reshoot."

"But didn't everybody ask how the fire started—and who set it?"

"We talked about confessing to the authorities, but it would have meant Elroy might end up in jail, especially seeing as how booze turned him into Mr. Hyde. And maybe we would have if people had died, but nobody did. I know what you're thinking: we should have forced him to turn himself in. And if we had our time over, we would've made more responsible decisions. But we didn't. We were young and stupid, and we slunk away like cowards the next day and agreed to never speak of it again."

Polly rejoined them at the table before her legs gave out. "I can see now why you've kept this a secret all this time."

Lois refilled Polly's sherry glass. "I've always regretted not doing the right thing. Guilt forces you to act in awful ways and make terrible decisions."

"But how was it between you all when you got back to LA?" Amelia asked. "It must have been unbearable."

Lois downed a deep swallow. "The irony is that after giving up booze, he became the distillery's best salesman. He kept his head clear while everybody else was getting smashed. Then Flora happened along. When your parents got hitched, Polly, Judd and I were thankful. Then they had you, and everything was peachy—until Flora died. So when Elroy came to us and said he was moving to Catalina Island to start over, we wondered if he was trying to make good in some way."

Cookie and Jewel were now pacing the living room. Polly knew how they felt.

"If I could have spared you all this, I would have," Lois said.

"Thank you," Polly said. "I appreciate that, but I feel like I've been pulled through the wringer." She drained her sherry glass and set it on the table. "Can we go now?" she asked Amelia.

"I'd like to spend the night here, Pol. Let's call you a cab."

Polly was relieved at the prospect of a night on her own. Her father had been a terrible drunk who had burned down half her hometown. She needed time to digest this news. Preferably alone. She picked up the photo she'd found at the tavern. "Did anybody learn your secret about the fire?"

"None of us ever brought it up again. Why would we? It was our big, shared shame we wanted to forget."

"What happened to Bernice?" Amelia asked. "Why haven't I heard about her?"

"She didn't enjoy making movies. A little while later, she met a traveling salesman. He sold candy to movie theaters. Did well out of it, too, but he had to travel a lot, so she went with him." Lois made a tsk of regret. "It didn't take us long to lose touch."

"And Sibyl?" Polly asked.

"*Pretty Pennies* made tons of dough, especially for her. And she needed it, because after that, she couldn't get another movie made to save her life."

"Do you know where she is now?"

"She's still kicking around. Last I heard, she was working on that big musical MGM is making out of *The Wizard of Oz*."

Generally, Polly believed coincidences were nothing more than mildly interesting happenstance. But that was the movie Gil was about to start working on.

And that was the sort of happenstance that got a girl thinking.

23

Through the week following Lois's revelation, the same thought whirlpooled around Polly's mind.

My father burned down Avalon.

Over her chicken salad sandwich at lunch.

In bed at night reading *Rebecca.*

My father burned down Avalon.

Memos to the production department about the Atlanta railway station. "We will have a spectacular crane shot with hundreds of wounded soldiers, so don't build it near any other set."

My father burned down Avalon.

Memos to the costume department: "I want the female underclothes historically accurate. The audience won't know, but the actresses will."

My father burned down Avalon.

"It's like I never even met Elroy Maddox," she'd later said to Amelia.

"We always think our parents are these old fuddy-duddies with no past," Amelia had responded. "Who knew yours and mine had such topsy-turvy lives?"

The next morning, Mr. Selznick had announced *Wind*'s first day of principal photography would be January twenty-sixth. Marcella, Polly, and Hazel had exchanged apprehensive looks. *Now the pressure begins in earnest.*

Selznick's Niagara Falls of paperwork were Polly's savior. As her workload increased, the intrusion of Lois's revelation diminished, each task providing a welcome distraction.

It was the lulls—folding sheets, brushing teeth—that she had come to dread. They cleaved a fissure, allowing apprehension and doubt to sneak in through the crack and menace her like buzzards.

What would all those people back home think about this?

Or worse:

Did they know Papa was the culprit? Was that why they kept me at arm's length?

Or even worse:

Did they treat him okay because his bourbon and his gambling attracted visitors and their money to the island, and then take it out on me instead?

"How close are you to finishing?" Marcella called from her desk.

Polly scanned the scrawled revisions. "Rhett has proposed. Scarlett has told him yes. He's asked her if she's said yes because of his money. So only a page or so."

"Take them straight in when you're done."

"Isn't someone with him?"

Marcella headed into the teletype room. "Just some camera department flunky."

After Polly had finished the scene, she straightened the pages into a tidy stack and headed for Mr. Selznick's office. But she stopped short of the doorway when she heard the flunky say, "Everyone calls him—let's just say they call him Dr. Jones."

"If I'm taking his shots," Selznick replied, "I should know his real name."

"Dr. Jones, Dr. Freud—what does it matter? It's a mix of vitamin B and thyroid extract. Nothing bad, nothing illegal, nothing fatal."

"Do you take it yourself?"

"When I have to pull an all-nighter, sure."

"I see. That'll be all, Mr. Marsh."

The guy exiting Selznick's office looked no older than Polly. Wasn't he a little young to be handing out medical advice? "The proposal scene." She stepped into the office and slid the stack of papers onto his desk.

He held a business card in his hands, pensively flicking it with a fingernail. "Thank you, Polly."

She lingered for a moment in case he needed anything further, but he said nothing, so she returned to her in-tray and retrieved her next task: a memo about the importance of the hair ribbons Scarlett wore in the opening scene, and how their color must match her lipstick. Polly threaded letterhead into her typewriter, but her fingers only sat on the keys.

Vitamin B and thyroid extract—whatever that was—sounded harmless enough. But if this so-called "Dr. Jones" didn't go by his real name, could Mr. Selznick trust him? So much rested on his shoulders; what would happen if he fell ill?

"Good morning!" Irene Selznick wore a festive red-and-green checked suit to match the holiday season. "Is he busy? Can I go in?"

She had every right to bypass the secretarial staff without a word. Fortunately, though, she had more style than that.

Selznick hurried out of his office and pecked her on the cheek. "What are you doing here?"

"The carful of gifts." Her explanation met with a blank face. "You agreed we'd go down to MGM and distribute them."

"You meant *today*?"

"We always make this trip on December twenty-third."

"A new version of the script—"

"Oh, David." She threw her lobster-red gloves onto Polly's desk. "I'm acutely aware there's only a month before the hurricane starts blowing, but life goes on." She caught her husband's secretary coming out of the teletype room. "Right, Marcella?"

Marcella waved the white handkerchief she kept tucked up her sleeve. "Think of me as Switzerland during the Great War: neutral."

"I'm so sorry, Pumpkin." Polly had never heard him sound so contrite. "There's no way I can take the time."

"There are far too many packages in the car for me to handle alone." Irene gathered up her gloves. "If you can't be bothered, I'm conscripting Polly."

* * *

Irene's black-and-white LaSalle smelled of Guerlain's Sous le Vent perfume.

"Oh, that is funny," Polly commented.

Irene turned on to Washington Boulevard. "What is?"

"I can smell Sous le Vent, which means 'Under the Wind,' and your husband's producing *Gone with the Wind*."

"I hadn't thought of that." Normally so forthright and direct, Irene sounded distracted. "A Guerlain girl, are you?"

The only reason Polly recognized the scent was that she and Amelia had done what Amelia called "sham-shopping" at the I. Magnin department store and had sampled a range of perfumes without buying so much as a hairpin.

"No, but my roommate is." It wasn't a complete lie. Amelia would be a Guerlain girl if she could afford it.

"Hmm." Irene tapped the edge of her wedding ring on the steering wheel.

"You weren't kidding about the Christmas gifts," Polly said, turning to look behind her. Over thirty boxes filled the back seat, each wrapped in red-and-white candy-striped paper and tied with a bright blue ribbon. "Do you have a system of how to distribute—"

"How's my husband?" Irene interjected. "I rarely see him anymore. We have almost no conversations unless it's about *Wind*, but those don't count. Please be honest. Is David all right?"

Polly only knew about Dr. so-called Jones and his thyroid extract because she had accidentally eavesdropped on an exchange she wasn't party to. "Depends on what you mean by 'all right.'"

"Does he eat lunch? Get any nourishment at all? Anything I should be aware of?"

"Mr. Selznick keeps all six of us busy."

"Good heavens!" Irene hit the brakes at a semaphore traffic signal that had changed from GO to STOP. "There are *six* of you now?" She lifted an elbow toward the glove compartment. "You'll find pen and paper in there. Please write everybody's names."

As Polly followed Irene's instruction, she crossed her mental fingers, hoping she had distracted her.

The delusion didn't last long.

"That fellow, the one skulking out of David's office like Benedict Arnold. Who's he?"

"He's from the camera department."

"And not high up, by the looks of him. Why would David waste his precious time talking to someone on the bottom rung?"

Had it been a rhetorical question? Polly spotted the huge *METRO-GOLDWYN-MAYER* sign that dominated the Culver City landscape. If she could distract Irene for a few minutes more—

Irene jerked the LaSalle to the right, cutting off an old Ford, more rust than paint, and pulled up at the curb. "I get it. You don't want to betray the man who signs your paychecks."

"It's not that I—"

"Which means you're a loyal person. I admire that. And I'm glad David has someone like you around."

"Marcella would do anything for him," Polly reminded her.

"Without a doubt."

So go ask *her*, Polly wanted to say. Don't put me in this position. She turned to Irene to say as much, but stopped when she saw tears spilling down the woman's cheeks.

"I'm beside myself with worry." Irene brushed away the tears with her fingertips. "I fear he might keel over in front of me and the boys and—and—"

"Your husband keeps us busy as little bees, occupied morning, noon, and night. So it's not like we can keep tabs on everything he does. But I can tell you he seems to exist largely on nicotine, coffee, and Benzedrine."

"I already know that!"

"I can try to ensure he doesn't skip lunch and that he takes in more nutrition than the cream he dumps into his gallons of coffee."

"Thank you. I'd appreciate it. But what about that camera minion? What did he want?"

Oh, brother. How do I answer when I'm not sure myself?

If Irene hadn't been imploring her with such weepy eyes, Polly might have declared herself Switzerland, too. But while everybody else was dissecting and analyzing, boosting or denigrating this sprawling movie, nobody was concerned with the price it was exacting on the people David O. Selznick came home to each night —if he came home at all.

"He was recommending someone who prescribes shots of vitamin B and thyroid extract."

"What's that supposed to do?"

"Give him pep."

"It's a doctor who administers these shots?"

More or less. Or at least that's how it had sounded. "Yes."

"That doesn't sound so bad." She swung the car into traffic and resumed their progress toward her father's studio. "Now tell me, any news with that embezzlement business?"

Before Polly could form a reply, Irene continued.

"I've thought a lot about Elroy since that night at King's. When I learned of his death, I couldn't have been more shocked."

Polly sank deeper into the car seat as Washington Boulevard swept past. Only after enduring the body blows of Lois's revelations had Polly become truly aware of how desperate she was to be reminded of Papa's popularity. But it wasn't easy to think of him that way all the time, not when the ugliness of Papa burning down half of Avalon during a drunken rage reared up.

"Yes," Polly said. "I've had better weeks."

* * *

Irene had only to wave a hand at the security guard, and the gate magically opened. The princess of this magnificent kingdom of make-believe parked outside the stark white Thalberg building, where her father, the monarch, reigned supreme.

As they climbed out of the LaSalle, Irene said, "I'll take the big ones up to Father's office." She walked around and opened the trunk. Inside it sat a large picnic basket, filled with smaller packages. "They're all marked with names on the cards. Ask anyone for directions."

Fortunately, most of the department heads who qualified for a Selznick gift were located close to each other, so Polly made good time handing out Irene's gaily wrapped presents.

Still, though, if only for the next hour, she thrilled at having the run of the "Tiffany of studios," which boasted "more stars than there are in heaven." A violin-and-clarinet combo floated through an open door in the music department. A young man wheeled a rack of pink-and-purple-striped Wild West dancehall outfits across Polly's path as she made her way to Costuming. As she passed a building marked *REHEARSAL HALL B*, a clear, sweet soprano voice soared through a window.

With twenty minutes to go, she had only a half-dozen gifts left, including one for MGM's ubiquitous set decorator, Edwin Willis. The script of almost every movie MGM released first crossed Willis's desk—including *The Wizard of Oz*. But would horse carriages come under his purview?

Yes, his assistant said, she had the right place. Yes, he was working on *Oz*. And yes, restoring that carriage was his responsibility. He directed her to the machine shop next to the blacksmith on Fourth Avenue.

She found Gil in an artist smock smudged with black paint, crouched at one of the carriage's rear wheels, inspecting his handiwork.

"No offense, but won't the audience only notice the Horse of a Different Color?"

"What a pleasant surprise!" He straightened up. "I'd hug you but—" He held out his smock to show how fresh the stains were.

"Yes, everyone'll be looking at the horse, which is why we're painting the carriage black. Except for this." He slapped the emerald-green leather upholstery, then flicked a finger at her wicker basket. "You brought lunch?"

"I did not." As she stepped closer to him, she was nearly bowled over by the heady stink of paint. "In fact, I didn't even come to see you." He mocked her with a *sure-you-didn't* grin. She flipped open the picnic basket. "I'm running Christmas errands for Irene Selznick."

He peeked inside. "Don't suppose there's one in there for li'l ol' me?"

He came across different from how he'd been up at the tavern. More relaxed, less eager to impress. Perhaps it was because he was in his element here, with his wagon wheels and his black lacquer. Whatever the reason, this change made him even more appealing. "Listen, I don't have a lot of time, but I was hoping that while I'm here, you might help me find someone named Sibyl."

He blinked in surprise as he put two and two together. "Sybil . . . Langley?"

Polly needed time to finesse the Sibyl-Catalina story into a bare-bones account before she was ready to share it with Gil. "I'll explain it to you when I'm not so rushed."

"I saw her this morning on the Munchkin set. Stage Twenty-Seven."

She thanked him and turned to leave, but he called after her.

"When?" he asked.

"When what?"

"When can I see you again?"

"After Christmas?"

"I'd prefer tonight."

Nobody had ever demonstrated such interest before. A frisson of excitement shuddered through her. "At the rate I'm going, I'll be lucky to get out of the office before midnight."

"After Christmas, then." He wasn't asking her. He was stating a fact.

"Promise," she said, and hurried out onto Fourth Avenue.

* * *

The Munchkin Village was a riot of vivid colors. The sky-blue lily pond near its center reminded Polly of Avalon Bay at the height of summer. Sunflowers the size of birthday balloons glowed under the lights. Around the perimeter, thatched-roof houses popped with window shutters painted vermilion and persimmon. And, most thrilling of all, the golden roadway weaved through the village, past a dilapidated house, and off the set. All of Polly's childhood memories of reading the Oz books had come to life. If only she had more time to explore this dream world.

She asked one of the bored stagehands if he had seen Sybil Langley. He indicated a fiftyish woman kneeling on the Yellow Brick Road repainting bricks. She looked up as Polly approached, offering a professional smile, but her eyes held no recognition.

"I'm the daughter of Elroy Maddox."

"Daughter, huh?" Sibyl laid her paintbrush across the top of the can and rose to her feet. Shrewd astuteness battled a seen-it-all world-weariness in her mint-green eyes. "I wasn't aware he had one."

"I came along a few years after *Pretty Pennies*."

Sibyl raised a wry eyebrow at hearing the name of her old movie, but said nothing.

"Look, I know this is coming from out of the blue, and it happened so long ago, and I probably shouldn't even bring this up—"

"How about you ask me anyway, and let me decide?"

"Could you share with me your recollections of the last night you and the crew were on Catalina, because of—when my dad—"

"Because of what he did?"

Polly nodded.

Sibyl approached the rim of an open trapdoor on the soundstage floor and tapped her heel against it. "Margaret Hamilton got burned this morning thanks to some shoddy special effects work. This area needs to be repainted by the end of the lunch break. I must keep at it, but we can sit down to lunch in the commissary later."

"I don't have much time before I have to meet up with Mrs. Selznick—"

"*Irene* Selznick?" Sibyl reappraised Polly with an arched eyebrow, then guided her to a patch of the Yellow Brick Road. "Take a seat." She settled to her knees, dipped her brush once again into the yellow barn paint, and resumed her rhythmic strokes over the blacked bricks of wood. "I've always had mixed feelings about Elroy."

Polly deposited the basket to one side and knelt beside Sibyl. "I've recently learned my father caused that horrendous fire."

"Who told you?"

"Do you remember Bernice's best friend, Lois?"

Sibyl stared off into the distance, past the Munchkin cottages. "Lois kept it to herself all these years, huh? Did she tell you that your father rescued the last two reels? If he hadn't, everything would have been for naught."

"And *Pretty Pennies* wouldn't have become a big hit."

"Followed by a slow downhill slide." Sibyl caressed her brush along the fake bricks, back and forth, dipping, back and forth, dipping. "Most people thought the flickers were merely a fad. The money men only took notice when we showed them motion pictures could turn a handsome profit. That's when they said, 'Okay, ladies, we'll take it from here.' And now I'm painting wooden roads, thankful for small crumbs."

"What have you been doing in the meanwhile?"

"I cleared out and didn't stop driving until I hit the Florida Keys. Winters working on a fishing boat and summers being a beach bum. But then I read a St. Augustine quote." Sibyl crawled to a fresh blemish. "'Resentment is like swallowing poison and waiting for the other person to die.' Moviemaking gets into your blood. This town has the memory of a tsetse fly with amnesia, so back I came."

"You must have heard about how Selznick plans to remake *Pretty Pennies*."

Sibyl looked up from her work long enough to smile. "Frankly, I get a perverse kick out of knowing MGM has the director of that movie under their noses. Mr. Mayer all but destroyed Lewis Selznick's studio, and now Lewis's son is in business with MGM over *Gone with the Wind*. When you get right down to it, everybody's a whore."

Polly didn't blame this woman for viewing Hollywood like that. And maybe it was truer than she wanted to admit, but that hadn't been her experience. Not yet, anyway.

"Mr. Selznick wants to remake his father's first hit to coincide with the twenty-fifth anniversary of Hollywood moviemaking. He also aims to restore his father's name, so if he has to jump into bed with Mayer to do it, he's prepared to do that."

"Did Irene Selznick tell you all this?"

"I work in David Selznick's office."

"Oh?" Sibyl's surprise gave way to a more neutral "Oh."

Did Sibyl consider Polly the enemy, or was she impressed that she knew what she was talking about? Either way, Polly had run out of time, and had more deliveries to make before heading back to the LaSalle.

"Do you have a print of *Pretty Pennies*?"

Sibyl leaned back onto her heels. "Is that what you came here to ask me?"

"Among other questions, yes."

"Extra points for honesty." She finished her work with a final stroke and scraped excess paint into the can. "The one copy I had got lost somewhere between here and Key Largo. But why are you asking me? Don't you have one?"

"Me? Why would I?"

Sibyl stared at Polly as though she'd realized this girl who had tracked her down was a batty simpleton. "A few years ago, I was at a big ol' fancy-schmancy party up on Mulholland Drive and got chatting to this grand dame. Oozing money from every pore. Somehow it came up that I'm the Sibyl Langley who made *Pretty Pennies* and how much I regretted losing my copy. She said that she had been gambling on the *Ning Po* and saw a bunch of film cans. They looked rather battered and rusty with the labels peeling off, she said, but she swore to me the faded labels said *Pretty Pennies*."

Polly clung to her basket. "On the *Ning Po*?"

"Or thereabouts."

"You didn't rush right over to Catalina to track them down?"

Sibyl picked up the paint can by its handle. "Water under the bridge."

Maybe for *her* it was. "I don't suppose you remember who told you this?"

"Nobody forgets a conversation with Mrs. DeMille."

Polly didn't need to check her watch to know how dreadfully late she was. Irene came across as a supremely punctual person who would think nothing of leaving Polly stranded. "Thank you," she told Sibyl, "but I have to dash."

"It's not a good idea to keep the boss's wife waiting." Sibyl waved toward the exit. "And thank *you* for an unexpected conversation."

The remaining gifts rattled around the basket as Polly tore out of Stage Twenty-Seven. After passing a long, narrow building signposted *MEN'S CHARACTER WARDROBE,* it was more or less a straight shot down Main Street to the Thalberg building.

Film cans.

Near the *Ning Po*.

Battered and rusty with the labels peeling off.

Polly came to an abrupt standstill, her feet rooted to the spot.

Had Sibyl been talking about the cans Polly and Amelia had seen in the shed at the Isthmus?

24

"Polly, dear," Marcella said as she walked out of Selznick's office and deposited a fistful of pages on Polly's desk with a devilish zest in her eye. "Get a load of this."

Final Revision of Contract between
David Selznick and Vivien Leigh

"He's made his choice?" Polly said, suddenly short of breath.

Marcella held up her stenographer's notebook. "Let's not leap to conclusions. Contracts first must be typed, then delivered, then scrutinized, then okayed, and *then* signed."

"But that'll take weeks." Could Polly hold on to this news without having a heart attack from the effort of keeping it to herself?

"DAMMIT, MARCELLA!" Selznick's voice bellowed from his office. "GET IN HERE!"

"He's been in a foul mood all morning. Stomping around,

barking orders, then taking them back." She headed into the lion's den.

"Are you talking about what I think you're talking about?" Hazel asked, looking up from her filing. Polly held up the memo for her to read. "The British dark horse?" She adjusted a mutinous wisp from her Gibson Girl hairdo. "Louella and Hedda will have a fit."

"Not to mention everybody below the Mason–Dixon line."

Hazel's eyes bulged. "The entire South will storm the studio gates with pitchforks and flaming torches!"

In the three months Polly had worked with her, this was the most animated she'd ever seen Hazel. "We'd better stock up on muskets and gunpowder. I wonder if the props department has—"

"IF IT COULD WAIT UNTIL AFTER CHRISTMAS, I WOULD HAVE DAMNED WELL SAID SO."

"Saying so is one thing," they heard Marcella retort. "Yelling is altogether different."

In Polly's eyes, Marcella's most admirable quality was her ability to remain unfazed by Selznick's ferocious outbursts. She and Hazel froze as they waited for more fireworks. When none followed, Hazel murmured, "Now that he's found his Scarlett, you'd expect he'd be less ornery."

"It's Christmas Eve, after all."

Polly returned to her desk and set about deciphering the chicken scratches Selznick had strewn across the previous draft of Miss Leigh's contract. Leigh's pay was to be $1250 a week with a guarantee of sixteen weeks. Could that be right? Scarlett O'Hara was in almost every scene. Weeks before, Polly had proofread Clark's contract. He would be paid four times that. Granted, he was a huge star and she was a relative unknown, but *Gone with the Wind* was Scarlett's story, not Rhett's.

Marcella stomped out of Selznick's office and hammered her blotter with her notebook. Her eyes darting around like an angered honey badger, she muttered an indistinct expletive as she cracked open her desk drawer.

Selznick appeared in his doorway. "And another thing—"

"Don't even *think* of asking me to work through Christmas. My husband is already upset over the hours I toil here."

"Your job is to do what I need you to do, whenever and however I need."

"He's had it up to—"

Selznick cut her off with a disdainful "Bah!" and kicked his office door shut behind him.

"I'm going for a walk to cool off." As Marcella marched into the corridor, she encountered George Cukor. Walking straight past him, she flung over her shoulder, "Proceed at your peril."

George watched her stomp away and then turned to Polly and Hazel. "Bad timing?" he said, eyeballing Selznick's closed door.

"He's been a grumpy old snapping turtle all morning," Polly replied.

"I'm here to ask a favor. Ordinarily I'd hold off until he's in a cheerier frame of mind, but it's Christmas Eve, so it can't wait." He caught sight of the contract draft, which instantly aroused his curiosity. "You heard, then?" Polly nodded. He perched on the edge of her desk. "I'm throwing a luncheon tomorrow. Vivien and Larry will be there. She and I have been working together on her screen tests and we've formed an extraordinarily close bond." He glanced at Selznick's closed door again. "I'd like to be the one to tell her, but I need to know if David is having second thoughts. I can't tell Vivien she's got Scarlett, only to have to renege later."

"That would be cruel and unusual punishment."

"However, if he's in there, spewing lava . . ."

"And I'd counter that by reminding you that you're up to the task of directing the biggest movie of the decade."

He acknowledged her point with a mute nod, then slipped off her desk and straightened the vest of his three-piece tweed suit. He walked resolutely over to Selznick's door and cracked it carefully open. "Dave, it's me, George. I'm coming in. Put away your knives."

There was no roar of protest, so George slipped in, leaving the door slightly ajar. The two men spoke so softly that Polly could only make out their tone of voice. Strident but not combative. Strained but not confrontational.

She returned to her work. She had made little progress, though, when George poked his head through the doorway. "Polly, dear, Mr. Selznick would like a word."

Inwardly, Polly grimaced. The man wasn't capable of saying "a word." Not when he could use five hundred instead. She entered his office; Selznick pointed to the vacant guest chair.

"Go on, David," George commanded. "Tell her what's upsetting you."

Polly steeled herself as Selznick chewed on his thick lips and then landed his elbows on the desk with a dull thud. "Yesterday. In the car. With my wife. You told her I exist on nicotine, coffee, and Benzedrine."

This was why he'd been prickly as a cactus all morning? "Yes, sir."

"Why?"

"Oh, David," George murmured. "Please tell me you're eating right."

He threw George a disdainful side-eye. "That's not what's been upsetting me. She then told Irene—"

"Tell *her*." George tilted his head toward to Polly.

"You tattled to Irene that I'm taking shots of vitamin B mixed with thyroid extract."

Uh-oh. Found out.

Polly stared back at her boss, unsure how to respond. She could deny everything, but that would be a lie, and she liked Irene too much to complicate things with her husband. But if she confessed, she could be out on the sidewalk by lunchtime.

"Don't let David's temper intimidate you," George said. "He's Anne of Green Gables hiding inside the Sheriff of Nottingham's tunic."

Polly doubted Anne of Green Gables lurked anywhere inside Mr. Selznick, but she trusted George.

"Your wife asked me if you were getting any nourishment, and

I can't remember the last time I saw you eat so much as a chicken salad sandwich. What would you have me do, lie to her?"

"Of course not, but dammit, the vitamin shots? How did you know about that?"

"Your office door wasn't closed when you spoke to the camera guy."

"As my employee, your loyalty is to *me*." Selznick tore off his eyeglasses and used his tie to polish them. "You had no right to blab confidential information to anyone, not even my wife. I've fired people for less."

Polly only had one more arrow left in the quiver of her defense. "Mrs. Selznick was in tears."

The polishing halted. "Irene was crying?"

"She's scared that you won't survive filming."

"Irene's hardly alone there, David," George said. "We have a marathon ahead of us, but if you assume you can get by solely on nicotine, coffee, and Benzedrine, you're in for a fall. All the way to the morgue. Human beings need *food*."

"Yeah, but I hate chicken salad sandwiches."

"If you asked nicely, they'd make you tuna instead," George replied amiably. Polly marveled at his ability to maintain an even keel in the face of such bombastic bluster. "Dave, you're lucky to have a wife whom you neglect but who still cares as deeply as Irene does."

Selznick repositioned his glasses. "She puts up with so much."

"I'd have told her the same thing. So no more talk of firing people, agreed?" He didn't wait for a conceding nod. "As for vitamin B, I hear it can give you a hearty boost. I'm not saying you shouldn't take it. That's for you to decide, but what I will say is: Be careful."

Selznick sank back in his chair. "I can't get everything done on tuna fish alone. Benzedrine usually does the job, but some days I need more. So if I get a goddamn doctor to come in here and shoot some goddamn vitamins into my goddamn ass, then that's my goddamn prerogative. And yes, I *will* fire any employee if I see fit."

Polly had hoped the spotlight of this conversation had swung away from her. Now was a good time to change the subject.

"I recently spoke with Sibyl Langley."

Selznick's brow puckered at hearing Sibyl's name. "The girl who directed *Pretty Pennies*? Where? When? How?"

"Yesterday, when I helped Mrs. Selznick distribute those gifts around MGM. She's working on *The Wizard of Oz*."

"You're kidding!" Selznick pitched forward. "My father often talked about how much he admired her."

"She thinks a copy of *Pretty Pennies* survives because Constance DeMille told her she saw film cans somewhere in my father's gambling joint."

"That's not much to go on."

"He also told Constance he had a copy of *Pretty Pennies*."

"I assume all this was news to you?"

"It was. And I thought of the time I saw film cans in the shed behind the *Ning Po's* bar."

Selznick ran his hands over his wiry hair as he fixed Polly with the same intense stare she'd seen on him the night of the Atlanta fire, when he'd first laid eyes on Vivien Leigh. "You need to go back to Catalina and find those film cans. And you have to do it tomorrow."

Polly looked at George. *Is he serious?*

"David, tomorrow is Christmas," George said. "I'm sure Polly has plans."

Amelia's parents had invited them for breakfast before they took off for Laguna Beach, where Judd's parents now lived in an old folks' home.

"I know I'm asking a lot." Selznick was on his feet now, his eyes wild with excitement. He skirted the desk with surprising agility and lodged his doughy frame on the edge of it, directly in front of Polly. He towered over her, close enough that she could smell his cigarette breath; the man was desperately in need of Clark's Sen-Sens. "If you return empty-handed, that's okay. If you find them, however, I want you to drive directly to my house."

"On Christmas Day?"

"I know, I know. Irene won't be happy. But if you do show up with the cans tomorrow, I'll be forever in your debt."

Only one steamer made a crossing on Christmas Day. It sailed from Long Beach at noon and left Avalon at six in the evening. That would give her six hours to hurry to the Isthmus, find the film cans, and get back to the pier. Was it enough time? Polly had no idea, but if she returned with the film cans, she'd have David O. Selznick in her debt, and that wouldn't be such a hardship, would it?

25

The briny sea air whipped at Polly's face as the *Avalon* glided past the Casino to starboard.

"Nervous?" Amelia whispered into her ear.

"I could've sworn the arches of the Casino were taller and wider. Everything looks so different."

"Maybe *you're* the one that's different."

Polly gripped the rail a little tighter and watched a cormorant skim the surface of the ocean, its obsidian wings shining in the anemic December sun. It soared upward, circled around, then plunged headfirst into the water.

"It sure has been a heady three months."

Polly's childhood Christmas mornings had, not so long ago, been a dependable routine. She and Papa would exchange several thoughtful gifts, followed by Papa showing off his lone cookery skill: blueberry pancakes big enough to fill a dinner plate and thick enough to last them until dinner at the Hotel Metropole.

Christmas morning at the Hartleys, however, couldn't have been more different if it had taken place in Alice's Wonderland.

Before the girls had arrived, Cookie had eaten several feet of tinsel she had ripped from the tree. As Polly and Amelia settled themselves on the sofa, Samuel and Sebastian played cowboys and

Indians with the BB guns Judd had thought made an appropriate Christmas gift for excitable boys. All the while, Faith's baby wailed until her husband, a reticent English literature professor, plugged the howler with a pacifier that he later admitted to dipping in rum. Breakfast had been a topsy-turvy circus parade of pandemonium, and Polly had loved every minute.

"I can't have changed that much," Polly said.

"Oh, no?" Amelia tapped a fingernail on Polly's new lacquered clamshell shoulder bag.

Black and shiny, it clipped shut with a "genuine sterling silver clasp." That's what Gil had claimed as she had unwrapped his surprise gift at Schwab's on Christmas Eve.

We're at the gift-giving stage? she had thought to herself. We haven't even been on a proper date yet.

Any gift would have surprised her, let alone one as expensive as this. Amelia had commented on the drive home that she couldn't decide who was happier—Polly for getting a gift she loved so much or Gil for finding one that had scored such a bull's-eye.

The *Avalon* made ready to come alongside the pier. Polly said, "Any other day of the year you'd see a pack of kids jumping into the sea to encourage passengers to throw coins to dive for."

"The aforementioned pretty pennies?"

"Gee, that's right. I guess it would have been pennies back then."

Polly and Amelia were the first of the steamship's few passengers to pass the information booth, where Eula Butts had drawn the short straw today. Although never effusive, snaggle-toothed Eula had been among the more pleasant islanders, greeting Polly with lukewarm smiles and good-mornings. But today her professional-greeter smile froze halfway to its destination, her sneering once-over undisguised.

It happened again with Mr. and Mrs. Jenson, who ran Catalina Radio and Electrical, and who took even less trouble to conceal their disdain as they passed her and Amelia, dressed in their Sunday best.

"I'm persona even more non grata now," Polly murmured to Amelia. "At least they used to pretend to be civil."

Amelia kicked an empty can of Pabst Blue Ribbon with enough force to reach Taylor's department store half a block away. "Now that they think your dad embezzled a ton of dough and got himself shot for his sins, they're showing their true colors."

"Papa stole that money, not me." Polly led her along a largely deserted Crescent Avenue to Avalon Canyon where they could saddle up Ol' Jim and Heidi. "So much for giving someone the benefit of the doubt." The heat of resentment fused with indignation swelled in the pit of Polly's stomach and surged into her chest. "When Elroy Maddox donated money to improve the town, they happily took it. But now he's buried in scandal, they run like cockroaches when the kitchen light flicks on." She boosted their pace from a stroll to a strut. "Let's find those film cans and amscray."

* * *

Amelia moseyed Heidi to a stop. "Well now, would you look at that?"

The sheriff's deputies had roped off the entire area. They had also driven a thick wooden stake into the ground and nailed to it a chunk of wood on which someone had painted:

NO ENTRY
THIS AREA IS
UNDER INVESTIGATION

Polly ducked under the rope and headed to the shed, where a bulky padlock hung from the door. In less time than it took to yell "Nuts to you!" she had catapulted a rock the size of her fist through a window facing the water. She pulled the stake out of the ground and used it to clear the space of any remaining glass shards and climbed inside.

The cans were where they'd left them. Polly pried open the top one and unspooled a length of film, holding it up to the light until she could make out the title.

"They look like opening credits. Too small to read, though."

"Try this." Amelia presented her with the magnifying glass Polly had noticed during their last visit.

"It says—" Her hand fell away of its own accord.

"What? *What*?" Amelia begged. "Don't tell me it's a stag film."

Polly returned the glass to eye level and read out loud, "Camera test. Cora Maddox on the stage of the Metropolitan Opera House. New York City, May 1912." She ran the film through her fingers. "This is my aunt at the peak of her opera career." Polly rested against the rough wooden counter. It had been a long day already, and it was only one o'clock. "Maybe Papa never gave up on reconciling with her."

Amelia opened the second can. "Empty."

"We're taking this with us," Polly said, holding up the first can of film.

They split up, hunting through the large shed, section by section, even though Polly knew the chances of uncovering *Pretty Pennies* lay somewhere between slim and none.

Aside from the usual gambling paraphernalia—poker chips, playing cards, spare roulette wheels—they found mostly items connected to Mad Ox: empty bottles, shot glasses, and ashtrays with the Mad Ox trademark, along with a faded, tattered poster. "Mad Ox bourbon," it proclaimed, "available only on sun-drenched Santa Catalina Island. You'd be mad as an ox not to try it!"

Sun-drenched Catalina—the place that had once been the entirety of her world now felt like a mere speck on its periphery. Where she had once found peace of mind in knowing what to expect from the coming day, these days she never knew what she might have to contend with. Paperwork, telephones, dictation, arguments, visitors. The nonstop bustle made her feel like she was a participant in life's hurly-burly. Once, LA's vastness had frightened her; now it filled her with excitement. What lay in wait around the next corner? A crisis over snoods? An emergency powwow with the legal department? A late-night roundtable to hash out the logistics of filming Sherman's march?

Polly stared through the broken window at the leaden December sky. *The legal department.* Papa must have left a will. He wouldn't neglect a detail like that. But he hadn't mentioned having a lawyer, and she'd never thought to ask. Goodness, what a trusting little ninny old Polly used to be. "Anything?" she called out.

"Nope." Amelia kicked a half-gallon-sized tin can.

Dented on all sides and missing its bottom, it was one of the old turpentine cans from when Papa was a bootlegger and transported his moonshine to the mainland in hefty cans labeled *WHITE ROCK TURPENTINE.* They had been such a ubiquitous sight in Polly's childhood, she hadn't taken much notice of them. It wasn't until she had reached high school and had gotten a whiff of real turpentine in the janitor's workshop that Polly had snapped the jigsaw pieces into place. These days, she rarely saw old White Rock Turpentine cans around. Seeing one now gave Polly a warm feeling of nostalgia. But for what? A life she was glad she'd left behind?

"What about you?" Amelia asked.

"Goose egg."

They climbed back through the window, Polly clutching the film can, and headed to Ol' Jim and Heidi.

"What now?"

"I want to go to the house and pick up a few things I missed in my mad scramble."

"What if it's roped off too?"

If this trip had demonstrated anything, it was that Polly was no longer the girl who had left Catalina three months before. *That* Polly wouldn't have hurled rocks. "All I need is a couple of favorite sweaters, some winter boots, a photo album or two."

"And then?"

"I used to type up manuscripts for Zane Grey—"

"No fooling? That guy who writes westerns?"

Polly untethered Ol' Jim and swung onto the saddle. "Yep. I'd like to say hi while we're here."

"Nothing else?"

Polly shook her head. She wasn't about to rush back to this place any time soon.

* * *

Sergeant Blackburn was the first to reach the top step of the Maddoxes' porch. "Now, remember," he said, stern as Wallace Beery, "fifteen minutes."

"Yes, sir." Polly smiled mildly. *Just play along.*

"Embezzlement is a felony. I'm answerable to the mainland. I'm only doing this because Mr. Grey has vouched for you."

"I'm terribly grateful to you for going out of your way like this." Anything to get him to stop treating her like an elementary school truant. "And to Mr. Grey, of course."

Grey snuck her a clandestine wink.

Polly shouldn't have been surprised to find the authorities had barricaded her house. Unsure what to do, Polly and Amelia had sought refuge at Mr. Grey's. After hearing her out, he proposed a visit to the police station, promising, "I'll have a quiet word with Sergeant Blackburn; you'll keep your yap shut."

"Just one question, if I may?" Polly asked Blackburn. "Do you know what became of Ben Worthington? He's run Mad Ox for my dad for years."

"Ben was boiling mad the day we showed up to shut down operations. If you ask me, he took as much Mad Ox as he could fit into his travel trunk and disappeared for good."

Polly had always found Ben to be efficient and matter-of-fact, but fair and professional. Papa would be so disappointed in him right now.

"Give me no reason to regret this," Blackburn said.

"If my friend can come in too, we might not even need fifteen minutes."

"Fine." He loosened the ropes crisscrossing the door.

Polly and Amelia ran inside as Mr. Grey engaged Blackburn in an animated conversation about a record-breaking marlin one of Reginald Hawthorne's customers had recently caught.

The scent of Papa's tobacco still lingered in the living room along with the citrusy notes of his aftershave lotion.

I haven't smelled it since—Polly mentally slapped herself across the face. No time for self-indulgence. Blackburn's stopwatch was ticking. "I'm guessing *Pretty Pennies* is anywhere between five and eight reels."

"But what if we find them? How can we hide so many film cans from Blackbeard out there?"

"There's an overnight bag under my bed. I'll shove some clothes and whatnot on top. Meanwhile, look in every cupboard, drawer, and wardrobe, under every bed, behind every chair."

She hurried into her bedroom. The sight of the olive-green chenille bedspread stopped her cold. She never did like that thing. The color was drab, and it smelled of the Cashmere Bouquet talcum powder her father always gave her for Christmas. She didn't much care for it either, but wore it to please him.

Focus, Doodlebug! Focus!

She ran to her bureau. Sweater. Sweater. Blouse. Cardigan. Underwear? No. Socks? No. Next stop, wardrobe. Sundress. Checked skirt. Plaid skirt? No, it's ugly. But yes to the gray wool suit. Yes to the lavender blouse and the white one, too. Matching shoes. She pulled three photo albums from her bookcase. Did she want all three? Yes. Absolutely.

The carryall under the bed was smaller than she remembered, but it fit all the clothes and one album.

Where to next?

Bag in one hand, albums in the other, she flew to Papa's study.

How stark it looked without his stacks of ledgers, bookkeeping folders, and all the other tools of his trade he needed to do his job. *And steal thirty-five grand.*

She rummaged through his drawers and peeked behind the damask drapes. What about his prized lithograph of a 1901 map of Catalina?

Her eyes fell on the pair of Mad Ox bottles Papa kept on a mahogany side table below the map.

That canard about Papa not touching a drop after the fire—Polly was willing to bet a week's pay it was only his mea culpa to Lois.

You'd be mad as an ox not to try it.

She inspected the two bottles more closely. One of them bore a tiny X in the bottom left corner of the back label. Its twin did not. She popped the cork on the unmarked bottle and took a swig. Yep. Mad Ox bourbon, all right. But the one marked X? "Son of a gun!" Iced tea.

"Miss Maddox!" Blackburn's voice rolled through the house. "Sixty seconds remaining."

The map would have been a welcome addition to the apartment, but it looked heavy.

Amelia was already on the patio, a cast-iron saucepan dangling from her fingertips. Her eyebrows twisted upwards into her crinkled brow as she met Polly's eyes. *I had to show up with something.*

With everything Polly had taken, plus the damned saucepan, as well as Cora's film, she needed a proper suitcase.

"I didn't count on taking so much back with me," she told Blackburn in her best Meek Mary voice. "There are some suitcases in the garden shed out back. I won't be two shakes." She dumped her loot in a pile at his feet and took off before he could protest.

The door hinges squawked as she stepped inside. Three suitcases stood in the corner, thick with spiderwebs and dust. The first one was too small; she pushed it to one side. Its neighbor would have done nicely, but was heavier than a pallet of bricks. She lifted the last case from its filthy tomb and stepped back into the shaft of sunlight etched into the concrete floor. It was one of the pieces of luggage that had accompanied Polly and Papa on their initial sailing on the SS *Cabrillo* and was now so decrepit that it would be lucky to remain intact for the trip home. But time was short and options were few.

She was only a few quick steps from the shed when that heavy suitcase tickled her curiosity. What in tarnation was Papa storing in there? Chunks of marble?

She stepped back inside and flicked open the flimsy locks. The suitcase split into two, each side falling onto the concrete with a hefty clunk. A stack of cans rattled against each other. Polly tilted the nearest one to the light.

PRETTY PENNIES (1914) – REEL 3 OF 5

Holy hounds of hell in a handbasket from Hades!

The *Avalon* was scheduled to set sail in fifteen minutes.

She poked her head around the corner of the shed. "Am-eee-liaaa!" she sing-songed. "Some help?"

Amelia slapped her hands together when she spotted the pile of film cans. "How heavy are they?"

"Too heavy to carry in a suitcase that might not hold together long enough to reach the pier."

Amelia kicked the smallest bag. "Put three into that one, and the other two into the carryall, and pretend they're filled with dandelions."

They'd nearly finished redistributing their cargo when Mr. Grey appeared in the doorway. "You two need to get a move on if —what's going on?"

"Is Blackburn still there?" Polly asked.

"He'd planned to accompany you off the island, but I assured him that you two flibbertigibbets weren't worth his time. Speaking of which, you've got four minutes."

Four minutes to get to a pier that was a seven-minute walk away.

Polly dashed up to the patio and grabbed her items from the

house, then ran back to where Amelia and Grey were waiting. They set off down toward Crescent.

"Would you happen to know the name of my father's lawyer?" Polly asked as they hurried along.

Grey shook his head. "Given everything that's come to light, I doubt he would have used the island's one attorney, seeing as how that guy is also Mr. Wrigley's." The ship sounded its horn. "I don't suppose you saw his address book?"

The film cans clunked around in the suitcase as Polly accelerated their pace. She could feel the handle loosening its screws. "The police didn't leave much behind."

"I guess they would've taken it."

The winter sea breezes cooled the sweat breaking across her hairline. "And put it where?"

"Wherever evidence is stored, I suppose."

They arrived at the steamer terminal as a single, final blast skewered the air. The gangway was still fifty feet away. This handle wasn't likely to make it. Polly yelled at a crewmember on the dock. "WE'RE COMING!"

They reached the gangway. Polly let Amelia head up first. "Who would I ask?"

"Sheriff's department. You shouldn't have too much trouble tracking down the deputy in charge." He eyed Polly's suitcase. "Whatever you're hiding in there, I hope it was worth it."

"Thanks for everything."

She dashed up the gangway and stepped onto the deck as the handle broke away from the suitcase with a sickening crack.

26

Polly set down the suitcase on Mr. Selznick's brick porch. It was now wrapped with a six-foot scrap of twine someone at the Long Beach pier had discarded; what a relief it was that she no longer had to lug it across town.

She rang the doorbell and peeled off her gloves. Would it be presumptuous to ask for a ham-and-cheese sandwich at eight-thirty Christmas night?

Polly had expected a maid or a butler, but it was Irene herself who opened the door. "What a delightful surprise—" She caught sight of the tattered suitcase. "Have you run away from home?"

"You won't believe it!"

Irene's welcoming smile dimmed. "God forbid you should have Christmas Day off."

"But I've found *Pretty Pennies*!"

"You'd better come in, then."

She ushered Polly into the living room where David and their sons, Jeffrey and Daniel, were gathered around a ten-foot tree draped with cranberry-red tinsel and matching tartan ribbons tied into bows. Mr. Selznick launched out of his easy chair as soon as he saw Polly's case and announced they must adjourn to the screening room.

"Absolutely not!" Irene jabbed a finger in his face. "YOU! PROMISED! ME!"

Unlike the near-tyrant Mr. Selznick could be at work, he quietly moved the case to the nearest wall.

"Having settled that non-debate," Irene turned to Polly, "we have four tons of leftovers, so sit yourself down and I'll bring you a plate. Come on, boys," she commanded her sons, "help Mommy decide what to serve our guest."

Mr. Selznick waited until his family had disappeared behind the swing door. "You've gone above and beyond, Polly. I'm profoundly grateful and deeply impressed. Tell me, were the film cans where Constance said they were?"

Polly explained that those cans had actually contained footage of her Aunt Cora. *Pretty Pennies* had been hiding away much closer to home. "However, this whole adventure brought up the issue of my father's estate."

"How so?"

"I don't know who Papa's lawyer was, but Zane Grey said—"

"*The* Zane Grey?"

Polly had impressed her boss twice in one day. It was hard not to smile. "I used to type his manuscripts."

"What did he suggest?"

"That I ask the officer in charge of the embezzlement case if I can go through Elroy's effects for a name."

"All his belongings are police evidence. No one can access them except officers working the case."

Irene poked her head through the kitchen doorway. "You have connections. Make a phone call. Explain the situation. Vouch for Polly, who, need I remind you, has achieved the impossible." She snuck Polly an artful wink. "Milk, ginger ale, or champagne?"

* * *

The Sheriff's office clerk glowered with disapproval as he led Polly and Gil into a basement storage area of the Hall of Justice, where he unlocked a steel-plated door. The square box of concrete on the other side reeked of the musty smell of rooms without windows. In the middle stood a table where five cardboard boxes sat in a row.

"Is there a time limit?"

The DA had authorized a maximum of thirty minutes, but Polly was counting on governmental bureaucracy muddying the channels of communication.

The clerk ignored her and looked at Gil. "You must know somebody to get special treatment."

"What makes you think *he's* the one with the connections?" she demanded.

Gil tapped the edge of his shoe against hers. "It's better you don't ask," he told the clerk, and threw in a man-to-man grin. *Women—whatcha gonna do?*

Polly swallowed her indignation like a lump of tripe. She didn't know what strings Mr. Selznick had pulled, but she guessed they were high up in the DA's office. Because of her workload, he had even managed to secure after-hours access.

"Thirty minutes." The clerk jacked a thumb toward the shadowy vestibule. "I'll be out here."

Polly lifted the lid off the nearest box and withdrew an inch-thick pile of papers. "Thanks for coming with me at such short notice," she told Gil.

When Mr. Selznick had given her the details of where she needed to go, at what time, and how long she'd have to sort through Papa's papers, she hadn't relished the idea of being in a deserted downtown office building, alone, nine o'clock at night. Amelia had an evening shift at Schwab's, and Ludlow was taking Margaret Mayer to Earl Carroll's newly opened nightclub on Sunset Boulevard.

"Gil's not likely to turn you down," Amelia had suggested.

Polly hadn't wanted to presume anything, but had called him anyway. He had finished refurbishing Lincoln's *Wizard of Oz* carriage on Christmas Eve and was free to join her.

He'd told her, "I would've been pacing my living room, knowing you were here by yourself."

Polly doubted that was true, but gosh, it was awful nice to hear. "Papa's address book has a brown leather cover with his initials embossed in gold in the top right corner. I couldn't see it anywhere at the house, so I assume it's here."

Gil lifted the lid off the second box and took out a pile of papers. "Their suspect's known associates are the first thing they look at."

Polly flipped through the contents. Contracts. Proposals. Every single sheet was the typical businessman humdrummery she expected. More and more papers. Agendas for the town council. Letters to street-lighting contractors. Other than correspondence to and from the law firm Mr. Wrigley and the Island Company used, they found nothing to or from anyone that sounded like an attorney.

Polly fished out another folder thick with notes for meetings and addenda on agreements. "Imagine filling your days with this party-of-the-first-part tedium. At least what you do is interesting."

"I'm glad you think so," he said.

"Doesn't everybody?"

"Nobody says it out loud, but their eyes say, 'Horse carriages belong in the nineteenth century. Why don't you find work that's more up to date?'"

"But they're for the movies."

"Most people think, 'Whoop-de-doo. Everybody here works in films. That doesn't make you special.'" He prodded her shoulder with his. "But you were different."

That nudge, playful and friendly, sent a jolt through Polly. This was the first time she'd been alone with a boy whom she found appealing and attractive. And who, unless she was misreading the signs, returned the sentiment.

She ran a finger along a narrow stack of paper-clipped proposals to resurface the airstrip at Hamilton Cove. "Different, how?"

"Your face didn't glaze over." He paused for a moment, squinting at her as though he were trying to gauge the height of a cliff he was about to leap from. "In my book, that counts for a lot."

Their eyes locked, earnest and unblinking.

Anticipation twitched inside Polly's chest like a trapped sparrow. She licked her lips to prepare for the coming moment.

He broke away and tapped his watch. "Eighteen minutes and counting."

Polly's little sparrow flew the coop.

Digging through the rest of the box took only a minute or two. More mundane documents: repainting the fire station, leveling the bridle path, plans for the Wrigley Memorial.

The next box, however, revealed exactly what Polly had been hoping for. She flipped to the A tab. "A for attorney, right?"

"In case there's nothing—" Gil dragged the third box toward him "—I'll keep looking."

Polly encountered no attorneys listed under A, so she thumbed through the alphabet.

C for Catalina High School.

P for Pacific Wireless.

R for Reginald Hawthorne.

By the time she got to Z for Zippy's Bicycle Sales, she felt heavier than an anchor. "It's all been a wild goose—"

"Not so fast!" Gil lifted a second address book from the box and passed it over to her.

About the size of Polly's dictation notepad at work, it had a plain navy-blue cover with no embossing or embellishments. The edges of the pages were frayed; the ink on the entries had faded over the years. Out of curiosity, she turned to H.

Hartley, Judd & Lois. 5115 Maplewood Ave., Los Angeles.

Polly found no attorneys listed under A or counsels under C, or lawyers under L. "How much time have we got left?"

"Seven minutes."

Letter by letter, she methodically ran through the book, her heart sinking deeper as she approached Z. "These pages are so old, so well-thumbed and raggedy. Half these people are probably dead by now." She reached the final tab, XYZ. "Unless Papa's lawyer was named Zachary Zane Zimmerman, I'm out of luck."

She ran her finger down the page and stopped at the bottom, where she found a name written in fresher ink.

Roscoe Brodsky, attorney-at-law

"That's weird."

"Don't tell me your father's lawyer was Zack Zimmerman."

"There's a newer entry here, and it doesn't belong in XYZ."

Gil started placing the papers back in their boxes. "What's the name?"

"Roscoe Brodsky."

Gil's hands froze in midair. Polly wasn't sure, but she thought she detected a sharp intake of air. "Ever heard of him?"

"Nope."

The clerk rapped on the door frame. "Time to wrap it up, folks."

Polly jotted down Brodsky's telephone number and dropped her father's old address book into its box.

Wintry breezes gusted along a deserted Temple Street. "It's so much cooler now that the sun's gone down." Talking about the weather felt so trite, but Gil had been uncomfortably silent since the moment after she had said the name of Papa's lawyer. She breathed a little easier when he said he'd walk her to the streetcar stop.

She waited until they'd walked half a block. "When I said that name out loud—"

"What name?"

"The guy who might have been my father's lawyer."

"What about him?"

"You said you didn't know who Brodsky is—"

"Never heard that name before." The words sling-shotted out of him.

"I got the impression you do."

They came to a pawn shop, the lights in the window display blazing bright as day. He came to an abrupt standstill, reached into the pocket of his woolen overcoat, and pulled out a flat parcel wrapped in holly-green paper dotted with Christmas trees. "I was waiting for the right moment to give you—"

"But you already gave me that beautiful clamshell purse."

"And now this."

She peeled off the paper. He had given her a copy of *Lost Horizon* by James Hilton.

He opened the front cover and tapped at the signature on the title page. "Signed by the author and everything. Have you read it?"

"No," she said. "I've been wanting to since I saw the Ronald Colman movie."

He was beaming now that he knew his second gift had also scored a hit. "I figured you for a bookworm—" He jutted out his hands in self-defense. "In a good way! I like a girl who's smart."

"Do you also like to kiss smart girls?"

He gave her a long look, and then steered them into the pawn shop's alcove and brushed his lips across hers; they were soft as cashmere. When he came in for a second pass, he pressed them more urgently. He drew her gently into a clinch, every part of his body from shoulders to knees grinding against her in slow motion . His tongue forced itself against her teeth, tenderly prying them open. She hadn't been prepared for it and tensed. But not for long. Movie kisses were nothing like this. How could they be? The real McCoy was so sensual, so lush. No wonder every movie featured them.

He loosened the belt of her overcoat and wormed one hand inside. Hovering at her waist for a moment, he worked his way up to her chest.

We're already at that stage?

He cupped her breast slowly—lovingly, even—and thrust his groin against hers. She sensed a firmness *down there*. When she mirrored his motion, he responded with a low, almost guttural moan, then retreated.

"What did I do wrong?" she asked, confused.

He slung an arm around her shoulder and guided her back into the deserted street. "I need to see you onto a streetcar before I insist we get a hotel room."

It was the most romantic sweet-nothing she could ever have imagined.

27

Polly was already seated at the desk against the back wall of the screening room when Mr. Selznick and his brother walked in, accompanied by a slim, dark-haired woman who carried herself with Irene's self-assured confidence. Mr. Selznick led them to the middle row. "This is Polly," he said, waving a hand over his right shoulder, "who'll be taking notes."

The woman turned around. "The intrepid adventuress who unearthed *Pretty Pennies*? Pleased to meet you. I'm Virginia Van Upp." The woman had the vigorous handshake of someone who was nobody's fool. "Bravo for pulling off the impossible. *Très impressionnant*."

"Virginia is an ace screenwriter," Mr. Selznick told Polly. "However, she's under contract with Paramount, so she's most definitely not here."

"What about Sibyl Langley?" Myron asked.

"I invited her." Mr. Selznick sat down. "She declined."

"Did she say why?"

"Nope."

"That's a shame. By the way, did you give any thought to my idea of Dorothy Arzner directing?"

"I wanted to see her most recent picture first."

Van Upp settled into her seat. "*The Bride Wore Red* doesn't show Joan Crawford at her best, but that's not Dorothy's fault."

A female director *and* a female screenwriter? Was Mr. Selznick thinking of going for another all-women production team like the original?

"And what about this Swedish remake of yours?" Virginia asked. "Still on the books?"

"It is."

"Assigned a screenwriter yet?"

"Throwing your hat into the ring?"

"Simply reminding you I have a hat worth throwing."

"Trust me, Ginny, I'm acutely aware of your millinery—as is Paramount, whom we can fool once, but twice might be pushing our luck. And besides, I've been wondering. Is *Intermezzo* or *Pretty Pennies* one remake too many?"

"I don't think so," Myron commented.

Of course you don't. Polly threaded her sharpened pencil between her fingers. You've now signed Vivien Leigh and Ingrid Bergman as clients. The more pictures your brother makes, the more opportunity you have to slot your clients into lead roles. What was it Sybil had said? *When you get right down to it, everybody's a whore.*

Polly could still feel the heat of Gil's hand cupping her breast from the previous night. She hadn't resisted like nice girls did in the movies. Would he soon make his move? And if he did, might she follow him into the bedroom? It would depend on the when, where, and how of it all. But if she agreed, Gil wouldn't consider her a whore, would he?

"I want to make *Pretty Pennies* as much as you do," Selznick told his brother, "but Irene'll murder me in my sleep if I take on a fourth project."

"In the interests of avoiding husbandicide," Virginia said, "let's first see the movie Polly here went to so much trouble to locate."

Selznick inhaled from his Don Francisco cigar and hit a button. The projection room descended into darkness, save for the dim light over Polly's desk. The screen glowed to life.

. . .

Lewis Selznick's
Equitable Pictures
Presents
PRETTY PENNIES
Directed by Sibyl Langley

Polly poised her pencil over the dictation pad. She hadn't been prepared for the torrent of notes she'd needed to make when they watched *A Yank at Oxford*, and had vowed to never make the same mistake again.

The credits gave way to a vista of the Pacific that Polly knew only too well: the view from Three Palms. The camera panned around to reveal a close-up of Lois's friend, Bernice. Despite having too much white makeup caked onto her skin, Bernice exuded an ethereal beauty; longing and hunger reflected from her limpid eyes. Put Amelia in a Mary Pickford sausage-curl wig and rim her peepers with kohl, and she could play that role.

According to Lois, she and Polly's mother resembled each other. So Flora and Bernice must have, too. Watching Bernice on the screen hinted at what Mama was like in real life.

The girl scampered into town down the path that Polly had taken more times than she'd licked Carver's double fudge ice cream cones. The action cut to a small cottage where the girl's grandmother lay bedridden with an unspecified disease. The title cards talked only of an unnamed treatment that would save her life.

Four minutes had passed and Mr. Selznick had remained silent. By this point in *A Yank at Oxford*, she had filled two pages with notes. Polly kept her pencil in position.

The girl, Juniper, is an orphan brought up by her loving grandma. But now Granny is old and infirm, and her only hope lies in an expensive treatment that can only be carried out on the mainland. So Juniper learns to dive for pennies thrown by tourists arriving into Avalon Harbor.

A handsome man spots her and throws not pennies but quarters. His actions incur the jealousy of an older boy considered Catalina's best diver. He can see the handsome tourist is favoring Juniper, so he and his gang take out his resentment by robbing her afterwards. The handsome tourist later seeks her out, and she's forced to explain how she lost the money. He offers to replace it, but she declines because the others will guess what happened, and she must face them after the end of his vacation. In the climax, Juniper's diving skills save the life of the mayor's daughter, and the handsome tourist reveals himself to be the new island's new doctor who can save Granny's life.

The film finished, leaving the screen stark white before the lights came up.

Myron stubbed out his Pall Mall. "Better than I remember."

"Such an emotional story," Virginia commented. "I wasn't prepared for that."

"What my contemporaries often fail to grasp," Mr. Selznick said, "is how a character's emotional trajectory hooks an audience. It's what I'm trying to do with Scarlett."

Virginia faced him more squarely. "So you're still keen to remake this one?"

"Now more than ever."

"I'm glad to hear it. So many possibilities."

Mr. Selznick surprised Polly by turning all the way around to face her. "As a real-life girl from Catalina, what did *you* think?"

"Well, you know . . ." She bought herself some time by closing the cover of the dictation notepad. *Don't act so coy. He's asked for your opinion.* "I do have a suggestion."

"We're listening," Virginia said.

"Instead of saving the mayor's daughter, why doesn't Juniper save the bully who's been taunting her? The bully's father turns out to be somebody important, like Mr. Emerson."

"And who's that?" Mr. Selznick asked.

"He runs the Catalina Country Club."

"Socially prominent and loaded with dough?" Myron mused out loud.

"What if he's so grateful that he thanks Juniper by paying for Granny's operation? And the handsome tourist turning out to be a doctor is too convenient. Wouldn't it be better if he was a pilot looking to set up a regular seaplane service to the mainland?"

Virginia snapped her fingers. "Grandma can be his first passenger!"

"We're off to a great start." Mr. Selznick rocked to his feet and led Virginia out of the room, leaving Myron and Polly to follow.

"Tell me," Polly said, taking Myron aside, "is Rita Hayworth still in the running for Juniper?"

Myron squinted at her. "What gives you that impression?"

"Mrs. Harry Cohn told me her husband wants the role to go to Rita."

"Is that a fact?" The tip of his right shoe tapped against the polished wooden floorboards. "Now that I've seen the movie, your friend Amelia could be right for the role—although she didn't seem too enthusiastic. On the plus side, she would be much cheaper than having to borrow Rita Hayworth from crusty ol' Cohn."

"I expect you've had your fair share of powwows with him?"

"Of all the merciless cretins I have to deal with in my line of work, Harry Cohn is, without a doubt, *the* most merciless of the whole damn bunch. I'd cross Sunset in peak hour, blindfolded, wearing nothing but my BVDs, rather than have to talk to him. Why do you ask?"

Because I suspect he's the reason my father is dead. "Just wondering."

* * *

Mr. Selznick called Polly into his office later that day and pushed eight pages of scribble toward her.

"You have some thoughts about *Pretty Pennies,* after all?"

"Come now, Miss Maddox, you knew I would." A schoolboy giggle rippled through his voice.

"By the bye, I haven't yet thanked you for pulling the necessary strings to gain access to my father's belongings."

"What good are favors if you can't call them in? Did you find what you were looking for?"

"I did, yes."

"Remind me what that was."

"My father's lawyer. Roscoe Brodsky." Mr. Selznick's double-take resembled Gil's reaction. "Heard of him?"

"He's got several high-profile Hollywood clients. If you're in trouble, Roscoe Brodsky is a powerful guy to have on your side."

"The way I figure it, if a suspect is accused of a crime, but then subsequently dies, wouldn't the authorities drop all charges?"

"One would think so."

"I want to ask him why the DA is still keeping the case against my father."

"A sharp operator like Brodsky is likely to know."

It wasn't until Polly had returned to her desk that the words "sharp operator" began ricocheting around her skull like a pinball. Had Mr. Selznick meant that as a compliment or as a warning?

* * *

Brodsky's offices were on Wilshire Boulevard at Gale Drive, which provided him with a Beverly Hills address, but only just. While the nondescript building lacked the charming Art Deco sunbursts, medallions, and colorful mosaics of its neighbors, it was at least freshly painted.

Inside the foyer, a list of the building's tenants directed her to a frosted-glass window announcing *BRODSKY & ASSOCIATES*. The unremarkable reception eschewed aesthetics for functionality: chairs to wait on, low-slung tables stacked with magazines, drab ferns in corner planters, and a couple of generic paintings on the wall; a beach, a mountain, a park.

A matching pair of secretarial desks, both empty, sat on each side of a middle door. Polly walked to the open doorway. The fiftyish gent behind a broad desk was balding on top, gray around the sides, and sporting the pallor of someone who spent precious little time outdoors on the tennis court.

"Mr. Brodsky?"

He looked up from his correspondence. "I didn't hear you come in. Miss Maddox, I presume." He gestured toward the chairs on the other side of his desk. He waited until she had taken a seat and shed her gloves. "I've been trying to track you down since your father's death."

She wanted to suggest he hadn't tried too hard, seeing as how she worked for Hollywood's most talked-about producer. But to point that out might undermine what she'd come here to learn.

"I don't wish to take up too much of your time," she said.

"Was there anything specific you want—"

"Just before the cops shot my father to death, he told me that he was guilty of this embezzlement charge. It came as quite a shock because my father was hardly the embezzling type."

"There's a type?"

Polly hadn't stopped to consider what an embezzler looked like or how he acted. She had, instead, fixated on the idea that Papa didn't fit her arbitrary notion. "My father was at his wits' end that day, so I'm not convinced he was telling me the truth before everything went haywire."

Brodsky reached for a dark brown cigarillo and a plain gold lighter. "He was."

Polly had laid her hands in her lap, out of sight of this lawyer with his interchangeable art and his barely-Beverly-Hills address. She interlaced her fingers and tightened them until her knuckles ached. "He was what?"

"In his right mind, and guilty of embezzlement. All thirty-five grand."

She hoped he hadn't noticed the way her shoulders slumped. How deeply she'd been hoping Brodsky would wave away her worst fears. Or that he had a rational explanation for this whole mess.

But no. Papa really had taken all that money from Mr. Wrigley.

"I don't understand any of this! Were you aware of what he was doing?"

"I had inklings."

"Did they include what the money was for?"

He flicked tobacco ash into a coffee cup with the indifference of a hanging judge. "I'm sorry, Miss Maddox, but I can't break client–attorney confidentiality."

"Your client is dead. Surely that rule doesn't apply anymore."

"Your father isn't the client I'm talking about."

"Who *are* you talking about?"

"I'm not at liberty to say."

Oh, so it's like that, is it?

They played a staring game, each daring the other to blink first.

Confidentiality be damned. He was using it as an excuse. To protect whom, she didn't know, but to jerks like this, a dead client was a useless client. "What *are* you at liberty to say?"

Brodsky softened his stoic face and tempered his stern lawyer-in-the-courtroom voice. "It's best if you drop the whole thing. Your father got involved with some nasty people. It wasn't his fault. He got dragged in."

"So you're saying ne'er-do-wells forced him?"

"Ne'er-do-wells is a genteel term, but yes. Again, I suggest you walk away."

Oh sure. I'll walk away from this horrible black mark against my father's name, and therefore mine, too.

This line of questioning wasn't getting her anywhere. It was time to change tack. "When will the DA drop the charges?"

"Mr. Wrigley has insisted they remain open. As head of the Santa Catalina Island Company, he's the injured party, and has therefore put a lien against your father's estate. In due course, the authorities will dispose of the material goods—"

"You mean our house."

"—and its contents to recoup as much of the debt as possible. As sole beneficiary in your father's will, you're entitled to anything left over."

Polly needed a moment to take in this news.

Papa had a will? Not that it mattered that he'd named her as his beneficiary. Even with the house thrown in, everything Elroy had left behind wouldn't add up to anywhere close to thirty-five grand. Except for maybe one thing.

"Does that include the distillery?"

Brodsky took an unhurried pull of his cigarillo. "Did you help your father run Mad Ox?"

"No."

"Miss Maddox." Brodsky sucked a morsel of food from between his teeth. "Manufacturing bourbon isn't like taking up knitting or learning how to raise orchids."

Polly thought of Judd Hartley, Amelia's father. He must know someone who could step in. And if this swellhead wanted to play the Lean Forward and Talk Down to People game, she'd give him a run for his money. "Mr. Brodsky," she said, adopting the same patronizing tone, "all that equipment could be enlisted to repay my father's debt. So if I'm able to restart it—"

"A mighty big if, Miss Maddox."

"You can see value in the idea, right?"

"I'm not the person you need to convince."

"Who is, then?"

"The DA officer in charge."

"May I have his name?"

He picked a strand of loose tobacco from the tip of his tongue. Polly wondered if the man smoked those pungent stink-bombs solely for delay tactics. "Gerard Donovan."

"Thank you," she said, getting to her feet. "I'll see myself out."

She collected her bag and gloves, strode past the empty secretaries' desks, and stepped out into the corridor. God, how she hated the idea of everybody in Hollywood remembering Papa as a dishonest embezzler.

Even if she got to plead her case to this Donovan guy, would he be open to releasing the equipment? Polly didn't relish the prospect of facing the DA, but she'd do it for Papa.

Wait a minute.

She turned around.

Wait a goddamn minute.

Polly marched back into Brodsky's office.

His hand rested on his telephone receiver. "Yes?"

"I'd like a copy of my father's will."

Brodsky retracted his hand. "It was written up quite a long time ago—"

"I assume you have duplicates."

"Of course."

"I work at Selznick International Pictures. For Mr. Selznick himself. You can send it there. Shall I write down the address?"

Brodsky's jawline hardened. "That won't be necessary."

"One more thing: When my father set up Mad Ox, he had a partner. Harry Cohn, if I'm not mistaken?"

Polly might have missed the astonishment that flitted across Brodsky's face had she not been looking for it. "It was a confidential agreement," he replied, emotionless as an undertaker.

"Rose Cohn didn't seem to think so. Perhaps you can tell me this: When Prohibition was lifted, did my father and Mr. Cohn formalize their partnership with a written contract?"

"As I mentioned before, confidentiality prevents me—"

"As my father's beneficiary, am I or am I not entitled to a copy?"

Polly hadn't the slightest idea what she was entitled to, but Brodsky's slow-burn, steely-eyed stare told her that she had won.

"I'll take care of it. Anything else?"

"No. That'll do it," Polly replied with all the annoying cheerfulness that she could summon.

She left the office a second time and made her way down the corridor feeling as though she had, at the bare minimum, established that Mr. Roscoe Brodsky knew that Elroy's daughter wasn't the most gullible sap to walk into his office. Not this week, anyway.

She stepped outside into tepid sunshine. The more she thought about Mr. Hartley running Mad Ox for her, the more she liked the idea. Mixing friendship with business wasn't the smartest move, but a concise and fair agreement outlining who would do what and when and how would overcome that.

Brodsky was the only lawyer she knew. Polly halted. Could she trust him, though? Probably not, but if she asked Mr. Selznick to recommend one, she'd have to spend the next five years paying him off. And Brodsky already knew how Mad Ox worked, so if she could find a way—

The sound of running footsteps derailed her thoughts. She looked behind her in time to see Gil dash around the corner and into Brodsky's building.

What the—?

She tiptoed to the front doors and cupped her hands against the glass to watch him bolt through Brodsky's office door.

Where had he come from?

Why had he been running?

She walked to the corner. Only two vehicles were parked along the street: a white van with a large, dark blue logotype painted on the side and a bone-shaking Ford old enough to qualify as a jalopy. She touched the van's hood, then jerked her hand away. It was hot: the engine had recently been shut off. She stepped back to take in the artwork on its side panel. Her stomach leapt up into her throat when she saw a woman holding a torch with two words below it: *Columbia Studios.*

28

Cora abruptly parked her Packard a block from the Selznick studio. "I don't know that I can do it!"

Gil groaned in a low voice, "But we're nearly there." Poor Luddie, Gil, and Benji had wedged themselves into Cora's back seat like jigsaw puzzle pieces, all interlocking elbows and knees.

It was now two days since Polly had seen him running into Brodsky's office. She should have marched back inside and demanded to know what was going on, and why he'd been driving a Columbia vehicle.

No need for amateur dramatics, she had told herself sternly. There's bound to be a reasonable explanation. All you need to do is ask him like you're a calm, rational, mature woman of the world.

However, Polly Maddox wasn't a calm, rational, mature woman of the world. At least, not when it came to members of the opposite sex.

It was different at work, though. Selznick's office was no place for shrinking violets. She had soon mastered the art of typing while answering the phone, as well as playing traffic cop to the cavalcade of people who "just want five minutes with the boss." It had been a while since she had given anyone at Selznick International a reason to assume they could walk over her.

Why, then, couldn't she muster that same spunk with men? Especially one who had shown romantic interest?

And so, like a lily-livered coward, she had said nothing, done nothing, challenged nothing. But if she had to bring it up—and she did—what better time than a lavish party when a glass of bubbly might lend her a measure of Dutch courage?

"You don't know that you can do what?" Polly asked.

It took Cora a conspicuously long time to reply. "This will sound revoltingly egotistical—"

"Egotistical for regular folk?" Amelia butted in. "Or by Hollywood's standards?"

"I was only twenty-five when I stood in front of that motion-picture camera. I was at the peak of my talents. My Countess Almaviva in *The Marriage of Figaro* wowed audiences."

When Polly had called Cora to tell her what she'd had found on Catalina, Cora had been thrilled—at first. But as the conversation had lengthened, her aunt's enthusiasm had waned. When she told Cora that she had secured Mr. Selznick's authorization to use the screening room on the night of the studio's New Year's Eve party, Cora's muted reaction had been an ambiguous, "Won't that be fun?"

"You don't have to compare yourself with *that* Cora Maddox," Polly said.

"*That* Cora was at the peak of her beauty, too. There, I've admitted it out loud. Revoltingly egotistical."

Luddie bent forward. "You should replace 'revoltingly egotistical' with 'understandably human.'"

Cora shook her head. "You're just saying that to indulge a vain prima donna."

"Aww, come on. Your life ain't too shabby now," Amelia said. "You work at the classiest studio in Hollywood. Thousands of people would sell their firstborn to be in your Mullen-and-Bluett pumps."

"You're working on *Wizard of Oz*," Gil pointed out, "and it's one of the most anticipated movies coming out of Hollywood next year." He had tried to say it lightly, but Polly could tell what he was thinking: *If you're not going in, then let us out now before we cramp up like English Channel swimmers.*

* * *

The screening room still reeked of the cigar Selznick had smoked earlier in the day as he'd watched the screen tests Cukor had made of actors under consideration for Scarlett's sisters, Suellen and Carreen. As the projectionist dimmed the lights, Cora groped for Polly's hand.

The title card appeared.

Camera test
Cora Maddox
on the stage of the
Metropolitan Opera House
New York City, May 1912

A milky haze grew clearer until it revealed the profile of a woman dressed in a lavish gown. With a squarish neckline and three-quarter-length sleeves, it nipped at the waist before flaring over panniers that spread out a foot and a half from each hip. Screen Cora lifted her chin until her face found a spotlight. Half a lifetime of triumphs and disasters had melted away, leaving a vibrant, youthful diva staring into the camera with an intense defiance.

"Holy cannoli, Cora," Gil said. "You're breathtaking."

She groaned. "That dress! It weighed a god-awful ton. The bodice with the starbursts? The thread was pure gold. On opening night, when I sang 'Dove Sono i Bei Momenti' in the third act, I got a four-and-three-quarter-minute ovation. The next morning, I was the darling of New York."

The Cora on the screen unclasped her hands, raised them

higher than her shoulders, and executed a three-hundred-and-sixty-degree turn.

"The director kept saying, 'This is a motion-picture camera. For chrissakes, *do* something!'" Screen Cora executed a slow, controlled deep curtsy. "Okay now, *that* I knew how to do." Screen Cora rose to her feet and lifted the hem of her skirt to reveal a pair of high-button boots. A smile broke out across her dignified face as she improvised a lively jig. "Now the director's yelling at me, 'I'm running out of film. Wave until I tell you to quit.'" Screen Cora waved at the camera until the screen dwindled to black and the lights came on.

Polly asked, "When did you last watch this footage?"

"Never! Nobody thought the flickers would amount to anything. It was a fly-by-night novelty. The director was a pal of the Met's general manager. He wanted to test a new-fangled motion-picture camera inside a theater." She tapped a contemplative fingertip against her chin. "How on earth Elroy got ahold of this, I can't imagine."

She had opened up an opportunity for Polly to ask her a question that had been nagging her for weeks. "When you landed back in LA, how come you didn't track him down?"

Cora turned to Polly, regret filling her eyes. "My desire to perform made me the Maddox black sheep."

"But you were an opera singer," Gil said, "not some tacky burlesque stripper."

"Our strictly religious parents held such rigid views, I'm surprised they didn't die from congenital rigor mortis. They would've left no opportunity untapped to condemn me to my brother. Especially after my fall from grace when my affair with the very-married manager of the Met was made public. That's the problem with success. When it falls apart, you have such a long way to tumble." She indulged in a sigh. "I got by doing my 'ten arias in ten minutes' gimmick in vaudeville. When the MGM offer came along, I was down to my last fifty dollars. I crept back into town poor as a church mouse. I didn't want to spoil everything for him with my soiled reputation."

"Even though Papa had been a bootlegger?"

"When you find yourself embroiled in a notorious public scandal, you learn to maintain a low profile. I've kept to myself. And then up you popped." She sandwiched Polly's hand between her own. They were kid-leather smooth, but chalkboard dry. "If I had known your mother had passed away and your father was doing his best to raise you alone out there on Catalina Island, I might have reached out. I should have anyway, and deeply regret that I didn't." She squeezed Polly's hand extra hard. "But at least you and I are making up for lost time, and I'm so grateful for that."

The room fell into silence until the projectionist cleared this throat over the intercom. "Do you need me to run it again? Because there's this party outside . . ."

Polly told him he was free to go after he rewound the film and left it on the counter.

As they filed out of the room, Cora said, "Oh, and one other thing. Purely out of curiosity, you understand." She had tried to sound blithe, but an undercurrent of trepidation gave her away.

"Would you like to have it?" Polly asked.

Cora blinked at her like a flashbulb, then wrinkled her nose. "I was the cat's meow, wasn't I?"

Polly ducked into the projection room and picked up the film can. Tucking it under her arm, she said, "It's time we got ourselves some giggle water."

* * *

Countless dozens of guests had clustered around the long bar set up next to the dance floor in front of Tara. Few of them were dancing to the band's version of Tommy Dorsey's "Once in a While," but the wandering waiters, their trays loaded with cocktails, would soon fix that.

Polly hoisted Cora's film can onto her shoulder. "I should store this on my desk for safekeeping," she told the others. "I'll be back in ten." She was about to ask Gil if he'd like to join her when Amelia piped up.

"I'll come with." She hooked their arms and the two girls marched toward the admin building known as The Mansion because it resembled George Washington's Mount Vernon home. As soon as they were outside of earshot, she cried out, "I slept with Benji!"

They halted by the water tower in its shadow cast by the gibbous moon. "When? Where?"

"Last night. Some doddering old codger spilled his lemon-lime phosphate on my dress at the Carthay Circle Theatre, so we hurried back to his place to wash it out."

Polly shifted the heavy can to her other arm. "And when the dress came off, nature took its course?"

Amelia nodded. "I thought all that business about murmuring sweet nothings into a girl's ear was malarkey Bing Crosby warbled in his ballads. But it's true! So dreamy, so romantic." she giggled like an adenoidal tommy gun. "When he caught me in my step-ins, his eyes became golf balls! Gosh, Pol, I like him so much. Even more, now that we've . . . taken the plunge, as it were."

"About that," Polly said, "how was it?"

"The way my mother described it during our sex talk, I was expecting to feel like he was stabbing me with a bayonet."

"Doesn't sound too romantic. Did it hurt?"

"It did. Until it didn't. And then quite the opposite."

A twinge of jealousy tugged at Polly's heart. Did mothers sit their daughters down and explain the mechanics of sex? Polly had gleaned the sum total of her knowledge from an old zoology book she'd found in the Avalon City Library called *Primate Husbandry*.

"This was your first time?"

"Hey! What kind of floozy do you take me for?"

"That depends." Polly held open the glass door into the executive offices. "How many different kinds of floozies are there?"

Amelia whacked Polly with a playful slap. "It wasn't until this morning that I learned Benji lives in a rental with three roommates. All four guys work in the movies, each at a different studio: Paramount, Columbia, MGM, and Fox. They've got personal contacts all over town. Picture it: this morning, I sat around a kitchen table crowded with strangers."

"You mean—"

"Every guy had brought a girl home! Well, three of them did. One didn't, but he spent most of the morning talking to us girls. So there we were, all seven of us, sitting around having coffee and sweet rolls like we were a bunch of Greenwich Village bohemians!"

They reached the short corridor leading to Mr. Selznick's suite of offices. "Sounds to me like you were in a pre-code Kay Francis movie."

The grin fell away from Amelia's face. "Here's a nugget to chew on: Benji told me he and Gil aren't the greatest of chums; they're only acquaintances at Paramount. It was Gil who had suggested they go to Kreiss's that night we met them."

This was sobering news. But not necessarily ominous.

They had now arrived at the brass plaque.

DAVID O. SELZNICK
President

Polly swung open the door with a theatrical flourish. "Ta-da." How strange to see the offices empty, the telephones silent, and the typewriters still. She deposited the film can onto her desk. "Sometimes I feel like I'm glued to that chair."

Amelia picked up her telephone. "Polly Maddox here. Why yes, Mister Zanuck, if you want to speak with Mister Selznick, you'll have to go through me first."

The band's jaunty melody drifted in through the window. "Let's skedaddle," Polly said. "We're missing the party."

"Can I peek into his office? I want to impress the girls at Schwab's."

"Okay, but make it quick."

Amelia took in the thick drapes, three-foot mahogany barometer, pair of standard lamps, and the white sofa he often napped on when the stimulating effects of the Benzedrine drained away. "This is how the muckamucks decorate? Fancy, but not over the top."

Polly tugged at the sleeve of Amelia's woolen coat. "I'll notify him of your approval."

"Will Myron Selznick be here tonight?" A note of wistfulness tinted her voice.

"Bound to be. Why?"

She ran a finger down the length of Selznick's desk before replying. "Luddie's suggestion about auditioning for *Pretty Pennies.*"

"You're interested now?"

"I've been rethinking it."

"Because I told you how much the role would pay?"

Polly had spent a recent afternoon typing up the initial budgeting projection for *Pretty Pennies* and learned Rita Hayworth's asking price was ten times what an unknown actress would cost. And that paycheck was almost ten times what Amelia would make in a year. Mighty tempting for a couple of months' work.

"Partly."

"Is it because it would give the also-ran daughter, caught between the perfect sister and the hellion brothers, a chance to shine?"

Amelia chewed over Polly's suggestion. "It's not like I yearn to be an actress, but acting in a movie would make for a fun story. I plan to lie on my death bed, muttering, 'What an interesting life I led. I even starred in a movie once back in the thirties.' When we were watching the film, I noticed how Cora's face went from 'This will be utter torture' to 'I was the cat's meow.' *That's* the face I plan to make when I look back on my life." The dreamy light in her eyes dropped away. "Am I being silly?"

"Sounds like a worthy goal, if you ask me."

Amelia fluttered her hands. "It's all pie-in-the-sky. Even a screen test would be a thrill. However, I'd rather not be one of those dummies who signs the first contract shoved in front of them. I'll need to get a lawyer. Wouldn't your boss know someone?"

"Oh, honey. If you and I pooled all our money, we couldn't afford anyone Mr. Selznick recommends." She headed for the door. "Let's go. I want a glass of Dutch courage before I ask Gil about—" An idea sparked a flurry of excitement, and she turned back to the desk. "Go stand in the doorway and keep a lookout."

"What are you up to?"

"I'd lose my job if I did this during the day."

Polly opened the side drawer where Selznick kept an address book almost the size of the directory for a medium-sized town. She skipped to the C tab. The listing for Harry Cohn included his home address and telephone number, but no details of his lawyer. She ran a finger down the page to a separate entry for Columbia, but again, there was nothing to tell her who the company's lawyer was.

"What are you doing?" Amelia whispered from her post.

"Remember that shifty lawyer I visited?" Polly flicked to the D tab.

"The one Gil's tied up with?"

"Allegedly."

Nothing under D, E, or F.

"Do they have security guards patrolling the offices at night?" Amelia asked.

Polly looked up from K. "I hadn't thought of that." She flipped to L. "I'll just—OH!"

Ludlow (escort). Marjorie, Margaret – Alameda & Firestone

Amelia ran to Selznick's desk. "Luddie! But who are Marjorie and Margaret?"

"Myron's wife, Marjorie, and Mayer's wife, Margaret."

"Our Smooth Sam sure swans around in high-falutin' company, doesn't he?"

Polly pointed to *Alameda & Firestone*. "What might this refer to?"

"Alameda is a street that starts in downtown and heads south."

"To where?"

"All the way to Long Beach."

"Is there a Firestone tire factory down there?"

"Couldn't say. But honestly, when I hear Alameda Street, I picture—Oh, Pol!" She grabbed Polly's wrist. "Remember how I told you about the Hooverville shantytowns? The most notorious one was at the corner of Alameda and Firestone."

"So—Luddie—he was—" Polly struggled to piece together incongruous clues to a paradox that made no sense.

"Our darling boy dug himself out of a horrible situation," Amelia said. "And I'm talking no running water, no heat, no bathroom."

Polly pictured him with his silk ties and merino wool suits, not a hair out of place, and shoes so shiny a girl could fix her lipstick in their reflection. "We can't say anything, though."

They crossed their hearts.

Outside, the dance band's trumpeter blasted out a long, strident note that dissolved amid enthusiastic applause.

Polly slipped Mr. Selznick's address book into the drawer and led Amelia into the corridor. They had reached the door leading onto the lot when it occurred to her how odd it was that only home addresses and telephone numbers filled Mr. Selznick's book. Where were all the business contacts?

She ran back into the office, with Amelia close on her heels, and sat herself at Marcella's desk. She found no listing in Marcella's address book for Brodsky in the Bs, but when she reached the Cs, there he was.

Brodsky, Roscoe

8390 Wilshire Blvd. (corner of Gale Dr.)

Beverly Hills

Personal attorney to Harry Cohn (Columbia)

Telephone CRestview 3811

So. Roscoe Brodsky was Cohn's lawyer? He used to be Papa's too, but Papa was gone now, so Brodsky's loyalties now lay with Cohn. Steadfastly and staunchly.

* * *

The crowd had more than doubled by the time Polly and Amelia rejoined the festivities. They lifted coupes from a nearby waiter's tray and picked through the throng until they spotted Luddie. It wasn't only how he held himself, erect as a ballroom dancer, or his stylish clothes. It was almost as though a halo surrounded him. Polly had always thought of it as charisma, but maybe it was more like determination? Tenacity? Ambition? Whatever it was, he possessed oodles of it—enough to stand out in a town filled with people who had built careers by being conspicuous.

"What happened to 'meet you back here in ten minutes'?" he asked.

"I needed to see where Pol works," Amelia said. "She's tied to that typewriter morning, noon, and night, so I wanted to stick my nose into every nook and cranny before her boss ranted for another fourteen hundred pages."

A dark-haired woman stepped out from behind Luddie. "You're not Polly, are you?" Her teeth were so white they almost glowed in the twinkling lights strung out across the front of the band stand. "The girl who helps keep Marcella sane, no thanks to my brother-in-law?"

"Polly Maddox," Luddie said, "I'd like to introduce Myron's wife, Mrs. Marjorie Selznick."

"You should work for my husband instead," Marjorie said. "He'll only *half*-drown you in dictation."

Gil and Benji had been talking to the man from props whose girlfriend had hauled him away to foxtrot around the dance floor. "Willow Weep for Me" had finished now, and they joined the huddle.

"I keep hearing about how David Selznick's addicted to putting everything in writing," Gil said. "Is he as bad as all that?"

"Oh-HO!" Marjorie squealed. "You have no idea."

"And may I present Gil Powell and Benji Fletcher," Polly said. "Gil is Hollywood's most skilled builder of horse-drawn carriages. He worked on *Stagecoach* at United Artists. And more recently, on a special carriage for *The Wizard of Oz* originally made for President Lincoln himself."

"Is that right?" She drifted a hand down the fur lining the collar of her sable. "What else have you worked on?"

"*Union Pacific* at—"

"Paramount!" Marjorie proclaimed, although it came out more like *Parmunt*. Evidently, she was as fond of a drink as her husband. "*My* old stomping ground." She let her fur fall open, revealing a flimsy dress of salmon pink silk. "I used to be an actress. Went by Marjorie Daw before I hitched my misguided wagon to Myron the Maniac. But then"—she beamed the smile of a moony teenager who'd drunk too much at her first adult party—"I met this bon vivant." Her arm encircled Luddie's waist like a boa constrictor. "Now I have the best of both worlds." The group stood in silence, expecting her to continue babbling, but when she didn't, Polly seized the opportunity.

"Have you ever worked at Columbia?" she asked Gil. "I hear Harry Cohn can be a real tyrant."

"Nah," he said. "I saw *In Early Arizona*, though. They had a stagecoach that I . . ."

A murmur ran through the crowd.

Heads turned.

Necks craned.

Vivien Leigh, in calf-length white ermine, and Laurence Olivier, in a brown houndstooth pea coat, meandered through the cleft created for them by the parting multitudes.

Polly whispered into Marjorie's ear. "It must be killing her knowing that she's got the part but can't tell a soul."

"The sixteenth can't come fast enough." She treated Polly to a saucy wink. *We know a secret the rest of the country is dying to learn!*

Had circumstances been different, Polly might have asked her why she considered hitching her wagon to Myron to be "misguided." Or maybe it wasn't such a great mystery. Being married to a Selznick couldn't be easy.

She felt a subtle pressure enclosing her elbow. Gil was luring her away from the spectators. "Where can we be alone?"

She guided them past Tara to the Atlanta railway set. It had no roof yet, but the walls were completed and afforded them a modicum of privacy.

"What's going on?" he asked.

Polly hadn't counted on him being so perceptive. "How do you mean?"

"Was it that clinch we got into the other day after sorting through your father's evidence? Did I move too fast? You only have to tell me to put the brakes on."

"If you recall, it was me who asked if you liked to kiss smart girls."

"I'm all discombobulated! I like you so much, Polly. Honest, I do." He raked his fingers through his hair. The soft, brown curls registered silver in the slanting moonlight. "But some days you're all fun and open, and other times you're shut off, like you've been all night tonight."

"I've been concerned about Cora and what she'd make of that old footage."

He planted this hand against a wall that had only been built in the last few days and fixed her with a face as earnest as a puppy's. "If you're cooling, let me off the hook. You don't have to be gentle about it. I'd prefer—"

It was time she let him present his side of the story, even though she wasn't sure she'd believe him. "Remember how we found my father's lawyer in his address book?"

Gil shoved his hands deep into his pockets. "Yeah."

"I went to see him."

"How'd it go?"

"He's a lawyer, so . . ." She seesawed her hand. "Afterwards, I was still standing on the sidewalk thinking things through when I saw you come roaring around the corner and into Brodsky's building."

Gil blinked slowly as though it were a herculean effort.

"Give it to me straight. Do you work for Brodsky? Or Columbia? or Cohn?"

He clamped both hands on top of his nest of curls. "What a relief!" he cried, loud enough to startle a trio of seagulls who'd been sitting on a nearby pile of bricks. "I was sure you were about to dump me."

He hadn't even tried to answer her question. "Is that a no?"

"It's a yes, and a no, and a kind of, and a maybe." He followed his non-answer with an amiable laugh and sagged against the wall, loose-limbed as a marionette. "In the dining room at Columbia, there is an electrified chair."

Of all possible starting points, that sentence wouldn't have made Polly's top one hundred. "You mean an electric chair? Like they use to execute murderers?"

"Yes. Only much, much milder. It's one of Mr. Cohn's practical jokes he reserves for newcomers. He invites them to lunch, where he waits for them to be in the middle of a bite, then presses a button with his shoe. The newbie gets a shock, and Cohn roars with laughter."

"So Cohn's as bad as everybody says he is."

"Only if he doesn't like you. At any rate, he did it to Frank Capra, who became so incensed that he smashed the chair to pieces."

"What did Cohn do?"

"He organized for a replacement, but secretly got someone from outside the studio to build it again."

"And that someone was you?"

"Uh-huh." Gil chewed at the inside of his cheek; it was the first sign of hesitation Polly had noticed. He raised his flattened palms toward her. "What I'm about to tell you is off the record, okay?" He continued only after she had nodded her agreement. "Cohn's deepest desire is to father a son. He's desperate to have an heir he can leave his empire to."

"Rose can't give him children?"

"Nope. It's his biggest frustration. However, he's the head of a movie studio."

The path of this story grew clearer. "Where beautiful women abound."

"Right."

"One in particular caught his eye?"

"Also right."

"Whom he asked to have a baby with him?"

"His plan was above board. Very businesslike."

Polly thought of Rose, and how her face soured every time she spoke of her husband. "I bet Mrs. Cohn loved this proposition."

"He never told her about it."

Rose didn't strike Polly as the dumb-wife-sitting-in-the-dark type. "As far as you know. And what did this pretty chorus girl say?"

"She told him she'd consider it. A few nights later, he came to her apartment for an answer. When she turned him down, he started shouting at her, which is how I got involved. I was living next door, and the walls of that cheapo apartment building were like cardboard. I could hear the fear in her voice, so I banged on the door to make sure she was okay. All we'd ever done was nod hello in the corridor, but she was a nice girl trying to make it in Hollywood. She answered the door, all pale and shaking, and asked me to get rid of him."

"You strong-armed Harry Cohn?"

"I grew up in a rough neighborhood, so I can handle myself with bullies. I grabbed him by the scruff of his neck and hauled him into the hallway. He calmed down and thanked me for intervening because he was so mad that he might have done something he'd later regret. That's when he asked how he could repay the favor. This was a couple of years ago when I was barely making rent. I told him I was a decent carpenter and asked did he need any woodwork done."

"Like rebuilding his mean-spirited electric chair?"

"Among other projects."

"I hope he paid you well."

"More than I would have asked for. In time, he got me work on some cowboy pictures. Hoot Gibson and Tex Ritter. Those are the jobs that gave me tons of experience on carriages and stagecoaches."

Over near Tara, the lively notes of a mariachi band bounced off the walls of the make-believe railway station.

Polly had dreamed up all sorts of shady scenarios explaining why Gil had been rushing to see Brodsky, but the truth had proved to be surprisingly prosaic. "What does Brodsky have to do with all this?"

"Cohn doesn't want my pay to go through the studio books or his own bank account, so we go via Brodsky."

"A little fishy, don't you think?"

"Men like Cohn are complicated people with complicated lives. Our arrangement is nothing more than his wanting to separate his work life from his personal life."

"So he's not the tough piece of work everybody insists?"

Gil took his time thinking through a response. "He has a favorite saying: 'I don't get ulcers. I give them.' He's tough but fair, which is okay in my book."

"And Brodsky?"

"I've done jobs for him, too. He must trust me because he has let me drive his customized Marmon with a two-toned, black-and-burgundy paint job." Gil whistled like a construction worker when a pretty girl walks by. "That dish drives like a pussycat. And by 'pussycat' I mean 'mountain lion.'"

The mariachi band had switched to a plaintive Mexican love song. Polly caught the words *amor no correspondido*.

"Mystery cleared?" Gil chanced a couple of steps closer. "Questions answered?"

"When we were in the evidence room and I read out Brodsky's name, I heard you react."

"I would've explained all this, honest, but we were pushed for time."

"And later?"

"We got busy in the back alley. And then I had to get you to your streetcar, and it's not a story I can tell in twenty-five words or less. In fact, I probably shouldn't have told you at all."

"Am I the first you've told?" Polly lifted her face toward the moonlight so that he could see her smiling.

"First, last, and only."

"I think that calls for a kiss."

He slid his arms around her waist. "A thank-you-for-trusting-me kiss, or a New Year's Eve kiss?"

She liked how he tightened his embrace until she was breathless. "It could start out as one and end as the other."

29

Amelia filched a french fry as she slid Polly's plate onto the counter. "Mr. S. better not ask me to work on New Year's Day next year. I didn't get to bed until three a.m."

"Get to *sleep* till three." Benji ignored her insistence that he hush his mouth and turned to Polly. "That boss of yours sure knows how to throw a swell party."

Polly saw no sign of Gil walking through the door. "Did you try the ginger crumb cake they brought out after the midnight champagne?"

"Did he ever!" Amelia scoffed. "*Three* slices."

"Is that why there was none left by the time I reached the dessert table?" Luddie asked.

"Serves you right for twirling Marjorie Selznick around the dance floor like she was a swizzle stick," Benji told him. "No wonder those old broads pay you good money to paint the town red."

"It's their dough," Luddie replied. "They get to paint it any color they like."

"We left that party at the same time." Amelia planted her hands on her hips and glared at Luddie. "How is it that I feel like a bag of rocks run over by a steamroller, while you look as though you've flown in from the Bahamas?"

Polly tried to picture him as a youngster, scrounging to stay alive in that woeful Hooverville, but he always showed up freshly shaved and nattily dressed. The best she could manage was William Powell in the early scenes of *My Man Godfrey*.

"When did Gil say he'd be here?" Luddie asked.

He was changing the subject, and now that Polly knew why, she didn't blame him. "All he said was"—she retrieved Gil's telegram from her clamshell purse—"'Meet me at Schwab's. Nine a.m. Big news.'"

"I hope he's not too much later," Amelia said. "Overenthusiastic partygoers will have roused from their stupor by noon o'clock, and will start packing this counter—there he is!"

Wearing no hat, no tie, and the fevered look of someone who hadn't yet been to bed, Gil came rushing at them, breathless as a sprinter. He planted a hurried kiss on Polly's cheek. "Good news, everybody. I got a new job. A *great* one!"

"When? At four in the morning?"

"Closer to five. I received a telegram from Raymond Klune."

"*Wind*'s production manager? You know him?"

"Not till last night. When Twinkle Toes Sinclair was taking you for a spin, I found myself chatting with the guy standing next to me. When I learned he works in your props department, we started talking about my experience building carriages and wagons. He got all worked up and asked how he could get ahold of me. I wrote my address on a paper napkin and he disappeared into the crowd."

"You didn't mention any of this on the drive home."

Gil shrugged. "A ten-minute conversation with some stranger I never saw again? But then this telegram arrived, urging me to call Klune. He asked how soon I could start. I told him, 'Tomorrow is New Year's Day, so how about the day after?' He said, 'Report to me at eight.'"

"Oh, Gil!" Polly exclaimed. "You realize what that means?"

He wrapped an arm around her shoulders. "We'll be on the same lot."

What a relief she no longer had to feel guilty working long hours to suit Mr. Selznick's insane schedule. Maybe, just maybe, it might help get them to the stage that Amelia and Benji had already reached.

"This calls for a round of root beers!" Polly turned to Amelia. "Waitress, line 'em up!"

"Sorry, honey." Gil kissed the top of Amelia's head. *Does he realize he called her 'honey' for the first time?* "I gotta go over to MGM to fetch my tools."

"I'm taking off, too," Benji said. "I'm heading out to Yuma, Arizona, tomorrow."

"Tomorrow?!" Amelia snapped. "*Beau Geste* doesn't start filming until the middle of the month."

"That was the plan. Shooting in a remote desert will be a tough as blazes, so Bill Wellman wanted the script to be as solid as possible so that we can swing into action." Benji managed to scrunch up his face in a way that looked guilty *and* sheepish. "I'll be gone for thirty-five days."

"How long have you known this?"

He pulled a crumpled telegram from his back pocket. "Gil wasn't the only one."

She helped herself to another french fry. "There's a fine New Year's how-d'ya-do."

"Gotta rush." Gil tilted Polly's chin and kissed her tenderly on the lips. Not that she had much experience in the smooching department, but he was a world-class kisser as far as she was concerned.

Benji then leaned in to kiss Amelia, but she pulled back with a wintry fish-eye. "I'm not sure I want to give you a goodbye kiss, leaving me like this with no notice."

"Sure you do." He bent farther over the counter and puckered up. "I gots to goes when m'job calls me, honey-bun."

She planted an extra-long smooch on his kisser and then waited until Gil and Benji had left the drugstore and turned to

Polly. "Serves me right for taking up with an art director. They're always going to be disappearing to the Grand Canyon or the Rockies or the goddamned Buttercup Sand Dunes—" She jolted upright. "He's back."

Benji lingered down the far end of the counter. "Polly?" he called. "A quick word?" She joined him next to an elaborate display for Westmore cosmetics. "I was hoping to get you alone, but the opportunity didn't present itself."

"What's wrong?"

"I couldn't head out of town without mentioning what my roommate told me this morning."

"MGM, Columbia, or Fox?"

"Noah's been at Columbia for years, working his way up the finance department. Spends all day looking at ledgers and balance sheets. How he doesn't fall asleep at his desk, I'll never know. At any rate, the week your dad got shot by the police, he told us that your dad and Cohn had a smooth business relationship all through Prohibition."

This confirmed what Rose Cohn had told Polly during their horseback ride. "Yes, that's right."

"He admitted Cohn got him to fudge the accounting for all the money Cohn spent on your dad's bootleg. The IRS wasn't aware Cohn was in business with your dad, so he had to justify those expenditures somehow."

"So cooking the books was hiding less-than-legal cash flows?"

"All those guys do it to some extent or other, but what is curious is that Noah talked about how one day the studio had a Mount Everest of Mad Ox, and the next it was like Cohn had turned off the spigot. No more Mad Ox, period."

"Did he say why?"

"Cohn and your father had had a falling-out. *Real* bad."

"Over what?"

"A bunch of people came into the kitchen before he finished telling me."

"But he knows?"

"He could."

Thirty-five grand was nothing to sneeze at and needed to be accounted for—fudged or otherwise. And who cooked the fudge? The accountants. "Do you think he'd tell me?"

"It's worth asking."

"But why would he blab his boss's secrets?"

"Because in the fourteen years Noah has worked there, Cohn has never, not once, not ever, thanked or complimented him, or shown him any gratitude for cooking the books so expertly that Columbia has avoided Tax Department audits. He's not stupid, so he won't say anything over the phone."

"Should I go see him?"

"It'll need to be today; tomorrow he's taking the Super Chief. He always spends the first week of the year in the New York office."

"He's at home packing?"

"Noah Briggs is the most conscientious guy I know. On New Year's Day he's at the office making sure he's all caught up. If you want to see him, you'll have to go to the studio. I'll call him when I get home so that he can put you on the list to stop security from giving you a hard time." He wished her luck and hurried into the street.

Polly's eyes fell on a Westmore compact. Its shiny brass casing reflected her image. Her hands grew clammy at the thought of venturing further into enemy territory. But if she wanted to clear her father's name and restore his reputation, risks would have to be taken. Besides, what was the worst he could do? Strap her into his electric chair?

30

It was almost three o'clock when Luddie braked at Columbia's Gower Street gate. The guard had the nose of a prizefighter who had bitten the mat in the fifth round at the American Legion Stadium. "Didn't anyone tell you it's New Year's?"

Polly called out from the passenger seat. "My name should be on the list. Polly Maddox."

The guard held up his clipboard. Aside from the date at the top —*Sunday, January 1, 1939*—the page was blank.

"We're here to see Noah Briggs."

"If Mr. Briggs drove through this gate, I'd have seen him."

"Not if he used the pedestrian entrance on Fountain," Luddie countered.

He scowled at them like a bulldog.

"I hate to play this card," Polly said, "but I go horseback riding with Mrs. Cohn. Whom I will call. If I must. So either you place a call or I do."

The guard shifted his unblinking scowl to Luddie.

"And I take Mrs. Cohn dancing at the Biltmore Bowl," Luddie added, as amiable as Roosevelt giving a fireside chat. He rapped a knuckle against the guard's empty list. "Go on, buddy, make the call."

The bulldog retreated into his booth.

"Typical man," Polly muttered. "I play the wife-of-the-boss card and he looks to another guy for approval."

Luddie maintained his artificial smile. "Keep your eye on the prize. Getting in is all that matters."

"Without you, Maxie Rosenbloom over there would've dismissed me as a crazy old lady with fourteen cats and a nervous twitch."

"One of us playing the missus card wouldn't have been enough. But both of us? That's a team sport."

The guard hung up and stepped outside. "Mr. Briggs is on the phone and needs about fifteen minutes. The finance building is on the west side. As for parking"—he waved a flaccid hand across the deserted roadway—"take your pick."

With ten minutes to spare, Luddie suggested they find Stage Six, though he didn't say why. The Selznick studios bustled with escalating intensity as *Wind*'s production start date approached. By stark contrast, Columbia's empty roads and the deserted alleyways between buildings and soundstages left Polly feeling distinctly uneasy.

The movie set in Stage Six smelled of fresh wood polish and turpentine, but had been designed to resemble a backwater South American saloon. They wandered around the battered chairs and aged poker tables arranged as though they had barely survived the previous night's brawl.

"I wonder what they're shooting," Polly said.

"The new Howard Hawks movie, *Only Angels Have Wings*." He ran his fingers down the keyboard of a honky-tonk piano; its plunkety-plunk notes rang out across the stage. "But Hawks hasn't been getting along terribly well with his leading lady, so the picture is what's known as 'in trouble.'" He stood at the bar, where photos lay in an untidy pile. "Here are some production stills."

Polly joined him.

Cary Grant in a leather aviator jacket.

Jean Arthur in a figure-hugging double-breasted suit.

Richard Barthelmess in a wide-brimmed fedora.

The last shot revealed a young girl around Polly's age with thick, dark hair parted down the middle. She wore a loose, low-cut dress designed to emphasize her impressive bosom.

"Harry Cohn's new sex bombshell," Luddie said. "Rita Hayworth."

Amelia's *Pretty Pennies* turnaround had taken Polly by surprise. Had she thought this through? She'd be up against hundreds of ambitious girls, all of whom were prepared to do whatever it took. Amelia would need more than a striking resemblance to the original star. Still, a refined British actress was to play the world's most famous Southern belle, so anything could happen.

"I can see why Cohn is pushing this girl for *Pretty Pennies,*" he said. "Do you think Amelia is serious?"

Polly thought about Amelia's admission about feeling like she was the invisible middle child. "You think she's not?"

"Benji's in the picture now. They seem taken with each other."

"You say it like being smitten is a bad thing."

"Not at all. Quite possibly, my evening work has made me cynical, but I see what happens. Almost every woman I've escorted around town gave up a career to marry her husband. These women weren't born Mrs. Selznick or Mrs. Zanuck. They've got more to give than dinner parties. Amelia is so full of beans that I'd hate to see her fade away in anyone's shadow." He returned the photo of Rita Hayworth to its place in the stack. "Speaking of smitten, have you and Gil—?"

"We've kissed a few times."

"Is he any good at it?"

"I think so, yes."

"Is he pushing you into doing anything you don't want to do?"

If anybody else had asked questions like these, she would've blushed and stammered and changed the subject. But Luddie was one part big brother, one part trusted confidante, one part you-can't-shock-me.

"He's tried his luck—with some success, I might add." She laughed. "But he's quite respectful in that way."

"Glad to hear it." Luddie's voice had taken a surprisingly solemn turn.

"Why are you asking? Is there a boys-only secret I ought to be aware of?"

"Gosh, no."

Her attempt at flippancy seemed to have struck a rare, jarring note with Luddie. "Don't stop now," she told him, sensing he was holding something back.

Luddie shrugged. "I have a disquieting feeling about him. Nothing I can put my finger on, so pay me no heed."

She debated telling Luddie about Gil's confession of doing odd jobs for Cohn. But even as she tried to imagine describing how there'd been nothing shifty in his manner or his voice, she knew how suspicious it would sound in the retelling. "I don't want to miss this Noah guy before he heads to New York. Let's shake a leg."

* * *

Noah Briggs' office was a cluttered hodgepodge of strewn papers, files, and ledgers stacked on every surface. The smell of burned coffee hung in the air like a thundercloud. He looked up from a fistful of receipts. "You must be Polly?" His voice had a slight squeak to it, as though it hadn't fully broken yet, and matched his youthful baby face.

"Yes, and this is Ludlow Sinclair." Polly surveyed the haphazard detritus. "Is this a bad time?"

"When your office looks like this, nobody goes searching through it." He dropped the receipts in his hand onto a messy pile. "Benji called me earlier, but was light on details."

Stacks of papers towering two feet high filled his two guest chairs, leaving Polly and Luddie no choice but to stand.

"Mr. Briggs—"

"Call me Noah."

"My name is Polly Maddox—"

"Elroy's daughter?" The question hurtled out of him.

She watched Noah's initial hospitable demeanor cool. "I'm looking for information about the agreement Mr. Cohn and my father entered into when they set up Mad Ox."

He returned to the handful of receipts he had tossed aside. "How much do you know?"

"Precious little. I get roadblocks at every turn." He kept silent as he turned over each receipt, no longer looking at Polly and Luddie. He wasn't nearly so forthcoming as Benji had led her to believe. "They were partners all through Prohibition and beyond," Polly went on. "But I was still puzzling through the specifics when the police gunned down my father right in front of me."

"I was sorry to hear about that."

"As far as I can make out, their partnership was somewhat murky, which I found odd because my father wasn't the murky type. But also, he and Mr. Cohn enjoyed a mutually beneficial arrangement with Mad Ox. So when Benji told me that you told him my dad and Cohn had a falling-out—"

"I was speaking in confidence. If I'd known he was going to blab—"

"Please don't be mad. He didn't tattle anything I hadn't already learned."

Noah arrived at the bottom receipt. He turned it over with the careful deliberation of a surgeon. But still he stayed silent.

"Rose Cohn also told me that her husband and my father had a bitter falling-out."

That did it.

Noah looked up. "You've met Mrs. Cohn?"

"I recently had tea with her and Constance DeMille."

This guy had no poker face. Polly could almost see him follow the breadcrumbs until they led him to Luddie. He squinted at him for a moment.

"You're that guy who escorts her around town, aren't you?"

Luddie feigned modesty with a tucked chin and aw-shucks smile. "I do accompany ladies around town when their husbands are otherwise occupied. Suits me, though. I get to eat dinner in the swankiest joints."

Noah continued to nod slowly. "You're looking at the guy who pays you."

"In that case, thank you very much."

Noah planted his hands flat against his blotter. "Cohn put up eighty percent of the Mad Ox money to your father's twenty."

"You've seen the figures yourself?" Polly asked.

"Who do you imagine has been juggling those books all this time?"

Now we're getting somewhere. "Does that mean Cohn took eighty percent of the profits, too?"

"My boss drives a hard bargain. Always."

"Did they make much money?" Luddie asked.

"Not at first. Setup costs, refining the product, shipping to the mainland, distribution. There were lots of moving parts, so it took them a couple of years."

"And after that?"

"By the late twenties, they were minting so much money it was hard to hide. It got easier when Prohibition ended and they took Mad Ox legit, but eighty percent of a ton of money still takes maneuvering when there's no record of an initial investment."

"Is that what their disagreement was about? Did Cohn want to buy my father out?"

"Nah." Noah glanced at his watch.

"You need to get going?" Luddie asked.

On his feet now, Noah shifted his weight from one foot to the other, then back again. "It's not outside the bounds of possibility that Mr. Cohn could show up at the studio."

"On New Year's Day?"

"The man works like a fiend, but especially now that he's okayed a fifteen-million-dollar budget for the new Capra movie. *Mr. Smith Goes to Washington* won't start shooting for months, but he'll fret over his decision every single stinkin' day, and I'll have to listen to it." Polly and Ludlow followed him into the corridor and down the stairwell. "I should've met you at Nickodell on Melrose when I was done." He led them through the exit, then shepherded them into a narrow lane between towering soundstages. "I'm not giving you the bum's rush, but it wouldn't be great if Cohn discovered you—you, of all people—on the studio lot."

How quickly he'd become rattled. She hadn't meant to put him on the spot, but this might be her only chance to ask him. "What can you tell me about why things went sour between Elroy and Cohn?"

"Not much."

"Anything?"

"I do know that Mr. Cohn landed in some strife after he got himself into a fight with a guy who ended up being connected with the mob."

"He has mob connections of his own, doesn't he?" They rounded the corner of Stage Two and turned on to one of the main east-west roads cutting through the studio. "I'm referring to Longie Zwillman."

"You *are* well informed, Miss Maddox. Yes, wherever Zwillman is, Roselli and Siegel and Cohen aren't far away. Mr. Cohn figured he had the most muscle on his side, so he wasn't prepared for the other guy to have mobster connections, too."

"Who was this other guy?"

"Dunno. But they must have been heavy hitters because next thing I know, Cohn needs to raise fifty grand."

Fifty thousand dollars was a huge pile of clams. Luddie whistled. "For what?"

"Don't quote me on it, but I suspect the other guy put a hit out on him and fifty grand was the price to have it canceled. From what I understand, they don't normally charge so much, but when the victim is high profile—"

"—up goes the price tag." Polly tripped over her own heel. She stared at Luddie. *This is getting out of hand.*

He bug-eyed her back. *Should we quit while we're ahead?*

Noah was too intent on charging ahead to notice. "Mr. Cohn and I had a tense meeting late one night. He was unnerved, which is rare. I told him that amount was a lot to hide in the books, especially if the IRS decides to audit. Then I suggested he must have any number of well-padded friends who could help him out. He told me he was too much of a bastard to have friends, actual be-there-when-you-call pals. I almost felt sorry for him."

"First time for everything."

"When I asked him if there was anybody at all, he replied, 'Fifty grand is a truckload of lettuce.' To which I responded, 'Especially when you need it in cash.' *That's* when fireworks went off in his eyes, like he'd suddenly remembered someone who deals in cash."

Polly stopped walking. "My father and the *Ning Po*."

"I didn't know who until the grapevine started chattering."

"What did it say?"

"Your father turned down Cohn several times until Cohn sent Zwillman and his thugs to strong-arm him into forking it over. But here's the strange part: Cohn got his fifty grand, but not in a lump sum. Instead, it came in two payments: eighteen thousand seven hundred, and thirty-one thousand three hundred."

"That's strange," Luddie mused out loud. "Isn't it?"

"Yes, but who was I to question—"

"WHO THE FUCK IS THERE?" The gravelly voice javelined over their heads.

"Cohn!" Noah pushed them inside a soundstage. "If he recognizes you, it'll get me into more hot water than I can stand."

The crunch of marching footsteps echoed off the thick wall. "Don't make me come after you," Cohn growled. "If you show yourself now, I'll only beat you to a slight pulp."

Ludlow whispered to Noah. "Get Polly out of the studio." He squared his shoulders and walked into the sunshine. "Put down your dukes, Mr. Cohn."

A long pause followed before Cohn growled, "You're that

faggot gigolo who shows Rose a good time so that I don't have to bother."

Faggot *and* gigolo? Didn't one cancel out the other? Polly longed to hear how creative Ludlow was with his retort, but Noah was already guiding her toward a side door. The alley led to a gate that opened onto the sidewalk along Gower.

"For what it's worth," he said, "I am sorry for my part in this rotten mess. If I hadn't said what I said, Mr. Cohn might never have thought of your dad."

"Don't be so hard on yourself. You work for a crafty snake in the grass, so I'm sure the odds are pretty good that he would have landed on Papa sooner or later. Thank you for telling me all this. Cohn'll be out for your blood if he finds out what you've done today."

He threw her a pained look, like a prisoner who's been denied bail. "Mr. Cohn pays me very well, which he thinks compensates for all the dubious chicanery he forces me to do. At first, it was easy for me to justify my actions. My mother's a widow. She's quite ill and a shut-in, so a lot of my blood money pays her medical bills. But the more he's gotten me to do his dirty work, the harder it's become. And now I have matching stomach ulcers."

"So this is payback?"

He held the gate open and stepped aside to let her pass. "You'd better get going. I might have to provide reinforcements for your friend."

"They say cabbage juice and sweet potatoes are good for ulcers."

"I'll try anything."

"At least until your mom gets better and you can quit this job."

He adjusted his frown into a mild smile. "Scoot before the Gorilla of Gower Street eats us alive."

Polly stepped onto the sidewalk. She and Luddie hadn't come up with a fallback plan should they become separated. It was too far to walk home, but the morning's gloom had given way to a clear blue sky. Maybe she'd wander down Melrose Avenue until a taxi appeared. She had plenty to chew over. A mobster had put out a hit on Harry Cohn, who had turned to Papa for the cash to have it rescinded. And to think not too long ago, her biggest concern had been how far she could walk along Crescent Avenue without being snubbed.

31

When Polly walked into work the next day, she wasn't the least bit surprised to see Marcella at her desk, her ashtray already filled with cigarette butts and her telephone handset cradled between her ear and her shoulder as she continued to type.

"I understand, dear," she grumbled into the receiver, "but as I told you this morning, Mr. Selznick is building up to the big reveal any day now. I can't abandon ship at five because you want dinner at seven." She tapped a fingernail on a mess of handwritten sheets and mouthed to Polly, "Start with these."

All in Mr. Selznick's barely legible handwriting, and all dated January 1, 1939, there were memos to Legal about actors' contracts, to Publicity about the size of newspaper teaser ads, to Scenic Design about aging Tara's wallpaper, and to Casting about the protests from the NAACP. Had Mr. Selznick worked all day and night on these things?

Polly was threading letterhead into her typewriter when Marcella dropped her telephone receiver into its cradle.

"You'd think my husband would understand the pressure we're under. But no! It's all 'Why isn't my dinner ready on time?' And 'Why must you work Sundays?' Now I'm getting 'You're more married to Selznick than you are to me!'" She contemplated her telephone. "I suppose he has a point. I kept telling him, 'Until we cast Scarlett.' Then it was, 'Until we announce Vivien Leigh.' And after that, 'Until we start filming.' But if not *Wind*, then *Rebecca*. After *Rebecca*, then *Intermezzo*." She drummed the receiver with her fingernails until she plucked herself out of her reverie. "The good news is that two new girls will be starting tomorrow."

Polly paused from a memo to George Cukor about how to direct Miss Leigh and Miss de Havilland in Melanie's birthing scene. "And put them where?"

"The room down the hall."

"The utility closet?"

"Take out all the junk and it's quite roomy." Marcella pantomimed wide circles with her hands. *What other choice do we have?*

Her intercom buzzed; Mr. Selznick's voice boomed out, "Is Polly here yet?"

"I'll send her in." Marcella lowered her voice. "That guy from Legal is with him. The one with the Friar Tuck haircut. They've been powwowing since before I got in."

Polly patted down her hair. "Any idea why he wants to see me?"

"None," Marcella replied, "but the more he gives you to do, the better it is for my marriage."

Mr. Selznick and Friar Tuck—Polly was reasonably sure his name was Campbell, but not confident enough to address him directly—sat at the circular conference table.

"I tasked Legal with establishing who holds the copyright for *Pretty Pennies*."

"We saw it in the opening credits," Polly said. "Lewis Selznick's Equitable Pictures."

Selznick gestured to Friar Tuck. "Equitable was folded into World Films. Later still, the board ousted Lewis from World Films, in which event the copyright reverted to a company called Descanso Films. And Descanso Films belongs to Sibyl Langley."

Had Sibyl drawn on Descanso Beach, north of Avalon, for inspiration?

"When you talked with her at MGM," Selznick said, "did she mention anything about owning *Pretty Pennies*?"

"It didn't come up."

"We can go no further until I've secured the copyright. I want you to go down to MGM and find her."

"And when—"

"Immediately."

"But, sir!" Polly protested. "Isn't this a lawyer-to-lawyer negotiation?"

Selznick's face had darkened. "I want a soft-soap approach. You've already established a rapport. Talk to her, working woman to working woman."

His tone startled Polly. Neither snide, nor condescending, nor dismissive, there had been an edge that implied she was his best bet to secure *Pretty Pennies* for the smallest outlay.

Polly had now been in Hollywood long enough to know that money—astounding, life-changing, shop-at-Bullock's-and-hang-the-expense money—had the power to warp people. To turn laundresses into snobs, snobs into automatons, and everyone into greenback gluttons. Was Mr. Selznick planning to gyp Sibyl out of a decent windfall now that she'd been reduced to painting scenery? After all, he was no Cohn, Zanuck, or Warner.

Or was he not planning that at all?

You were the one who defended Mr. Selznick to Sibyl, Polly told herself. At least give him the benefit of the doubt like you're giving Gil, despite the mounting evidence that Gil works for a despot with no moral bearings.

"I'll give it a shot, but honestly—"

"The first question out of her mouth is bound to be 'How much?'" Mr. Selznick swayed a chewed pencil between his fingers like a crazed teeter-totter. "Offer her one thousand dollars." Polly bit back a yelp of surprise. He wasn't out to gyp Sibyl at all. She chided herself for doubting her boss. "If she plays hardball," he went on, "you can go as far as two. However"—he pricked the air with his pencil—"if you come back with a verbal agreement, I'll give you a bonus for the difference between the amount she agrees to and the two grand."

Would a thousand dollars fund Mad Ox's resuscitation so that she could reimburse Mr. Wrigley? Assuming, of course, that she could figure out a way to run the revamped distillery. Polly's job kept her so dreadfully busy. And if Marcella delegated more of her work, where would she find the time to run a distillery? To say nothing of the technical know-how. But she'd figure that out later. All of that was pie-in-the-sky stuff as long as she didn't have the funds to pull it off. But now she did. Or might.

* * *

Polly walked onto Stage Twenty-Four as *Wizard of Oz*'s director, Victor Fleming, was shepherding the leads through the final rehearsal of a musical number.

"No. NO!" Fleming shouted from his stepladder. "'The jitterbug' is supposed to be perky. Be bouncier. Jauntier. I need more pep."

"We've been peppy through five weeks of rehearsal," Ray Bolger said. "How much pep do you think we've got left in us? Especially poor Bert here." Bert Lahr lay sprawled out on the floor. "He'll be wearing his Cowardly Lion costume under those blazing Technicolor lights."

"What's the point of filming this number if you're not ready?"

This barking drill sergeant of a director was, in Polly's opinion, an odd choice to direct a kids' fantasy picture. She was relieved she didn't have to work with someone like that. And she was glad to spot the friendly face of the man who might have been directing this picture had he not already been committed to *Wind*.

George Cukor stood well back from the tree-lined set. With his arms crossed over his chest and thick brows drawn in pensive distraction, he brightened up when he noticed her approach. "Playing hooky?"

"I might ask you the same question." Polly motioned toward life-sized trees designed to obscure a grown man who could wave branches in time to the music. "Don't you have enough to do preparing for *Wind*?"

"Vic isn't convinced this jitterbug number will work and wanted my opinion. But tell me, what brings you to this neck of the enchanted woods?"

She asked him if he knew who Sibyl Langley was and where she might find her. George didn't, but he flagged down a passing assistant director, who suggested they try *The Adventures of Huckleberry Finn*.

"Oh, dear. How awkward," George said. "*Huck Finn* is being directed by Richard Thorpe, whom Mayer fired from *Oz*. And then he asked me to step in until he'd convinced Vic to take over."

"You're busy, but if you could tell me where—"

"Nonsense!" George walked her outside. "I've seen enough of this number to know it won't fit *Oz*'s tone."

"Shouldn't you be telling Mr. Fleming that?"

"Here's a lesson in moviemaking: wait until you're asked."

* * *

In gray overalls splattered with red and orange barn paint, Sibyl was easy to spot. As they approached the *Huckleberry Finn* set, George whispered that he ought to hang back in case Richard Thorpe happened by.

Sibyl brushed away a mutinous lock of hair with her wrist. "You again."

"I assume you've heard the news that a print of *Pretty Pennies* has been found." Sibyl stared at her blankly. "You don't read *Variety* or *The Hollywood Reporter*?"

"I'm more of a *Time* magazine girl."

She listened impassively as Polly ran her through recent events.

"And so, I'm here on Mr. Selznick's behalf to make you an offer."

A wrinkle of confusion passed over her face. "To direct it?"

"He wishes to acquire the rights to the original film."

"Shouldn't you be asking Equitable Pictures?"

"They were folded into World Films, who then later sent Lewis Selznick packing. When that happened, the rights reverted to Descanso Films."

"Descanso Films. I'd forgotten about that." Sibyl swiped her forehead, leaving a trail of cherry-red paint. "Are you saying *Pretty Pennies* belongs to me?"

"Yes!"

George stepped forward and adopted the paternal tone Polly assumed he used with his thornier actresses. "Your lawyer must have inserted a reversion clause in your contract."

"And now those rights, which I wouldn't have given two bits for—David O. Selznick wants to buy them?"

"For a thousand dollars," Polly said.

Sibyl's lips formed the silent words "thousand dollars."

Polly pictured herself requesting the DA to authorize access to the distilling equipment. *A thousand for me. A thousand for her. We both win.*

But as she mapped out her future, Polly took a fresh look at this woman who she guessed was around fifty and spent her days painting yellow brick roads and balsa-wood barns. Twenty-five years ago, she had dreamed up a story that was still relevant to modern audiences. Had the industry allowed her to continue, maybe she would be in a position to remake her own movie, but instead, the men in charge had cast her aside.

She deserves more than a thousand, Polly thought. But that would mean no money for Mad Ox, and no way to pay back Philip Wrigley, and if I couldn't—

"Tell Selznick he's got a deal." Sibyl wiped her right hand down her streaked overalls. "Do we shake on it to make it legal?"

Polly took Sibyl's hand, but felt like a dirty, stinkin', low-down, four-flushing skunk. And she was, too. "Where shall I tell our legal department to send the paperwork?"

"MGM art department. Gosh. Oh my!" Sibyl raised herself onto the balls of her feet and dropped back down onto her heels. "I can buy a decent car that doesn't break down every other week. Or rent an apartment with its own bathroom. Or maybe get myself a new wardrobe that doesn't include"—she shook the sides of her overalls—"this."

After telling Sibyl their legal department would be in touch, Polly and George stepped outside into the thin January sunshine and headed for the Washington Boulevard gate.

"How come you're looking blue?" he said. "Don't you think that went well?"

She kicked a discarded Nehi cola cap along the road. "I'm a scoundrel."

"Oh, really, Captain Kidd? And why, pray tell, is that?"

"Mr. Selznick authorized me to go as high as two."

"Securing the contract for half his maximum will make you a hero. Again."

"But he added a sweetener." The opening notes of a popular new song, "The Lady is a Tramp," percolated through a nearby window. Polly let a few bars wash over them before she was ready to confess. "I keep the difference between the two grand and what Sibyl agreed to."

He guided her hand into the crook of his elbow. "A thousand bucks is a lot of lucre."

"I could use it to get the Mad Ox distillery going again. And use the profits to pay back Papa's debt."

"Restoring your father's reputation is important to you, isn't it?"

"Very."

"Okay, so Sibyl gets a new car and you resurrect Mad Ox. Where's the problem?"

"Because that spunky, smart woman in there got a rotten deal the first time around and I had it in my power to get her a fair shake." Polly stopped walking. "But I took the money for myself like every other greedy little moneygrubber." She searched his face for signs that she had done the right thing, but found only cool detachment staring back at her. "You're going to tell me to follow my conscience."

"The only thing I shall tell you is to stop putting words in my mouth."

"Is this how you treat Garbo and Colbert and Hepburn? Clever innuendo and leading questions?"

A skewed smile distorted his lips. "I've never directed Claudette Colbert."

She shook her hand loose and marched back into the soundstage, where Sibyl had resumed painting the side of a barn.

"I hope you forgive me," Polly blurted out.

"Whatever for?"

Stumbling over her words like an illiterate dunce, Polly owned up to the full arrangement Mr. Selznick had charged her with and what she planned to do with her half of the loot. She punctuated the end of her confession with a croaky sigh, shook off the last vestiges of her guilt, and waited for Sibyl to berate her manipulative dishonesty.

But instead, Sibyl told her quietly, "Take the money."

"But—but—" Polly brushed away the tears threatening to spill from her eyes.

"Oh, sweetie. A thousand clams is a thousand more than I had when I woke up this morning. It'll last me a good, long while. You're putting your share toward a worthy goal, which means we both come out ahead. How often do women get to say that when most of the time men go out of their way to run us down and then throw their Pierce-Arrow into reverse to make sure we won't stand up again?"

"Is that why you turned down Mr. Selznick's invitation to join us in the screening room?"

"I don't believe in looking back. The past is a dead-end street. I learned that the hard way. So take Selznick's money and build your future."

. . .

Outside, Cukor was nowhere in sight. That man had better things to do than wait for a dolt like Polly Maddox to come to her senses, she thought glumly. She set out down Fourth Avenue, already dreading the Mt. Everest of work that had no doubt piled up in her absence. She ignored the staccato of running footsteps behind her until she heard Sibyl call her name.

"I don't suppose you've encountered Longie Zwillman?" Sibyl asked, panting from her sprint.

"No."

"Do you know who he is?"

"Papa told me he was some sort of go-between for Harry Cohn. Why do you ask?"

"One of my best-paying jobs was when I was on the team of muralists who helped Billy Wilkerson turn La Boheme into Café Trocadero. I even got to attend Myron Selznick's star-studded party. The whole place was so ritzy and high-class. But as soon as Wilkerson opened gambling rooms downstairs, the mob came sniffing around. Zwillman first, which meant Bugsy Siegel followed, and Mickey Cohen after that."

"Those three seem to come as a matched set."

"Nasty pieces of work, all of them, but Zwillman is especially barbaric. If you get Mad Ox up and running again, don't be surprised if Cohn decides he still owns a piece. And if he does, he won't show up demanding his cut. He'll send thugs."

"Zwillman?"

"Or someone like him. I'll warn you now: if you resist, life could get very ugly, very quickly. These people have no morals, no scruples. Nor will they care that you're a woman. If you want my advice, you need to stop things before they get to the Zwillman stage."

Polly swallowed hard. "You mean confronting Harry Cohn himself, don't you?"

"I do," Sibyl said. "And good luck with that."

32

The calendar on Marcella's desk now featured two dates circled in red: January sixteenth, the date Selznick had chosen to announce Vivien Leigh's casting, and January twenty-sixth, the start of principal photography. Every staff member felt like they had weeks of work left to do and only days to fit it all in. When getting into the office at eight a.m. wasn't early enough, Polly started showing up at seven. And when seven proved insufficient, she arrived at six. Some days, the only glimpses of sun she caught were through the window behind Hazel.

In the back of her mind, she knew that she couldn't keep up this frenetic pace forever, but the demands of the work drove her cogs and gears as she flourished in a job that required her to juggle more and more balls with ever-increasing dexterity. Memo by memo, phone call by phone call, decision by decision, David O. Selznick's screen presentation of *Gone with the Wind* was slowly crystallizing. And Polly took ineffable pride in her minuscule part in it.

True to his word, Mr. Selznick had immediately ordered the payroll department to draw up a thousand-dollar check. Not that Polly had had time to deposit it. The envelope still lay untouched in her desk drawer. She'd get to the bank eventually. For now, knowing she had the funds to revive Mad Ox bourbon was enough to settle her mind.

Except for one frustrating hitch.

To secure the District Attorney's okay to release Papa's equipment, she needed to plead her case. Her best bet was to do it in person, but how could she pull that off while working twelve to fourteen hours a day, six days a week?

She'd figure it out somehow, but not now. Today was about retyping the redrafted opening scene. She turned to the first page, where Mr. Selznick had scrawled directions on how he wanted Miss Leigh to sit on the porch step in her opening shot as she complained to the Tarleton twins how war talk was spoiling all the fun.

Hunger was already gnawing at her innards. Damnation. Was it only eleven o'clock? A quick ham sandwich was the best she could hope for. And even then, her chances were slim.

Mr. Selznick appeared in his office doorway. "Security called to say that Myron has arrived with final documents concerning Vivien's casting, start date, and overtime provisions. He's pushed for time, so someone will have to go down to collect it from him." He pointed to Polly. "You."

"Just to pick up papers?" Marcella snapped. "I'll send one of the new girls."

"They contain sensitive information, so either you or Polly."

"It's almost lunchtime," Polly said. "What if I swing by the commissary and grab sandwiches for everybody? Secretaries can't live on coffee and cigarettes alone."

Marcella's nod was brusque and grudging. "Make mine turkey. Heavy on the mayo."

* * *

Polly expected Myron to be seated inside his car, the motor running, an arm extended out of the window, and an envelope clutched between his stubby fingers. But instead, he was leaning against his sleek midnight-blue Lincoln Zephyr convertible with the camel top. His right foot resting against the front fender, he puffed from a Monte Cristo he held in one hand and swigged from a chrome hipflask he clutched in the other. "I figured he'd send you."

"Aren't you supposed to be in some god-almighty hurry?"

He took a swift pull on his cigar. "I needed a break from all the madness."

If he had time to drive all the way from his offices on Wilshire, how could this so-called madness stack up against the monstrous pressure his brother toiled under?

"What madness is that?" she asked.

"Take your pick."

"The worst one."

"Olivier." He kicked one of his white-walled tires. "His first lead in a Hollywood movie and he has to come down with a raging case of athlete's foot. He has to be carried to and from the set. What he doesn't realize is that it plays into Heathcliff's anguish, so Willie Wyler is happy for him to suffer through the utter hell he's making of everybody's life. Then he goes home to Vivien, who is preparing for *her* big break, and dumps out his frustration on her."

"Which she takes out on you?" Polly asked.

Myron eyed her with an appreciative raised eyebrow. "I can see why you're Dave's golden girl."

Polly took a deep breath to calm the blush creeping up her neck. She knew she ought to be heading to the commissary, but this opportunity was too good to waste.

"Can I ask you about the Trocadero?"

Her question caught him off guard. "What about it?"

"Did you throw a star-studded party for the opening?"

"That was five years ago."

"So you did?"

"Uh-huh."

"And when Mr. Wilkerson opened gambling rooms downstairs, did the mob muscle its way in?"

Myron needed another slug of whatever he had in his flask. "What's all this about?"

"Sibyl Langley brought it up when I struck that deal with her over the *Pretty Pennies* rights."

"Why would she do that?"

"Have you ever encountered Longie Zwillman?"

"Aw, jeez!" Myron winced as though Polly had dropped a brick on his wingtip brogues. "I'd rather give birth to a porcupine backward before I had to face him again."

So Sibyl hadn't been exaggerating. "She warned me things can get ugly when he's around."

"But why would you be anywhere near that psychotic cutthroat?"

He listened without reaction, comment, or interruption as she laid out her plan to repay Mr. Wrigley, concluding by saying she'd need to do it free of interference from Zwillman. "But all of that is moot because I first must convince the DA to let me take possession of Papa's distillery equipment."

"I see." The wind changed direction, blowing a scotch-saturated haze over Polly. Marcella had intimated that Myron drank to such excess that it might kill him some day, but Polly had never seen it for herself before. He fished a black address book from inside his jacket. "I'm pals with a well-connected fixer with the DA. Let's go to Dave's office and I'll make a call."

"No!" she cried out. "I want to keep this ugly business separate from my job."

He slid the book back in his pocket. "God knows I can understand that."

"They've installed pay phones near Tara. I need to run over to the commissary. Perhaps you could make your call and I'll meet you over there?"

* * *

Polly clutched the brown-paper bag containing twice the number of sandwiches she and the girls needed. But the possibility that Mr.

Selznick might need them to work late always hung over them like a guillotine blade, so the extras would come in handy. Myron was hanging up as she reached the trio of coin-operated telephones.

"I just spoke with the officer in charge of your father's embezzlement."

"Gerard Donovan?"

"The very one." Polly caught another whiff of expensive rotgut and shuffled a tactful half-step away. "What's he like?"

"Typical law enforcement. All rules, regulations, and requirements to start out with."

"And after a dash more blarney?"

"He's okay with releasing the distillery equipment—"

"Terrific!"

Myron held his hands out. "Hold your cotton-pickins. *If* it's okay by Philip Wrigley."

Mr. Wrigley reigned as Catalina's lord and master. A benevolent dictator, to be sure, but his was always the final word on everything. Still, what choice did she have? "Thanks again," Polly told Myron. "I owe you one."

He rubbed his hands together, then pressed them as though in prayer, which was a queer sight to see from someone who hadn't voluntarily been inside a synagogue since his bar mitzvah. "I left Vivien's paperwork on the passenger seat, so walk me to my car." He took off, leaving her to catch up with him.

"Ever since you uncovered *Pretty Pennies,* you've risen in my brother's estimation," he told her as she fell into lockstep beside him.

"That's nice to hear." *Where was this conversation heading?*

Myron stared grimly ahead. "Me and Irene and Marjorie, we're all concerned that Dave is working himself into an early grave."

This man had always struck Polly as the typical fast-talking negotiator who wouldn't hesitate to sweat the industry's movers and shakers if it meant securing a more lucrative deal. But instead of Myron Selznick, the aggressive talent agent, Polly now took stock of Myron Selznick, the concerned brother.

"It's not unheard of for him to work twenty-four hours straight," she admitted.

"He must have help."

"He smokes like a chimney and downs coffee like it's soda pop."

"And the Benzedrine?"

Please don't ask me, Polly wanted to plead. Your sister-in-law put me in the same position and I bore the brunt of it the next day. I only redeemed myself because I found *Pretty Pennies*. I can't pull off that trick a second time.

"I withdraw the question."

She hadn't noticed he'd been observing her.

"You're a good egg, Polly Maddox," he said. "Dave's lucky to have you. I have my answer now." He reached through the convertible's open window and retrieved a thick envelope. "God knows I'm hardly a Puritan finger-wagger, but we fear he's playing Russian roulette with his health."

"As David's family, you have more sway."

She tucked the envelope under her arm and turned to go.

"You need to get on Mr. Wrigley's right side, yes?"

"I do."

"Know him well, I suppose?"

"Not at all. But who'd blame him for refusing to see the daughter of the guy who swindled him? I need to figure out the best approach."

"As it happens, this coming Sunday I'm throwing a 'Welcome to Los Angeles' party for a British director."

"Alfred Hitchcock?"

"You *are* good, aren't you?"

"Who do you think typed up the contracts?"

"At any rate, this wingding I'm throwing will be a sprawling affair. Tons of guests. Some of them film folk, but the rest will be from all walks of life. What if I invite Philip Wrigley and his wife?"

"You know them?"

"I know the Longbottoms, who know the McCalls, who know

the Wrigleys. If you were there, too, who knows what opportunity might present itself?"

Polly squeezed the envelope more tightly. "That would be marvelous. I'm so grateful you'd go out of your way for me like this."

"Lewis was my dad, too. A successful *Pretty Pennies* will help restore his name, and I'm all for shoving it in the faces of people like Mayer and all his cronies."

"Does that include Harry Cohn?"

"Why him?"

"Sibyl Langley warned me that if Cohn finds out Mad Ox is back in business, he'll want a piece of the action."

"She's right. Cohn is the worst of the bunch, so yeah, he'll want to muscle in."

Polly lifted the bag of sandwiches. "If I don't get these to the troops, I might have a rebellion on my hands. Thank you again for your help."

It wasn't until she began racing toward the admin building that she became aware of the winter air cooling the clammy dew beading her face.

33

"It sure must be swell to have a home in Beverly Hills *and* a Santa Monica beach house," Gil said from behind the wheel of his faded-red Plymouth pickup. It didn't qualify as a jalopy, but its clunker days were looming on the horizon. He wasn't envious; it was more of a straightforward observation that some people are the Haves and others are the Have-nots. "Remind me who Hitchcock is."

"Marcella told me he's a big deal in England."

"So this'll be a snazzy affair, huh?" His tone turned solemn as Wilshire Boulevard veered around the old Sawtelle Veterans Home.

"I thought it would be a great way to spend an entire afternoon together."

"It's not that." He stroked her hand, which had been lying on his knee. "Although I must admit, I assumed we'd at least have lunch sometimes."

In his first week at Selznick, he had been assigned to restore three old carriages before principal photography began, which gave him only eighteen days, and then to build two from scratch.

"It won't always be like this," she reassured him, though in truth she was talking to herself. "Marcella says that once the cameras roll, a picture falls into a predictable rhythm."

"Huh," was all he had to say.

They passed several blocks in silence before Polly asked, "Anything wrong?"

"Nah," he said, attempting to buoy his voice. "I've never frolicked with the crème de la crème before. These people are a different breed."

Polly thought of Clark Gable's fear of appearing foolish in period costume, George Cukor's apprehension that Selznick might leave him out of the loop, Irene's concern that overexertion could cost her a husband, and Mr. Selznick himself, who worried and fretted and overthought every detail. "They're really not. And even if they were, you have an ideal conversation starter."

"Oh, yeah?"

"The Horse of a Different Color carriage in *Wizard of Oz,* and how it once belonged to Lincoln. Trust me, that'll bridge any awkward silences."

She hoped like mad he didn't expect her to be glued to his side the entire time. The demands of their jobs prevented them from the usual dating routine of going to the movies or strolling along a beach, so this party was a rare opportunity for them to enjoy each other's company for more than a few snatched minutes.

He had worked at studios where famous faces were an everyday event as unremarkable as paper napkins. It hadn't crossed her mind he would look at this party as anything more than an elevated lunch in the commissary.

"I guess you're right," he conceded after a long pause.

Polly was glad to hear it. Why, then, hadn't she told him about Mr. Wrigley and the opportunity she'd be looking for this afternoon?

Because a scaremongering voice inside her had been warning all week against showing her whole hand.

Gil works for Cohn, Polly's inner Cassandra argued. It might be broken doors and new window boxes, but he's still got a toe in

Cohn's camp. Don't be like every other moonstruck girl, all starry-eyed over her first romance. You're smart. Act like it.

"Anybody who knows how to build a horse-drawn carriage from scratch," she said, scooting over to kiss him on the cheek, "is someone who can make chitchat with studio wives and publicity hounds."

* * *

Myron Selznick's house on Coast Highway stood a few blocks north of the Santa Monica pier and south of the outlandish Georgian Revival mansion William Randolph Hearst had built for his mistress, Marion Davies. Bright red streamers hung in loops from rose bushes trimmed like giant lollipops. The burbling of party chatter wafted through the double front doors. A pair of slim platinum-blonde girls dawdled in the corner of the square foyer. Not much older than Polly, they flared defensive eyes at her, before returning to each other satisfied she represented no threat.

"If I've got any shot at getting the lead, I suppose I should read the book," the one in the sky-blue striped sundress drawled. "Tell me, do I look like a Rebecca?"

Polly was tempted to let Miss Blue Stripes know Rebecca was the title, not the lead, and that of the nine *Rebecca* memos Polly had already typed, all of them cited Joan Fontaine as the presumptive candidate.

The living room stretched across the width of the house. Expansive seascapes covered three of the walls; a six-shelf red-cedar bookcase was packed with books, most of them classics by the Brontës, Austen, Dickens, Trollope, and Melville. None of them looked to Polly as though they had ever been cracked open. French doors facing the ocean opened out onto an expansive patio. Dozens more people filled its large square tiles of glazed terracotta, which reached down to the golden sands beyond. Somewhere out of sight, a string trio played a lively waltz that belonged in a Jeanette Macdonald / Nelson Eddy operetta.

As Polly and Gil accepted glasses of champagne from a passing waitress, a familiar voice trumpeted, "WELL, IF IT AIN'T BURNS AND ALLEN."

With his olive skin and shiny black hair, Polly wouldn't have thought white would have suited Luddie as flatteringly as it did. But there he was in a three-piece linen suit and white shoes, with a miniature white camellia pinned to his lapel. For contrast, he had chosen a yellow silk tie the color of the Californian sand behind him. Did the man ever put a sartorial foot wrong? He was also squiring Rose Cohn, who had one arm linked in his.

"I should have guessed you'd be here," Luddie said as she and Gil approached.

"And yet I'm not the least bit surprised *you* are."

But Polly's retort fell flat. Crinkles puckered the edges of Luddie's smile. The toe of his right shoe tapped against the tiles as though keeping up with a jittery drummer.

Rose's tense smile was for public consumption only. As the perennial plus-one appendage to her husband, did her presence here mean that Cohn was here too? But if he were, why would Rose need Luddie?

Slowly, covertly, Luddie widened his eyes. *I'm trapped against my will.*

"What a relief to see a friendly face," Rose announced at a volume aimed at everyone within a twenty-foot radius. "Especially one who doesn't want to suck up to me thinking I have any power over my rat-faced husband."

"Rose," Polly said, "you know Gil, don't you?"

"As a matter of fact"—why was Gil trying to sound like Ronald Colman?—"we've not met." He lifted her hand and kissed the back of it. "Gil Powell."

Polly searched Rose's face for signs of recognition, but saw only a blank expression.

"Charmed, I'm sure." Rose guided them to the patio wall. It stood four feet high and featured a mural of Italian cypress trees. "Want to hear my news?" she asked in a way that told them they were about to get an earful anyway. "Last night, Harry notified me that—and I quote—'the formality of our marriage is too confining.'"

"He's leaving you?"

"He has plans to move into a penthouse at the El Royale on Rossmore, but I'll never divorce him. Maybe if he'd behaved differently, with some class and decorum, these past fifteen years. But he didn't. So screw him—and the whore he rode in on."

At the far side of the patio, where the trio was now playing a Gershwin tune, Paulette Goddard was leaning Myron against a wooden fence as though he were a department store mannequin. Kay Francis was doing her best to pry a highball from his hand. Hitchcock hadn't even arrived yet, and the host was already on his way to messy-drunk. Marcella had warned Polly, "At about cocktail number six, he loses his equilibrium. Two more and he turns into that loudmouthed drunk everyone backs away from."

Polly spotted Philip Wrigley with his wife, Helen. Belonging as they did to Los Angeles society, not Hollywood society, they were probably surprised to be invited. If she was going to make her approach, she ought to do it now while everyone was still sober.

She excused herself and made her way toward the Wrigleys, who had stepped onto the sand where a second, smaller bar covered with bamboo poles stood under twin papier-mâché palm trees. Halfway there, Walter Plunkett crossed her path.

Wind's costume designer was a regular visitor to David's office. With over five thousand pieces of clothing to prepare, he had never so much as given her the time of day, so she was flattered to find he had sought her out. But did he have to choose this particular moment?

"Mr. Plunkett. How nice to see you."

A slim man with a pencil mustache and tasteful clothes with the precise amount of restraint, he usually exuded a calm air.

But not today.

"I hate to talk shop at a fête such as this, but I'm terribly anxious about the costume Scarlett will wear for the opening scene."

"What about it?"

"It's the first one we'll be filming!" He had managed to raise his tone an octave before taking control of his agitation. "I need to know who I'm making the damned frock for."

"Mr. Plunkett, should you be asking—"

"George has directed full-color screen tests for Joan Bennett, Jean Arthur, Paulette Goddard, and Vivien Leigh. They each have different measurements. Once the official announcement is made, I'll have a little over a week and a half. Yet how can I build it if I don't know who I'm building it *for*?"

Along with Marcella and all the girls in the office, Mr. Selznick had sworn Polly to secrecy. If Walter let on that she'd told him, it'd be her head on the chopping block, not his.

"Come now," she said, as placatingly as possible. "Mr. Selznick will tell you when he's ready."

"He's not mindful of how long it takes . . ."

His voice trailed off as a surge of excitement billowed through the crowd: Clark Gable and Carole Lombard had arrived. Everyone had probably assumed Gable was there because of *Wind*. However, Polly guessed he was a Trojan horse. Hitchcock had a predilection for blondes, and Polly would have bet twenty bucks Myron had advised Carole it would be a good career move if she let Hitchcock get an eyeful.

"Look, Mr. Plunkett," Polly said, "Marcella is Selznick's right-hand man. You ought to be prevailing on her."

"Perhaps, but"—a sly smile slipped onto his face—"everybody knows you're David's favorite girl Friday."

She had put little stock in Myron calling her "Dave's golden girl," but she hadn't stopped to consider whether that distinction had leaked beyond the executive suite. "Oh, come now. I hardly think—"

"To quote Bill Menzies, 'Polly Maddox is the one who gets things done, so ask her, even though'—and remember, I'm quoting Bill now—'she can come across as somewhat of an ice princess.'"

A *what*?

Could nobody tell the difference between shy and aloof? She'd need to make more of an effort around the lot. But right now, the

Wrigleys were standing by themselves, scarcely bothering to hide their boredom.

Another tidal wave of turned heads and smattered murmurings.

Harry Cohn strode through the crowd, his face a grim mask as he approached Rose. All three of them—Rose, Gil, and Luddie—jolted. Even Cohn must know dirty laundry shouldn't be aired in public.

But he ignored his wife and confronted Gil.

"I'll beg if I have to," Plunkett said.

His plea jerked her back into their conversation. He had grown even paler in the time she had been tracking Cohn's invasion. *Poor thing. He's beside himself.*

"Let's play a little game."

"I'm at my wits' end and you're playing games?"

"Remind me of the actresses who've been screen-tested."

He counted off the names, finger by finger. When he reached Leigh, Polly theatrically cleared her throat.

"Thank you, thank you, thank you," he whispered, pulling her into a bear hug. "I owe you one."

"A big one." She pried herself loose from his embrace and hurried forward.

She shouldn't have blabbed. The news might be all over Hollywood by sundown, thus destroying the grand reveal that Mr. Selznick had been so carefully assembling for weeks. But Plunkett had a massive job to do and deserved to be kept in the loop.

Mr. Wrigley wore a cream-of-wheat-colored Brooks Brothers suit that he'd paired with a necktie of the same bland hue, only slightly darker. His wife had encased herself in a stiff ensemble of rayon that was neither pink nor red, but more of an unflattering sun-bleached puce. They couldn't have looked less at home if they'd been wearing hair shirts.

Business kept him in Chicago most of the year, so he was generally around for only the summer season. What a shame that their first conversation should be about her father's embezzlement.

"Good afternoon," Polly said. "These Selznick boys sure can throw one heck of a reception, can't they?"

Mrs. Wrigley turned to her husband. "What did I tell you? She's the one who put us on the invite list. These aren't our people. She's got a ploy up her sleeve. Like father, like daughter."

"Look," Polly said, perhaps a tad too forcefully, "I'm the last person you want to talk to—"

"I doubt we should be conversing at all," Mr. Wrigley said. "Legally speaking."

"Please hear me out." Polly expected them to stalk off, but they stood their ground. *Spit it out. We don't have all day.*

"I swear to you I had no idea what my father was doing; otherwise, I'd have talked him out of it. I can only presume he wanted to shield me from all that ugliness. As any father would." Both Wrigleys tried to interrupt, but Polly knew that if they did, they might nab the last word and walk out, so she plowed forward. "I know you've seized all the Mad Ox assets to recoup the missing money, which is fair enough. However, I have a proposal."

"Oh, yes," Mrs. Wrigley said. "Here comes the dodge."

"There's no dodge, I swear. What I want is to pay back all thirty-five thousand. Every last dollar."

"That's a lot of money, Miss Maddox."

"It is," her husband agreed. "But tell me, what's your proposal?" He tilted his chin toward Mr. Selznick, who was regaling Clark and Carole with a story that involved a lot of wild arm movements. "Ask your boss for a loan?"

"I'm asking you to permit me to gain access to the distillery equipment so that I can get the operation going again. Mad Ox bourbon is a respected brand, and exclusive to Catalina. After I've taken off running expenses, one hundred percent of the profits go directly to you until I've paid back the full amount."

Polly spoke with far more confidence than she felt. Who the heck knew what the profit margin was on hard liquor? Or how much income Mad Ox would generate each month? Or whether it was even possible to pay it all off in her lifetime?

The glacial resentment etched into Mr. Wrigley's face softened enough to show her spiel had impressed him. Behind the Wrigleys, Harry Cohn had clamped a fist onto Gil's arm and was dragging him across the sand. They disappeared around the south wall of the beach house.

Polly watched them for a moment and then returned her gaze to Mr. Wrigley. "What do you think?"

"Here's what I don't get." He tugged thoughtfully at his earlobe. "The whole time Elroy worked for me, not once did I sense underhandedness. Legalities at the *Ning Po* aside, I felt like I could trust your father implicitly. That's what really hurts. If I couldn't trust Elroy Maddox, who could I trust?"

The plaintive look on the man's face reminded Polly that when you're the heir to a chewing-gum fortune, intangibles like trust are more valuable.

"Imagine how I feel." Polly's voice had ebbed to a rasping whisper. "If I couldn't trust my own father . . ." Finishing that sentence felt unnecessary; she let the ocean breeze carry away the rest of it.

"I know it's a waste of time to ask you this, but"—Mr. Wrigley's chest caved in a little—"do you know what your father did with my money?"

Now, *there* was a question. If only Polly had the answer, maybe she would sleep better at night.

"I've only got a theory."

"Go on."

A raucous group of social butterflies, including the two blondes from the foyer, had carried their drinks from the bar to a vacant spot next to Polly. One of them made a full-throated toast—"Here's to Maxim de Winter!"—and clinked her champagne coupe with her friend's.

"Follow me." Polly led the Wrigleys farther onto the sand where they could be alone. Without naming names, she told them about how "a trusted source" had told her that "one of Hollywood's heaviest hitters" had forced Elroy to embezzle the funds so that the mob would cancel the hit they'd put out on him.

"The *Ning Po* casino must have been an all-cash enterprise,"

Mr. Wrigley pointed out. "Wouldn't he have had enough to cover the cost?"

"Not when the price of a mob hit was fifty thousand."

Mrs. Wrigley dug one heel into the soft sand. "They weren't kidding around."

"Evidently, the price gets steep for high-profile targets."

"This Hollywood heavy hitter," Mr. Wrigley said. "Are we talking about Harry Cohn from Columbia?"

"What makes you say that?"

"Just a hunch. I knew Elroy had a silent partner when he started Mad Ox. We didn't talk about it, but I used to hear him say the name from time to time over the telephone. I always thought he was saying 'Cohen.' There are tons of Jews in LA, so I thought nothing of it. That is, until I came across a Western Union telegram stuck inside a ledger."

"Did you read it?"

"It was an order from Columbia Pictures. Fifty bottles of bourbon. On the back, your father had scribbled a bunch of calculations, which came out at zero."

Would Cohn expect to get Mad Ox for free if Polly got it up and running again?

"I was tempted to ask Elroy, 'What does Cohn have on you that he can get fifty bottles gratis?' I rather wish I had now."

Polly stole a look toward the beach house. Cohn had looked mad as blazes as he had dragged Gil across the sand. "Anyhow," she said, "putting Mad Ox back into business is the only way I know how to repay the thirty-five thousand my father took from you."

"For the record, Miss Maddox," Mr. Wrigley said, "thirty-five thousand was an approximate guess. I can now tell you that our accountant has determined the actual number is only thirty-one thousand three hundred dollars."

Nothing about that amount was "only." She was no chewing-gum heiress. "That's good news."

"Indeed. But the mob leaned on your father for fifty thousand, and he took thirty-one thousand three hundred from me, which leaves eighteen thousand seven hundred. Where did the rest come from?"

Wrigley raised his eyebrows and kept them halfway up his forehead until Polly tumbled to his meaning.

"His *Ning Po* earnings?"

"So it would seem. Now, I don't know how much space it would take up, but I bet it wouldn't fit into the average box of Don Francisco Cabañas."

"It'd need to be bigger than a bread box," Mrs. Wrigley said.

Yes, Polly thought. More like the size of a—a— She squeezed her eyes shut, tight enough to block out the winter sun. In its place she pictured that old White Rock turpentine tin on the floor of the shed near the *Ning Po*.

Stop the presses and hold the phones.

Didn't Noah say that Cohn had made his payoffs to the mob in two installments? And weren't those payments $18,700 now and $31,300 later?

Had Papa emptied his tin-can stash and stolen the rest from Wrigley?

Papa, Papa, Papa. If only you had shared your burden with me.

"You've got yourself a deal," Mr. Wrigley said.

Polly's beleaguered mind battled the whirling fog. "I'm sorry, what?"

"Resurrecting Mad Ox is the best chance I have of seeing my money again. I do, however, insist we formalize it with a contract."

"Absolutely."

"I'll have my lawyer draw one up."

"Could I get two copies? I know someone who could take over operations."

"That's fine, but Mad Ox's appeal is that it's made on Catalina. I insist it continue to be."

Wrigley's stipulation might have put the kibosh on the whole scheme, but he was the locomotive driving this train and she was merely the caboose.

"And one more proviso," he said. "I'm not unsympathetic to your situation, Miss Maddox, but business is business. If you fail to come up with a workable plan by, say, the end of February, I will then sell the brand as an ongoing concern. I can also then claim ownership of all your father's effects, including the house, which I will offer at public auction. Are we clear?"

She nodded and assured him they were quite clear. With that out of the way, he confided that neither he nor Helen felt the least bit comfortable in this crowd and that they planned to slip away. Polly waited until they had left, then sprinted to the side of the beach house and peeked around the corner.

Fists clenched, Gil and Cohn were facing each other like a pair of pugnacious billy goats.

"What does she know?" Cohn demanded. Gil tried to reply, but Cohn cut him off. "Why can't you do what I'm paying you for? I cannot permit the DA to scrutinize what went down."

Gil responded, but his back was turned to Polly and the wind spirited away his defense into the late afternoon skies.

"After the *Lost Horizon* fiasco, my studio barely broke even last year." Cohn was screaming now. "I'm sinking a mill and a half into *Mr. Smith*. If it flops, I'm more fucked than a three-dollar hooker during Fleet Week."

He drew back his right fist and aimed a punch at Gil's face. Gil blocked it, but failed to see Cohn's left hook. It clobbered him on the side of his head, sending him staggering against the brick wall.

Polly jumped out from behind the corner and caught his arm, but he was too heavy for her. He slumped to his knees.

"Who the hell is *this*?" Cohn jeered. "Don't tell me it's your *girlfriend*?" He drenched the word with disdain. "And as for you . . ."

Polly faced Cohn squarely, gathering a volley of insults: bully, tough guy, thug, two-bit punk. And she might have let them fly, but they dissipated when she saw the blank look in his eyes.

He has no idea who I am. He's staring at the daughter of the man he betrayed, and he's oblivious. Strangers in drugstores have recognized me. Everybody who works at the studio thinks of me as a direct path to David O. Selznick. But Mister High-and-Mighty Harry Cohn of Columbia hasn't got a clue.

The wind changed and treated her to a blast of the man's

cologne. Her stomach roiled. *Oh please, dear God, no. Don't tell me he wears the same one as Papa.* But the rich, floral scent was unmistakable. Of all the aftershaves, did it have to be Carnival de Venise?

Gil climbed sluggishly to his feet. "I'm okay. No harm done." He was doing his best to sound unfazed, but the underlying tremble in his voice betrayed him. "Let's go."

Polly threw Cohn a parting glance to see if he'd figured out who she was. But the same stony, uncomprehending eyes glared back at her.

But that was okay. Preferable, in fact. His ignorance gave her an advantage she hadn't known she had: the element of surprise.

34

Polly burrowed her hands into the crunchy sand underneath the Santa Monica pier as she and Gil dropped onto their butts. The melodic waltz of Looff's carousel bled through the pier's weathered boards overhead.

Her attempts at conversation had failed during their trek from the Selznick beach house. Given what had happened, Polly had excused Gil his leaden silence.

But not forever.

"Ready to talk?" She got a nod for a reply, which wasn't much, but she'd take it. What she had witnessed was more than a squabble between a guy and his handyman. "Did you know Cohn would be there?"

"I was shocked when I saw his missus on Ludlow's arm."

"She didn't seem to know you."

"He keeps his wife at arm's length. Most of those guys do. 'Extracurricular activities,' if you catch my drift."

"What did he mean by, 'What have you told her?'" A lone seagull landed nearby on the sand and squawked. Gil threw a pebble at it. "Told me about what?"

He was drawing in and pushing out harsh, deep breaths now,

as though he had sprinted the half-dozen blocks. She gave him sixty seconds.

. . . fifty-eight . . . fifty-nine . . . sixty.

"The longer you clam up, the more you come across like you're hiding something. And that forces me to question everything about your association with Harry Cohn. You can see how that would drive me bananas."

He dredged up a handful of sand and patted it into a ball. It looked like a baseball in the dusk light slanting in from the pier above them. He flip-flopped it from palm to palm. "The 'she' Cohn was referring to wasn't you, so you ain't got nothing to worry about."

Polly wanted to believe him. She had always found his ability to hold a conversation one of his more appealing qualities. But now, when she needed him to open his trap and start yakking, he was handing her the silent treatment.

"So who's this mysterious 'she'?"

"An ingenue he's grooming for stardom." Gil launched the sandball into the ocean. It hit the water with a sharp plop. "She's been in a bunch of pictures and is getting more confident in front of the cameras. He would have put her into *Mr. Smith Goes to Washington*, but Jean Arthur owes him a picture."

"Yes, yes, I've heard all about Rita Hayworth. She's currently filming *Only Angels Have Wings*, and he wants to loan her out to Mr. Selznick for *Pretty Pennies*."

He looked at her, bug-eyed. *You're more informed than I imagined.*

A gloomy veil of guilt dropped across his face. "There's more going on than a simple loan-out."

"Isn't there always?"

The response made her sound more jaded than she'd have liked, but it was better than dead silence.

"Did it occur to you that you're poking your nose into confidential studio business?" he asked.

Why would a studio head talk about confidential studio business with his odd-jobber? She let his question slide by. For now. She wanted Gil to trust her, but it'd only work if she let him come around to the idea that he could, so she waited for him to speak again.

"All right," he said. "What I'm about to tell you is strictly off the record, okay?"

She pantomimed locking her lips with a key.

"Cohn's in financial straits. Deep."

"How deep?"

"Touch and go. He took a massive risk on *Lost Horizon*, shelling out way more dough on a Capra movie than he'd ever dreamed. But previews were rotten; editing was like torture. And then, the movie cost so much that it would've taken a miracle to make its money back. And ever since, Cohn's been scrambling to keep his head above water. If *Mr. Smith* bombs too, it might spell the end of Columbia. That three-story lamasery set he built for *Lost Horizon*—"

"Lamasa-what?"

"That's what I wondered, too, so I looked it up. You know how monks live in a monastery? Turns out, Tibetan lamas live in a lamasery. And the huge white one Columbia built on its ranch in Burbank, it alone cost more than most pictures, so he's left it standing in case they can use it in some other film. Meanwhile, his best cash flow comes from loaning out his stars. Problem is, he doesn't have many, but this Rita Hayworth girl, she's special."

"He's gunning for Rita to be cast in *Pretty Pennies*?"

"And how."

"Is that why you're working at Selznick International? To snoop for Harry Cohn?"

Polly hugged her knees to her chest. If she couldn't put her doubts to rest, she might soon be walking away from the only guy who'd ever shown interest in her. Sure, this town was full of guys. But most of them were lady-killers who thought anything in a skirt was fair game. She steeled herself for some variation of "How could you even *think* that?"

But Gil didn't explode. Nor did he vault to his feet and stalk off, outraged and offended. He sat still, taking her questions like a prizefighter absorbing punches in the fifteenth round. "All this must look mighty suspicious, but I swear it happened the way I told you. I got talking to a prop guy who talked to Mr. Klune about my work on *Oz* and *Stagecoach*. I got that telegram. The pay was good, and I'd be working on either the biggest success Hollywood's ever seen or its biggest flopperoo. Either way, why would I say no?"

Why indeed would he—as long as he was telling the truth.

"It wasn't until later, when Cohn learned I was at Selznick, that he doubled my pay to keep my ears open."

"Open to what?"

"Jean Arthur is still in the running for Scarlett. Her getting cast would be a huge win for Cohn that might help him salvage his studio."

"How much insider information does he expect you to get working in the prop shop?"

Gil smirked. "Nobody's ever accused Harry Cohn of being reasonable. That frustration you witnessed—it came from all the pressures pushing down on him."

Should she tell him what she knew about the hit out on Cohn and how he'd forced Papa to steal from Wrigley? This entire calamity could have been avoided if Cohn had done the decent thing and paid back the money. But he was a dirty rotten louse who had left her father holding the bag until he was gunned down by the cops.

A niggling, skeptical voice in the back of her head told her to hold off. But what if Gil had inadvertently gotten in over his head? You're not his mother, the voice replied. Nor his grandmother, his boss, his schoolteacher, or his zookeeper. He's a grown man who has given you reason to not trust him fully.

"Funny, isn't it?" she said. "Cohn stands to gain a lot if Mr. Selznick casts Jean Arthur, but there I was, the lowly peon who types up the memos, takes the dictation, overhears the meetings . . ." She let the rest of the sentence hang in the air.

Gil swiveled to look at Polly for the first time since they had planted themselves on this damp sand. "You know who's been cast?"

"I'm merely pointing out that my desk is thirty feet from the man who makes the decisions."

"You *do* know!"

The next few seconds were the real test. If he were Cohn's mole, he'd pitch all the woo in his arsenal of charm in three, two, one . . .

"Well, I'll be." He faced the shoreline again and sank back on his elbows. "The whole world is dying to know who's going to play Scarlett O'Hara, and my girl is one of the few people who do."

Polly melted a little at those two words: *my girl*. All those years spent in solitary confinement, mulling over my gossamer-thin chances I'd meet a nice boy. And now I have. What a crushing shame Papa couldn't see this. "Those Selznick wives know how to put on a mighty good buffet. And I hear this Hitchcock chap is quite the gourmand."

"The Thrifty at Wilshire and Fourth has a lunch counter that serves till midnight. It won't be no caviar and lobster Thermidor, but they make the best grilled cheese sandwich in town."

As they got to their feet and brushed themselves clean of sand, Polly snuck a look at Gil.

He hadn't pushed her to tell him who would be playing Scarlett. That was a huge point in his favor. And he had a credible justification for his ugly run-in with Harry Cohn.

But that's the problem, Polly's inner skeptic warned. When push came to shove, his explanation had flowed out of him, letter-perfect, without a stumble, backtrack, or contradiction, with nary an 'um' or an 'ah.'

Polly picked up her handbag. Can't Gil simply be what he appears to be? And why are you so suspicious? Not everybody in this town pretends to be someone else for a living.

In any other town, I'd agree with you, the cynic said. But this is Hollywood. Everybody's acting.

35

Every muscle and joint in Polly's hands ached. Wrists, shoulders, and back, too. She checked her watch.

Thirty-five minutes until takeoff.

Or would it be more like a detonation? The Bomb that Destroyed David O. Selznick's Career?

Or maybe there wouldn't be any takeoff. The three messengers were supposed to be here well before noon.

"MARCELLA!" Mr. Selznick's voice boomed from his office. "ANY NEWS?"

She pantomimed wrapping her fingers around Selznick's neck. "YOU'LL BE THE FIRST TO KNOW."

The three-year talent search would finally end today. Mr. Selznick was ready to announce whom he had cast in the most sought-after role in Hollywood history. At exactly twelve o'clock, Marcella was to teletype his announcement to every news and media outlet in the world that he had cast a Brit. In the same press release, he would also be announcing that he'd cast Leslie Howard as Ashley Wilkes and Olivia de Havilland as Melanie. But Vivien Leigh's casting would hog the spotlight.

Keeping Miss Leigh's casting a secret had been a monumental task; only essential personnel had been permitted to know. Polly was surprised that nobody had blabbed. Especially with those newspaper stringers who loitered outside all the studios in the hope they'd catch word of a breaking news story that they could sell to the wire services.

In retrospect, though, maybe their success in keeping the secret wasn't such a surprise. Only a week ago, Polly had typed up a letter Mr. Selznick had dictated to Ed Sullivan in which he had detailed a five-point list of reasons why Miss Leigh's casting was, by no means, a sure bet yet. The two-page letter was sheer nonsense. But by putting an influential entertainment journalist off the scent, Selznick could prolong the anticipation until the last-possible moment.

What Selznick had counted on was that he would have Leigh's contract, de Havilland's contract, and Howard's contract in hand. Yes, yes, yes, their lawyers and agents had promised. The contracts will be signed and delivered first thing Friday morning.

But here they were, twenty-eight minutes before Marcella was due at the teletype. They couldn't transmit the press release until they had the signed contracts in hand—but where in tarnation were the messenger boys?

Mr. Selznick sagged against the jamb of his office doorway. "I shouldn't have given Winchell the scoop."

"You had to," Marcella reassured him. "His three-hour head start let him make the early edition. But sharing the news with the West Coast gives everyone here a chance to catch their late edition. But this whole scheme falls apart if we don't have—"

Footsteps slapping against the linoleum floor accompanied a reedy voice. "Gangway! Gangway!" A beanpole of a guy with bicycle clips binding the cuffs of his pants held a large envelope aloft. "I don't know what this is, but some lawyer told me to ride like the wind."

Marcella's phone rang, so Polly plucked the package out of his hand and checked the return address. "Leslie Howard!"

Selznick wrapped his arms around his chest as though it might forestall his coming apart at the seams. "Make sure all the dotted lines are filled in."

She had typed every version of this contract and knew which eleven places required Howard's signature. She opened the envelope and eyeballed the contents. "All present and accounted for."

"One down, two to go." Selznick paced the patch of floorboards in front of Marcella's desk, waiting for her to finish her call.

"I'll let him know." She thanked her caller and hung up. "That was my spy at the *L.A. Times*. Hedda's already gotten wind of Miss Leigh's casting. And I quote." She read from her steno pad. "'After two years and out of billions of American women, Mr. David O. Selznick couldn't find one to suit him and has cast a British—yes, that's right, *British*—actress as Scarlett O'Hara. I encourage all my readers to join me in boycotting what is bound to be a misguided atrocity.'" Marcella dropped her notebook. "Her and Louella's noses must be so out of joint right now it'll take a croquet mallet to whack them back into place."

Selznick chuckled more affably than Polly would have expected. "They'll change their tune when they see what Vivien's capable of. Remind me to call them later for some buttering-up."

He disappeared into his office as Hazel came flying in from the corridor. She looked wildly around and her gaze landed on Polly. "One of the guys from props, the one who's building the horse-drawn carriages, he's waiting for you outside. He's got something to show you."

After the night of the Hitchcock party, Polly had excavated a sliver of time to share her plan with Judd. Naturally, her moving to Catalina was out of the question, but he told her that if she paid him a management fee, say, twenty percent of the profits, he knew someone who might be coaxed into supervising the day-to-day. Even more exciting was his speculation that *if* they could clear sixty dollars in profits per week, it wasn't impossible that Papa's debt might be paid off in ten years. Granted, that was a mighty big if, but in theory, everything felt achievable. It was a huge load off Polly's shoulders during the busiest week of her life. Consequently, she'd had little time to see Gil—especially seeing as how the admin office and the props shop lay at opposite ends of the studio lot.

. . .

Gil paced the flagstone path that meandered throughout the front lot, a rolled magazine in one hand, a lit cigarette in the other.

"I can give you twenty seconds," she told him.

"You know those stringers that hang around the gate?" He unfurled the magazine. "One of them gave me this. Came out this morning." He shuffled the pages of *Photoplay* until he found an article headlined *HOLLYWOOD'S UNMARRIED HUSBANDS AND WIVES.* "It names celebrity couples who live together but aren't married. Robert Taylor and Barbara Stanwyck, Charlie Chaplin and Paulette Goddard, Constance Bennett and Gilbert Roland."

"Gil, I'm in the middle of—"

"One of the other couples is Carole Lombard and Clark Gable."

Polly snatched the magazine away from him. The public had demanded Clark play Rhett, but they also expected him to be respectable. "This is going to cause a scandal!"

"The stringer specified how Vivien Leigh and Lawrence Olivier aren't married either."

"Oh, cripes. They're mentioned, too?"

"No, but only because they're not famous enough."

"So it's only half a PR disaster."

Hedda's reaction had been entirely predictable, but this had come from out of nowhere. Let Marcella decide when to show it to Mr. Selznick, Polly decided.

Maybe I've been wrong to question him or his motives. Maybe he's on my side, after all.

Another barrage of running footsteps came at her from behind. A kid considerably younger than Polly sped past them.

Two down, one to go.

Polly followed him. "Thanks, Gil." She held up the *Photoplay.* "I mean it."

. . .

When she walked back into the office, Marcella gripped the contract as though it were the Olympic torch. "Olivia!"

Mr. Selznick called back, "Guess who promised me, faithfully, absolutely, one hundred percent that he'd have Vivien's contract on my desk by nine, come hell, high water, or Hades? And yet, here we are, eleven minutes before this scheme unravels like a cheap rug."

"His secretary told me the messenger picked it up an hour ago." Marcella turned to Polly. "Where did you get to?"

Wordlessly, Polly laid out the *Photoplay* in front of her.

Marcella read the headline. "Christ almighty. This is all we need."

There was a loud clunk as Mr. Selznick dropped his phone into its cradle. "What's going on?" he said, getting to his feet.

Marcella told him nothing he needed to worry about.

"You'll have to show him," Polly whispered.

Marcella nodded. "If he flies off the handle, I'll come running—and I might not stop till I reach Cincinnati. In which case, you'll have to do the teletype."

Did Polly want to be tasked with sending out a teletype that would be read around the world? No, siree, she most certainly did not.

"I'll take the *Photoplay* to him if you handle the press release." She crossed her mental fingers.

Marcella's eyes bounced between the magazine and the boss's office. "Our lord and master will kill me if it doesn't go out exactly as planned. I'd hate for you to be splattered with my blood. We're getting down to the wire, so I'll play lookout for Myron's delivery boy." She shoved the *Photoplay* into Polly's hands. "It's sure been nice knowing you."

Mr. Selznick was checking his wristwatch as she approached his desk. "Four minutes. I'm going to kill my fucking bro—" He tilted his face up to hers. "'Scuse my French." His eyes dropped to the *Photoplay* in her hands. "What gives?"

Polly unfolded the magazine at the double-page spread and let him take in the photos of the soon-to-be notorious couples.

"Remarkable timing, don't you think?" His voice was drier than week-old toast.

"In a way, you dodged a bullet."

"How do you figure?"

"Miss Leigh and Mr. Olivier aren't married either; nor are they famous enough to be included."

A third set of running footsteps approached them. A breathless voice, barely past puberty, wheezed, "My boss sends his apologies. I got here as fast I could. Honest injun."

Polly and Mr. Selznick hurried to the outer office, where Marcella was already running her finger down each page, stopping momentarily to check for Miss Leigh's signature, until she arrived at the final dotted line. "And that makes eleven!" She grabbed the final draft of the press release and bolted into the teletype room.

Mr. Selznick slouched against the edge of Marcella's desk. "Three years and my knuckleheaded sibling has to drag things out to the last possible moment." He tucked the *Photoplay* under his arm as he rose to his feet. "Follow me."

"Where are we going?"

"Now that I know the announcement is going out as planned, I need to check on the construction of Tara. Specifically, the front porch, where, God willing, we'll start filming soon."

Polly listened for the sound of Marcella at the teletype's keyboard. "The big announcement is going out. The phones'll start ringing any sec—"

"Marcella is the most capable secretary in Hollywood. I can now attend to the ten thousand other details. The most pressing of which is our opening shot."

She followed him past the secretarial pool where Hazel was standing between her desk and Polly's with a telephone pasted to each ear.

"Hold the fort until Marcella is done," Selznick called to her as he went by.

They trekked past Stages Two, Three, and Four, each of them abuzz with hammered nails, sawed wood, yelled commands. As they drew alongside the drapery department, Selznick stopped and pressed a hand against the brick wall as the color in his face slowly waned.

"Sir? Are you okay? Do you—"

"Bit winded, is all."

"When was the last time you slept?"

He inhaled a series of deep breaths and wagged a warning finger. "Trust me. My wife and brother have been on me about my hours, my diet, my sleep, and how I might not last the distance."

"Mr. Selznick, we haven't even started filming yet."

She cringed inwardly: how awfully presumptuous that "we" had been for a Girl Friday to say. She wished she could pull this conversation out of her typewriter and start over.

A flush of pink tinged his ashen cheeks. He let go of the wall and resumed his march. "Civil war pictures never make a dime, they all told me. 'The book's too sprawling.' 'You've bitten off more than you can chew.' If we can make the movie I see in my head, we'll prove every goddamn naysayer wrong. And if I have to lose a bit of sleep, then so be it."

The man was losing more than "a bit of sleep," but he had asked her along for some reason, and she doubted it was to act as an emergency nursemaid.

He waited until they were passing Stage Twelve, where Belle Watling's hotel would soon be ready for painting. "I saw you talking to Philip Wrigley at Myron's party," he said. "Was it about filming *Pretty Pennies* on Catalina?"

"No, sir." Polly had to hotfoot it to match his momentum. "Something else."

"Might you be willing to tell me what?"

With everything else going on, this was hardly the time to talk about how a resurrected Mad Ox might pay off her father's debt. But Polly could see how it might serve as a welcome distraction.

"I'm impressed you want to honor your father's debt," he said, after she had recapped recent events.

"I couldn't bear thinking that people remember him as a swindler."

"Did I ever tell you about the time he helped me clear one of my gambling debts?"

They both knew he hadn't, but it was his way of prodding the edges of a tender scar. "I'm a gambler by nature. Professional or personal, every move I've made involves taking a chance. On this particular occasion, I'd been on a lucky streak playing poker with Darryl Zanuck and Eddie Mannix and Sam Goldwyn."

"I'd imagine those men play hardball."

"To say the least." A pair of set decorators, each holding a basket loaded with pink-and-white paper magnolias, slowed their pace long enough to duck their heads toward the general. He returned their salute with a courteous nod of his own head. "But my luck changed, and before I knew it, I was in debt to the tune of"—he paused for flagrantly obvious dramatic effect—"ninety-eight thousand dollars."

The total of all the annual salaries of every Selznick employee wouldn't reach half that number. Not even if Clark's paycheck was thrown in for good measure. "Mister Selznick!"

"I know, I know." He slowed his pace once again. "You can't chastise me any more than I have already berated myself."

"And Papa came to your rescue?"

"I had a third of what I needed. I groveled to my father-in-law for another third."

"That can't have been easy."

"I wouldn't wish such profound ignominy on my worst enemy."

"Did my father supply the other third?"

"Without even so much as an IOU."

That turpentine tin in the back shed on Catalina, empty and discarded. Had it once held that amount of money? How could Papa have been so reckless? But where else was he supposed to put all those ill-gotten gains? He had to store it somewhere.

"Look," Mr. Selznick said, "I owe your father for what he did for me."

"You didn't pay him back?"

"I did—and as soon as I could. It's his unhesitating loyalty and trust I feel indebted to. Now that he's gone, I consider that debt transferred to you."

"What are you saying, sir?"

"I'd like to pay what your father owes Wrigley. Please let me do that. Okay?"

Polly's stomach contracted in on itself. If her boss hadn't been so rash, so gosh-darned irresponsible about gambling money he didn't have, Papa would have had more than enough to lend Harry Cohn without having to embezzle a dime. He'd still be alive today. 'Pay me with what money?' she wanted to ask. According to your wife, you overspend like an Ottoman sultan.

They crossed into the Forty Acres backlot, where *Wind*'s larger outdoor sets were under construction. She turned away from him to conceal her disgust.

"Thank you, Mr. Selznick, but I have the situation well in hand."

"You're an independent little thing, aren't you? And I admire that, but I also wish you'd change your mind." When she said nothing, he continued, "You're probably wondering why I asked you to come walking with me."

The shock that Papa had had enough money in his backyard tin had chased away any questions Polly might have had. "Because you want me to take notes?"

"I have a sensitive question to ask you. If the answer is no, I'll apologize immediately and we'll speak no more about it."

Polly kept her eyes fixed on the brick path as it veered to the left. "Sounds fair."

"Have you been planted here by Harry Cohn to spy on me?"

Polly stopped walking. "Excuse me?"

"Is that a no?"

Selznick either ignored or had failed to notice that he had rendered Polly immobile, forcing her to catch up yet again. "What on earth put that idea into your head?" she demanded when she was beside him once more.

"I happened to look out the filing room window and was shocked to see you talking to Harry Cohn's henchman." He slid the *Photoplay* from under his arm. "The one who handed you this."

"That's Gil," she said.

"Strangers don't stand so close to one another."

"He's not Cohn's henchman. More like his handyman. Broken doors, that sort of thing."

"You're dead wrong, Polly, my girl. That punk plays henchman to the meanest son of a bitch in Hollywood."

Polly felt as though someone had sucked the air out of her lungs. She kept walking. Up ahead, Tara's four freshly painted columns glowed in the winter sun. A dozen workmen buzzed about with hammers, buckets, and brushes. The decorators were knotting their paper magnolias to bushes lining the front porch. Polly wished Mr. Selznick would order her back to the office. She needed time to unscramble her chaotic mind.

"I can see I've burst your bubble." He'd taken the trouble to soften his voice, but still goaded her along the path.

"But how do you know?" Polly asked. "For *sure*, I mean."

"Back when I was at MGM, I made *Dancing Lady* with Clark, Myrna, and Franchot. Clark was still having an affair with Joan Crawford, but she and Franchot were making with the bedroom eyes at each other, which of course Gable was having none of. That picture had all the earmarks of a hit, so I wanted him for *Manhattan Melodrama*. As all that was going on, Cohn was campaigning to get Robert Montgomery and Myrna for *It Happened One Night*. Mayer wasn't going to hand over two of his biggest stars to a prick like Cohn. He said to me, 'Let that low-rent huckster find his own goddamned stars.' What did Cohn do? He asked for Gable instead. This was back when Gable was still on the way up, so he had to do what he was told."

"I bet he resented Mayer for shunting him over to Poverty Row."

Selznick appraised her with an admiring eye. "Very much so. But I told him, 'Look, Clark, working without complaint at that second-string outfit will demonstrate you're a good team player. This business is built on relationships, and doing this movie will show those who are watching you—and trust me, everybody is—what you're made of.'"

"In other words, you stroked his budding movie-star ego."

"And then I sweetened the pie and let him know he'd be working with one of Hollywood's best directors. Even back then I could tell Frank Capra was a talent to be reckoned with. 'Show up,' I told him. 'Know your lines. Be professional to Claudette. Watch how Capra works and learn from him.' What I neglected to tell Clark is that I tried to steal Capra out from under Cohn's nose and add him to my production unit. I might have pulled it off, but Cohn's spies blabbed and he talked Capra into staying. Meanwhile, he saved all his ire for me."

Selznick stopped and stared at Tara in the distance. He laid one arm across his thickening waist, and rested the elbow of the other on it, absentmindedly pinching his lower lip. "Perhaps when Scarlett is running to meet her father. Hmmm."

They were halfway to Tara. Once they arrived there, he'd be all business. "And Gil? How does he figure in all this?"

Mr. Selznick jolted himself out of his preoccupation. "I wanted to keep tabs on Gable because of *Manhattan Melodrama,* so I paid a camera assistant on *It Happened One Night* to report back to me. At first, Gable, Claudette, and Capra clashed and clashed. But two weeks in, things clicked into place, and they started getting along famously. By the end of filming, Prohibition was repealed, so I sent over to Columbia half a dozen bottles of one of Gable's favorite liquors: Mad Ox bourbon."

Polly remembered Clark drinking lots of it during that summer of *Mutiny on the Bounty,* but she had grown up surrounded by Mad Ox, so she had thought nothing of it.

"The next day, my spy reported that Cohn had found out about my delivery and sent someone to intercede."

"But he was partners with my father in Mad Ox bourbon."

"It wasn't the Mad Ox that stuck in his craw." Mr. Selznick permitted himself a satisfied smirk. "It was me. I was infuriated by the underhanded pettiness of it all. And I was still steamed a couple of days later when I was in the Field and Turf Room at the

Ambassador and saw Cohn across the room. He was with his wife and a couple of yes men. Now, remember, Prohibition had been repealed, so everyone was out getting as soaked as humanly possible."

"You were all tanked."

"To the gills."

"You took a swing at him?"

"Verbally, yes. Faster than you can say 'What Price Hollywood,' he's insulting my *King Kong*. I'm insulting his *Lady for a Day*. He's insulting my *Christopher Strong*. I'm insulting his *Mr. Deeds Goes to Town*. But when he started in on my *Dinner at Eight*, that's when I took a literal swing at him, hard enough to knock him on his keister."

But how did Gil figure in all this? They were so close to Tara now that Polly could hear the hammering. "Did he retaliate?"

"One night later, I was leaving the Trocadero when I caught one of his minions attacking my brand-new Chrysler Imperial. He'd punctured all my tires, and was now scraping a jackknife along the paint job. I've never been so mad. This all happened late at night, so neither of us could see each other well. But when I called out, 'Hey you!' he turned around long enough for the streetlight to reveal his face. And I saw that it was—what's his name, this guy you're sweet on?"

"Gil."

"Right. So, what I want to know is what the devil is he doing here?"

"Harold Coles liked his work on *The Wizard of Oz*. His specialty is horse-drawn carriages, and we need a whole bunch for *Wind*."

Mr. Selznick's face fell into a glower. "I will *not* have one of Cohn's henchmen on my lot."

"He's the best carriage maker in Hollywood."

"I don't care if he's the best goddamn carriage builder since the Civil War." Selznick handed her the *Photoplay*. "Put this on my desk when you get back to the office."

Polly felt like Selznick had clobbered her over the head. Cohn's handyman, she could live with. But *henchman* wasn't a word she could pretend she hadn't heard. She would have preferred to hear Gil's side of the story, but Mr. Selznick's word was law.

"You're right about dodging a bullet, about Vivien and Larry being omitted because they're not famous enough," Selznick admitted. "But still, my two leads are living in sin."

"Shall I take this magazine to Mr. Birdwell?"

He stared at the *Photoplay* in Polly's hands. "Russell has done a masterful job coordinating the search for Scarlett. Containing this crisis should be a cakewalk. So, yes, take it to him."

"Anything else, sir?"

He started out for Tara. "Go find Harold Coles and tell him to get that hoodlum the hell out of my studio."

36

Polly poked at a shrimp in her salad with a chunk of Ry-Krisp cracker as Gil told her, Luddie, and Amelia of his firing. "Just like that!" He pounded the Schwab's lunch counter with his fist. "Out on my ass."

"Did your boss give you any reason?" Luddie asked.

"All I got was, 'Sorry, kiddo. Things haven't worked out.' I was shocked. I'm *still* shocked. There's a scene where Scarlett gets attacked while she's driving a wagon through the countryside. It's a beauty, but I hadn't finished it. Good luck finding anyone who can do the job half as well. Let alone start immediately, seeing as how filming kicks off Monday."

He slid a finger along Polly's bare forearm until he reached her wrist. "I needed to see you after the crazy day I had yesterday."

She wanted to pull away from him. Revoke his touching privileges. All of them. *You're Cohn's henchman*. Harder still was this act, feigning ignorance of his firing. "You and me both."

Luddie slung his arm around her shoulders. "I can only imagine how tired you must be with the entire country talking about Selznick's decision."

"What's three levels beyond 'exhausted'?"

"Debilitated?" Amelia grabbed up a double order of fried-egg sandwiches and took off. Eight o'clock Saturday night was the start of Schwab's busiest evening of the week.

"Until the movie comes out, half-day Saturdays are a dim memory."

Gil picked a shrimp out of Polly's salad. "But that's a whole year away."

"Exactly."

At seven the evening of the Vivien Leigh press release, Marcella had called a ceasefire and escorted the girls out of the building. All the others were most likely out cold in their beds already. For Polly, however, there would be no rest until she settled the Gil situation.

"Has Hedda Hopper stormed the castle yet?" Amelia picked up a hot corned beef club sandwich and a root beer float. "Her column this morning! Boy howdy! That woman is angrier than a poked bear with distemper."

"This place will get packed soon." Polly shoved a menu across to Gil. "You should order. Meanwhile"—she slid off her stool—"I'm shanghaiing Mister Sinclair."

Luddie looked at her with skeptical eyes.

"I need a second opinion on a perfume I'm thinking of getting Aunt Cora for her birthday."

She led him to the retail side of the store, where floral scents intermingled with citrusy notes.

"Since when do women need help with perfume?"

"Since Mr. Selznick told me about an ugly run-in he had with Gil, and how Gil doesn't only do odd jobs on the side for Harry Cohn. He's one of Cohn's henchmen." She paused to let Luddie insist, "I knew it!" But he merely nodded, slowly and calmly. "This is the part where you say, 'I told you so.'"

"I was thinking about Gil's New Year's Eve story," he said, earnest as a preacher, "and how he said he struck up a conversation with some random stranger who happened to be next to him."

"It wasn't like that?"

"Nothing random about it. Gil approached the prop guy and did most of the talking, standing over him like a Doberman pinscher. 'You owe me, buster, and I'm now calling in the favor. Get me that job!'"

Polly wanted to look across the drugstore, but didn't dare in case Gil caught her eye. "You saw all this from the dance floor?"

Luddie nodded. "I asked him about it later on, but by then he was no longer steamed."

"How was he?"

"Just his usual self."

"Why didn't you tell me about any of this?"

"I figured I could be wrong. You work such long hours and now your beau is working on the same lot, so I hoped things would settle down. And I thought they had until I saw all those scrapes and cuts."

"What scrapes and cuts?"

"His hands are covered with them."

"They are?"

"All over."

"How come I haven't noticed?"

"He's been keeping his hands in his pockets."

They returned to the counter as Gil was handing his menu to Amelia. His hands were scabby battlefields. "They're awfully banged up," she said, sliding onto her stool. "Where have you been, the Battle of Verdun?"

"Between the hammers and the nails, handsaws, and circular saws, carpentry is a messy job."

It was a reasonable explanation, but his hands had never looked like that before. "They're bound to have a salve for that in the retail section."

She skewered a shrimp with a tiny salad fork, deep in thought.

Selznick and Cohn had feuded.

Papa and Cohn had, too.

Gil got a job at Selznick International, where Elroy's daughter works.

She squirmed in her seat. All this felt way too coincidental. She had to break up with him. But she'd never had a boyfriend before.

How do people do that?

* * *

Dread and apprehension prevented Polly from enjoying the rest of her shrimp salad. She picked at a banana split until the invading after-theater crowd jammed the Schwab's counter so tightly that it was time to call it a night.

Wishing Amelia the best of luck with the onslaught, Polly, Gil, and Luddie stepped outside into the wintry night. A light rainfall had slicked the Sunset Boulevard sidewalk; the red neon rimming the *SCHWAB'S PHARMACY* sign bled across the asphalt.

Luddie pointed west toward the Garden of Allah Hotel. "I'm thataway." He raised his eyebrows at Polly. *You okay?*

She winked back. *Yep, thanks for asking.*

Gil slid his arm around her waist. "I'll walk you to your car."

"No need. I'm parked close by on Laurel Avenue."

"Nonsense." He was shooting for a mix of flippant and gallant, but managed to fall short and ended up sounding condescending.

She replied with silence and set off toward her car. Gil fell into lockstep beside her, his arm still firmly around her waist.

The streetlight nearest to her Chevrolet was fifty feet away; the rest of the street was in near-darkness. She wished him a noncommittal, "G'night," but he turned and ground his hips into hers, and her hips against the passenger door, and moaned into her ear, "How about a proper goodbye kiss?"

She pushed him away. "Not tonight."

"What gives?"

"Nothing. I—"

"Don't give me any of that 'Nothing's wrong' crap. You've been chillier than Jack Frost all evening. When I told you I lost my job, you barely reacted."

Even though he was right, she figured she should make a token objection. "That's not true."

"The hell it ain't. I got canned with no notice, no warning. For all the sympathy I got from you, I may as well have said I'd lost a button. I had to walk off the lot like I was some sort of criminal. Is it too much to expect my girlfriend—"

"I don't want to see you anymore." Her words erupted forth, startling her like a thunderclap.

"What?! You're breaking up—with—me?" Gil staggered back as though she had walloped him with a roundhouse.

Oh, I get it. Putting on a performance, are we? "Stop embarrassing yourself with this" —she flicked a scornful wrist at him—"display." He went to respond, but it would only be more hot air. "You know why I'm breaking up with you."

"THE HELL I DO!" He punched a nearby telephone pole with the side of his fist. "Jesus, Polly, talk about kicking a dog when he's down."

"That's not—"

He lunged forward and grabbed her shoulders, crushing them with his powerful hands. "I thought you were different, but you're like all the others, aren't you? Fickle as weather vanes. Smiles and flirty when the sun's out. But when things take a turn for the worse, you're off and running"—he sank his jagged fingernails deeper into her skin—"like I've got enough syphilis to infect half of LA."

"Stop!" Her shoulders burned from the pain. Anger flared in his eyes and consumed his face. "You're hurting me." She cast around, peering through the dreary night, hoping there might be someone walking their dog or putting out the trash. "Quit it, Gil." She raised the pitch of her voice in the hope it sounded more playful. "Quit squeezing me like a ripe tomato."

"You're all ripe tomatoes. Plump and red and juicy. All the prop guys at Selznick call you Miss Aloof. I've been defending you to them. Telling them, 'No, you've got her all wrong. She's only shy, is all, until you get acquainted.' What a joke. You ain't nothin' but a—but a—"

Polly wrenched herself free. "At least I'm not some tyrant's henchman."

"You talking about Cohn?"

"You know I am."

"I'm his handyman. Odd jobs. That's all."

"Does that include stabbing car tires and carving off paint?"

He turned his head to the side. "Selznick."

"And how Cohn needed fifty grand, but came up short, so he bulldozed my father into embezzling the rest from Wrigley, and then reneged on paying him back. That's why my father got chased down by the cops. And why they ended up shooting him. Dead, Gil. They shot him *dead*."

"Just because your gutless father—"

GUTLESS? The last sprig of fear inside Polly disintegrated. "Have you been spying on me for Harry Cohn? To keep tabs on what I was doing? And did you finagle your way into Selznick International to spy on David Selznick too? Or to sabotage *Gone with the Wind*?"

"You're not half as clever as you think you are." Gil tensed his hands into fists and paced the wet sidewalk. "This whole town—no, this whole world—you can't count on nobody for nothin'. Everybody's out for themselves."

"Harry Cohn, worst of all."

"Lemme tell you this." He stood close enough now that she could feel the heat of his breath. "He's the only person who has always, always, *always* kept his word. Okay, so maybe he's forced me to do some crummy things—"

"'Maybe'?" He was dead wrong if he thought shoving his face up against hers could be an intimidation tactic. "You're justifying your actions because the guy pays you. He's a heartless tyrant who's only out for himself—"

"I ain't listening to anyone condemn—" He shoved her against the car, knocking the wind from her lungs. She felt the door handle bite into the flesh over her hip. He raised a fist. She had to think fast.

She gripped the shoulder strap of her clamshell purse and swung it like a sockful of quarters. She had meant it as a warning shot and wasn't prepared to hear its rigid exterior thwack against his cheek. The blow sent him staggering backward into the low brick fence behind him.

"Harry Cohn is the wrong horse to back," she said icily. How delightfully ironic that Gil had given her this weapon she'd used to slug him off his feet.

His knees buckled and he dropped to the ground. He muttered, "Screw you," before getting unsteadily to his feet and slinking into the shadows without so much as a backward glance.

Fighting to still her trembling fingers, she opened the door and heaved herself into the driver's seat. Doubt wrapped itself around her like the legs of a spider. Had she done the right thing? Could she have handled that better? Might she have been able to turn this situation around?

NO! She slapped the wheel hard as she could. *You fell for a louse.* This town is lousy with louses, so chances are you'll tangle with at least another one. Meanwhile, you've got a demanding job and a bourbon distillery to set up.

She turned the key and the engine roared to life.

"Good riddance," she muttered as she pulled away from the curb.

37

The biting ocean winds died down as the crew of the *Avalon* ran through their assigned tasks to guide the steamship alongside the pier. Polly turned to Judd and Desmond, the guy from City of Angels Distillery whom Judd wanted to talk into moving to Catalina.

"Try not to read too much into the chilly reception from the natives," she told them. "Since the news of my father broke, I've been as welcome as a pimple on prom night."

Amelia harrumphed. "As far as they're concerned, you stole that money yourself."

"In other words, don't be surprised if our rooms overlook the laundry."

Two long blasts from the ship's horn announced the gangway was in place.

Polly had been in no rush to return to Catalina. It had been no fun seeing people she'd known her whole life treat her like she was a clown at a funeral.

But a week ago, Amelia had bounded into the apartment with the news that one of her father's trusted lieutenants, Desmond Clift, was open to resurrecting Mad Ox. With *Wind* starting in five days, Polly doubted she could get a Saturday off, but when she asked Marcella, she'd told her, "Take it. The good Lord knows you've earned it."

Mr. Selznick had approached her later that day. "I hear you're off to Catalina." She had tried to explain the trip's purpose, but he had cut her off and suggested she do some advance location scouting for *Pretty Pennies*. How could she say no when he offered to foot the bill for passage on the steamer, meals, and rooms at the MacRae on Crescent, right across from the water?

It wasn't until Catalina Island had appeared on the horizon that it had occurred to her it was far too early to scout for locations. Mr. Selznick's offer was a tacit helping hand.

Polly had been the lone passenger on deck. Everyone else had elected to stay indoors, enjoying afternoon tea and a few laps around the dance floor while the six-man band played chipper tunes for spirited vacationers. The main cabin had felt too crammed with cheerful faces, so she had fled to the bow of the ship, where she braved choppy seas and lashings of salt spray to distract herself from revisiting that ugly scene with Gil. She could still feel his fingers digging into her shoulders, his humid breath heating her face, and the caustic way he had called Papa "gutless."

"What a low-down, dirty crumb," Amelia had said over eggs and waffles the following morning. "But you're rid of him now. There's bound to be a cute scenic artist or greensman somewhere around." But Polly had wet her feet enough to last her into the foreseeable future, thanks but no thanks.

She led them from Steamer Pier and along Crescent and pointed to the block along Sumner. "Our hotel is right there," she told Desmond. Earlier that day, Judd had taken Polly aside and told her to highlight the advantages of living here. "That's what's so great about island life. Nothing is more than a couple of blocks from anywhere. No traffic jams!"

Mr. Selznick's back lot is bigger than this place. How could I have been content living in such a small town?

"Do you miss it?" Desmond asked. With his handlebar mustache and thinning hair combed down the middle with medical precision, Desmond looked like he'd walked out of a

Roaring Twenties speakeasy, but he had his rarely-gets-home-before-two-a.m. charms.

"A bit," she said, not dishonestly. "I'm still new to LA, where everything is bright and exciting." She pointed out Piper's Cafeteria. "Decent meals for decent prices. You can't go wrong with the squab or fried scallops, but their Chinese Chow Mein?" She pinched her nose as Mr. Piper stepped outside. When he spotted Polly, he waved his hand in a wide crescent. "Hey, Polly! How's it going?"

Had the man not been reading *The Islander*?

She returned Piper's enthusiastic wave. "Fine, thanks."

Hotel MacRae was not as plush as the St. Catherine, but its location was more convenient for an overnight stay. Black-and-white tiles checkerboarded the floor of the dark foyer; a pair of lighthouse-shaped lamps bracketed the front desk. The clerk peered at them through gold-rimmed glasses. "Polly!"

"Roger?"

This boy had always been nice enough to her, even though they'd barely spoken the entire time they'd gone through high school. He spun the check-in book on its turntable and handed her a fountain pen. "I brightened up this morning when I saw your name among today's incoming guests."

First Mr. Piper and now Roger? How had she transformed from disgraced grifter to distinguished guest in less than a month? "When will our rooms be ready?"

"I've already aired them out. You're in nine and ten, upstairs, facing the water."

"Thank you, Roger. We appreciate that."

He handed over two keys, each hanging from a polished brass disk. "The café opens at six-thirty each morning."

Polly led the others to the stairwell. What the heck was going on?

* * *

Amelia blew a raspberry as she and Polly hiked up the road. "You told Des nothing in Avalon is more than a couple of blocks away."

"It isn't," Polly said. "But Papa's distillery sits outside the city limits."

"That's inconvenient, I must say."

"Not to the townsfolk. The stink can be dreadful."

Amelia surveyed the sharp hairpin turn ahead of them where Stagecoach Road angled upward into the hills. "It's why I didn't like to visit Pop at work. That corn-yeast-malt mash? What a god-awful stench."

"Almost as bad as that jerk I dumped." Polly kicked a pebble up the hillside; it didn't get far before it rolled down toward her again. "Honestly, how could I have missed all the signs?"

"What signs?"

"That he was such a stinker."

"O-o-o-h!" Amelia stretched a two-letter word into five syllables. "Guys come with red lights and neon warning signs, do they? Listen, some of them excel at hiding who they are. Especially in Hollywood. The place is swarming with actors. Some of them even act on the screen."

Stagecoach Road sloped more steeply than Polly recalled. Had her backside grown a little too soft sitting at that typewriter for days on end? At least here on Catalina, she'd had that daily climb up the hill to the telegraph office. "Is this the part where I chalk one up to experience?"

"Besides, if you married him," Amelia added in a stage whisper, "you'd have become Polly Powell, and that's a ridiculous name."

Her wisecrack generated a laugh Polly hadn't realized she'd needed. "You lucked out with Benji. He seems like one of the good guys."

"Yeah." Amelia was now breathing harder than Polly. "Except that right now, he's rolling around sand dunes where Arizona meets Mexico." She threw up her hands like she was being robbed at gunpoint. "I asked for interesting, so I ain't complaining. But holy Moses, doesn't Mr. Wellman care how long a month is?"

They meandered up the gravel path and around several more tight bends until they had reached Stagecoach Viewpoint, which presented a broad vista across the channel to the mainland.

Polly hadn't often ventured this far out of town and had forgotten what an eye-popping panorama it provided. "I wish I'd appreciated this place more." She jotted down *Stagecoach Viewpoint* in the notebook she'd brought with her, and added a brief description in case Mr. Selznick truly expected an inventory of potential locations.

"At the risk of stating the obviously obvious," Amelia said, "the locals are treating you differently now, aren't they?"

Polly looked up from her notebook. "You noticed it too?"

"I'm surprised that kid at the hotel didn't ask you out on a date."

They returned to the path, where the road leveled out. "Four weeks ago, everyone was shunning me like I was the town witch. But it appears I'm no longer the Typhoid Mary of Catalina."

A final curve revealed Mad Ox's red-brick building. One story, but tall, with half a dozen broad windows lining the south wall, it was pretty much as she remembered.

An envelope marked *Santa Catalina Island Company* in gold-embossed lettering had awaited Polly in her hotel room. It held a key wrapped in a sheet of paper on which was written in elegant copperplate, "Front door, distillery. Return to hotel front desk when finished." She inserted the key in the lock, but it was unnecessary. The door's rusting hinges squeaked a half-hearted protest as she pushed it open.

The chaotic fiasco spread out in front of them like a war-torn disaster zone. From one end of the hall to the other, mesh baskets, glass jars, rubber-stoppered bottles, and metal canisters lay strewn and battered. Hessian bags, once filled with yeast and malt, were ripped to shreds, their contents dumped all over the floor.

Tiny fragments of shattered glass crunched underfoot.

"Jumping Jesus!" She walked over to one of the large mash kettles and examined dents bigger than her fist.

They stood in silence, taking in the rubble that had once been the heart of a thriving business. A blue jay hopped into the open doorway. He chirped his quiet melody of clicks, whirrs, and whines like a one-bird Greek chorus tsk-tsking this calamitous turn of events.

Polly absently caressed the kettle's damaged copper surface. It was useless now. Everything was. "Let's go." She stomped past Amelia and escaped outside. The blue jay skittered out of her way, still trilling his condolences. She returned to Stagecoach Road and headed downhill, Amelia trotting to keep up with her. "All that stuff back there, I can't imagine any of it comes cheap. Why not steal it? Nobody's around. Sell it off piece by piece with nobody the wiser. What vindictive son of a bitch—"

Gil's hands.

Those cuts and scrapes.

Polly lurched to a stop and stared at Amelia, eyes wide.

"No!" Amelia said. "You think?"

"Too far-fetched?" Polly asked.

"He'd have to be awfully angry to come all this way. Doesn't sound likely, does it?"

Only if we're starring in a Cagney–Bogart crime picture, Polly thought, with tough-guy racketeers, man-eating femme fatales, and machine guns with enough slugs to end every argument.

Or did she only want to think that? How could someone she'd been so awfully keen on be capable of reducing all that expensive equipment to heaps of junk?

"Harry Cohn is a vindictive pig," Amelia said. "By letting Mad Ox pay back the debt, he gets off scot-free. Why endanger that when he's still financially wobbly?" She lowered her voice into a grating snarl. "'If *Mr. Smith* flops, I'm more fucked than a three-dollar hooker during Fleet Week.'"

"You're right. It doesn't make sense. But you know what does?"

"Noah-the-accountant's theory."

"Cohn thought he was Mister Big Shot Tough Guy, hanging around with Zwillman and Roselli and Siegel and Cohen—until he learns there's a fifty-thousand-dollar hit on him. Then all those gangsters back off. 'Good luck with that, buddy boy.'"

"I bet it was a bitter pill for him to swallow. Too bad he didn't choke on it."

They had reached the road's sharpest hairpin turn. Around the tight corner lay the edge of town. Polly riffled through every name she could think of. "All it takes is one influential journalist to do some digging."

"You're planning on taking this to Hedda Hopper? She'd run hog wild if this got out."

"I need someone with more heft than that old bag." The exact right name came to Polly like a bolt of electricity. "Aggie Underwood loves to sink her teeth into the dramas that play out at the corner of Hollywood Boulevard and Gangster Avenue."

Amelia clutched at Polly's arm. "Are you sure talking to Aggie is the best course of action?"

"That shambles at the distillery was no coincidence. If there's one lesson I've learned from working for Selznick, it's that no problem is insurmountable if you keep chipping away at it. But," Polly added with a laugh, "if you see me starting in on the Benzedrine, that's when you call the loony bin."

Roger was still behind the desk when they returned to the hotel. He had a note from Judd saying the meeting with the harbor master had gone well, and to meet them at El Encanto at two o'clock. It was almost that time now, so they were on their way when Polly hesitated at the stained-glass doors.

"I don't suppose you had a Gil Powell registered with you recently?" she asked Roger.

"Not that I recall. But the St. Catherine got flooded with a busted pipe, so we took some of their guests." Roger ran a finger down the names listed in the hotel register. He was two pages in when he stopped. "We had a Powell Gilbertson."

Polly eyeballed Amelia. *Jackpot.*

"Do you remember him?" Amelia asked.

"Yeah . . ." Recognition filled Roger's face. "Quiet guy. Almost sullen. I tried to draw him out. Told him with a name like that, he should be an actor or a writer. He wasn't flattered or amused."

"Did he have brown eyes and a mop of dark curls?"

"Hmmm. I do remember thinking he'd need cement to keep those curls at bay. Oh, and by the way"—Roger leaned across the counter—"we're all thrilled you're starting Mad Ox up again. It'll be a real shot in the arm for the island's economy."

Polly looked at Amelia. *This is why everybody's been so nice.* How could they know their bonhomie was wasted effort? Without the equipment, and without the funds to replace it, Mad Ox was dead in the water.

* * *

Aggie Underwood suggested they rendezvous at the It Café on Vine Street at nine. Polly and Amelia had arrived home from Long Beach only an hour before, so it had been a Keystone Kops scramble to get there on time. She walked in to find the place three-quarters filled with a lively crowd, most of whom were on their third or fourth highball if the volume of their cocktail chatter was anything to go by.

Underwood's *Herald-Express* articles had always impressed Polly with their candor. Whether she was reporting on gambling raids, bank robbery shootouts, or the Long Beach earthquake, Underwood wrote with appealingly frank directness. She also sounded like the kind who'd stick to her word when asked to keep their conversation off the record.

Booths lined the north wall. Upholstered in diagonal stripes and backlit with chrome Art Deco lamps, each one was occupied. Tucked into an unobtrusive corner sat a single woman with a squarish face, wavy hair parted to the side, and the air of a pragmatic gal-in-a-rush.

"Miss Underwood?"

The reporter snuffed out her cigarette butt in a brass ashtray. "You're Elroy's kid, aren't you?"

Before Polly had finished peeling off her gloves and unpinning her hat, a waiter had appeared to take her drink order. Underwood was having an Old Fashioned—"though sadly not with Mad Ox bourbon"—so Polly ordered the same.

"I chose this place on purpose." Underwood lit another cigarette. "Phil took this place over from Clara Bow after she and that movie-cowboy husband of hers decamped to Nevada."

"Phil?"

"Selznick, your boss's uncle. Never mentioned him to you?"

This woman was sharper than Polly had supposed, which helped allay any fears she might have turned to the wrong person. "Mr. Selznick keeps us on our toes all day long, Miss Underwood."

"Oh, I bet he does." Hers was a throaty, nicotine-stained laugh. "And call me Aggie. So, why are we here?"

"I need some advice, and I wasn't sure where to turn."

"I assumed you had a story to pitch me."

"I do. It involves the mob."

Aggie set down her drink hard enough to rattle the brass ashtray. "Now you have my attention."

"First, let me say that everything I've cobbled together is circumstantial, so I could be way off the mark."

"Duly noted."

"I feel like I've sunk neck-deep into a pit of quicksand and nobody is throwing me a rope. For that matter, I don't even know if there's a rope within a hundred-mile radius. I'm in—I'm out of my depth, and I just—"

Polly cringed at the thought of losing her composure in front of this hard-boiled dame. Courage was easy on faraway Catalina, but now she was sitting with someone who possessed more streetwise sass than everybody in this bar combined.

The waiter appeared with their drinks and told Aggie he figured she was due for a second round.

Aggie clinked her glass with Polly's. "Let's start at the beginning."

"I'm not even sure where the beginning is."

Aggie took a gulp of her drink and a deep drag from her cigarette. "Your dad was a bootlegger who turned legit. Then he opened up a gambling den next to some old Chinese tub. Let's go from there."

A jumbling waterfall of names and dates and places gushed out of Polly. None of it was in chronological order, or any sort of logical order at all. As the words tumbled from her mouth, she doubted Aggie was following along. But she persisted until she had staggered to the end and then, lifting her glass, nearly emptied her Old Fashioned.

"I've heard worse," Aggie said.

"I'm normally more articulate than that."

"Want to hear what I think?"

"Desperately."

"Okay, so first off, we all knew about Elroy's bootlegging on Catalina back in the day. And we all agreed he made the best bourbon in Southern California. However, I doubt many people were aware your father's silent partner was Harry Cohn."

"Sounds like you did, though."

She tapped the side of her nose. "It's my job. Elroy and Harry enjoyed an amicable relationship based on mutual advantages. And when your father went legit, Harry understood how making Mad Ox available only on Catalina was a plus." She took a sip of her drink and eyed Polly speculatively. "Okay, so now I have a confession."

If this woman had a confession, it must be a doozie.

Aggie wasn't the type to wear makeup, so when she bit down hard on her lower lip, there was no lipstick to ruin. "I'm friendly with Mickey Cohen, who arrived in LA when Bugsy Siegel called him to the West Coast to be his lieutenant. He and I discussed your father."

Oh, brother. This didn't sound good. "And?"

"We'd been talking about Bioff and Browne. D'you know who they are?"

Polly shook her head.

"Willie Bioff and George Browne are medium-level East Coast gangsters sent here to infiltrate the studios by taking control of the unions. Took them a while, but they did it."

"How long ago was this?"

"A few years. And now those two schmucks call all the shots."

"Mayer and Zanuck and Warner must love that."

"HA!" Aggie blew a plume of smoke straight up in the air, where it mingled with the cloud forming on the restaurant's black-tiled ceiling. "For some reason, Harry Cohn was immune to all this intrigue and manipulation."

"Why would these Bioff and Browne characters let him off the hook?"

"My gut tells me it's connected to a strike from a few years ago. Sound Local Six-Ninety-Five downed tools against Columbia. Harry, being Harry, refused to budge. The strike was crushed and union membership plummeted. Skip to last year. Mickey's now in LA and he hears about Mad Ox bourbon and wants Harry to get him lined up with a few bottles. It wasn't like Mickey wanted the hooch for free. He likes his bourbon and wanted to sample the local brew he'd heard so much about. But Harry exploded at the idea."

"Did Mickey say why?"

"He got the impression that things had gone sour between your father and Harry. When I asked him for particulars, he shrugged and said he didn't know, but the story he'd heard was that Clark Gable had a front-row seat."

Clark *again*? Why did it feel like all roads in Hollywood led not to fame, but to Gable?

"Did you ever bring it up with him?" Polly asked.

"All that glamour malarkey isn't my beat. Mickey made out like he knew about how Bioff and Browne tied into all this, too. I might have chased that story, but not long afterward, I went to a fundraising dinner at the Biltmore for the Hollywood Anti-Nazi League, which was more my beat. So I'll say to you what Mickey said to me: Go ask Gable."

Polly knew that Clark's final costume-fitting session was this coming Thursday; it would be the only chance she would have to see him before he nosedived into production the following Tuesday.

And, Polly mused, Walter still owed her that favor from when she told him Vivien Leigh had been cast. "I can't thank you enough for your help, Aggie."

The reporter shrugged off Polly's compliment. "If it helps square things for your dad, I'm all for it."

Polly surveyed the restaurant for signs of a waitress. "How's the food here?"

"They do a nice minute steak. Veal scallopini's good, too. Why? Are we eating?"

"It'll please my boss if I go into work tomorrow and mention that I've dined at Uncle Phil's."

"In that case, we're ordering the Roast Chicken Parisienne. It's for two and the most expensive item on the menu. If Phil's paying for it, we might as well order up big."

"Who says Uncle Phil's paying?"

"I do." Aggie tapped her on the wrist. "David is famous for working his secretaries to death. Take the perks where you find them."

38

The week after her meeting with Aggie Underwood, Polly walked up to the security gate, half-heartedly covering up her yawn. It wasn't yet six a.m. and already the studio was buzzing with activity. Now that *Gone with the Wind* had finally, thankfully, and excitedly commenced production, she sensed the vigor in the air.

The guard, a sun-weathered version of Fatty Arbuckle, greeted her with a tip of his cap. "Yesterday was a big day, huh, Miss Maddox?"

"At long last, yes."

"When I saw you hoisting the Confederate flag up the pole out front, I hadda blink to make sure I wasn't dreaming."

Flying the Confederate flag to publicize the start of production had been Russell Birdwell's idea. Polly had been the only person in the executive office who'd run any sort of flag up a pole, so the job had fallen to her.

"How did filming go yesterday?" Buck asked.

"After Mr. Selznick, Mr. Cukor, and Miss Leigh shook off their nerves, the porch scene progressed fairly smoothly."

"I love how the first scene they shoot is the first scene in the book."

Most studio guards were humorless men who took their gatekeeping role seriously. Buck, however, was always ready to chat. Polly would have spent a few more minutes, but she needed to make a stop before heading into the office. Bidding him farewell, she skirted past the screening room and carpentry shop and into the wardrobe department.

Elaborate hoop skirts, voluminous petticoats, bustles, and corsets filled the long western wall. The droning of dozens of sewing machines choked the air, and the unmistakable trill of Walter Plunkett soared above it all. Polly found him at the workbench next to his office, hacking at a dark green skirt with a pair of scissors. Huge singe marks had blackened the hem.

"You had a fire?" she asked him.

"Last month, some girl showed up thinking she was testing for Scarlett, obliviously unaware it wasn't her test but Hattie's. Somehow, this skirt caught fire. The luckless creature was lucky to escape getting burned; however, she wasn't wearing any underwear—*and* the cameras were rolling."

"Oh, no!"

He shot her a wary look. "I swore everyone to secrecy. I do *not* need our boss doubting my ability to run a tight ship." Walter slid the blades straight upwards and cut out a panel of silk. "So now I'm reusing the dress for color tests and dye sampling. By the way, I know why you're here."

"You do?"

"Mr. Selznick hates the patio dress, and now I have to come up with something more virginal." He took in her blank expression. "What?"

"I'm here to call in that favor you owe me."

He snipped the panel into strips. "You've picked a hell of a time."

"All I need is ten minutes with Gable."

"He's only got one more fitting. Cukor has decided Clark should wear a black velvet jacket when we introduce the audience to Rhett."

"The fitting's at eleven. Yes, I know."

Walter smiled for the first time. "I'll send a studio runner with a message that you're needed in Costuming. Gable is causing a ruckus and is asking for you. But drop everything. I've only got him for an hour. He needs to be back in his car by noon."

* * *

Selznick's secretarial staff had been clinging to the hope that once production started, Mr. Selznick would be on the set and their workload might lighten. But he knew the location of every phone on the entire lot, each of which he used to bark orders and request reminders.

"Wouldn't it be nice to eat lunch in the commissary?" Marcella mused.

"One day," Polly told her, "we'll have the baked pork chops."

"With whipped potatoes and creamed spinach."

"Maple nut layer cake for dessert.

"With coffee—no. *Two* coffees."

Fantasizing about a day that wasn't likely to arrive helped relieve the pressure of awaiting a tidal wave that nobody was certain would ever reach the shore. However, it wasn't so bad that Polly couldn't monitor the time as she plowed through a busy morning. But when eleven o'clock became eleven-ten, then eleven-fifteen, then eleven-twenty, Polly's attention strayed from Selznick's memo to the Breen Office, a pre-emptive strike centering on his determination to insert the word "damn" into Rhett's final line.

If she told the girls she was in the filing room, she could slip out the side door.

If she ran full tilt, she'd reach Costuming in three or four minutes.

If she had five or six with Clark and then three back, she'd only be gone for ten.

"Which one of you is Polly?"

Studio runners were like messenger delivery boys: fresh out of high school and brimming with enough boisterous energy to last the day hurtling around the lot.

"I am."

"Mr. Selznick wants to see you on set."

Polly gaped at him. "When?"

"Immediately."

* * *

Selznick finished dispensing instructions to *Wind*'s cinematographer for their next setup, then turned to Polly. "I have thoughts I need to get down on paper." They sat on the steps of Tara's porch, away from the flurry of activity. "I'd forgotten how being in production can be so stimulating," he said, surveying the crew. "I'm brimming over with ideas. They're bursting out of me like butterflies from a cocoon!"

Polly poised her pencil at the top of her notebook and waited.

He had been right about the bursting butterflies. *Gone with the Wind*, *Rebecca*, *Intermezzo*, *Pretty Pennies*—how the man was able to juggle four disparate projects still astounded her.

Selznick's dictation lasted until they were ready for the next take. "Type these up by this afternoon. Separate pages for each picture." He didn't stick around to ask if Polly had any questions.

It was now nearly twelve-thirty. Clark would be long gone. But Costuming would be on her way back to the office if she took the path via the water tower.

She knocked on Walter's doorjamb. "I don't suppose . . .?"

He pulled his scrutiny from a sketch of a crimson dress with feathers enveloping bare shoulders. "I tried to hold him. We worked past the hour, but he kept muttering about meeting Carole for lunch. It's a pity that you missed him—"

"Where'd he park?"

"South, near the writers' bungalows. He—"

Polly didn't hear the rest. She was already sprinting.

. . .

She spotted him with one foot on the running board of his cream Duesenberg, a half-smoked cigarette in his hand. "CLARK!" It wasn't until she drew closer that she could make out the tense lines burned into his face like a cattle brand. Had she caught him at a bad time? But then he smiled that devilish Gable smile that had earned him millions of dollars, and at least as many female hearts. "If it ain't the intrepid Miss Maddox."

"Mr. Plunkett told me about your lunch date with Carole," she panted, "but I wanted to catch you before your first day in front of the cameras."

Gable took a final drag from his cigarette and crushed it under the heel of his brown suede wingtip. "We're not meeting until one, but I hate fitting sessions, so I said that to hurry things along. What's with the hellfire rush? You looked like your tail was on fire and the nearest water was the Atlantic."

She told him about her encounter with Aggie and how Mickey Cohen had told her that Clark had had a ringside seat to the fight between Elroy and Harry.

"Is it true?" she asked when she'd finished. "Aggie Underwood is nobody's chump, so when she tells you, 'Go ask Gable' . . ."

Gable kept mum for an uncomfortably long time.

Is he going to say anything? Have I asked that one question too many?

When he broke his silence, he was more thoughtful and contemplative than she'd ever seen him. "I'd hoped you'd never find out about that fight."

"Why not?"

"It reveals a sordid side of Hollywood that I prefer a nice girl from Catalina wouldn't have to think about."

"I'd rather know the truth."

"Come on," he said. "Let's you and me take a walk."

He led her past the vast building that held Stages Eleven, Twelve, and Fourteen, where most of the interiors would be shot over the coming months. "Aggie was right, but for the wrong reasons. This goes back to filming *Mutiny* on Catalina. One day, I bumped into your dad. He had some Mad Ox on him, so we installed ourselves on the porch of the Hotel St. Catherine. We were having a pleasant visit when I spotted Harry Cohn charging toward me. He's a vile bastard, but he cast me in *It Happened One Night*, which nabbed me an Oscar, so I smiled and said hello. But it was like I was invisible. He was boiling mad over some dang-fool incident from the year before."

Clark slowed his pace to a stroll as he retrieved a brushed silver cigarette case from his pocket and scraped a match against the wooden fence that ran along Van Buren Place. On the other side of it, he'd get mobbed within ten seconds. But here inside a movie studio, he was safe to be himself. He let the match flare before holding it to a fresh cigarette.

Polly asked, "Do you know what the dang-fool incident was?"

"Took me some time to thread the needle. Dave Selznick had asked Elroy to send hooch to Columbia during filming on *One Night*. Harry saw that as David interfering with his production, or some such horse hockey, so he was throwing his weight around because he's Mister Big Shot."

"Mr. Selznick already told me about what took place during filming."

"He did, huh?"

"But what happened when Cohn turned on my father that night?"

"He got himself worked up so bad that Elroy did, too. Suddenly Cohn's yelling, Elroy's yelling."

Polly couldn't remember witnessing her father yell at anyone. "Did you say anything?"

"When I couldn't take it anymore, I dished out a speech from one of my old hoodlum roles."

"Did it work?"

"Cohn stalked off muttering to himself like a lunatic. Your dad and I kept drinking until it got too dark to see our shot glasses. I hoped that would be the end of that."

"But it wasn't?"

Clark's "No" was a long time coming. "Here's the part where you might get mad at me." His smile was too forced to be convincing. "I saw your dad one more time before the raid that killed him."

Polly was too stunned to push out anything more than a couple of words. "You what?"

"I have this buddy. Owns a sporting goods store. We get out of town from time to time. Hunting. Fishing. The weekend after our night at Club New Yorker, he called me up. Told me he was itching to go on a long, hard, challenging hike, and did I know of one? I thought about one your dad told me about: the hike up to the old Dawn Mine, which is a tough trek high into the mountains past Mount Lowe Tavern. So there we were, my buddy and me, slogging our way up the hillside. Steep terrain, no trail, real outdoorsman stuff. I loved it! But then we came into a clearing, a rocky outcrop, with a waterfall and a stream. We're filling our canteens when someone calls my name. And I'm thinking, 'Goddammit. Even up here in the middle of nowhere?'"

"Papa?"

"In the flesh and desperate for conversation. My buddy took the hint and said he'd scout around. Elroy and I pulled up a rock, and I let him yak."

"About what?"

"Cohn and the embezzlement charges, mostly. But then he got onto Bioff and Browne. Did Aggie mention them?"

"Just that they're East Coast mobsters who infiltrated the Hollywood unions and somehow Cohn was immune to their chicanery."

"They've been screwing over the workers to line their own pockets."

"Why would the studio bosses allow that?"

Clark flicked cigarette ash into a geranium bush, a cynical smile slinking onto his lips. "Simple Hollywood economics. It's cheaper to pay them off than fork over decent union wages. Someone told me mob payoffs have saved the studios fifteen million."

Polly fanned her overheating face with her notebook. Fifteen million dwarfed the thirty-two thousand plus change that she'd been worrying about. "What's all this got to do with Papa and Cohn falling out?"

"Because Harry ran around town making out like he was forking over a fortune like the other moguls, but the skinflint bastard isn't paying a dime, which is par for the course for Cohn."

"But how can he get away with that?"

"Way back in the early twenties, Harry set out to gain controlling shares of Columbia stock. To do that, he needed extra money and so he got himself a loan on the QT."

"From the mob?"

"Specifically, Longie Zwillman. Cut to ten years later. Cohn is faced with having to pay off the mob over this union business, so he asks Johnny Roselli to intercede. Bioff protested, but Roselli sided with Cohn."

"So Cohn has never shelled out a dime, and the other moguls don't know?"

"Nope."

"But you do."

"Only because your dad told me all about it, sitting by a burbling waterfall. And even then, Elroy would have kept out of it except that Cohn had gotten into a fistfight at some swanky New Year's Eve party. The other guy got the better of him, so Cohn tried to retaliate, not realizing the bruiser was all mobbed up himself. The next thing Cohn knows, the mob's changed its mind and there's a hit out on him."

If I lie on the lawn along this fence, maybe this lightheadedness will pass.

Clark slung an avuncular arm around Polly's shoulders. "Cohn wasn't ponying up any money to Bioff and Browne, which meant he should've had enough dough to pay off the hit. But he forced your dad to embezzle and then refused to pay him back. Elroy threatened Cohn he'd tell all the other studio heads that Cohn wasn't paying his fair share. A couple of phone calls is all it would've taken and ol' Harry would have been hung out to dry."

"I have to admire Papa. Taking on Harry Cohn isn't nothing."

She thought for a second. "Hold on!" She shrugged away Clark's arm. "If Cohn was in the good books with the mob, how come they ordered a hit?"

"Well, now, you're assuming there's only one gang of hoodlums. The ones who helped him seize control of Columbia and who are letting him get away with not paying Bioff and Browne aren't the same gang Cohn fell afoul of and who put out the hit."

"Couldn't he go to the first gang to pay off the second one?"

"That's when he learned there really is honor among thieves. When push came to stab, they closed ranks."

"And hung Cohn out to dry."

Gable guided them back toward the parking lot. "Pretty much."

"Giving him no choice but to strong-arm Papa."

"Sadly, yes. That's how it played out.

"I wish you had told me all this before now."

"Fair enough. But the day after I saw him, the coppers gunned him down. There didn't seem to be any point. But now that you do know, what's your plan?"

"You mean after I raid Mr. Selznick's liquor cabinet for a stiff drink?" She threw up her hands in frustration. "I had a nifty scheme to pay off my father's debt by relaunching Mad Ox." There was no time to tell him about the smashed equipment and the telltale state of Gil's hands. "It's no longer feasible, though. But now I've got the full picture about why it wasn't Papa's debt to pay, I don't know that I can sit on the sidelines."

"Watch your step, Missy," Gable warned. "It's a game the big fellas always win."

"Once *Wind* comes out, the biggest fella in town will be *you*."

"I'm just the guy standing in front of the camera trying to learn to dance the Virginia reel. Swear to God, Polly, Cukor arranged the Atlanta charity bazaar to be my first scene out of spite."

"As someone who helped type up the timetable, I can assure you Mr. Cukor had nothing to do with scheduling."

"Everybody knows how uncomfortable I am dancing on screen like a big sissy."

"You did okay under Cora's tutelage for *Idiot's Delight*."

Clark reared back, genuinely shocked. "You know about that?"

"Cora Maddox is my Aunt Cora, the Maddox family's infamous black sheep."

"She is? How come? What'd she do?"

"Made a life for herself in the theater. It's all so silly now, but the two of us have rediscovered each other, so that's good."

Clark beamed. "It's important to find your gang. We all need people who have each other's back."

They had arrived at his car. His intense scowl from before had evaporated.

"Get the Virginia reel out of the way," she told him, "and it'll be smooth sailing after that."

He shook his head and gave her a distrustful half-smile.

She hugged him goodbye and hurried past the electrical power plant.

It's important to find your gang.

Amelia. Luddie. Cora. Who else did she have? Benji, maybe? And Noah at Columbia was no fan of his boss. She put him in the Maybe column, too. Marcella and Hazel? Definitely. She smiled to herself. A year ago, she'd had nobody. And now she had a gang.

With a gang, someone's always got your back.

But as she drew close enough to the office to hear the interminable clack-clack-clacking of Marcella's Remington, she thought of Cohn's gang. Literally a gang of gangsters. Her bravado dissolved like a handful of soap bubbles.

39

Polly clumped up the apartment stairs, straining with each step as though her shoes were made of granite. This had most definitely not been the day to wear heels. She had closed the door behind her at five that morning, and now it was ten at night. Fifteen hours is a darned long haul, she told herself. You can't keep working like this.

Not that all those hours had been Mr. Selznick's fault. She had arrived at work extra early to catch Walter Plunkett before his day had turned into a whirligig, too.

She slid her house key into the lock and shoved open the door with her left hip.

"Hello."

The greeting came from a figure sprawled out on the sofa, silhouetted by the streetlight bleeding through the venetian blinds behind him.

"Benji?" Polly dumped her handbag on the floor. "Aren't you supposed to be miles away in the desert?"

He called out, "SHE'S HERE!" before lowering his voice again. "The last place you want to be is the Buttercup Dunes when a once-in-a-decade sandstorm blows up. We were told it'd be at least four days before shooting resumes, so Mr. Wellman gave us the choice of sticking around Yuma or returning to LA. Enough of us elected to come back that the studio rented a bus. We drove all night and arrived this morning."

Amelia bounded into the living room with more energy than a girl who'd been standing for nine hours ought to have. "Tell her!" she said, jumping into his lap. "Or *I* will."

He sipped from a half-finished beer. From the smell of him, Polly guessed it hadn't been his first. Or even his third. "I was starving for breakfast when we arrived at the studio, so I headed straight to the commissary. I was finishing my coffee when who should walk past the window?"

"Gil?" The relentless grind of Polly's day faded away. "At Paramount?"

"And acting all jumpy!" Amelia put in.

The fine hairs on Polly's neck stood upright. "Did you follow him?"

"You bet I did. He walked up to the Paymaster window, so I figured he'd gotten a job. However, after a brief exchange, he was shown *inside*."

"Is that unusual?"

"They allow nobody—and I mean *nobody*—in there because that's where all the cash for the pay envelopes is kept. Strictly off limits to everybody, from DeMille down."

"You must have been floored."

"To say the least. So I stick around because now I'm curious as hell. Three or four minutes later, Gil reappears holding a hessian bag. Real bulky-looking."

"Bulky, how?"

"Like it was filled with bundles of cash. Like in bank-heist movies."

"Did you approach him?"

"I was still debating, but someone called him back. He turned around, listened to whatever he was being told, then hid the bag under his jacket as he walked away. That's when I followed him to the parking lot, where he got into an expensive car."

"But Gil drives a beat-up old Plymouth."

"This was a Marmon—with a two-tone paint job. Black and burgundy."

"Black-and-burgundy Marmon?" Polly cried out. "Are you sure?"

"Those little beauties are hard to miss."

"Gil told me Roscoe Brodsky drives a two-toned Marmon." She could still hear the thrill in Gil's voice. *He must trust me because a couple of times he's let me drive it.* "What's the word for a guy who collects payoffs for crooks?"

"Bagman."

"You think that's what Gil is?" He was in cahoots with Cohn, who was in cahoots with Bioff and Browne, who in turn were extorting God only knew how much money from the studios every month. What else was Polly supposed to think?

"Do we have any Mad Ox around here?"

"We've got some Four Roses in the kitchen cabinet," Amelia said. "Will that do?"

"Close enough." Polly swung to her feet. "Because I now understand what I should do."

* * *

Luddie stood at Polly's office window as she finished a memo about Bonnie Blue Butler's riding outfit. "I'd bet my favorite bow tie that's them."

"Are they standing under the Confederate flag as per my instructions?" Polly freed the paper from her typewriter and laid it in her out-tray.

"He's in a Brillo-pad-gray Harris-and-Frank three-piece with his Sunday-best necktie that's neither red nor orange. She's in a woolen suit. Mullen and Bluett, I'd say. Half-size too small but a pleasant shade of jacaranda that not many women can get away with."

Thank goodness everybody had left for the day. Polly checked her lipstick in the hand-mirror Marcella kept on her desk. "Do they look nervous?"

"He's stiff as a corpse."

"And her?"

"She looks like she's wolfed down a can of Mexican jumping beans." He studied her some more from his concealed vantage point. "Oh, yes. The missus cannot wait to visit Tara."

When Polly had called Gerard Donovan, the officer from the DA's office in charge of Elroy's embezzlement case, to see if she might meet with him, he had dithered like an old maid who couldn't decide which hat to wear in church until he'd come up with Tuesday at two. Polly couldn't get away from the office during the day for anything longer than a sandwich run, so she had countered with, "How about Saturday afternoon at the Selznick studios? We'll take care of business and give you a tour of our *Gone with the Wind* sets." She had sensed the hesitation in his voice, so she had thrown in a sweetener. "And by all means, bring your wife."

She straightened Luddie's Chinese silk shantung tie. "Remember, you're with the publicity department."

"What are my primary duties?"

"Charming and disarming."

"I'm pretty sure that's not an actual job."

She playfully smacked him on the rump. "The Mrs. DeMilles and Mrs. Selznicks of this world beg to differ."

Polly extended her hand as she approached the couple. "And right on time, too."

"I don't have a lot to spare."

Donovan possessed the mildly florid complexion of his Irish heritage, but it complemented his sun-faded strawberry blonde hair. Mr. Selznick had described him as "Typical law enforcement. All rules, regulations, and requirements." And had then added, "To start out with," which was all Polly needed to know.

Soundstages with various interior sets were all well and good, but the Tara set was the jewel, so Polly steered them around the Mansion toward the back lot.

"This is Mr. Sinclair from our publicity department."

"And you must be Mrs. Donovan." Luddie had been right. That jacaranda suited her black hair and jade-green eyes. "Welcome to Selznick International Studios. We're so happy you've joined us."

"Are you kidding?" the woman said. "I'd be plumb loco passing up a chance to visit *Gone with the Wind*."

"Not to mention the envy of your mahjong club." Luddie waited until Mrs. Donovan's eyes flew open. "Or is it pinochle?"

"Your first guess was on the money, Mr. Sinclair. Do you play?"

"Constance DeMille taught me when she was laid up with a twisted ankle."

"DeMille? As in 'Cecil'?"

"As in 'plays to win and takes no prisoners.'" Luddie unobtrusively slowed his pace so that he and Mrs. Donovan fell in behind Polly and Gerald, giving them the space she needed.

Mr. Donovan's brittle shell softened a little as he heard his wife chirp and chatter in Luddie's expert hands. "I've been working on several major cases, so my wife hasn't seen much of me."

"Is this visit your way of telling her, 'Let me make it up to you'?"

He smiled for the first time. It wasn't a face-splitter. Not much more than a glimmer. Gerard Donovan, Polly decided, would have experienced enough of the tawdry side of life to know that nothing good came from letting down one's guard. "She's a huge fan of the book."

"Mrs. Donovan?" Polly drew alongside Stage Twelve's gaping elephant door. "Belle Watling's house of ill-repute."

Mrs. Donovan jabbed an elbow into her escort's side. "Wait till the girls hear about this!"

Polly waited until Donovan ran his eyes up the water tower. "I have pertinent information about my father's embezzlement case."

He kept his eyes on the tank at the top. "Figured as much."

"Harry Cohn from Columbia forced my father to embezzle those funds from the Island Company."

"Any proof?"

"My father and Cohn had a mutually beneficial arrangement during and after Prohibition."

"Mad Ox?"

"Yes. But then the relationship turned sour and I struggled to understand why."

"Now you do?"

"Cohn got into a fistfight, but it was his bad luck to take on some thug who was a better boxer *and* who had mob connections."

"Could we cut to the chase, Miss Maddox?"

"Their animosity turned ugly, and then deteriorated to where a hit was put out on Cohn's life."

The Forty Acres backlot stretched in front of them, but Luddie and Joan had lagged behind, arm in arm. Luddie was beguiling her with a wild story that was inducing her to pepper his yarn with an escalating "No. No! *NO!*"

"A hit on someone as high-profile as Harry Cohn carries risk."

"Which is why the price tag was fifty thousand." Polly watched Donovan's face for a reaction, but the guy didn't flinch. She doubted he'd blink if he took a bullet to the chest. "It was a lot, even for someone of Cohn's caliber."

"Did he have the fifty grand?"

"He did not."

"So he turned to your father?"

"'Leaned heavily on my father' would be more accurate."

"Which is why Elroy stole from his employer."

"Cohn refused to pay it back, which is why Papa went on the lam. He had to buy himself some time to get the money out of Cohn somehow, return it all, and negotiate down to a lesser charge."

Joan called from behind them. "Is Tara far?"

"Off to the left," Polly threw over her shoulder. "Nearly forty feet tall. You can't miss it." Luddie guided her away.

"Still sounds like conjecture to me," Donovan said.

"You know who Bioff and Browne are, right?"

"What am I, in a coma?"

Sheesh. This combative posturing was more than she'd bargained for.

"I assume you're aware that all the studio bosses are outlaying huge kickbacks to keep the unions in line. But can you name the one who's not?" Polly waited for a snappy comeback, but received only silence. "Cohn isn't coughing up a dime. And *that* means he should have had plenty of money to pay back my father. But even worse, one of his henchmen is serving as a bagman."

"This is all speculation. I'm with the DA's office. I need proof—"

"I've got a witness."

Donovan's head twisted around.

"My, oh *my*!" Joan squealed. "It's how I pictured it." She trotted ahead. "Do you see, Gerry? Tara come to life!"

Polly continued, "Someone who watched Cohn's henchman go into Paramount and walk out with a sack full of cash."

"How could he tell the sack contained—"

"And then the henchman climbed into a Marmon that belongs to Roscoe Brodsky, who is Cohn's lawyer. He was also my father's lawyer." Donovan stared at her, his face as hard as ice. "Elroy Maddox wasn't the bad guy. This situation has Cohn's fingerprints all over it. Surely this is enough to spark a ton of leads to exonerate my father."

"But your father was guilty."

"Only because Cohn forced him to embezzle and then refused to pay him back. If Mr. Wrigley wants his money, he needs to get it from Cohn."

They had caught up with Luddie and Joan now.

"Darn it!" Joan said, hands on hips. "I should've brought my camera! The girls will simply perish."

"If it makes you feel any better," Polly told her, "these sets are copyrighted, and so taking photos is a big no-no."

"Get your fill, dear," Donovan said. "We must be going."

"So soon?"

"I have business to attend to."

"Don't you always?"

Joan sighed the sigh of a wife accustomed to second place. "Truly, Miss Maddox, I can't thank you enough."

"Yes," Donovan said, now distant and pensive. "Thank you for everything."

As they accompanied the Donovans past Aunt Pittypat's Atlanta house, Luddie's deft skill at small talk filled the silence, mostly about Vivien Leigh's casting as Scarlett. It was a facile topic; everybody had their opinion but craved an insider's angle.

They waved as the Donovans took off down Culver Boulevard in their blue Nash.

"Did you convince him?" Luddie asked through a frozen smile.

"I know a DA has to be suspicious, but good God."

They turned back toward the office. "You didn't mention Benji by name, did you?"

"No, but his whole attitude changed when I told him I had a witness."

Polly chewed on the inside of her cheek. Had Donovan asked, she might have given him Benji's name. She saw now it was fortunate she hadn't. "How about dinner at Schwab's? My treat."

"No can do."

"More mahjong with Constance?"

"I'm taking Mrs. Hitchcock to a recital at the British Consulate. Alma's quite a bright spark, which is more than I can say for the consulate crowd. But they do serve high-quality gin, so that's a plus. Tell our favorite Schwab's waitress hello."

"I will, and"—Polly kissed his cheek—"thanks for today. You make a superb studio PR flunky."

"All for one and one for all."

* * *

All the stools were taken, but when Amelia spotted Polly, she held up four discreet fingers: Their secret code for "Fourth from the end is finishing up, so start jockeying into position."

Amelia slid a menu at her. "I bet Luddie charmed the brassiere off Missus DA."

"She was putty from the get-go."

"And the mister?"

"Touch and go, at first. But then I mentioned I had a witness to Gil playing bagman at Paramount."

"How nice to see you again." Leon Schwab had appeared next to Amelia. "I hear you've got a job at Selznick filming *Gone with the Wind* singlehandedly."

"Quit it, Mr. S!" Amelia whacked him across the arm with her order pad. "I said 'virtually.'"

Spending nine hours on her feet wasn't Polly's idea of a swell job, but now that she saw the rapport Amelia had with her boss, she understood how her roommate could spend a day slinging hash to an interminable stream of ravenous customers and still come home full of pep.

"Have you taken Miss Maddox's order?"

"No need. Her usual is a cup of the chili con carne, club sandwich number five, and a Black Beauty if she's got room for dessert."

"Which I do," Polly put in. "And don't forget my root beer float."

Amelia took off to place Polly's order.

"I haven't seen you since the night we surprised each other at Club New Yorker." Leon stretched across the counter to create a more intimate space amid the social hurly-burly around them. "I was so sorry to hear about your dad. No one deserves an exit like that, least of all him."

"Thank you." The heat of tears prickled her eyeballs. Would that feeling ever go away? "I must say it's been . . ." How to sum up the past few months in only a few words? "A lot."

"If it's any consolation, I—" A disturbance behind Polly thwarted Mr. Schwab's response. He straightened up, alarm filling his face.

Amelia joined him, a frosted glass of root beer in her hand. "What the—?"

The noisy crowd fell into a hush as a pair of uniformed cops, serious as tightrope walkers, wended their way to the counter.

"Officers," Leon said, "what can I do for you?"

The taller of the two turned to Polly. "Miss Polly Maddox?"

She stared up at his Mt. Rushmore face. "Yes." The word popped out more like a question, as though she wasn't sure who she was.

"Come with us."

Polly turned, open-mouthed, to Amelia, then to Leon, then back to the cop. "Where?"

"We're placing you under arrest."

"Under—? What—?"

"Excuse me," Leon said evenly. "On what charges?"

The other officer looked like he shot-putted bowling balls for fun. "Supplying false testimony, making spurious accusations without substantial evidence, and interfering in the due process of the law."

The two cops frog-marched her past every diner and customer, and out onto Sunset Boulevard. They opened the rear door of their car and bundled her inside as though she were a sack of potatoes. The car stank of bargain-basement cigarettes and Bay Rum after-shave. As Polly peered through the vehicle's window, she could see Amelia's face through the diner window, her mouth a silent "O."

The car pulled abruptly into traffic. Polly held onto the door handle. "May I ask where we're going?"

"Downtown," cop number one said. "Women's jail."

The lights of the stores along Sunset blended into an indistinct blur.

Jail?

The Crossroads of the World shopping plaza rushed into view. She stared at the rotating globe perched on top of the soaring tower out front and thought of Donovan. It had only been four or five hours since they'd parted company. She had no idea how the police department worked, but she doubted it could swing into action that fast.

Or could it?

40

The holding cell reeked of stale alcohol, sweat, and cheap perfume. The inmate next to Polly smelled like rust. Or was it gunpowder? She wore her neckline too low and her hemline too high, or maybe it was exactly the right balance for a hooker. She had been moaning to herself all night. Eight and a half hours of it, and there appeared to be no end in sight.

They couldn't hold Polly indefinitely, could they? Surely, they had to charge her or let her go?

Minnie the Moaner shook her wig as though she expected fleas to tumble to the mottled cement. "Don't buy your wigs from Zelda's of Hollywood," she said to nobody in particular. "She'll cheat ya, soon as look at ya."

The cell door slid open with a metallic clang. A female officer with the red hands of a laundress yelled, "MADDOX!" The woman stepped into the corridor and unhooked a large ring of keys from her belt. "Someone's posted bail."

"Who?"

The officer threw her a scornful look. *You think I give a tinker's damn?*

Formalities dispensed with, Polly was released into the visitors' waiting room, where a slim woman in white linen stood rooted to the floor, careful to touch nothing.

Polly could hardly believe her bleary eyes. "What in God's name—"

Irene Selznick half-pushed, half-pulled her out into the street. "They didn't hurt you, or—anything?"

"A little worse for wear, but no, I'm fine. But how did you—why are you—?"

Irene opened the door of her LaSalle. "I packed peanut butter sandwiches in case you're hungry."

Polly ripped the wax paper off the sandwiches sitting on the dashboard, grabbed one off the top, and crammed as much of it as she could into her mouth. After the night she'd had, who cared about being a lady?

"Your roommate—Amelia, is it? She called the house, frantic as can be, asking for David, but of course he was at the studio. She told me what transpired at Schwab's."

Oh, God. Poor Leon. How horrified he must have been to witness an arrest in his own establishment. How does a person make an appropriate apology for a calamity like that?

"And then Amelia asked if I knew of a reputable lawyer to spring you from jail. I told her, 'None who'll accept your call, but all the sheriff wants is bail money. I'll go down there first thing and get her myself.'"

Polly wolfed down another gooey mouthful of peanut butter sandwich. What a relief to eat again. "I don't know how to repay you."

Irene started the car and threw Polly an impish smile. "Liberating reckless actresses from the consequences of their indiscretions comes with the territory of being the daughter of one movie mogul and the wife of another."

"Ride this merry-go-round often, do you?"

"During Prohibition, I knew the names of all those turnkeys in there." She patted Polly's knee. "You're in fine company."

The pale winter sun was now crawling above the horizon, lending the concrete of the Spring Street bridge an unforgiving, sterile, off-white hue. "I'm not guilty of those charges," Polly said.

"Goes without saying, my dear."

Polly let her head flop backward. What she wouldn't give for twenty minutes' shut-eye. "Does Mr. Selznick know?"

"You're assuming I've seen him." Irene's tone had turned mildly caustic.

"I expect you'll have to tell him."

"Those asinine charges didn't come from out of thin air. Suppose you tell me what events preceded your arrest."

Polly took a hefty bite out of the second sandwich and brooded over how much she should and shouldn't share with her boss's wife. Then again, the woman hadn't hesitated to drive all the way to Lincoln Heights when it was still night out; she deserved the full story.

As they skirted the perimeter of downtown, past the tower of the new Union railway station emerging from the chaos of its vast construction site, Polly took her through the events of the past week. Irene kept quiet until she had finished.

"Those charges were intended to frighten you."

"They did a bang-up job."

"What they are is cooked-up hogwash warning you to walk away."

"From what?"

"How well are you acquainted with this Gerard Donovan?"

"I only met him yesterday. Why?"

"He has the most ghastly reputation."

"How ghastly?"

"Whenever Cohn needs to extricate one of his minions from a serious scandal, Donovan is his fixer within the judicial system. And if we draw a short line from Cohn to the mob, it won't take the brains of Oliver Wendell Holmes to find an equally short line from Donovan to the mob."

Polly stared out the passenger window. "It's time to back off." It was bad enough that she'd been hoodwinked not only by Donovan and Brodsky, but by Gil, too. She had seen signs, and had questioned them. But in the end, she had accepted all his explanations, just like those dummies who'd been taken in by Orson Welles and his *War of the Worlds* broadcast.

"Backing off is one option," Irene said evenly.

The vibrations of the tires thrummed through the floor, lulling Polly into a fuzzy-blanket stupor. "There are others?"

"They want you to back off," she said, crisp and decisive.

"Harry Cohn runs a studio. Men like that—"

"Those studio heads—pfft!" Irene turned on to Ninth Street "They're not as powerful as you think."

It was all very well for her to say. Nobody was going to throw *her* in jail. Nobody could intimidate *her* father into breaking the law. "I'll take your word for it," Polly said.

"You've got a secret weapon."

"And what might that be?"

"Ludlow Sinclair."

Polly jackknifed upright. "How do you figure?"

"He has squired around town Mrs. Cecil B. DeMille, Mrs. Louis B. Mayer, Mrs. Myron Selznick, Mrs. David O. Selznick, Mrs. Darryl F. Zanuck, and, most important of all, Mrs. Harry Cohn. Did you know how Olivia got the role of Melanie? Jack Warner wouldn't lend her out to David, so Olivia took Jack's wife, Anne, out to lunch. And bingo!" Irene snapped her fingers. "The husbands get all the spotlights in this town, but who thinks about the wives? Not even female journalists! God forbid Louella or Hedda should ever call the house to speak to *me*. Not that I'd want them to, but you get my point."

"You included yourself on that list," Polly said. "You've been using Ludlow's services?"

"Seeing my husband so infrequently has forced me to adopt a for-the-duration mentality. But that doesn't mean my entire life has to be put on hiatus."

"What happened to your regular escort?"

"Tom? He took Barney Balaban's wife, Tillie, skiing and ended up breaking his leg in five places. Won't be back on his feet for months. He was the one who suggested Ludlow, so we've been out and about several times. Holy cow, that man knows how to show a girl a good time. He makes you feel like you're the only woman in the room. What a remarkable conversationalist. It's been forever since any man has asked my opinion."

Irene Selznick was one of the sharpest and most astute women Polly had ever met, and, she guessed, hard to impress.

"He's also the epitome of discretion," she told Irene.

"I know he's only doing his job, but for us attention-starved Hollywood wives who are crawling out of the Sahara, desperate for a drop to drink, he's a frosty bottle of Pommery champagne."

"I don't doubt that for a minute, but . . ." A yawn dredged up from the depths of fatigue pushed to the surface. Polly couldn't wait to slip between the sheets of her own bed. "But why, exactly, is he my secret weapon?"

"Put all those married ladies into a room, stir in a generous dollop of Ludlow Sinclair, tell them what you've been through at the hands of Harry Cohn, and you'll see."

41

Amelia plumped the last of the sofa pillows. "Jiminy Christmas!"

Polly poked her head out of the kitchen. "What have we forgotten? They'll be here soon."

Trepidation filled Amelia's face like a rash. "These women, they're kinda intimidating, y'know?"

Oh, cripes, Polly thought. I'm barely hanging on to my composure. I need Miss Nothing Fazes Me to be all bright and bubbly. Please don't lose your nerve. Not when they're en route.

"They live in big, fancy Beverly Hills mansions," Amelia said. "I'm sure they have cooks and nannies and gardeners and maids. And what have we got?" She swept her hands in a wide circle.

Polly looked at their apartment with fresh eyes.

Sure, it could do with a new paint job, and the rug was fraying at the edges. What little furniture they owned was second-hand, which was fine because the living room was on the small side. But it was *their* place, decorated as best they could. Better than that, nobody could tell them what to do or how to be, or judge them on their fathers' actions or who they used to be a million years ago.

"What are they going to do?" Polly asked. "Turn up their noses at our fifty-cent thrift-store lamp and leave?"

They had bargained the salesclerk down from two dollars to fifty cents and had walked out as though they'd inherited the crown jewels. "Aww," Amelia said, "I love our lamp."

A sharp rap on the door.

Polly wished Amelia had kept her trap shut. She hadn't considered how "the Mrs. Moguls," as Luddie called them, might feel once they'd found themselves in a somewhat gimcrack, one-bedroom, one-bathroom apartment.

Polly opened the door to find Luddie looking relaxed as a golfer. "Ready, ladies?" Her secret weapon sauntered inside with an enviable swagger. "All spic and span, I see."

Amelia picked up the same cushion and plumped its sides again. "We've been lamenting that our place isn't up to their usual standards."

"So we might not impress them as much as we need to," Polly added.

"Are you kidding? Except for Irene, most of these women were starving actresses from humble beginnings. I'd bet my next steak dinner your adorable little nest is a darned sight better than the fleabags they started out in. If anything, it'll remind them they were once where you are now. And that's a point in your favor."

He makes you feel like you're the only woman in the room. Luddie may have crawled his way out of a squalid Hooverville, but Polly lacked for nothing if he was on her side. "Any last-minute instructions?"

A second knock prevented him from replying.

"Be yourselves," he whispered. "Otherwise, what's the point?"

He opened the door with a dramatic whoosh. "LADIES!" All six women had crowded together on the tiny landing. "You didn't all squish into one car, did you?"

"Oh, Ludlow, you *are* a caution," Mrs. DeMille said as she led the way inside. "It would look ridiculous if we drove out of Beverly Hills like a military convoy, so we took two cars." She extended her hand. "Lovely to see you again, Polly, dear." As the other Mrs. Moguls filed in, she cupped a gloved hand to one side of her mouth and whispered, "We're all so intrigued about why you've asked us for tea."

Virginia Zanuck was the only wife Polly hadn't met before. In her early thirties, she was around Irene's age, but lacked the somewhat austere lines of her friend's face. She carried herself like a small-town girl who, much to her own surprise, had married far beyond the situation of everybody she'd left behind.

Each woman now standing in Polly and Amelia's living room wore an outfit that cost more than the apartment's weekly rent. Though nothing flashy or conspicuously expensive, they reminded Polly that she was swimming in a whole new ocean.

The apartment contained seating for nine people, so although everybody had to jam into close quarters, the setup encouraged a chummy camaraderie. Or so Polly liked to tell herself. It might be an altogether different story after she'd told them why she had asked them here.

The tea poured and the petits fours passed around, Polly said, "Ladies." Her voice cracked on the second syllable. "I have recently experienced a series of—let's call them eye-opening revelations."

"Sounds like somebody has crash-landed to earth in the land of make-believe," Marjorie said, though not maliciously. "It's a sickening thud when you realize life here isn't anything like it is on the screen."

"Hush up, Marj." Irene slapped her sister-in-law on the wrist. "Polly's in a jam not of her own making." She waved her fingers. *Go ahead, honey, and don't stop until you're done.*

Earlier that morning, Amelia had insisted Polly practice her speech. "I'll be Mrs. Cohn with my arms crossed until you've convinced me." After a couple of false starts, Polly had cobbled together a cohesive account of the past few weeks. But Amelia's arms had remained folded. "Do it again, but don't hold back. These dames aren't ingenues. They know what's what."

Polly saw that she'd been soft-pedaling her own story, so she had started over, throwing in every detail: Papa's fight with Cohn, the mob, the destruction of the distillery on Catalina, Brodsky,

Donovan. Amelia hadn't unfolded her arms until Polly had talked about Bioff and Browne. "When the Mrs. Moguls hear the full story and they still want to help," Amelia had said, "that's the sign they're on your side."

"And so," she finished up, "that's my story, and I thought you should know."

Rose Cohn was the first to speak. "This Gil person you were dating, did he tell you how he came to be working for my husband?"

Polly had left out that part of her story because this was neither the time nor place to lift the lid on that particular cookie jar.

"Gil was friendly with his neighbor, a girl under contract at Columbia."

"Did they work together at the studio?"

"Not as far as I'm aware."

"So Gil met Harry when Harry came calling next door." Rose smoothed out the front of her skirt, a heavy tweed that needed no flattening. "This girl next door, was it Della?"

"Gil didn't mention her name."

"Why?" Irene asked. "Who's Della?"

Rose tsked. "Every once in a while, Harry becomes preoccupied with a contract player. They're always young, pretty, leggy—"

"And ambitious," Constance put in. "Don't forget 'ambitious.'"

"I can always tell when he's got his eye on one. A name comes up in conversation, always with the same tone."

"They try so hard to be casual and nonchalant, don't they?" Virginia said. "'Oooh, do you remember that girl I mentioned last week?' as if I'm some backward five-year-old."

"Suddenly it's Della this, Della that," Rose continued. "Same old routine."

"What made this particular chorine stick in your memory?" Irene asked.

"Once he's lost interest, the name peters out over weeks. But this girl dropped from his conversation overnight."

"Why was Harry at this Della's apartment?" Margaret asked Polly.

Any promise she had made to keep Gil's story off the record had been swept aside the minute he'd tried to manhandle her outside Schwab's. But that baby business was a whole different hamper of dirty diapers. Fair or not, society had decreed that the inability to give husbands a child was a wife's ultimate failure. "All he said was how he knew a single girl lived in the apartment next door, and when he heard yelling, he hurried over to see if she was okay."

"The yelling came from my husband, I suppose?"

"Gil didn't realize who he was. He figured it was some boyfriend—"

"Sugar daddy, you mean."

"—so Gil gave him what-for."

Irene plopped a second spoonful of sugar into her tea and stirred it vigorously. "I'd have paid top dollar to see that."

"I guess Harry admired Gil's nerve because he asked Gil to fix a prank chair in the commissary."

"That damned electric chair!" Rose thwacked the side of her armrest. "My husband would have thrived during the Spanish Inquisition." She smoothed her skirt again. "Oh, ladies, I'm appalled at my husband's behavior."

"Men are *all* a bunch of stinkers." Irene shot Luddie a sardonic smile. "Present company excluded."

"I mean more than that Della business." Rose counted off, finger by finger. "Funding a bootlegging operation and taking eighty percent for himself; forcing a business partner to embezzle money; reneging on repaying it; weaseling out of paying off the mob while all his peers are forking over gobs of money. And all because it's cheaper than doing right by their thousands of employees." Rose had inched to the edge of her chair as though she were Joan of Arc preparing to launch herself into battle. "I knew he was a rat, but this is beyond the pale. If he were in this room right now, I'd slug him across the puss with Polly's teapot."

"And then I'd take it from you and clobber Louis with it."

Of all the women in the sparse living room, Margaret Mayer

had come across the meekest. Her outburst now surprised even Luddie.

"Why, Margaret!" he said, laying a hand on his chest, his eyes twinkling. "Such violence. Coming from you?"

"Well, I would," Margaret insisted. "Paying the mob to save on salaries for their workers who give it their all? I'd throw in a second wallop for good measure."

"I'll tell you this for sure," Virginia said. "When Darryl learns that Harry isn't paying his way, I'm vacating the house with all sharp objects in my purse."

"Are you sure he doesn't already know?" Constance asked. "This town is like Swiss cheese when it comes to keeping secrets."

Virginia set her teacup on the table with a loud clatter. "I guarantee Darryl knows nothing about Harry colluding with Bioff and Browne. There are a lot of things he doesn't share with me—such as the little room he has off his office where he keeps a bed with fresh sheets for 'entertaining purposes.'"

"You know about that?" Luddie asked.

"Like Constance and Virginia and Marjorie, I, too, was an actress in my early days. And I knew Darryl couldn't keep it in his pants when I married him." She lifted a self-deprecating shoulder. "It's the devil's own bargain you make with men like that. But this Bioff and Browne business? He'll burst a blood vessel when he learns Cohn isn't coughing up his fair share. And if Darryl's in the dark, I'll wager the others are, too."

The Mrs. Moguls all nodded in agreement.

"Harry Cohn shouldn't get away with not repaying the money he forced my father to swindle from Mr. Wrigley," Polly said, "but these Bioff and Browne crooks are too much for me to take on alone."

"But"—Irene raised a finger and traced a large circle in the air—"you aren't alone."

"Count me in," Margaret said.

Constance waved her hand. "Me too."

A vivid image flashed through Polly's mind. She's sitting alone in the old Avalon amphitheater. Reading an Edna Ferber with a bright red cover. *So Big* or *Show Boat*. It's late summer. The warmth of the day still dawdles, and the sun hasn't yet dunked itself into the Pacific. The cicadas, quiet. The air, still. It's a crystalline moment, almost cinematic in its perfection. And she has no one to share it with.

But look at me now.

"So," Luddie said, "you all agree that your husbands should be aware they're being gypped?"

"Indisputably," Constance said. "But they also hate it when their wives interfere."

Irene harrumphed. "They're rarely the partner-in-everything we expected and wanted. So, yes, we want to help you bring Cohn down a peg."

Polly looked to Rose. "Including you?"

She nodded with a resolute chin. "Me most of all."

"I doubt we can take on the likes of Bioff and Browne," Polly said, "but what about getting Harry to pay back those embezzled funds and clear my father's name? Do you think that's within reach?"

Rose absently twisted an emerald ring the size of a giant pea. Polly couldn't imagine how much it cost, but it would have had to be more than a factory-fresh Hudson. "I'd say so."

"Harry isn't easily threatened," Virginia cautioned.

"If you want to get him where it hurts, threaten what he loves most."

"Profits?" Luddie asked.

"Exactly. What'll get his attention is to endanger the picture he's pouring a small fortune into."

"*Mr. Smith Goes to Washington,*" Constance said.

"Bull's-eye."

She ran a fingernail back and forth along her triple strand of pearls. "Virginia and Tillie Balaban and I were at the Academy luncheon at the Biltmore. Typical boozy, all-afternoon affair. While we were visiting with each other, Frank Capra's wife, Lou, approached us."

"She's been busy with her toddler, so we haven't seen her

much lately," Virginia said. "She was especially excited because half the room was saying *You Can't Take It with You* was the odds-on favorite for Outstanding Production and for Best Director."

"It got seven nominations," Rose said, "so it's likely to win big later this month, which lays the groundwork for *Mr. Smith*'s publicity campaign. Harry hasn't said as much to me, but I get the impression that if this picture tanks, Columbia might not recover. Harry is hoping to repeat *Can't Take It*'s success. Same director, same male star, same female star. He can't afford *Mr. Smith*'s one-and-a-half-million-dollar budget right now, but also, he can't *not* take a big swing."

"He's sailing that close to the financial wind?" Margaret asked.

Rose crossed one leg over the other. "My husband loves Santa Anita. To give him his due, he is rather skilled at picking horses."

"Is that a bad thing?" Luddie asked.

"It is when he dips into the payroll to place bets."

"No!" Margaret gasped.

"*That's* how close to the brink my buzzard of a husband sails. Pile on another enormous debt like this fifty grand and it might break him altogether."

"Hold on! Hold on!" Constance waved her hands in the air. "We don't want to sink Frank's movie any more than we want to sink Cecil's *Union Pacific* or David's *Gone with the Wind*."

Relieved that one of them had brought up a valid point, Polly said, "We're better off threatening him that we'll expose his contemptible behavior. And if he doesn't—"

The women burst out laughing. "Contemptible behavior?" Virginia asked. "Did you not hear me when I talked about Darryl's little side-room?"

"My dear," Margaret said, patting Polly's knee, "every husband represented here today has committed the crime of contemptible behavior. Sometimes weekly."

"Seems to me this Bioff and Browne situation is our best leverage," Polly said.

"Absolutely, it is," Margaret agreed. "Daryl isn't the only husband who'll burst a blood vessel when he hears Harry isn't pulling his weight. Mine will too—and probably all over our new carpets."

Irene said, "Perhaps if we go our separate ways, it'll take off the pressure of coming up with a solution right here and now."

The group took Irene's suggestion as their cue to leave. The six women rose as one and departed amid a flurry of hats, gloves, handbags, and kisses to the cheek.

"Phew!" Luddie said, sagging against the door. "Got anything stronger than tea?"

"Whatever we've got, make mine a double," Amelia said. "Right, Pol?"

Polly stared at her, then swung her gaze over to Luddie, then back to Amelia, a look of consternation creasing her brow.

"What?" Amelia asked.

"Can we really take on Harry Cohn?"

42

Polly was glad Luddie had parked his Pontiac several blocks from the Beverly Hills Hotel. Nobody would have recognized it—least of all Harry Cohn. But Luddie had sensed she needed time to clear her head.

"You look smart," he said as the three of them assembled on the sidewalk. "Is that new?"

"Thank you, yes." Polly patted the front of the navy-blue suit with white piping and wide lapels. "But Harry Cohn won't care what I'm wearing."

Polly had intended to place that telephone call herself, but Luddie had remarked how Cohn wasn't the type to take a girl seriously. Especially an anonymous one telling him she had crucial information about his "shady business dealings with persons currently of interest to the LAPD," so if he knew what was good for him, he'd show up at seven p.m. at the Polo Lounge. And if he didn't, Aggie Underwood would be her next port of call.

Luddie had made the call from a phone booth in the foyer of the Ambassador Hotel, with Polly and Amelia pressed beside him. When he'd finished speaking Cohn had told him curtly, "Whoever you are, go fuck yourself, hard, fast, and twice over."

The three of them had stared at each other. *What now?*

Polly had whispered into Luddie's ear, "You wouldn't want another fifty-thousand-dollar mob hit, would you?"

That had clinched it.

The week since the Mrs. Moguls tea party had been an especially tough row to hoe. On top of the interminable landslide of memos, letters, contracts, and teletypes, she now had to ignore the fights waged between Marcella and Mr. Selznick.

They were all working under such pressure that fissures were bound to mar the veneer of civility they had all been laboring under. The occasional testy word had blistered into cross exchanges.

But this past week had been different. Their fights had raged more often and longer, but most telling of all, behind closed doors, where they honked at each other like quarrelsome geese.

The most Polly could glean was that Mr. Selznick was working his way up to firing a member of the *Wind* company, whom he didn't want to sack, but felt he had no choice. Marcella was having none of it, however, and had argued against such a drastic step. Earlier that day, Polly had pressed her ear to the keyhole, hoping to deduce the gist of their ongoing argument, but the honking had degraded to hissing.

Thick with the expensive cars of Hollywood executives and big-timers, Sunset Boulevard was a river of Friday evening peak-hour headlights. Luddie slowed his pace along the sidewalk and turned to Polly and Amelia. "What else is going on?" he asked Polly. "Outside of this whole Harry Cohn puddle of puke, I mean. Is it Selznick? Gil?"

"I think Mr. Selznick is about to fire someone from *Wind*."

"Who?" Luddie asked.

"I don't know, but it must be someone major because he and Marcella have been going at it like the Montagues and the Capulets."

"It can't be Gable," Amelia said. "He's the only acceptable Rhett Butler. So do you think it's—"

The three of them stopped walking at the same time.

It was Luddie who said it out loud. "Do you think he's caved in to the pressure of casting the Brit?"

"Louella and Hedda all but set their fox furs on fire at the news."

Good lord, Polly thought. After all that. The *years* he spent looking for his Scarlett. The agony he put himself through, narrowing down the field to the final four and then whittling those down to Vivien Leigh, knowing she wasn't American, let alone from the South. It wouldn't be quite so bad if they hadn't started filming yet. But they had.

Polly could already picture the press release she'd be typing, but the Beverly Hills Hotel was in sight now. She needed to put the Scarlett crisis out of her mind—but she was no automaton. If only she'd thought to drop some sachets of Goody's Headache Powders into her purse.

They were at the foot of the driveway now. The hotel that everybody referred to as The Pink Palace towered over them like a gigantic frosted cupcake.

"Mr. Selznick is bound to be losing sleep over it."

"He must do right by his picture," Luddie countered. "If *Wind* is in trouble and fixing it means firing his star, then he has no choice. His job is to produce the best possible film, so let's let Mr. Selznick do his job. Meanwhile, you do yours."

"Type memos until my hands fall off?"

Luddie grabbed Polly's shoulders and aimed her at the hotel's portico. "Restore your father's name."

* * *

The hotel had laid out its dining room tables in ten rows of ten. Potted ferns hung from the ceiling in bronze flowerpots the size of enormous mixing bowls. The room was larger than Polly had expected, and only half-filled. She would have preferred more diners. The more spectators, the less likely Harry Cohn was to detonate.

The maître d' gathered up four menus and told them to follow him. Polly spotted Irene and Marjorie at one table and Constance, Margaret, and Virginia at another. But where was Rose?

The maître d' stopped at a four-top where a woman hid behind a menu. She lowered it to reveal her identity. "Hello!"

"Rose! No!" Polly took a seat. "We talked about this. It—"

"I want to see the whites of Harry's eyes when you drop your bombshell."

"We need a card up our sleeves in case your husband bolts."

"I still say Amelia and I should be with you," Luddie said. "I don't like the idea of you taking on Harry Cohn alone."

"Neither do I," she admitted, "but if he doesn't feel threatened, he won't be nearly so vigilant."

Rose laid her menu on the table. "Harry'll dismiss Polly before she's even opened her mouth. The same applies to Ludlow, whom he calls 'that faggot gigolo.' But I know how to handle him if things go off the rails."

Luddie conceded her point and decamped with Amelia to the other table.

"Rose," Polly said, taking care to be as gentle-but-firm as she could, "you're forgetting about the element of surprise. If Harry sees you sitting with me—"

"Don't look now, but we've got another element of surprise heading our way." She lifted a finger, pointing to the left.

An attractive young woman, mid-twenties, with dark brunette hair bobbed like Louise Brooks', approached them. "You're Rose Cohn, aren't you?"

"I am." Rose gave her plain yellow rayon dress a once-over. "Have we met?"

The girl sat down at their table. "I always promised myself that if I ever got a proper chance, I'd introduce myself."

Rose shifted in her seat. "Now's your opportunity."

"I'm a contract player at Columbia. Or rather, *was*. I had to leave after your husband approached me—"

"You're not Della, are you?"

The girl's shoulders drooped. "You know what happened, then."

Rose sucked in her cheeks. "Being merely the wife, I'm in the dark. How about you light a candle for me?"

Oh, Jesus! Polly thought. Not here. Not now. Not this girl. But the Super Chief locomotive couldn't have budged Rose Cohn from her chair. With any luck, a phone call or screening had delayed Harry.

Della fiddled with a hotel matchbook, revealing her elegant fingers. She possessed all the movie-star prerequisites: large eyes, straight teeth, glossy hair, creamy skin. Who knows how far the kid might have flown if Harry Cohn hadn't—

"I'd been working on the lot for five or six months before your husband made me an offer—"

"Oh, sweetie, I bet he did."

"So when he asked me to have his baby, I was shocked."

Rose took in a terse breath. "I know how that feels."

"He'd given it a great deal of thought."

"Harry is nothing if not thorough."

"He wanted us to rendezvous twice a week."

"My husband loves a regular schedule."

Polly laid a gentle hand on Rose's wrist. "Just let her tell her story." *The quicker she does, the sooner she'll be gone.*

Della met Rose's eye, composed and self-assured. "So, like I said, twice a week till I fell pregnant. He'd pay all the bills: doctors, hospitals, and what have you."

Rose went to fling out a caustic retort, but Polly squeezed her wrist. "And after the baby came?" Polly asked. "Who'd raise it?"

"Me. Being his mother and all." Polly felt tension rippling along the tendons in Rose's forearm. "Mr. Cohn would pay an allowance until the kid reached twenty-one. He was no tightwad. It was more than generous, and would've doubled it if I had a boy."

"A little baby boy," Rose sighed, almost to herself.

"Mrs. Cohn, I want to make it clear I wasn't the slightest bit tempted to accept his offer."

"How'd he take it when you turned him down?" Her voice had turned cold.

"Not well."

"I bet."

"Especially when I told him it wasn't fair on you. Wasn't your fault you can't conceive. He all but spat at me. '*I* want an heir and that old broad can't give me one, so *I'm* goin' out and gettin' me one.' I said to him, '*Buy* one, you mean.' That's when he started screaming and hollering and stomping around my apartment."

"That's my Harry. Figures if he screams loud enough, he can bully anyone into submission. Usually works, too."

"Not with me, it didn't. I stood my ground."

"Good for you."

"Naturally, that was curtains for me at Columbia. Now I live paycheck to paycheck, sharing a two-bedroom apartment with three other girls. I can barely afford one pair of stockings at a time, and haven't bought a decent hat since I can't tell you when. Anyway, I wanted to put you in the picture because none of this seemed fair to you."

Rose shook herself free from Polly, her voice now calm as a pond. "I must say, this is an odd coincidence, you being here."

In other words: *Can a girl like you in a dress like that afford to eat in a place like this?*

"I often work as extra waitress at charity balls and Academy Awards dinners," Della said. "I've served you on a number of occasions."

"You have?"

"The last time was at the Mayfair Ball. You were telling Myrna Loy about how you loved the food here at the Polo Lounge. I know the maître d' quite well. He said you're generally here on Fridays."

"You went to a lot of effort to square things."

"It's been on my conscience something awful."

"You have nothing to feel guilty about," Polly said.

"If some guy did me the dirty like that, I'd want to be told."

"And I thank you, Della," Rose said. "If you're strapped for cash, will you let me send you some money for your trouble?"

"Oh, no, no!" Della stood up. "That's not why I approached you."

"It would be Harry's money. There's satisfaction in that, don't you think?"

No, Della did not think. She thanked Rose for the offer, but said she had to be going now, and scurried toward the exit.

Rose sat in her chair, still as a statue.

"You okay?" Polly asked.

"Nothing a double rye whiskey won't fix."

She lifted her hand to flag the nearest waiter, but Polly yanked it down. "Your husband's here."

Harry Cohn stood in the doorway, fists jammed onto his hips, scanning the room like he was Alexander the Great surveying Babylon. He muttered an order over his shoulder to some yes-man behind him. The flunky stepped out from Cohn's shadow.

It was Gil.

But not the Gil Polly had fallen for.

He was deathly pale, as though he'd spent the last couple of weeks chain-smoking his way through every dive bar and gin mill between the Pacific Palisades and Rancho Cucamonga. Dark smudges rimmed his eyes, and he needed a decent haircut.

Gil spotted Polly at the same time Cohn saw his wife.

"What in God's name are you doing here?" Cohn demanded, marching over to their table.

Rose stiffened her backbone. "I'm here to support my friend."

"I'm the one who asked for this meeting," Polly said.

Cohn's eyes, dark as pitch and hard as basalt, held no recognition. "I talked with a guy."

"Because I figured you wouldn't agree to meet with someone like me."

"You got that right, girlie."

Polly gestured to the two empty chairs. "Take a seat." Gil's lips were now a thin, mean line, his face suddenly so red he resembled a balloon on the brink of popping.

Cohn lowered himself into a chair. "Two minutes."

"We'll need more than that," Polly said.

"What the fuck is this about?"

"Bioff and Browne."

"Bioff—?" The name caught in Cohn's throat like a bug. He grabbed a water glass at his elbow. As he gulped, Gil bent at the waist to whisper into his boss's ear, but Cohn shoved him away. "Cut the crap, whoever you are, or I'll have you brought up on charges."

Like the ones he had drummed up through Brodsky and Donovan? His threat caught Polly off guard, paralyzing her for a moment. Why had she taken on a mountain when all she had was a shovel?

"What do you mean about Bioff and Browne?" Cohn calmly folded his arms across his chest, his voice low and controlled. "This had better be good because my time is too valuable to waste on rumors and"—he treated his wife to a venomous sneer—"gossip. In case you haven't heard, I don't get headaches; I give them."

God knows there are countless egotistical, self-important, pompous, swell-heads in Hollywood, but Mister I Give Headaches must be the most insufferable of the bunch. Polly kept her hands in her lap, twisting her fingers until they were a strangled pink. "You know what I mean when I say Bioff and Browne." Polly made a point of looking at Gil. *And you do, too.*

Cohn emitted a low, growling sound, like a cornered bear. "If you think you can hurl around those names to me, in public, and get away with—"

"I'll tell you what this is about!" Rose jumped to her feet. Polly tried to pull her down, but she wrenched her arm out of reach. "It's about Della."

"I've met tons of Dellas," Cohn shot back.

"Which one did you throw money at to give you an heir?" Cohn was probably a first-class poker player, but even he couldn't act fast enough to veil his surprise. "I'm fully aware of your plan to sublet the womb of the latest kewpie doll to catch your eye. She's cute, I'll grant you that, but did you think I wouldn't find out? Do you think you're the only one in this family with busy little spies running all over town?"

"Rose!" Cohn spat out her name, curt and terse.

"And worst of all, how could you give no thought to *my* feelings in all this?"

Every face in the dining room had turned toward them now; all conversation halted.

Cohn vaulted to his feet. "I'm not listening to this garbage." He threw Gil a cursory nod. *We're leaving.* Gil cast Polly a dark look she couldn't interpret, and followed his boss through the exit.

Polly buried her face in her hands. *Oh, Rose, if you only knew how much courage it took for me to confront your husband.* But what good would it do? Cohn was gone. The opportunity had crumbled away and the entire room was staring at them.

A shadow fell across her. Ludlow, Irene, Marjorie, Virginia, and Margaret had gathered around.

"Want to vamoose?" Amelia asked.

Polly nodded. "Come on, Rose. Let's go."

They picked up their handbags and gloves and trudged out of the restaurant, single file, avoiding all eye contact.

The hotel's glass doors opened on to the portico, where several uniformed parking attendants were lined up like infantrymen.

But they weren't the only ones.

Cohn and Gil stood face to face, barely a foot apart. Cohn, still red-faced and angry, was yelling at Gil. "Where the blazes is my car?"

"How d'you expect me to know?" Gil yelled back, the cords in his throat taut.

"When I want my car, it must be *where* I want it, *when* I want it—"

"You need to give me a head start. I can't pull it out of my ass."

"And you need to learn to read my moods, anticipate my needs—"

"What am I, a mind-reader?"

"Good heavens," Irene muttered. "He's interrupting He Who Must Not Be Interrupted."

"You insolent little shit." Cohn clamped his right hand into a fist and took a swing. Gil blocked it with a well-practiced forearm, but not before Polly had involuntarily called out his name. Cohn turned at the sound and stared at each face, one by one, until he'd landed on Irene. "So, this is a *Selznick* ambush?"

"Don't talk utter rot," Irene threw back. "It's nothing of the sort."

"Now I get what's going on here. That fat oaf of a husband of yours—"

"Harry!" Rose cried out. "Enough!"

"You can run home and tell Mister David O-for-oaf Selznick that if he wants to play ball, then I'm prepared to do everything I can to sabotage that four-hanky, Southern-belle schmaltz he's peddling."

"Oh, Christ," Irene muttered, so softly that only the women could hear. "He would, too."

Polly stepped forward. "Irene had nothing to do with it. This was my idea."

"You again. And who the hell are you?"

It looked like she was going to get her chance with him after all. "Polly Maddox."

"She's Elroy Maddox's daughter," Gil said.

Harry whipped around. "You knew who she was and didn't tell me?"

"I tried, but you cut me off."

"You shoulda tried harder." He turned back to face the Mrs. Moguls and sucked in a deep breath.

In that brief pause, Polly saw her opportunity and stepped forward. "I know all about the fifty grand and how you forced my father to embezzle it."

"Pah!" Cohn swiped the air with a contemptuous flick of the wrist. "If he'd hung on a bit longer, I'd have paid it back. But what does it matter now? It's all history."

"Not to me, it isn't." Polly wished she had that teapot in her hand; she could do a heck of a lot of damage. "If Mr. Wrigley doesn't get his money back, I lose everything. Be. Cause. Of. *You*." She spat out those last words as though they were a mouthful of sour cherry pits.

"We don't always get what we want." He turned to Gil. "Why the fuck isn't my car here yet?"

Polly waited until Gil had taken off to the huddle of parking attendants. "We aren't finished yet."

Cohn's head whipped back toward her. "Christ on a cracker, are you still here?"

"It's all bluff," Rose murmured. "Mostly. Don't let him intimidate you."

Polly had no intention of letting him trample all over her, but she would've preferred it if Rose hadn't added the 'mostly.' "What about your fellow moguls?"

He eyed the women who had formed a semi-circle behind Polly. "What about them?"

"They'll be mighty interested to learn you're screwing them over and using Bioff and Browne to do it. They're forking over God knows how many hundreds of thousands. Meanwhile, you're not paying one thin dime."

"Be careful tossing around accusations you can't prove."

"Not only are you not paying your fair share, but"—Polly jerked a thumb in Gil's direction—"you've got your lackey picking up the dough from the studios. Bags filled with cash. I've got witnesses."

Thank heavens Benji was safe in the California desert.

A deep, guttural snarl was the best retort Cohn possessed in his arsenal.

"I took it to Donovan, but he's in your pocket as well. And now that we"—she drew a circle in the air indicating the women behind her—"know about Bioff and Browne, the way forward to get justice for my father is a lot clearer."

Clearer yes, but feasible? Polly was far from sure. Confronting Cohn was one thing; taking on the mob was an altogether different barrel of tommy guns.

"Girlie"—Cohn's arctic stare made Polly feel like a moth caught in a searchlight—"you're dreaming if you believe you can intimidate me. You're nothing but the naïve ball-of-fluff offspring of a hapless small-fry. Only a fool would get himself shot by those flat-footed coppers."

"He got you the money you needed to have a mob hit taken off you."

Cohn stared in mute surprise.

Rose stepped up to the front, pressing her shoulder against Polly's. "And all because some drunk got the better of you in a fight. Except you were too cocky to realize he's more mobbed-up. Who's the fool now?"

He threw wait-till-we-get-home daggers at his wife before facing Polly again.

"At least I didn't set the fire that destroyed half of Avalon."

Polly hated the involuntary cry that erupted from her. But it was out there now, and she couldn't suck it back in.

Cohn smirked at her. "How do you think I coerced your father into lending me that dough?"

Irene joined Polly and Rose. "You were never going to return any of it."

"The next time your husband wants to borrow one of my stars," he retorted, "tell him he can go fuck himself. And the same goes for the rest of you dusty old hags."

"What did you call us?" Constance demanded.

A sleek Cadillac Sixteen with gleaming bronze chrome trim whisked up the driveway. The driver's side door opened and a parking attendant slid out.

"You battle-axes, with your bridge parties and tearoom lunches. What a useless bunch of parasites."

Polly was closer to Cohn's sedan than Gil was. She dashed around the hood and yanked the keys out of the ignition. "We're having this out. Here and now."

"What're you standing there for?" Cohn yelled at Gil. "Take them from her."

Gil froze. For the briefest, most fleeting moment, Polly caught a flash of the Gil she'd met at Kreiss's Coffee Shop. The one with the floppy hair and the talent to build carriages more skillfully than anyone else. The one who didn't hesitate to help her hunt through that tavern in the mountains, and who was genuinely thrilled to be working on *Gone with the Wind*. Why couldn't he have kept on being that Gil?

But his hesitation lasted only a second. Irene, Rose, and Marjorie stepped in to create a barrier. He shunted them aside like they were sacks of potatoes. Ludlow dodged around them. Anchoring his weight onto his back foot, he tried to throw a punch. Gil blocked him as easily as he had thwarted Cohn, and landed a nasty uppercut squarely into Luddie's chin. The force sent Ludlow staggering backward. He sprawled onto the ground, gasping for air.

Gil plucked the keys from Polly's grip.

Cohn was now in the passenger seat. "Drive, dammit. DRIVE!"

Gil vaulted behind the wheel and jammed the keys into the ignition. The engine rumbled to life. He shifted the car into gear and roared down the driveway.

43

Marcella didn't look up from her typewriter when Polly arrived at the office the next day. Polly repeated her "Good morning," a little louder, a little brighter. No response. She put away her hat, bag, and gloves, and approached Marcella's desk. "Anything going on?"

Marcella held up a finger, signaling for Polly to wait.

Had word already gotten out about last night's awful scene at the Beverly Hills Hotel? Any of those half-dozen parking attendants might have been well-paid snitches for Louella or Hedda. She should have known that shaming Cohn into doing the right thing because they were in public wouldn't have stopped him from behaving like a fink. Instead, had she brought shame to the Selznick studios? Was Marcella working her way up to asking for Polly's resignation?

Marcella extracted the memo from her machine. "Get a load of this."

February 13, 1939

Joint press release from David O. Selznick and George Cukor

As a result of a series of disagreements between us during the production of Gone with the Wind, *Mr. Cukor and I have mutually decided that the only solution is for a new director to be selected as early a date as is practical.*

"Those arguments you two have been having," Polly said.

"It took me a couple of brawls to realize he was desperate for me to talk him out of firing George. It's been churning him up inside. Take a look at the first line of the second paragraph."

Polly read the sentence out loud. "'Mr. Cukor's withdrawal is the most regrettable incident of my rather long producing career.'" She lowered the paper. "How did this happen?"

"He's got a definite vision of how he wants the picture to be. George wasn't achieving it, so he had to pull the trigger."

"It'll look terrible changing horses at this point. Especially seeing as how everyone loves to call *Gone with the Wind* the biggest white elephant Hollywood's ever given birth to. Mr. Selznick firing George will only confirm their suspicions."

"So you can imagine the agony he's been going through."

Polly nodded. Despite contending with all this, Irene had still shown up at the Beverly Hills Hotel, been her usual unflappable self.

"Where is he now?"

"He said he couldn't listen to the clackety-clack as I typed up what he called 'George's Obituary' and took off for a lap around the studio. To clear his head, he said. But if you ask me, he's in his car having a jolly good cry."

Polly placed the memo on her desk. "What happens now?"

"We close down the entire picture."

"Mr. Selznick must have a replacement in mind, though."

Marcella drummed her fingernails against the space bar of her typewriter. "Victor Fleming."

"Isn't he directing *The Wizard of Oz*?"

"Uh-huh."

"Mayer would pull him off one of his biggest movies before they've completed filming?"

"Your guess is as good as my guess is as good as Louella's guess is as good as the janitor's. But"—Marcella leaned forward onto her elbows—"my husband will welcome this slowdown." She took the memo and stood up. "While I send this out on the teletype, you can make a start on the Hitchcock deal. They've finally agreed on terms."

Polly scanned Hitchcock's seven-year deal at forty thousand per picture. The contract ran to eight pages, with Selznick's notes, corrections, and clarifications crowding the margins.

But she was paying it no heed. Poor George. How dreadful he must feel right now.

Hazel cannonballed into the room. "Is it true? About Cukor?"

"'Fraid so."

"I caught a streetcar with Gertie from Wardrobe, who heard it from Thelma in Casting, who heard it from Katharine Hepburn."

"How could Hepburn possibly know?"

Hazel peeled off her gloves. "Last year she made *Holiday* with Cary Grant at Columbia, and Mr. Cukor was her director."

An idea pinged in a tiny corner of Polly's mind. "Yes, he was, wasn't he?"

"According to Thelma, they're real close pals."

After the previous night's debacle, Polly had returned home with Amelia and Luddie for an autopsy over highballs. Could she have handled it differently? Yes. No. Maybe. Was there any hope for restoration of Elroy's reputation or the money he'd stolen? Possibly not. Probably not. Nope. Polly had gone to bed stumped, trying to think of a single person to whom she might turn.

Until now.

The Mrs. Moguls shared a viewpoint on all this, but filtered it through the prism of their husbands' perceptions. Having worked for Harry Cohn, might George have a broader, higher, wiser perspective?

"I suppose Marcella's at the teletype?" Hazel stowed her gloves in her handbag and lifted the cover off her typewriter. "It won't be long before we're inundated by every columnist and reporter between here and Hong Kong."

And so would George. Not only that, if this were to be his last day at the studio, the next hour might be her only chance to ask him.

The other four girls in the typing pool arrived in a giggling gaggle. Once Marcella returned from the teletype room, there'd be all hands on deck to man the telephones. More than enough.

"Bring them up to speed and tell Marcella I'm out on an emergency."

* * *

George's office was empty. Had he already left the studio? Not that she'd blame him. Fortunately, one of the prop makers happened by and told her that Mr. Cukor was on Stage Fourteen blocking out the scene where Melanie gives birth.

How very George Cukor of him to continue working even though he had been fired.

She hurried onto a bedroom set at Aunt Pittypat's house and found him down the back in a snug recess tucked away from the milling crew. "Hello there."

He steeled himself as he turned around. The smile he'd arranged on his face drooped. "Have you typed up the press release yet?"

"Marcella did."

He nodded, somber as a pallbearer. "So, that's that."

She stepped inside the alcove. It was big enough for two people, but barely. The faint scent of his expensive aftershave hung in the air, fighting for space with melancholy. "For what it's worth, I think Mr. Selznick has made a dreadful mistake."

"Thank you, Polly. I appreciate that." He clamped a hand on her arm and dug his fingers in harder than she was expecting. She tried not to flinch. "All the preparatory work we did was based on Sidney Howard's script. But when we started shooting, I was forced to use Dave's version, and it simply doesn't play the same."

"But you're too much the gentleman to tell him, 'Look, you silly bonehead, your writing's not up to snuff.'"

George managed a feeble smile. "I had to direct what I considered unplayable scenes to the best of my ability. He's the boss;

what he says goes. In this specific case, what goes is my lumpy Jewish tuchus!"

"Oh, George. Should I be laughing or crying?"

"The professional in me wants to see this behemoth through to the bitter end. But confidentially, I don't know that I have it in me to go the distance. I haven't been sleeping, but now I can go home and snooze like a baby." He gave an uneasy, strained laugh. "Maybe *tomorrow* night. And besides, if I play my 'Poor me' cards right, all this drama puts me in a splendid position to manipulate Mayer into giving me a consolation prize."

"You've got one in mind, haven't you?"

"*The Women.*"

After MGM had handed over an enormous sum for the screen rights to Clare Booth Luce's hit play, conjecture over which actresses would be cast had filled almost as many column inches as *Wind*.

"That's a gem of a consolation prize," Polly said.

"Always seek the silver lining, kiddo. But tell me, why are you here?"

Polly ran a hand down a frilly gingham drape that framed their intimate nook. "It's just that I . . ." *Yes, kiddo, what* are *you going to say? That you came to him with your own problems, today of all days, you self-absorbed, self-interested, self-centered knucklehead?* "The press release didn't mention when you'd be leaving, and I didn't want you to slip away without saying goodbye."

"How thoughtful of you."

"If I'd known you were still directing, I wouldn't have rushed."

"Come now, Polly, you didn't run all the way over here solely to bid me farewell, did you?"

"I . . ." She looked into his eyes and saw only compassion and understanding. "I had a thorny dilemma I wanted to run past you, but given what's going on—"

"I'd consider it a favor if you were to distract me."

The last of Polly's resolve to not be a selfish old so-and-so fell away. She told him about Gil, and Cohn, and the Mrs. Moguls, and that appalling scene at the Beverly Hills Hotel.

"So," George said, "that wily coot isn't paying his fair share to Bioff and Browne, huh?"

"Nope."

"Even though the top dogs are saving money in the long run, you can bet they're comforting themselves, secure in the knowledge that they're all in the same boat called the good ship USS *Paying Through The Nose*."

"Except Cohn."

"I assume the wives have told their husbands?"

"They wish their husbands would include them more in their work, but they don't, so they feel somewhat powerless in this situation."

"Those women have more clout than they believe, but as a man, it's not my place to tell them."

"When you were working at Columbia making *Holiday*, did you hear anything about him that might help us?"

George thought for a minute, raising Polly's hopes, but dropping them again when he admitted nothing came to mind. "But, if you confront him, do it with witnesses around. If you try it in private, he'll squash you like a steamroller."

"But we tried that already. It was a disaster."

"What does a bastard like Harry Cohn care if a bunch of parking attendants see him swing a punch? No, no, I mean take it public."

"Mr. Cukor?" a voice called from the front of the set.

George and Polly stepped out of the alcove. "What is it, Paul?"

"Miss Leigh and Miss de Havilland have heard." The young man pulled a *Yikes!* grimace.

"Where are they?"

"Rehearsal room B, but you ought to hurry. They're threatening to march on Mr. Selznick's office."

"I'll leave you to it," Polly told him. "Best of luck."

"Walk with me." He set off at a brisk pace.

"Vivien and Olivia need you far more—"

"And they shall have me. It takes three full minutes to get to the rehearsal room." George nodded at a pair of passing workmen, each loaded down with department store mannequins dressed as Confederate soldiers for the big Atlanta railway station scene. "Voting on the upcoming Academy Awards doesn't close for another three days. If word got out that Harry Cohn is playing dirty, the tide might turn against *You Can't Take It with You,* which could have a bleed-through effect on the reception of *Mr. Smith Goes to Washington*—"

"Which Cohn is risking everything on."

"And *You Can't Take It with You* is up against *Robin Hood, Boys Town,* and *Jezebel.*"

"If people learn what Cohn's been up to, votes could easily swing to those three pictures."

"Harry would have the conniption fit to end all conniption fits. You ought to find a way to face him *before* voting closes."

"Won't everybody have sent their ballot in by now?"

"Nobody submits early unless they're voting for themselves. Scandalous details surface. Loyalties turn on a dime. Grudges and fights can erupt. Everybody holds off until the last minute."

"But it's not fair to Capra to sabotage his chances because of what Cohn's up to."

"Naturally. Which is why you need to get to him before Monday." They were now standing in front of a door with a large "B" painted in red.

She kissed him on the cheek and whispered, "Whatever happens, I'm on your side."

He acknowledged his gratitude with a brief nod. "Ditto, kiddo."

Polly listened long enough to hear the two actresses wail his name before turning on her heel and scurrying back to the Mansion.

44

Compared to the bustling streets of Culver City, Burbank felt like a country town. Not that Polly had ever seen a country town—Avalon didn't count, as far as she was concerned—but this was what she'd always imagined: wide streets, light traffic, easy parking, and the citrusy aroma of lemons and oranges drifting over from nearby groves.

Polly turned onto a side street, and then right again before she felt safe enough to pull to the curb. Was this subterfuge necessary? Noah had assured her that he'd double-checked with the guards at the Columbia Ranch security gate.

Yes, her name was on the list.

No, she wouldn't have a problem.

Yes, Mr. Cohn was spending all afternoon there to ensure everything for tonight's party would unfold according to his exact plans.

No, he wouldn't be surrounded by flunkies because this was strictly a hands-on operation.

And that was all well and good, but even if she got onto the ranch where Columbia shot westerns and war pictures, and any movie requiring a large outdoor set, would she get anywhere near Cohn?

Still, as George had pointed out, today was her last shot at getting him to change his mind.

And she wouldn't even have that had two things not occurred.

First, George's departure had forced *Gone with the Wind* to close down, which led directly to Marcella letting go two typists and giving Polly and Hazel time off.

And second, Columbia's *Only Angels Have Wings* was barely midway through production, but Cohn had announced a huge party to celebrate. "Celebrate what?" Winchell had groused. "Is the flick in such poor shape that he needs to whoop it up because they've made it halfway through?"

Neither Cohn nor his PR people had confirmed nor denied the reasons for this everybody's-invited bash, but Noah had confirmed Polly's suspicions: It was a last-ditch effort to impress Academy members to vote for *You Can't Take It with You*, because if they did, it boded well for *Mr. Smith Goes to Washington*."

"It's a risk, though," Noah had said. "Nobody's having fun on the *Only Angels* set, so this cast and crew most certainly do *not* want to attend a studio party and pretend to be all palsy-walsy. But when Cohn commands, you salute. And besides," he'd added, "that rickety lamasery set from *Lost Horizon* is tagged for demolition. It cost so much to build that he wants to get his money's worth. They're using it for *Only Angels*, but after that, down it'll go, so this'll be your last chance to see one of the most beautiful outdoor sets Hollywood has ever built."

Polly gave her name at the Columbia Ranch entrance gate. The security guard looked over her shoulder. "You walked?"

"I parked around the corner," Polly said.

"Visitors parking is over there." He threw a thumb over his left shoulder. "You could've driven onto the lot." Not a chance in hell, Polly thought. What if I need to bolt out of there only to find my car impounded by the man who's baying for my blood like a werewolf? "If you're here for the big party tonight, you're six hours early."

Polly mounted a stiff smile. "I'm what you might call an advance scouting party."

"For the Paul Whiteman Orchestra?"

Polly knew of Paul Whiteman and his dance-band orchestra from their gigs at the Casino on Catalina. NBC Red often broadcast them live to air. Polly would listen at home and marvel that people as far away as Billings, Montana, and Galveston, Texas, could be listening to the same music at the same time. If Cohn was shelling out for Paul Whiteman, he was sparing no expense.

Polly propped an elbow on the window ledge. "Confidentially," she said without moving her lips, "these musicians are a delicate bunch. Everything has to be just so. Know what I mean?"

"Like actors, huh?"

"Worse."

"In that case, you're a saint." The guard snapped his spearmint gum. "Need directions to the *Lost Horizon* set? Or have they changed their minds about where they're putting the dance floor?"

Cohn had to be around here somewhere, so it was as good a place to start as any. "Can you aim me in the right direction?"

He pointed to the road heading into the heart of the lot. "Follow it until it veers off to the right. The damned thing is three stories. The only way you can miss it is if you're blind or dead."

The road led Polly to a Wild West town with hitching posts, swinging-door saloons, roughly hewn wooden sidewalks, and barrels to catch rainwater. In the distance, a man's voice screamed instructions, fraught with cursing and short on tact. Polly couldn't determine the direction, but there was no mistaking the grating tirades of Columbia's sheriff.

Only three blocks long, the town gave way to empty land after the blacksmith shop. Ahead lay a hillock, its slopes dented with cannonball-sized pockmarks. A stunted ponderosa pine stood at its summit with branches sloping skyward as though beseeching the heavens. And beyond that, Polly found Noah hadn't exaggerated.

A reflecting pool, fifteen feet wide and lined on each side with low shrubs, stretched fifty feet to a wide flight of shallow steps. They, in turn, led up to the first level where a team of workmen in grimy overalls were laying down planks of wood. Behind them, a narrow staircase of steps sandwiched between two broad pylons ushered the way to the second platform thirty feet in the air.

A third level reached another twenty feet into the crisp January air. A single pane of frosted glass etched with a tapestry-like design ran up the center. Lit from within, it glowed like translucent snow.

It may have been cobbled together with balsa wood, plaster, and whitewash, but it reminded Polly of a Beverly Hills mansion Luddie had shown her once on a drive around town. It sat at the end of a brick driveway, rising two stories, gleaming white in the blinding sunshine, serene as a cathedral.

Cohn started up his harangues again. Now that Polly was closer, she could follow the sound to the roof of the lamasery set. No wonder she'd been able to hear him from so far away: he held a bullhorn to boost his big mouth.

She hooked the leather strap of her clamshell shoulder purse over her head and positioned it behind her. Skirting past the workmen setting up a temporary dance floor and bandstand, she flew up the narrow steps to the first landing, where she headed for the second flight of longer, narrower steps.

A familiar voice stopped her. "Not so fast."

Wearing dungarees cuffed at the ankles and streaked with dirt and paint, Gil looked more disheveled than she'd ever seen him. He lolled against the lamasery wall, although he probably shouldn't have; it reeked of fresh whitewash. Not that his faded flannel shirt with the torn pocket could have looked any worse for wear.

"What a gorilla you turned out to be. And hitting Luddie proves it." She turned her back on him and headed for the steps.

"I can't let you go up there."

"You plan on slugging me, too?"

"I will not let you anywhere near him."

She faced him more squarely now. He could knock her out with a single well-aimed punch, so she'd have to talk her way out. "Harry Cohn is the last person you should hitch your little red wagon to."

"Mr. Cohn pays me to do what needs to be taken care of. And he pays me plenty."

"It should be about more than a paycheck."

"Easy for you to say."

She could see now that he needed a new razor, hairbrush, and nail scissors because he sure wasn't using the ones he had. "Everything I left behind on Catalina—every last stick of furniture, crystal bowl, bath towel, and toothbrush—is out of bounds. I have access to nothing from my past, and all because—"

"*You* didn't grow up in a shantytown hovel." Naked resentment shook his voice. "No hot water, terrible food, barely any schooling, no prospects. I should think you'd be more sympathetic seeing as how you're friends with Luddie."

This encounter had pivoted into a direction Polly didn't see coming. "What's he got to do with this?"

"Ludlow Sinclair." Gil said the name as though Luddie had kidnapped the Lindbergh baby. "He's not who he pretends to be."

Polly rejoined Gil on the landing. "Care to explain?"

"For starters, his name is Rufus Klinger."

Polly had no reason to believe anything that Gil said, but he hadn't conjured a name like that out of thin air. "And how do you know that?"

His lips narrowed into a resentful line. "He was my neighbor."

"You were *neighbors*? Where was—?" But Polly already knew the answer. "You both lived in that Hooverville at Alameda and —and—"

"Firestone. The Klingers were such poor white trash they made everybody there feel good about themselves. A whole slew of kids when they couldn't feed one. Raggedy clothes. Dirt floor. Drunken dad, beaten-down mother. Everybody looked at them and thought, 'Our life is one miserable, hopeless, desperate day after another, but at least we're not the Klingers.'"

So that was why Luddie avoided talking about his past, and why he'd become so deft at deflecting any question that reached back further than the day they'd met. "And look at him now," Polly said.

"He was a filthy, snotty-nosed brat dressed in rags and covered in scabs. The youngest of six raggedy guttersnipes; not a decent one in the bunch. He's so completely different now, and with a whole new name, I didn't even recognize him."

"Do you think he recognized you?"

"I don't look much like how I used to, either. Plus, he knew me as Bert, so it's no wonder neither of us cottoned on to the other. That is, until we were all in front of the Beverly Hills Hotel and he was taking a swing at me. The way he tried to deflect my punch jogged my memory. I was still putting two and two together as I slugged him. We were blocks away before it hit me like a bolt of lightning. I nearly drove us into a hedge."

"Mr. Cohn wouldn't have been pleased."

"I'd be lying if I said I didn't want to turn that Cadillac around and go back to the hotel to flatten him but good."

Was Gil aware that he'd tightened his hands into fists?

"Why?"

"Hooverville wasn't just a time and a place. It was a whole way of looking at the world and seeing there was no place for you in it. But he figured a way out. Him with his fancy suits, and his champagne cocktails, and his swanky nightclubs, and his dinner-and-dancing with Mrs. DeMille and Mrs. Zanuck and Mrs. Selznick."

"Nonsense!" Polly had had enough of this self-pity. "He's not the only one. You're now the best carriage maker in Hollywood."

"You know how I found I was good with my hands? By punching people. You didn't survive Hooverville if you couldn't slug every no-hoper in your way. That's why Rufus was so pathetic and downtrodden. He couldn't handle himself in a fight. But I could. And I punched and kicked and lied and bullied my way out. All he had to do was learn to waltz and match his neckties with his socks."

Luddie's escape from that awful Hooverville would have entailed more than that, but time was ticking by and she needed another shot at Cohn.

Two stories above them, Cohn's voice boomed from his bullhorn. "And make sure that bandstand is level. The last thing we need is to watch the Paul Whiteman Orchestra topple over like they're on the fucking *Titanic*."

"I can't let you up there," Gil said.

"He and I have unfinished business." She stepped toward the next set of stairs once more, but he leaped ahead, blocking her path.

"Part of my job is to protect him," he said, low and even.

"Him?" she said. "The guy is a rotten bastard with no morals—"

"He's the only person who has kept me in regular employment. And for a Hooverville fugitive, that means a lot."

"And I sympathize, Gil, I do, but that's no reason—"

She could see him preparing to grab her, so she took a half-step backward, far enough to put her out of reach, then stepped to the left and concaved her body so that when he took a swipe at her, he grabbed only air. The maneuver would have worked had it not been for the strap of her shoulder bag. He grabbed hold of it and yanked it toward him and down. She caught herself before she sprawled headlong into the stairs. Regaining her balance, she lashed out at him, fists flailing, but he blocked each attempt at landing a punch as though she were a four-year-old throwing a tantrum.

But then Gable's advice came back to her. *Knee 'em in the groin. Don't warn them. Don't hold back.*

But she needed leverage.

The flannel shirt hung from his shoulders in loose folds big enough for her to grip.

She shot out her hands and seized his shirt, bunching the material between her fingers. She wrenched him into her raised right knee. Strangled gurgling sounds heaved out of him as it barreled into his crotch. His face turned red with agony, the tendons in his neck straining.

He staggered backward, closer to the edge of the landing than he knew. Only a couple of steps away. It wouldn't take too much effort.

She closed the space between them in two strides, wedged the heel of her shoe against his hip, and shoved.

He hung in midair for a moment, his arms swinging, his mouth gaping in astonishment.

Polly didn't stick around to watch him tumble down the lamasery stairs like Laurel and Hardy's piano. She flew up the second flight, reaching the top as Cohn bellowed more orders through his bullhorn. "The witless wonder with the bags of ice. The party doesn't start for another couple of hours. TAKE 'EM BACK."

Polly peeked behind the two-story stripe of frosted glass. Zigzagging flights of stairs so steep they almost qualified as a ladder led to the roof where Cohn stood.

She felt them wobble under her feet as she scampered up and up and up. If they're sturdy enough to take Harry Cohn, she told herself, they can certainly hold me.

First flight.

Second flight.

Third flight.

Fourth flight.

Then, finally, an open hatchway.

He stood at the roofline, one hand holding the bullhorn to his mouth, the other swiping the air. "You goddamn morons. *This* side of the dance floor. I don't care if the musicians can see the set. Do I have to do this all myself?"

The craggy wooden boards creaked as Polly approached him. He swung around. "What the fuck are you doing here?"

"More to the point," Polly said, "what are *you* doing? Isn't it a mite unsafe for someone in your position to be—"

"I can see everything all the way up here. Make sure my minions—why the hell am I justifying myself to you? Whatever the reason, I ain't buying, so make yourself scarce."

"I've come to finish the conversation we started at the hotel."

"I've got nothing more to say to you."

"My father—"

"I can have you arrested for trespassing."

"And thrown into jail? Again?"

A malicious smile surfaced. "Wasn't once enough?"

"I'm not as easily scared as you'd like."

"You're not getting the dough."

"You have an unpaid debt, and I'm—"

"The *fuck* I do!" He lunged at her. She felt the force of his foot slamming into the floorboards as the wind blustered down from the back of the Hollywood Hills and whipped across Burbank. The lamasery roof shuddered and swayed.

Except that it wasn't a real lamasery but a movie set built to last a couple of months. *Lost Horizon* had come out two years before, so it was a wonder the three-year-old set was still upright. And here she was, four stories up, standing on rickety floorboards that had long outlived their intended purpose, with a madman who was growing more and more enraged.

"You and my father were friends."

"Business partners," Cohn growled.

"He made a lot of money for you."

"Which he wouldn't have done if I hadn't invested his idea with capital. Without me, there wouldn't have been any Mad Ox."

"You both came out on top. When he needed you, you came through with the goods. But when you needed him, you forced him to embezzle."

"Shows what you know."

"I know about the fire. And I know that you threatened to get what you needed from him. All I'm asking—"

"FORGET IT!"

Polly felt a whisper of air on her neck: the wind had changed. It blew across them from the east now, out San Bernadino way, warmer and stronger. Amelia had warned her about the Santa Anas. *They can be sudden and blustery. You gotta watch 'em.* The walls creaked in protest.

Cohn spread his feet to steady himself. "Your father lost because he couldn't stand up to me. And I don't respect anyone who lets me steamroll over them like they were nothing but a doormat."

"My father—"

"—is dead. Only a sucker would pay back a dead man, and I'm no sucker. So get lost, girlie."

He turned his back on her and raised the bullhorn. "I hope you blockheads aren't planning on putting the bar next to the reflecting pool. I don't want drunk people falling in. Give it at least ten feet. No, make it twelve. There's no telling how stupid people can be when they're stinko."

Polly joined him at the edge. The tower furnished a rare three-hundred-and-sixty-degree panorama of the San Fernando Valley. Under different circumstances, Polly would have enjoyed taking in this bird's-eye view of the orchards and farmhouses, wide-open fields and pockets of houses springing up around Warner Brothers, but there was no handrail, no balustrade. Nothing but a two-foot parapet along the wall, and then a thirty-foot drop.

"Gerard Donovan isn't the only one I can go to," she persisted. "There are other authorities."

"Authorities, huh?" He worked up a gob of spit and launched it over the edge. "From Donovan to Buron Fitts, I've got 'em all in my pocket. Plus the LAPD and the Sheriff's office. How do you think I got away with making Mad Ox during Prohibition? You think the Avalon police were above taking bribes?"

Aw, jeez. Them, too? There had been weeks when the local policemen were the only people who had talked to her. So, they were only being nice to the daughter of the guy who paid them to look the other way?

"Yes, that's right, sweetheart," Cohn said, reading her face. "They may have liked Elroy personally, but they were there to uphold the law, and needed an incentive to look the other way. And trust me, we gave them plenty of incentive. Every month."

"You can't have every single officer of the law in all of Los Angeles in your pocket." Polly had hoped she'd sound more sure of her facts, but the quaking in her voice matched the tremble beneath her feet.

"You naïve little runt. LA's got the most corrupt government since Tammany Hall."

"You're paying nothing to Bioff and Browne. Meanwhile, Mayer, Zanuck, Selznick, Warner, and Balaban are paying tens or even hundreds of thousands of dollars to keep the unions out of their studios. And those men will be mighty unhappy if they learn you've weaseled out of paying your fair share."

"And you're the cheerleader to tell 'em, I suppose?"

"Have you cast your ballot for the Academy Awards yet?" Polly asked him, changing tack. Confusion wavered in his cold, gray eyes. "I didn't think so." She didn't try too hard to keep the satisfaction out of her voice. "Like everybody else, you wait until the last minute. Which means there's time for people to change their vote for *You Can't Take It with You*. And even more time for them to sour on *Mr. Smith Goes to Washington*. The future of your studio is dependent on *Mr. Smith* doing gangbuster business; otherwise, you're in a suffocatingly tight financial pickle. Isn't that right?"

He slammed the bullhorn onto the low-slung parapet. "Tell me where you got that information, or so help me—"

"I don't have to tell you a damned thing."

"Was it my wife? Did she run her mouth off as usual?"

"Rose is a better wife than you deserve. And no, it wasn't her."

The red blotches breaking out on Cohn's face grew brighter and angrier; instinctively, she retreated a step.

The Santa Ana picked up again. It had changed direction and begun to intensify; it now howled over their heads in unpredictable gusts. The set quivered like Jell-O, worse than before. Polly felt the board beneath her feet give way just a little. The movement was so negligible it might have only been her imagination—but it was enough for her to question how smart it had been to follow him up here.

Cohn grabbed the parapet for support, but a hefty chunk of plaster crumbled in his hands and cascaded over the edge.

"Neither of us should be up here," Polly said.

"You shouldn't be here at all. And you won't be." He straightened up and screamed, "SECURITY!" The workmen peered up at them. The supervisor grabbed the shoulder of the nearest laborer and sent him running toward the Wild West town. Cohn lowered his bullhorn. "You come at me with Bioff and Browne. Who the fuck do you think you're dealing with? I squash bugs like you before I even get out of bed."

Polly stared back at him. *Don't blink. Don't blink. Don't you dare blink.* "I'm not dealing with you," she lobbed back. "I'm dealing with *Mrs.* Mayer, *Mrs.* Zanuck, *Mrs.* Selznick. They, in turn, will deal with their husbands. And when they learn you're not paying your fair share because you're in bed with the mob, *they* will be dealing with you. I don't know how many bugs you kill before you get out of bed each morning, but I can't imagine you've taken on any quite as big as them."

The bright pink flush of anger faded from his cheeks. His beady eyes lost their flinty malice. "You've turned my wife against me." His growl had lost some of its obnoxious self-confidence.

"You did that all by yourself. Rose is deeply—*deeply*—angry over how you approached that starlet about giving you a child."

"Hey! What about me?"

Now he was sounding like a petulant little boy who didn't get his after-school Tootsie Roll.

"What about you?"

"I want a kid to carry on my name and my legacy. Rose can't give me that."

"You could've handled it more diplomatically."

"How?"

"For starters, you could have talked it over with her."

"Fat chance."

"You men—you're all the same. You never ask your wives what they think, how they feel. God forbid you should ask them for their opinions or viewpoint."

"Tell me, Dorothy Dix, how many marriages have *you* had?" He had her there, and she probably would have let it go. But then he added, "You shoulda stayed on Catalina. This city is too damn big for small-town rubes. Leave the important stuff to people who know what they're doing."

Polly took a step forward. To do what, she didn't know. Hit

him? Slap him? Punch him? Trip him? He had a good thirty pounds on her and knew how to deliver a right hook. A rotted plank gave way, sinking her foot up to the ankle.

But Cohn didn't see because a voice called from down below. "Hey boss, you still up there?"

Cohn leaned onto the same chunk of parapet that had fallen apart. "WHAT?"

As Cohn and his supervisor screamed their discussion, Polly retracted her foot from the fissure, slowly and gingerly, but the wood deteriorated even further. They shouldn't be standing up here. Nobody should. The whole structure was one monumental sneeze away from collapse.

"GODDAMMIT!" Cohn pounded the low-slung wall with his fist, sending up plaster dust into the wind.

"Don't do that!" she said. "Can't you see how brittle everything is?"

Cohn ignored her. "I don't care where you put the damned catering tent," he boomed, "as long as it's out of sight."

She joined him at the wall, but kept back from the edge. The parapet now had two gaping holes; she wasn't keen to make a third.

"You're wasting your time." He faced her with a snarl. "I ain't paying nobody nothing. Least of all you."

"If you're broke—"

"Shut your mouth before I shut it for you."

"—you could go to your mobster pals for a loan. They've got the fifty grand you paid to take their hit off you."

He laughed a grim, cheerless laugh. "That's not a bad scenario for a movie. Thanks, kid. Here's what I'll do: A hundred bucks for the story idea, and for the rest, you can GO FUCK YOURSELF."

He kicked the wall as hard as he could. The plaster broke apart like it was made of sawdust. He lost his balance, clutching at the air as his leg crashed clear through to the other side, slowing his momentum, but not halting it. The entire set shuddered. "JESUS!" He flung out his hands to hook the parapet's edge. It held firm, but for how long? "Don't just stand there, for Chrissake!"

There would be time enough to tell him "I warned you" later.

She shuffled over to him and gripped him by his underarms. "Promise to pay Wrigley back."

"Are you fucking kidding me? I'm about to plummet to oblivion and you're haggling terms?"

His fingers started to slide. Despair filled his eyes, naked and helpless.

"It's a three-story drop." She peeked over the edge. "All your workers have gathered down below, watching how their boss is being saved by a girl. And—" she laced her voice with enough mockery to fill a carnival sideshow—"at least half of them are hoping I lose my grip."

His eyelids fluttered as grim realization filtered through his desperation.

Yes, that's right. Half the people down there don't give a fig about you.

"The money," he said. "I'll think about it."

"I need more than a vague promise from a desperate son of a bitch."

Was calling a powerful studio head a 'desperate son of a bitch' going too far? Her grip on him was quite firm and she had every intention of pulling him to safety, so he was unlikely to be biting the concrete any time soon. But he didn't know that. Another gust blasted over them. He was sweating worse than a prisoner on a chain gang. "Ever thought of selling your stake in Mad Ox?" she asked.

"No."

"It'd be worth a fair amount."

"And you've got a buyer all lined up, I suppose."

"I might." How hard could it be to find one?

"Fine," he spat at her.

She'd have preferred a more substantial answer, but she could now hear workmen climbing the steep stairs. Cohn would only keep his word—assuming he would, which was far from guaranteed—if *she* were the one to save him.

"Can you get your leg over the parapet?" She used the word

'parapet' because she knew he probably had no idea what it meant. One last chance to twist the knife.

"Para-what?"

Another breeze whipped up, stiffer and colder than the others. The set swayed.

"Your leg that's dangling like a carcass. Swing it over the wall enough for me to grab your ankle. It'll be easier to pull you up sideways."

He grunted and threw his foot over the edge; she caught it on the first attempt. Bracing her feet and leaning back, using her own weight as leverage, she hauled him slowly, slowly, slowly toward her.

"I can't hold on much longer," he said.

The dead weight of his burly body grew lighter and lighter as he regained his grasp on the edge of the structure and helped pull himself back onto the top. "We're . . . nearly . . . there . . ."

She let out a boorish grunt as she hoisted him those final few inches. But she was stronger than she supposed. He plowed into her like a wrecking ball. She staggered backward. They hit the floorboards together. A sickening crack rent the air.

Polly and Cohn looked at each other, fear reflecting fear.

They tried to scramble free, but their combined weight was too much. The wood splintered under their efforts, and they plunged through the gaping hole.

45

Polly inserted her knitting needle into the top rim of the cast encasing her leg from foot to thigh. It didn't reach the itch that had been driving her nuts all morning, but she had to try.

Two months she'd have to wear this damned thing, hobbling around on crutches, needing help to do almost everything.

Still, as Amelia had reminded her, "better a broken tibia than a broken neck." At least she and Cohn had landed on soft lawn. But did he have to land *on her*? All he had to show for it were two dislocated toes. They were his big toes, so they hurt the most. That, at least, was something to be thankful for.

Luddie walked out of the kitchen carrying a steaming coffee cup in each hand. "How's the bruise?"

"Inconveniently placed."

"So it's on your butt?"

"And hip, and into my—well, never mind about that."

"Ouch." Luddie screwed his handsome puss into a sympathetic pucker as he handed her one of the cups.

The coffee had an unusual woody-nutty taste to it. "What did you put in this?"

"There wasn't much left in the can, so I added some chicory I found beside the cod liver oil, which you're also nearly out of."

"Amelia said she'd stop at the market next to Schwab's."

It was three-thirty. Amelia's shift had finished at noon. Where was she?

"Have you been able to sleep?" he asked.

"Not much. Every time I shut my eyes, all I see is Harry Cohn's ugly mug staring back at me."

"Did he ever apologize?"

"Surely you jest."

Whatever had happened following the fall was a hazy blur now. She remembered the sound of running boots, and someone shouting for a medic. Of more comfort was the voice of one workman commenting to his colleague how embarrassing it was for "Mister He-Man" to have his fall broken by a girl.

Later on, when Polly and Cohn had been waiting in the studio's sick bay for ambulances to whisk them to the Olive View Receiving Hospital, Cohn had attempted a conciliatory gesture that registered more like a begrudging mumble about how much worse the mishap could have ended. But by then, the fog of confusion had given way to a delirium of pain, so Polly wasn't sure of anything. After the ambulances arrived, she hadn't seen Cohn again.

A loud knock sounded on the apartment's front door. "Yoo-hoo! Polly?" It was Cora. "Are you there?" When Luddie let her in, she marched into the sitting room and ran her eyes up and down Polly's cast. "I came as soon as I heard."

"How did you hear?"

"Are you kidding? The whole industry's talking about it. Nobody's clear on what you were doing up there in the first place—"

"Trying to get justice for my father."

"I figured as much. But you should hear the theories. Polly darling, I do wish you'd told me you're a hired assassin."

Polly yipped at the sheer absurdity. She might have enjoyed the notion more, but her monstrous bruise throbbed with pain. "Hired by who?"

"Depends on the gossipmonger. Bugsy Siegel. Mickey Cohen. Longie Zwillman."

How ironic. They were probably the same people who'd taken out a hit on Cohn, and now people thought they had enlisted her to finish the job.

Cora harrumphed. "That's what he gets for bulldozing everyone in his path."

Enough talk of Harry Cohn, Polly thought. Hasn't that man brought enough disaster into my life? "Tell me, what's news at MGM? How's *The Wizard of Oz* progressing?"

Cora settled into the sofa. "They're all in a tizzy because your boss wants Mayer to release Victor Fleming so that he can take the reins on *Wind*. Fleming's reluctant as hell because, let's face it, who wants to be dragged down by Selznick's Folly?"

If only people knew the mammoth effort Mr. Selznick was putting into his magnum opus. What a dreadful shame if it were all for naught.

"Meantime," Cora continued, "George Cukor's back on the lot, happy as a clam at high tide."

"They've given him *The Women*?"

"Look at you! Falling through movie sets like a stuntman, but still up on the latest."

Another knock on the door.

It wasn't Amelia, but Irene Selznick holding two enormous picnic baskets.

"For the patient!" She handed one to Luddie and deposited the other on the dining table. "I bought out half of Jurgensen's on Rodeo. I don't know what you like, so I got a bit of everything: bread, Vienna sausages, Bick's pickled eggs, some gorgeous smoked Gouda, which will pair well with those posh Carr's crackers from Britain. Some plums. Apricots. And a ton of Campbell's soups. I even got Spam. That stuff's not to my taste, but my boys love it, so I figured what the hell."

"Irene!" Polly said. "This is very generous."

She waved away Polly's thanks. "The food was my idea; the doctor was David's."

"Doctor?" Cora asked.

"David insisted our spunky little daredevil be well taken care of, so our personal physician will come house-calling soon."

"That's so thoughtful," Polly said, "but the staff at the receiving hospital were all so nice."

"And I have a message from Marcella," Irene said, ignoring her protests. "She said to take your time coming back to work. There's no rush now that *Wind* has closed down temporarily."

Inwardly, Polly breathed a sigh of relief. The most she could cope with right now was lying on the sofa, her leg elevated on cushions as she read *Rebecca*. Goodness gracious, what a ripper of a tale. No wonder Mr. Selznick had been so keen to secure the rights. Also on the coffee table was Gil's copy of *Lost Horizon*, which now held less appeal. However, after a week or two, she'd be desperate to fill her days with more than thumbing through *Life* magazine.

"Here's some news to cheer you up," Irene said. "After what happened, someone took it on themselves to cancel that party at the Ranch. When Harry heard, he was furious."

"He would've spent a ton of money on it," Luddie said.

"Got so mad he went to throw his *It Happened One Night* Oscar, but it slipped out of his hand and broke one of his dislocated toes. The bastard is in the most horrendous pain!"

"Best news I've heard all year," Cora said. "Any coffee in those baskets?"

Irene fished a can from the one she'd handed to Luddie. "Freshly ground at Nate and Al's. Point me toward the kitchen—" A knock on the door interrupted her. "That's probably Dr. Grodeski now."

"Will he have an extra-long knitting needle?" The unscratchable itch had wormed its way past Polly's knee.

"Entrez-vous, whoever you are," Irene called.

But it wasn't Grodeski. Rather, Benji stood there, holding a glass vase filled with sunflowers the size of clock faces.

He set them down and greeted Polly with a kiss on the cheek. "Amelia said she'd meet me here."

"She's not home from work yet." Polly ran a finger across the bright yellow blooms. "These are darling. And very thoughtful of you."

"Thoughtful, yes," Benji said. "Of me, no. I was walking past a florist's van parked out front and the delivery guy asked for a hand. When I saw your name"—he plucked out a card hidden among the arrangement—"I tipped the driver and told him I'd take it from there."

Polly pulled the folded card from its snowy white envelope and checked the signature. "It's from Rose Cohn."

"What did she say?" Cora asked.

Irene and Luddie dragged some dining chairs closer, and Benji parked himself on the end of the coffee table.

"'Dear Polly,'" she read out loud, "'Flowers don't make up for what happened, but they'll do for a start, and I hope they cheer you up. As for my rat-faced husband, his near-miss must have scared the ever-loving bejesus out of him. Since he got home, he's been saying all the right things, including—are you sitting down? Yes of course you are!—an apology for attempting to rent that starlet to have his baby.'"

Irene tsked. "When I told David about that Della girl, he said, 'That's pretty much par for the Cohn course, isn't it?'"

Polly returned to Rose's card. "'Will wonders never cease? Call me when you've recuperated enough to go out for lunch. We can go anywhere as long as it's the Vine St. Brown Derby. I'm kidding. Not really. Get well soon. P.S. Fear not. I shall be busy at this end pushing Harry to do the right thing and pay up everything he owes. Between the two of us, we'll get him!'" She tucked the card back into its envelope. "I trust Rose isn't fooling herself into thinking Harry won't revert to type." She caught the sheepish look on Benji's face. "Why are you looking like that? What do you know?"

Benji chose his words carefully. "You won't believe who's outside screwing up the courage to knock on your door."

Cora sat upright. "If it's Harry Cohn, I'll drop that glass vase on his other toe."

"Not Cohn," Benji said.

"It's Gil, isn't it?" Polly looked at Luddie. *What do you think?*

"At the first sign of trouble, Benji and I will haul his carcass out of here, pronto."

Gil's description of Luddie came back to Polly. *He couldn't handle himself in a fight*. She turned to Benji. "Go fetch him."

Gil surveyed the room, cautious as a gazelle. Only a few days had passed, but already those telltale dark blotches under his eyes had faded a little. He'd given himself a close shave and had shelled out for a haircut. Inflamed veins no longer spiderwebbed the whites of his eyes. "How's the leg?"

"I can't see how that's any of your business." Polly clipped her words, curt and brusque. "Why are you here?"

A slight tremor twitched through his body. "I'm probably the last person you want to see right now—"

"That would be Harry Cohn, which makes you the second to last." She tapped her wristwatch. "Two minutes."

"I need more than that to tell you everything—"

"Tick-tock, tick-tock." Anger mixed with resentment bubbled up from within her, distracting from the irritation along her leg. "You've got some nerve coming here."

"I never—"

"You sized up Harry Cohn and thought 'Yep, he's the guy for me.' Yeah, well, get a load of what that led to." She rapped on the plaster cast. It hurt like hell, but it was worth it to make her point. "So excuse me if I question anything that comes out of your mouth."

"I quit being Cohn's flunky." He paused, waiting for Polly to respond. What was he expecting? A hug and a kiss and a twenty-one-gun salute? "I've found work on a dude ranch outside of Reno. That's where women go to get a divorce."

"I know what happens there." Polly kept her voice flat and detached. She liked what she was hearing, but was far from ready to drop her guard.

His fidgety hands took refuge deep in his pockets. "The place needs fixing up. And I need to start over because this town . . ." His voice trailed off. "Too many memories. All those years scraping by in"—he shot Luddie a pointed glance—"Hooverville."

Polly wished Luddie would look at her so that she could comfort him with one of their glances that said everything, but he had turned away. No need to be ashamed, she wanted to tell him. What about my father and the Avalon fire? Doesn't everyone have a gangrenous wound from their past?

"Moving to a place where you can put your skills to better use," she said, softening her tone a tad, "sounds like a good idea."

"I hope so. By the way, I came straight from Cohn's bedside."

"Is the dirty rat in agony?" Cora asked.

Gil responded with a sly smile. "He talked about selling his share of Mad Ox."

Polly grabbed at Cora's hand. "I told him it'd be worth a decent amount."

Once he'd embroidered his fall into an amusing after-dinner story, a guy like Cohn could easily decide against hawking his interest in Mad Ox. But for now, the hope of repaying Papa's debt was enough to keep Polly's spirits up. If Judd convinced Desmond to move to the island, maybe she could rent him the house, which would help pay off the debt even faster. *How 'bout them apples, Papa?*

"Please don't suggest he sell to David," Irene said. "It's the last thing I need."

Polly crossed her heart, then returned to Gil. "Thanks for stopping by."

He risked a step closer, but stopped when he saw Cora stiffen. "I really am sorry about everything."

It would be a long while before the memory of Gil's words faded from Polly's memory. *I can't let you up there. Part of my job is to protect him.* "I hope you are." She flicked her eyes toward the front door as though to say, This is your cue to exit. But before he could take the hint, the door flew open and hit the wall with a startling thump.

"HERE I AM!" Hoisting a bag with *Western Costume Co.* printed down the side, Amelia hurled herself into the living room like a Chinese firecracker. She'd hung the bag on the top of the kitchen swing door and tossed her hat and gloves onto the table next to Irene's baskets before she spotted Gil. "What's *he* doing here?"

"Long story." Polly wiggled her finger at the bag. "Explanation, please?"

"There's nothing like knowing your best friend almost died to wake you out of a stupor."

Polly had never seen her roommate in anything close to a stupor. An extra-lively sparkle now vibrated the air around her.

"If you live life right," Amelia continued, "it opens you up to a whole panoply of experiences."

Polly looked at Luddie. *Did she use 'panoply' in a sentence*? But he had a faraway look in his eyes as he took fresh stock of Gil.

Amelia fetched the bag and ran the zipper to the bottom to reveal a middy blouse in a pastel green paired with a deep emerald silk scarf, and a pleated skirt with a zigzag trim. "I'm auditioning for *Pretty Pennies*!"

"You really are?"

"A regular of mine at Schwab's is a talent agent. He received the casting announcement calling for actresses to audition for Juniper."

"My David's *Pretty Pennies*?" Irene asked.

Amelia nodded. "I was still of two minds about the whole thing, but Farley read me the character description, and gosh darn it if I didn't fit the bill!"

Polly remembered Marcella giving Hazel that casting notice to type up, but she had been too busy to read it.

"Making a movie could be a wonderful experience. Just because I don't want to turn it into a career doesn't mean I shouldn't give it the ol' college try."

"Gosh, dear," Irene said. "David will want to sign you for a long-term contract, the way he's doing with Ingrid Bergman and Alfred Hitchcock. I'd be happy to put in a good word for you, though."

"Thank you, but please don't." Amelia rezipped the bag. "I want to earn this on my own merits." She eyed the overflowing baskets. "What's all this?"

"Irene 'Florence Nightingale' Mayer-Selznick raided Jurgensen's."

"I'm famished. Shall we dig in?"

Polly assigned Amelia to get plates and cutlery and Luddie to fetch glasses and bottle openers. She sent Cora to the radio with instructions to "find us a station playing appropriate feasting music."

"What about me?" Irene asked.

"You unpack these horns of plenty. Benji, you're on condiments duty." She turned, at last, to Gil. "When are you leaving for the dude ranch?"

"Day after tomorrow."

"You've got some packing to do, then."

He pantomimed a noncommittal shrug. "Not really."

Irene held two bottles of champagne in the air. "We need ice. Is there a place close by?"

"Three blocks east," Polly replied. "Luddie, would you mind making an ice run?"

He emerged from the kitchen and slid a tray loaded with glasses onto the table. The two men stared at each other for a prolonged moment. "How about you walk me as far as the market?"

Gil nodded taciturnly and followed him onto the landing.

Amelia landed a stack of plates on the table. Polly patted an empty spot and waited for Amelia to join her. "Auditioning for Juniper, huh? Is this the also-ran daughter talking?"

"A cry for attention, you mean?" She tried to sound flippant, but her voice fell short. "I got to thinking when you told me how much I looked like the girl in the movie. So, when Farley mentioned how Selznick wants an unknown young redhead, I thought, 'Hey, *I'm* an unknown young redhead.'"

"It's free to audition," Polly said.

"I'm highly aware the chances are real slim that I'll get past the thanks-for-coming-in stage."

"What were the chances that a British actress would play Scarlett O'Hara?"

Amelia squeezed Polly's hand. "I've watched you take on Philip Wrigley, Harry Cohn, and his cunning fox of a lawyer, not to mention the DA's office. No small potatoes in that bunch."

Polly had been so intent on dealing with each new hurdle life had thrown at her that she'd never stopped to take in how far she'd come. "I suppose not."

Amelia squeezed her hand extra hard. "And so I decided, 'If Pol can do all that, *I* can throw my hat in the *Pretty Pennies* ring.'"

"And when you do, I'll be in the front row, cheering you on."

"Which'll be handy if your boss hands me the lead and I have a nervous breakdown."

"Not so fast, chum." Polly wiggled her fingers over the cast. "One crisis at a time, please."

"Deal." Amelia pecked her on the cheek and rejoined Cora and Irene at the table.

Irene nestled a champagne bottle in the crook of her arm and twisted its cork. It popped open with a startlingly loud bang. "You know you've bought the good stuff when it sounds like a gun going off," she told the room. "Hey over there, Queen Sheba of the Sofa, should we set up this buffet on the coffee table?"

"No, no," Polly said. "I'll come to you."

Her leg aching from hip to ankle, she swung the cumbersome cast off the couch and set her foot on the floor as gently as she could. Launching herself upright onto her crutches, she paused to regain her balance, and didn't move until she was satisfied she wouldn't end up face down on the rug. She took the first step.

Suddenly, the twenty feet to the table looked like twenty miles, but every step was going to bring her closer to a generous bounty of food, French champagne, and, above all, the cherished friends who had given her back a family.

THE END

Did you enjoy this book?

***You* can make a big difference.**

As an independent author, I don't have the financial muscle of a New York publisher supporting me. But I do have something much more powerful and effective, and it's something those publishers would kill to get their hands on: a committed and loyal bunch of readers. Honest reviews of my books help bring them to the notice of other readers. If you've enjoyed this book, I would be so grateful if you could spend just a couple of minutes leaving a review.

Thank you very much,

Martin Turnbull

AUTHOR NOTE

As with most historical fiction, *Selznick's Girl Friday* is a blend of fact and fiction. To help you sort out which parts were real and which I invented, here are some clarifications and links for further reading.

1939 is known as "Hollywood's Greatest Year" because many of the most memorable movies that Hollywood ever produced were released in that one year. Not just *Gone with the Wind* and *The Wizard of Oz,* but also *The Women, Stagecoach, Gunga Din, The Hunchback of Notre Dame, Ninotchka,* and many more. I always thought that it was one of those stranger-than-fiction quirks of timing, but it wasn't until I started my research for this novel that I learned there was a specific reason. In his 2013 book, *Majestic Hollywood: The Greatest Films of 1939.*

Mark A. Vieira explains that 1939 was the 25th anniversary of the arrival of Cecil B. DeMille and company in Los Angeles to film *The Squaw Man,* one of the first feature films to be shot in Hollywood. It was also the 50th anniversary of the first moving picture developed on celluloid film in London, England, by William Friese Greene. Vieira says that late-1930s filmmakers were aware of these two coming anniversaries, and wanted to maximize the opportunities for publicity. They upped their game and made extra effort to turn out the very best product possible for 1939. I think it's safe to say they met that goal.

A couple of other books I read from cover to cover when planning this novel were:

1939: Hollywood's Greatest Year, by Thomas S. Hischak

Gone With the Wind: 1939 Day by Day, by Pauline Bartel

Adventures of a Hollywood Secretary: Her Private Letters from Inside the Studios of the 1920s, Edited by Cari Beauchamp

I didn't read this collection of letters, written by Sam Goldwyn's secretary to her friend back East, until I was half a dozen drafts into the writing of this novel. Nothing in this book influenced or inspired the plot in my story; it is, nevertheless, a fascinating insight into what it was like to work at a Hollywood studio in the 1920s.

One of my all-time favorite books about studio-era Hollywood is Irene Mayer-Selznick's autobiography, *A Private View*. Being the daughter of Hollywood's most powerful movie mogul and wife of the producer of Hollywood's most successful movie, Irene's straightforward and matter-of-fact account of her life makes for captivating reading.

Polly Maddox and her father, Elroy, were fictional, but Harry Cohn from Columbia Pictures was very much a force to be reckoned with in studio-era Hollywood. Liked by few and feared by many, he managed to bootstrap an also-ran film studio into one of the industry's major players. However, in 1937 and 1938, Columbia Pictures was still striving to overcome the economic effects of Frank Capra's *Lost Horizon* (1937). The film's original budget of $1.25 million was much more than Cohn liked to spend on a single picture, and ballooned to over $2.6 million. Consequently, the film lost money. Following a million-dollar plummet in profits in 1937,

Columbia's fiscal 1938 showed a net of only $2,046. So, going into 1939, the studio's finances were in real trouble. As an author, I saw his precarious situation as a juicy plot complication. Coupled with the fact that practically everybody in Hollywood hated Harry Cohn (with good reason), in my mind he made an ideal antagonist.

Columbia's *Only Angels Have Wings* (1939) did have a troubled production; however, Cohn did not throw a party on the lamasery set. That event was fictional.

Harry Cohn's involvement with organized crime was true. On January 28, 1932, Cohn spent $500,000 to buy out his business partner, Joe Brandt, which allowed him to become the head of Columbia. He did it with the help of Longie Zwillman, Mickey Cohen, and/or Bugsy Siegel. (Sources differ.) The mob hit on Cohn's life was my own invention, but it was partially inspired by an incident that happened in 1957. Columbia star Kim Novak fell in love with Black entertainer Sammy Davis Jr., and Cohn retaliated by ordering a mob hit on Davis, saying it would be rescinded only if Davis left Novak and immediately married a Black woman. Within hours, Davis paid an African-American woman to marry him.

The plotline about Cohn paying a starlet to have his baby came directly from the biography *King Cohn* by Bob Thomas, which talks about how Cohn did exactly that.

In Chapter 21, I talk about a feud between Cecil B. DeMille and Harry Cohn over a poker debt. In real life, there was no feud; however, hours-long, high-stakes poker games among the Hollywood elite were commonplace during this time, as were the mind-boggling amounts they would gamble. The $35,000 IOU mentioned in that chapter would translate to nearly a million dollars in today's money.

Cohn's electric chair was real. It was in the executive lunchroom, and Cohn would gleefully use it on newcomers, preferably those who were timid. The first chair met its demise when an angry Frank Capra demolished it. Cohn went ahead and had another one built.

Author of many Western novels, Zane Grey had a long history with Santa Catalina Island. A world-class fisherman, he first visited Catalina on his honeymoon in 1906. He was attracted to the challenge of deep-ocean fishing and had heard tales of the big game fish in Catalina waters. After making many annual trips to the island, he built a vacation home, the Zane Grey Pueblo, in 1925.

In the scene where Polly meets Sybil Langley on the Munchkin Village set of *The Wizard of Oz*, Sibyl talks about how Margaret Hamilton got burned during filming. This is based on fact. In the movie, she makes a dramatic entrance and exit amid billowing smoke. On one take, the special effect went awry. Hamilton was burned as she descended through a trapdoor and was taken to the hospital. I would imagine that the first choice for the role of the Wicked Witch of the West—Gale Sondergaard—was glad she turned down the role. That trapdoor in soundstage 27 is still there.

Believe it or not, the carriage used in the Horse of a Different Color sequence in *The Wizard of Oz* really had been a gift to Abraham Lincoln during the Civil War. You can see it in action on YouTube.

The scene in Chapter 31 when Polly and Cukor watch a *Wizard of Oz* musical number in rehearsal is based on "The Jitterbug," which took five weeks to rehearse and shoot, but wasn't used in the film. Fortunately, we can get an idea of what it was like on YouTube.

The scene in Chapter 15 where Luddie takes Polly to meet with Irene Selznick takes place at King's Tropical Inn at 5939 Washington Blvd. in Culver City. It was a real place, extremely popular in the 1920s and 1930s, and known for its chicken dinners. Of all the Los Angeles restaurants I have posted about on my social media, King's is probably the one that generates the most nostalgia.

The reference to Laurence Olivier's misery on the set of *Wuthering Heights* was based on fact. During production (December 1938 to March 1939) he developed a raging case of athlete's foot and was in such torment that he had to be carried to and from the set. It played into Heathcliff's anguish, so director Willie Wyler was in no hurry to get it fixed, even though Olivier made everybody's life hell. Hopefully not Vivien Leigh's, though. Both Larry and Vivien were the leads in important Hollywood movies, so it must have been an exciting, invigorating, exhausting, and stressful time for them both.

The plotline about organized crime figures Willie Bioff and George Browne using Hollywood unions to shake down the studios was based on fact. It was also true that the studio heads paid up because it was cheaper to pay them than it was to allow their workers to unionize and pay higher wages. When I read that Harry Cohn refused to give in to the shakedown, I wrote it into the plot of this novel. If you'd like to know more, here are a couple of worthwhile accounts of that era on AmericanMafia.com and Film-NoirFoundation.com.

David O. Selznick did not throw a New Year's Eve party prior to the start of principal photography on *Gone with the Wind*. That party in Chapter 28 was my own invention, as was the party in Chapter 33 to welcome Alfred Hitchcock to Hollywood. On March 3, 1939, Hitchcock signed an exclusive seven-year deal with Selznick, and on March 15, Selznick announced their project would be *Rebecca*. So the real-life timing of all this fits reasonably well with the plotline of this novel.

David Selznick did see some sort of a doctor who provided his "patients" with injections of vitamin B mixed with thyroid extract.

He also took copious amounts of Benzedrine to keep him going during the extremely stressful production of *Gone with the Wind.* Not surprisingly, by the time the movie was finished, Selznick was a wreck. In her autobiography, his wife, Irene, talks about how she was forced to adopt a "for-the-duration" mentality. David was so completely swamped that she felt all she could do was lie low until the ordeal was over.

For more information on the Selznick International Pictures studio, I can recommend *Hollywood's Lost Backlot: 40 Acres of Glamour and Mystery* by Steven Bingen.

You can watch a five-minute "tour" of it on YouTube: The Selznick Studios Retrospective Backlot Tour

In Chapter 35, Polly types up a letter Selznick had dictated to Ed Sullivan (who, back then, was a newspaper columnist) in which he listed the reasons why Vivien Leigh's casting was, by no means, a sure bet yet. This did actually happen and indicates how skilled Selznick was in prolonging anticipation for the official announcement of the casting of Scarlett O'Hara.

In Chapter 38, readers of my Hollywood's Garden of Allah novels might have caught the oblique reference to the disastrous *Gone with the Wind* screen test that my character Gwendolyn Brick endured in book two, *The Trouble with Scarlett.*

During the time that this novel covers, David Selznick's secretary was Marcella Rabwin. In 1998, she was interviewed by the *San Diego Reader* about her experiences. You can read the article on the website of the San Diego Reader newspaper

At the same time that David Selznick was working on *Gone with the Wind,* he was also developing his first movie with Alfred Hitchcock, *Rebecca,* as well as the remake of *Intermezzo* in which Ingrid Bergman would make her Hollywood debut in the same lead role she had in the Swedish original. *Pretty Pennies* was entirely my own invention and not based on any movie.

Schwab's Pharmacy opened at 8024 Sunset Blvd. in 1932, and quickly became a social hub for Hollywood people to see and be seen, meet and be met, schmooze and be schmoozed. There were four Schwab brothers (Leon, Bernard, Martin, and Jack) who owned six different pharmacies. I don't know if Leon Schwab was the one who ran the famous location; I chose his name more or less at random. (And no, Lana Turner did *not* get discovered there—she was discovered at Top Hat Café, farther down Sunset.)

The Avalon fire actually happened. It broke out sometime between 3:30 a.m. and 4 a.m. on November 29, 1915. The most reliable account I've read said that it most likely started behind the Rose Hotel, where it quickly spread to destroy half of the town's buildings, homes, and hotels, including the Metropole, Central, Bay View, Rose, Grand View, and Pacific, as well as the Pilgrim Club, the Grill Cafe, the Tuna Club, the Bath House, and virtually every home between Whittley Avenue and Hill Street. You can read about it on the website of The Catalina Islander.

The Mt. Lowe Tavern where Polly's father hid out was a real place. It stood in the mountains above Altadena, north of Pasadena.

Hoovervilles were named after President Herbert Hoover, who was in the White House during the onset of the Depression and was widely blamed for it. The Hooverville where Ludlow and Gil lived actually existed at Alameda St. and Firestone Blvd.

In January 1939, *Photoplay* magazine published an article called "Hollywood's Unmarried Husbands and Wives," as described in the novel. Written under a pseudonym by gossip columnist Sheilah Graham, it caused a scandal. Selznick announced Leigh's casting on January 13, 1939. The two events didn't happen on the exact same day, but they were both big Hollywood news, so I conflated the dates for plot purposes.

In Chapter 37, there is a scene where Polly meets Aggie Underwood at the It Café. Located inside the Plaza Hotel south of Hollywood and Vine, it was opened by actress Clara Bow (aka "The It Girl") in September 1937. She and her husband owned it for about a year, after which it was acquired by David Selznick's uncle Phil.

Aggie Underwood was a crime reporter who was noted for her ballsy coverage of LA's seedier side. You can read more about her in a biography of her, *The First with the Latest!: Aggie Underwood, the Los Angeles Herald, and the Sordid Crimes of a City*, by Joan Renner.

ALSO BY MARTIN TURNBULL

The Hollywood's Garden of Allah novels

Book 1 – *The Garden on Sunset*

Book 2 – *The Trouble with Scarlett*

Book 3 – *Citizen Hollywood*

Book 4 – *Searchlights and Shadows*

Book 5 – *Reds in the Beds*

Book 6 – *Twisted Boulevard*

Book 7 – *Tinseltown Confidential*

Book 8 – *City of Myths*

Book 9 – *Closing Credits*

Chasing Salomé: a novel of 1920s Hollywood

The Heart of the Lion: a novel of Irving Thalberg's Hollywood

The Hollywood Home Front trilogy

A trilogy of novels set in World War II Hollywood

Book 1 - *All the Gin Joints*

Book 2 - *Thank Your Lucky Stars*

Book 3 - *You Must Remember This*

The Hollywood's Greatest Year Trilogy

A trilogy of novels set in 1939 Hollywood

Book 1 - *Selznick's Girl Friday*

ACKNOWLEDGMENTS

Heartfelt thanks to the following, who helped shaped this book:

My editor: Jennifer McIntyre for her keen eye, unfailing humor, and the willingness to debate every last letter and comma placement.

My cover designer: Damonza

My beta readers: Steven Adkins and Gene Strange for their invaluable time, insight, feedback and advice in shaping this novel.

I'd like to thank John Luder for his time and efforts assisting my in research of the history and layout of Santa Catalina Island, which does, indeed, as the song says, lay 26 miles from Los Angeles.

My extraordinarily eagle-eyed proofreaders: Bob Molinari, Susan Perkins, and Leigh Carter, whose final polish raised this manuscript to gleaming perfection.

ABOUT THE AUTHOR

A lifelong love of travel, history, and sharing his knowledge with others has led Martin Turnbull down a long path to authorship. Having made the move to the United States from Melbourne, Australia in the mid-90s, Martin staked his claim in the heart of Los Angeles. His background in travel allowed him to work as a private tour guide--showing off the alluring vistas, mansions, boulevards, and backlots of the Hollywood scene. With stints in local historical guiding with the Los Angeles Conservancy as well as time on the Warner Bros. movie lot, Martin found himself armed with the kind of knowledge that would fly off the very pages of his future works. As a longtime fan of Hollywood's golden era and old films, Martin decided it was time to marry his knowledge with his passions and breathe life back into this bygone world.

The product of his passions burst forth in the form of Hollywood's Garden of Allah novels, a series of historical fiction books set during the golden age of Hollywood: 1927-1959. Exploring the evolution of Hollywood's most famous and glamorous era through the lives of its residents, these stories take place both in and around the real-life Garden of Allah Hotel on iconic Sunset Boulevard. Although Martin's heart belongs to history, his energy remains in the present, continuing to put his passions on paper and beyond.

CONNECT WITH MARTIN TURNBULL

MartinTurnbull.com

Facebook: facebook.com/gardenofallahnovels

Blog: martinturnbull.wordpress.com/

Goodreads: http://bit.ly/martingoodreads

Amazon author page: http://bit.ly/martinturnbull

Be sure to check out the **Photo Blog** for vintage photos of Los Angeles and Hollywood on Martin's website: martinturnbull.com/photo-blog/

To hear about new books first, sign up to my mailing list:

http://bit.ly/turnbullsignup

I won't fill your inbox with useless drivel or I email you too often or never share your information with anyone. Ever. (And you can unsubscribe at any time. No hard feelings.)

* * *

Made in the USA
Las Vegas, NV
03 July 2024

91841817R00256